Praise for
THE READING LIST
by Sara Nisha Adams

"[A] quietly beautiful novel about the magic of books and the joy of human connection."

—*Newsweek*

"A remarkable, heartwarming debut about the power of fiction."

—PopSugar

"Thoughtful and heartwarming. . . . An absolute delight to read, it will be catnip to book groups craving a story to remind them why we read and how very important libraries and bookshops are."

—*Library Journal* (starred review)

"A lovely story about how a love of reading can transport us to other worlds and also bring us together."

—*Toronto Star*

"This moving debut demonstrates the power of novels to provide comfort in the face of devastating loss and loneliness, with relatable characters and a heartwarming tone throughout. Readers who enjoyed Gabrielle Zevin's *The Storied Life of A. J. Fikry* and Nina George's *The Little Paris Bookshop* will find themselves drawn in by this book."

—*Booklist*

"The most heartfelt read of the summer. . . . A surprising delight of a novel."

ndaland

"The story is an absolute joy. A captivating and exquisitely crafted debut."

—Heidi Swain, bestselling author of *The Winter Garden*

"If you love books, read this. If you love people, read this. If you love crying with sadness, crying with happiness, and feeling like you have been wrapped in the blanket of someone else's life, read this."

—Debbie Johnson, bestselling author of *Maybe One Day*

"A wonderful read about the fundamental power of books to lift our lives from the mundane and to transform them into something truly magical."

—Imogen Clark, bestselling author of *Postcards From a Stranger*

"*The Reading List* absolutely captures the magic of reading and of libraries. I felt a part of Mukesh and Aleisha's book club, revisiting some of my favorite novels alongside these new friends."

—Louise Hare, author of *This Lovely City*

THE READING LIST

THE READING LIST

A Novel

SARA NISHA ADAMS

wm
WILLIAM MORROW
An Imprint of HarperCollins*Publishers*

Grateful acknowledgment to Andrew Nurnberg Associates for permission to quote the line on p. 102 from *To Kill A Mockingbird* © Harper Lee, 1960.

HarperCollins books may be purchased for educational, business, or sales promotional use. For information, please email the Special Markets Department at SPsales@harpercollins.com.

A hardcover edition of this book was published in 2021 by William Morrow, an imprint of HarperCollins Publishers.

FIRST WILLIAM MORROW PAPERBACK EDITION PUBLISHED 2022.

Library of Congress Cataloging-in-Publication Data has been applied for.

ISBN 978-0-06-302529-5

23 24 25 26 27 LBC 10 9 8 7 6

In loving memory of Granny, Grandad, Ba, and Dada

For Mum and Dad

Love you lots x

THE READING LIST

PROLOGUE

THE READING LIST

2017

The doors are new: Automatic open. Fancy. That has changed since Aidan was here last. The first thing he notices are the sparse rows of books—when he'd been younger, *smaller*, the shelves seemed to never end, teeming with books of all shapes and sizes. Even when he'd been a teenager, working here over his summer holidays, this place had been a sanctuary for him and, though he'd never have admitted it to his friends, he'd loved getting lost between the stacks and stacks of reference books. Maybe he is just looking back with rose-tinted spectacles, imagining some kind of magical, bookish wonderland that has never really existed. But now, at twenty-two, no longer a boy but a man, here he is again, looking for a place to hide—from the world, his friends, his family.

The librarian looks up for a moment as he steps through the doors, and smiles. Aidan is greeted by silence. In his memories, this place was *never* silent. Obviously, it *is* a library . . . so it has always been quiet, but there had been that hum—of people shuffling about, of kids whispering to their mums, people flicking pages, moving chairs, wiggling around, coughing and snuffling too. Today, barely a sound. Someone tapping out a text on their phone. The librarian drumming away on that clunky old keyboard. Nothing else. Recently, he has spotted posters about saving Brent's libraries stuck up on community boards: in Tesco; at the gym; even plastered near the Tube station, advertising cake sales, knitting clubs at the library, sit-ins, petitions. But it has never crossed his mind that Harrow Road Library needs saving. In his mind, it is popular, well loved, but now that he is here, his heart begins to sink . . . Maybe Harrow Road Library will be the next to go.

He wanders over to the fiction shelves, the crime section, and runs his fingers over the spines, landing on *Black Water Rising* by Attica Locke. He has read it before, years ago. Maybe even more than once. As he starts to turn the pages, looking for an escape, memories rush in . . . of Attica Locke's Houston, the city alive, vibrant, dark, full of contradictions and contrasts. Today he needs that kind of familiarity, he needs to step back into a world where there are scares, twists, turns, but a world where he knows how everything will end.

He needs to know how *something* will end.

The table he'd once curled up under as a kid is gone, everything rearranged. Nothing was going to stay the same just to please him, not here, not in his life. This is another bad summer. But as the words of the story wash over him, he traces the sentences with his fingers, trying to re-create that feeling of being grounded, rooted to the spot, nothing more than a body, reading words, allowing his mind to wander elsewhere. He can feel the story take control of his mind, pulling him away. His own thoughts, his worries, that voice, begin to buzz at the back of his mind, and eventually they become nothing but white noise.

When he was younger, his mum would bring him here with his little sister, Aleisha; Aleisha was always more interested in playing and she'd kick and she'd fuss and Leilah would have to take her outside. Aidan would never have more than a few minutes of alone time, but those few minutes calmed him, they stopped his mind racing, they helped him breathe, escape . . . whatever he needed most.

A loud *thwack* alerts him to someone beside him. He averts his gaze, keeping his eyes on the page, unwilling, for now, to allow someone else to break his spell. Out of the corner of his eye, he spots a large stack of books piled high. A barricade.

There's the scraping of a chair, and scraps of paper are pulled from a bag, creased receipts, a library slip, the back of a crossword puzzle, leaving a crumpled cloud of white on the desk beside him.

He tries hard to quiet his breathing as his neighbor begins to mutter almost inaudibly. He can't tell if it's a song, or a tune, or complete nonsense. He spots a pen poised above the first scrap; then follows the rhythmic scratching.

Aidan keeps his eyes fixed on the page, running over the words in his book, taking them in, trying to conjure up the feeling he'd had the last time he'd read these words in this order.

For minutes, Aidan allows his focus to flow in and out of the book, into the library, and then out onto the road, over to Wembley. He wonders how his mum is doing now. Has Aleisha noticed he's vanished? He brings his mind back to the room, back to the library, to the person sitting beside him, scribbling as if their life depends on it.

And then, suddenly, his neighbor stands up abruptly, leaving a heap of little folded pieces of paper littering the desk. He watches from the corner of his eye as slips of paper are pulled into a line, as if in slow motion, a finger tapping each one in turn . . . counting *one, two, three, four, five, six, seven, eight* . . . Then the scraps are all tucked away into the first book, at the top of the pile—he sees now that it is *To Kill a Mockingbird*.

His neighbor's hands rest for a moment on the cover of the book. Aidan realizes he hasn't turned his page in a while. He wonders if *they* realize he's watching. He wonders why he's watching at all. Then, a moment later, their arms, wrapped in a thick black sweater, reach forward and pull the books toward them. With a soft groan, the pile of books is swept from the corner of his eye and he hears the *swoosh-swoosh* of shoes against the tacky library carpet, shuffling toward the front desk. He allows his mind to return to his story.

When he eventually stands up from his chair, the evening light is streaming through the window, and the library looks exactly how he remembers it: magical. It feels like a miracle, but he's never believed in those before. The sun is casting long shadows on the scruffy library, dousing everything in a warm amber—it looks as if it has been carved out of gold. He tucks his chair in, lifting it up, trying not to make a sound—though there is barely anyone left here to disturb.

Then he spots one lonely folded scrap of paper sitting on the desk beside him—the crossword puzzle.

For a moment, he turns his head to the left, to the right, and slowly over his shoulder. No one is watching him. His arm reaches forward, pulling it toward him, and he unwraps it—one fold at a time. His fingers treat it delicately; it is barely thicker than a cigarette paper. He doesn't want to break it. He thinks of the person, his anonymous neighbor, writing, scrawling, intent.

As he unfolds the final corner, the mystery is suddenly revealed. The lettering is neat, looping, warm, inviting.

Just in case you need it:

To Kill a Mockingbird

Rebecca

The Kite Runner

Life of Pi

Pride and Prejudice

Little Women

Beloved

A Suitable Boy

To Kill a Mockingbird—the first book in the massive pile. He runs his eyes down the list. It doesn't mean anything to him—just scribbled words on a scrap of paper. But, for a moment, he thinks about taking the list with him, popping it in his pocket, but he stops himself. This small scrap of paper, so neatly folded, is nothing more than a stranger's reading list. What does he need with something like this?

Instead, he lays it back on the table, and picks up his book, sending Attica Locke a secret thank-you, and tucks it back on the crime shelf, for someone else to enjoy. He heads out of the library, the doors closing automatically behind him. He turns once more, and he can see the note sitting exactly where he left it. The shadows of the library close in behind him; the books read and unread forming a barrier between him and the list. As he steps away from the library, he feels the peace, the silence, slide away from him as he heads toward the lights and sounds of the city he calls home.

The Time Traveler's Wife

by

AUDREY NIFFENEGGER

CHAPTER 1

MUKESH

2019

Beep. "Hi, Papa, it's Rohini. Sorry, sorry to be calling you again, but you know how I worry when you don't pick up or return my calls. We're going to come and visit you on Friday, me and Priya, so let me know if you need me to bring anything, food or drink. I'm not convinced the food you make yourself is nutritionally balanced, Papa—you need to eat more than just mung. And remember it's bin day today, black bins only today, ha. Green bins next week. Call Param at number eighty-seven if you can't do it, okay? I know your back has been playing up."

Beep. "Dad, it's Deepali. Rohini told me to give you a ring because she hasn't heard from you. She said to tell you it's your bin day today, so remember, okay? Not like last time when you had to run out in your dressing gown in the morning! Call me later, okay? I am going to work now, okay? Bye. The twins say bye too! Bye, Dada."

Beep. "Hi, Papa, it's Vritti. You doing all right? Wanted to check how you are. Let me know if you need anything. I can come round soon, just let me know when you're free. I've got a busy few weeks, but can sort something out, yeah?"

And just like that, Mukesh's day started like almost any other Wednesday: with three identical voicemails from his daughters—Rohini, Deepali, and Vritti—at the unsociable hour of eight A.M., before they started work; often Mukesh wasn't even awake by then.

On another day of the week, he might have called each of them in turn, to let them know he was on top of his bins, even if he wasn't, and that he had no clue who Param at number 87 was, even though he did—he liked to keep them on their toes. But he had no time for that today.

Today was his shopping day. Naina had always done the shopping on Wednesdays. To deviate from that routine now would be wrong. First things first, he checked the fridge and the cupboards, organized just the way Naina had liked them to be, by which he meant not at all. Just as he suspected: he needed okra and mung beans. He *loved* mung beans, regardless of what Rohini said. He had never cooked much when Naina was alive, except in the last few months of her life, but he knew a few recipes by heart. They kept him going. What did he need with "nutritionally balanced" at his age, anyway?

As he stepped out of his house, slamming the door behind him, the early July heat bowled him over. He had worn too many layers *again*. And he *always* felt the heat. Some of the other "elderly" people at the mandir laughed at him—when they were too cold, Mukesh was too hot. He worried about underarm sweat patches, though they would often say, "Mukeshbhai, why do you worry about such things? We are old now. We don't mind."

But Mukesh did not want to be old, and if he stopped worrying about sweat patches, belching in public, that sort of thing, he might stop caring about other more important things too.

He adjusted his flat cap, which he wore whatever the weather, to make sure the sun was out of his eyes. He'd had this cap for fifty years. It was wearing away and wearing out, but he loved it. It had outlasted his marriage and, while he didn't want to be a pessimist, if he lost it, it would be like losing another fundamental part of himself.

Every week, the walk up the slight hill from his house to the high road got a little bit harder, his breathing a little bit shallower, and one day he would need to order a Dial-a-Ride for the five-minute stroll. When he eventually reached the top of the hill and turned left, he took a deep breath, steadied himself against a bollard, readjusted his mandir-branded canvas bag, which was slipping off his shoulder, and carried on toward his usual grocery shop on Ealing Road.

Ealing Road was a bit quieter on a Wednesday, which was why Naina had nominated it as her shopping day. She always said it reduced her chances of bumping into someone she knew, which always had the potential to turn a ten-minute shopping trip into an hour's social catch-up.

A few people wandered in and out of the shops that had beautiful mannequins showing themselves off in the window, draped in jewels and bright material, but the majority frequented the fruit and vegetable stalls, or hung around near the Wembley Central mosque. Mukesh waved to his neighbor Naseem and Naseem's daughter Noor, sitting on a wall sharing a packet of cassava crisps between them. They hadn't spoken for more than a few minutes since Naina had passed, but whenever he saw Naseem, and Noor on school holidays, they never failed to brighten his day.

Mukesh finally reached his favorite shop, overflowing with all sorts of vegetables, fresh and fragrant, kept in the shade by the awning. It was swarming with shoppers and buggies and children. Mukesh felt a little bubble of panic in his throat. Nikhil was standing in the doorway, as though he had been waiting just for him.

"Hey, Mukesh!" Nikhil was thirty, and the son of an acquaintance from the mandir. So really, he should have called him "Mukesh*fua*," meaning uncle, as a sign of respect, but Mukesh let this slide, as he often did. He didn't want to be fua to this young man, who still had all his original hair, all his original teeth, and was a while away from the muffin-top belly Mukesh had been sporting for the last ten years, steadily maintained by a diet of rice, mung, and kadhi. He liked feeling like Nikhil's friend rather than his doddery old uncle.

"Kemcho, Nikhil," Mukesh replied. "Can I have mung, plenty of it—and some bhindi too?"

"Wonder what you're making today, eh, Mukesh?!"

"You know what I'm making."

"It was a joke. You know mung and okra don't even go together, right? Make something different. For *once*, Mukesh." Nikhil mock-rolled his eyes, a toothy grin on his face.

"You know, young man, you should be calling me fua! I must

tell your mother of your rudeness." He smiled to himself. Even if he tried, he'd never be able to earn the respect Naina had once had. She had been the public-facing figure in their marriage. She'd run the satsangs at the mandir on Saturdays, and led the bhajans. The younger ones *and* her peers looked up to her.

Mukesh watched Nikhil weave his way in and out of the crowds. Finally, he presented Mukesh with a blue bag, teeming with greenery. Okra and mung beans aplenty, but many other bonus vegetables thrown in too. They didn't call it "Variety Foods" for nothing.

Mukesh said thank you, quite quietly, and jostled back through the shoppers to the street, where cars were tooting and beeping, their windows open and music of all kinds blaring out.

When he reached the top of his road, he began to walk "briskly," helped by the downward slope. He unlocked his door, hobbled to his kitchen, and unpacked his groceries (bonus veg today: spinach and coriander, and a bread roll or two, perfect for pav bhaji, which Mukesh had no clue how to make). Finally, he sat himself down in front of the television.

Usually, on a Wednesday, he'd unpack his shopping and then sit on his chair with his feet up, drinking a cup of hot and just-right sweet chai, as Naina used to make it (now made using ready-mix sachets), and he'd turn on Zee TV or the news, to keep his eyes away from the empty chair beside him, Naina's chair—and to fill his ears with sound, laughter, and stern conversations, important world affairs, to keep his mind away from the deafening silence that had welcomed him home every day for two years now.

For months after Naina's death, Mukesh hadn't been able to sleep in his own bed, because being in there alone felt like being in someone else's home entirely.

"Papa, you take your time," Rohini had said to him at first, and Vritti had set up a bed in the living room for him.

"He can't sleep there forever, he'll do his back in," Deepali had whispered to her sisters after tucking him in. A strange role reversal that made him feel an immense sense of shame. How could he be whole again when his whole had gone for good?

"He'll be okay. He is grieving. I can't bring myself to go in the bedroom at all, but we're going to need to clear Mummy's stuff away. She kept it so messy!" Rohini whispered back.

Lying on the living-room sofa, Mukesh had shut his eyes, hoping to block out the sound of their laughter. Soft, comforting laughter. He was the father; he should be looking after his girls. But he couldn't. He didn't know how to without Naina.

Once a year had passed, and Mukesh Patel's Time of Eternal Quiet had begun, that silent, lonely stage of grief, where everyone but you had moved on, Rohini, Deepali, and Vritti had insisted on finally clearing out Naina's room. "Papa, we're not letting you put this off for any longer. It's time for you to move forward with your life."

So, they began sorting through the detail and debris of their mother's life, reorganizing the organized chaos Naina thrived in. Deepali, who conveniently had dust allergies, opted to cook a lunch for them instead. For that one day, his house was full of life again—but for all the wrong reasons. As he listened to Deepali mixing batter in the kitchen, he stood in the doorway of his and Naina's bedroom watching Vritti and Rohini. They didn't know he was there. He was silent and invisible in his own home, a ghost of himself.

Rohini took the lead, shouting instructions to Vritti to root out the boxes under the bed, while she dashed around the room, returning a comb to its rightful place in a shoebox on the top of the wardrobe, folding up shawls and tidying them away into a big wheely suitcase, and packing away handfuls and handfuls of bangles. Mukesh watched as they dragged box after box out from under the bed. Vritti knelt to the floor, her cheek pressed against the carpet, and ran her hand to the left, and to the right.

All of a sudden, there was a clinking, clattering crash.

"Oh God! What have you done?" Rohini groaned, staring down at her sister. Vritti pulled the box out, revealing a now half-emptied yogurt pot of mismatched earrings. Next came the Clarks shoebox of photographs that had entertained them all for hours on end when the girls were little, sitting on Naina's or Mukesh's knees, asking about their paisley-patterned clothes and garish flares. Mukesh had always thought they looked rather fashionable. The girls laughed at that.

Then followed several pieces of empty Tupperware. And finally, one lonely, dust-covered library book.

Vritti slowed her pace for a moment and held it in her hands, as Rohini knelt down beside her sister.

"Papa," they called, loudly, still oblivious he was only a few feet away. Deepali trotted into the room then too.

"Mummy's book—well . . . library book," Rohini said. "I thought I'd returned them all, but I must have missed this one." She held it up to him and he walked forward, not quite believing it. As though this dusty, icky, sticky book was some kind of mirage. When he'd seen the other relics of her life, he'd barely felt a thing. But here, seeing this book, the gray dust sticking to the plastic cover in splotches, it was like Naina was here in the room with them. Here, with his three girls, and one of Naina's beloved books, for a moment, just a moment, he didn't feel so alone.

Once upon a time, a huge stack of library books sat on Naina's bedside table. They'd kept her company in her last year. She'd read the same ones over and over again. Her "favorites." Mukesh wished now that he'd asked her what they were about, what she loved about them, why she'd felt the need to read the same ones again and again. He wished that he'd read them with her.

And now all he had left was this one library book: *The Time Traveler's Wife.*

That night, with the room devoid of Naina's mess, Mukesh cracked the spine, feeling like an intruder. This wasn't his book, it was never chosen for him, and perhaps Naina would never have wanted him to read it either. He forced himself to read one page, but had to stop. The words weren't making sense. He was trying to turn the black letters and yellowed pages into a letter from Naina to him. But no such message existed.

The next night, he tried again. He put Naina's reading lamp on and turned to page one once more. He flicked through the successive pages, trying to be gentle, trying so hard not to leave his own mark on this book in any tangible way. He wanted this book to be Naina, and only Naina. He searched, forensically, for a clue—a mark on the page, a drop of chai, a tear, an eyelash, anything at all. He told himself that one day he would have to return it to the library—it's what Naina would have wanted. But he couldn't let it go. Not yet. It was his last chance to bring Naina back.

He took it page by page, chapter by chapter. He met Henry, a character who could travel through time. Through this gift, he could meet a past or future version of himself, and it was also, importantly, how he met Clare—he traveled in time to meet her when she was just a girl, and returned again and again over the years. The love of his life. And Clare had no choice but to love him, because he was all she had ever known.

He began to see these characters not as Henry and Clare but as love itself—that kind of love that feels fated, inescapable. That's what he and Naina had. Eventually in the story, Henry leaps forward into the future and learns he is going to die. He tells Clare he knows when it will happen, when they'll be separated forever.

As he was reading about Clare and Henry's tragedy, the phone beside him had begun to trill. It was Deepali. He'd not been able to speak, he could only cry.

"I knew she was going to die, my beta," he said to her, when his voice could finally escape. "In the same way Clare knew Henry was going to die in that book. They could almost count their last days together. I had that warning too. But did I do enough? Did I make her last few months happy?"

"Dad, what are you talking about?"

"Your mummy's book—*Time Traveling Wife*."

"What about it, Dad?" Her voice was soft, he could hear the pity ringing through it.

"Henry and Clare . . . you know . . . they loved each other ever since they were very young, just like me and your mummy. And they knew when he was going to die. And they lived their lives as best they could, making the most of every moment. I don't know if I did the same."

"Dad, Mummy loved you, and she knew you loved her. That was enough. Come on, now. It's late, Papa, go to sleep, okay? Don't worry about it at all. You gave her a good life, and she gave you a good life too."

Naina had died. But this book felt like one little glimpse into her soul, into their love, their life together. A snapshot of the early days of their marriage when they were still all but strangers to each other. Married, with no idea of what the other one was really like. Naina would do everything—she'd cook, she'd clean, she'd laugh, she'd cry, she'd sew, she'd mend, and at the end of the day, she'd read. She'd settle into bed as though she'd had the most relaxing day, and she'd read. From their first few weeks together, he knew that he loved her, and he'd love her forever.

I'll never be lost to you, Mukesh, she had said to him then as he gripped the book in his hands. He heard the words. Her voice. The story—it had brought her back—even if just for a moment.

Now, as Mukesh reached for the remote control to continue today's routine, his hand collided with a book. *The Time Traveler's Wife* was staring up at him from the sitting-room table. *Time to go to the library, no excuses*, the book whispered to him, in a voice that sounded uncannily like Naina's. It was time to leave this book behind, to move forward. Now it was time.

After a few deep breaths and a little stretch of his legs, he stood up, tucked the book into his canvas bag, checked his pockets for his bus pass, and headed straight out of the house, up the hill. He crossed the road at the traffic lights to get to the closest bus stop. He waited, struggling to read the timetable.

A young woman was standing next to him, with a messy bun and a huge mobile phone, held in two hands.

"Excuse me, where on earth is the library and which bus would I need to get, please?"

The woman sighed and began to tap the screen. He had irritated her, he would have to find out another way, but, squinting, he couldn't make out any detail on the map. He would be here forever.

"You've got to get the ninety-two from here," the woman said suddenly, making Mukesh jump. "It's in the Civic Center."

"Oh *no*! Surely there is another one. The Civic Center is so full of people. Too, too busy for me. Can you check again?"

The woman chewed her gum loudly, grumpily. She looked at her phone. "*I* don't know. They're all closing down round here, aren't they, the libraries?" She inhaled sharply. A moment later: "Yeah, okay, there's Harrow Road Library, down there—same bus. You've got to cross the road though."

"Thank you, thank you. I'm so pleased." He smiled at her; and then, against all the odds, she gave him a smile back. As he stepped off the curb—in his excitement he had forgotten how slowly his limbs moved—he felt a stabbing pain in his knee. The woman grabbed him, firmly but gently. "Chill a bit, you need to look both ways first." She checked right, she checked left, she checked right again and gave him a nudge when the coast was clear.

On the other side, he turned to look for her, his hand held up in a wave. But her bus had arrived, and he was already forgotten.

As the 92 came to a stop in front of him, he clambered on, pulling himself up onto the deck with all his might, tapping his Oyster card on the reader. "Excuse me," he said to the driver, "please tell me where to get off for the Harrow Road Library." He enunciated the words as though it was a Highly Important Place of Interest. The bus driver looked at him blankly.

"Ealing Road stop," he replied eventually.

"Thank you, my friend, thank you. Today's quite a big day for me."

CHAPTER 2

ALEISHA

"Aleisha." Thermos Flask Dev tapped his hand on the desk. "I'm out for the rest of the day. Look alive a bit, if you can. I know this isn't Tiger Tiger, or wherever you kids like to go these days, but people still expect good customer service here."

Aleisha was slumped over the desk, her expression molded into her "resting bitch face," as her brother so lovingly liked to call it. She looked up at Thermos Flask Dev, without bothering to sit up to attention. Thermos was her manager. A tall, rather scrawny, sweater-vest-wearing Indian man who could be irritating, but over whom she also felt slightly protective. In the library he was The Boss. The librarians ran around after him, trying to please him, even when he was just sitting in the corner drinking from a thermos flask (she always wondered if there was actually booze in the thermos flask because they had a swish—well, sort of—coffee machine in the staff room. Why would he need to bring his own?). But outside, she imagined that he shrank by half, because the outside world, especially Wembley, wasn't quite so accepting of thermos-flask-drinking, all-year-round-sweater-vest-wearing men who loved to boss people around. She worried people might shout at him on the street if he was walking too slowly, or barge past him and spill his "coffee."

"Don't worry, boss, it's completely dead today."

He raised his eyebrows at her, but he couldn't disagree. A few children, whiny and loud, had been in earlier with their uninterested parents. They'd taken out one book each and promised to pay their overdue fines the next time they came in. Those fines (20p and 67p) had been sitting on the account for the past three months, set to become fines forever unpaid. Aleisha let it slide—she had no urge to police this. This wasn't her dream job—was it anyone's?—she was just working here for the summer. She'd finished her exams in May, so this was literally the longest summer of her life.

"Do people even still use libraries?" her school friends had asked her when she got the job. So quiet. Dying. Boring as hell. She'd tried for a job in Topshop in Oxford Street—for the discounts and for a chance to get out of Wembley for a bit. But this is where she'd ended up. "It's a place of peace," Thermos Flask had said to her after her interview. "We pride ourselves on that. Lots of libraries have been closed down recently—I'm sure you've heard all about it—and we're doing everything we can to highlight to the powers that be how *vital* this space is for our community." His arms were open wide, basking in the library's stuffy silence. "Lots of our regulars come here for that lovely sense of quiet companionship, you know? Your brother used to love that about this very special place too, didn't he? How *is* your brother?"

Aleisha nodded and shrugged in response. Her older brother, Aidan, had worked here when he was her age. "The people are *endlessly* fascinating," Aidan had said to her when she'd told him she'd actually gotten the job. "Like, just watching people sit and be quiet, or browse, or whatever, when they don't realize they're being watched . . . It's like, I don't know, no one's trying to be someone they're not in a library."

Aleisha hadn't understood his fascination. Aidan had always been the bookish one. He was studious, often learning for learning's sake, whereas she did her work only to get the grades, and would never have just curled up with a book in the way he used to.

Their mum would bring them here on the odd occasion as children, and Aleisha couldn't bear the silence. She'd kick and scream, wanting to run around in the park just outside. As they'd grown older, Aleisha had never made her way back to the library by herself, but Aidan used to head there after school, sometimes to do his homework, but mostly to read books for fun.

So as soon as Aleisha said Topshop wouldn't take her, Aidan had suggested the small, quiet, musty Harrow Road Library. She was sort of doing this job for him, hoping, in some small way, to make him proud.

"I'm off out too, Aleisha, you'll be all right on your own for a bit?" Lucy, one of the two library volunteers, scooted out from between some shelves. Thermos said there just wasn't enough funding to actually employ any more staff—there wasn't enough of an incentive to have two perfectly good libraries going, when the Civic Center one was super swish, so they needed to do all they could to cut costs while also providing "the best service possible." Lucy had lived in Wembley for years, and Harrow Road had been her go-to library, when it was fully funded. She loved to talk about the good old days, when children would pile in at the holidays. "This library used to be so full and vibrant, you know, Aleisha. I like coming back here a couple of times a week, it just brings back memories of my little ones. They became readers here." Lucy loved to reminisce. She'd told Aleisha this story at least fifteen times already, always saying, "Stop me if I've said this before."

"It's quieter these days, kids playing Xbox and stuff, I guess!" Lucy continued. "My little ones, though, they inhaled every page they got their hands on."

One of Lucy's kids had gone on to run her own hair salon, opening up two or three in the area, and they were doing really well. The other had trained as an accountant working for some law firm in the city. Lucy was endlessly proud of them, and always put it down to "this library."

"It's so peaceful today, isn't it?" Lucy looked at them both, throwing her summer jacket on and wandering toward the doors. "The perfect day for chilling out with a book." She winked at them. "I'll see you next week!"

It *was* peaceful. Lucy and Aidan were both right about that. But, with peace came boredom, and today was a real struggle.

"Maybe," Thermos Flask said, turning to Aleisha as he reached the door, "you could look through the returns pile? You need to make sure you take out any scraps or bits of rubbish. Some of our regulars"—*What? All five of them?* Aleisha thought to herself—"have complained about finding bits and pieces stuck in the pages. There are latex gloves in the drawer. I know Kyle usually enjoys this job, but it would be a huge help if you could get it done today."

Of *course* goody-two-shoes Kyle loved the gross, super-diligent jobs. She thought about ignoring his instructions completely . . . but she looked around, surveying the room. Silent. There was a guy reading in the corner, a mum and her toddler in the children's section, all getting on with their days. No one needed her. Her phone sat on the desk: no new messages. The old clock hanging above the door said one thirty. She still had hours and *hours* left and, with nothing to do, time would seemingly stand still. So, she pulled out the desk drawer, put on two latex gloves, all clingy on her skin, and got started.

After ten minutes, she'd already succeeded in forming two piles. Stuff to chuck: a few train tickets, old receipts, and a torn ticket to see Stormzy dated 2017. Stuff to keep: one lonely chicken-shop loyalty card—with just one stamp left to go. Poor Kyle would be gutted he'd missed out on this piece of treasure.

Just as she began to open a particularly disgusting copy of *War and Peace*, she spotted, out of the corner of her eye, an old man on the other side of the library's glass doors. He was trying to push the doors open. When that failed, he tried waving his arms around.

Bloody hell, she thought to herself, *there's a push button right in front of you.* Just when she thought she might be left alone for the rest of the day. She rolled her eyes and waited for him to work it out. With enough luck, he'd lose patience and wander off on his next errand.

But she was wrong. He persisted, fruitlessly. He stood there, reaching up, one hand on the small of his back, his neck as long as it could go, peering at every inch of the doors, searching for a clue. His eyes went from left to right—his head followed, just a moment behind.

Nothing.

She waited a little while longer, but as his hands began to reach up to the top of the doors, she gave in. She didn't need Thermos Flask Dev yelling at her for neglect if this guy toppled over or something, trying to climb through an upstairs window.

She pulled her earphones out, walked over to the entrance, and pressed the button to open the doors. She watched as they slid apart.

"*Aha!*" the man said from the other side, delighted with himself.

"I just pressed the button. There's a button outside too."

"Oh, thank you, miss." He nodded his head.

Aleisha wandered back to the desk, plugged her earphones in again, latex gloves at the ready.

But when she looked up once more, the old man was standing exactly where she had left him. On the wrong side of the doors, which had now closed automatically behind her. She rolled her eyes, and resolved, this time, not to help him.

"Excuse me, miss!" He was now knocking on the door with one hand, frantically feeling around with the other, looking for the button he'd missed. She didn't get paid enough for this.

After thirty seconds of him fumbling and knocking on the door, the mum decided to take her toddler home, letting the old man in on her way out. He didn't miss his chance this time and hopped straight in, walking right up to Aleisha at the desk. She fixed her eyes on her scrap-paper pile, pretending to concentrate, hoping he'd realize she was busy and leave her alone.

Even through her music, she could hear his repeated "Excuse me, miss." Then he started tapping on her desk. When his finger began to worm its way over to the bell, she looked him straight in the eyes.

"What can I help you with, sir?" She smiled, sweetly, using her polite "Look at me, I'm a librarian" voice.

"I am wanting to return . . ." and after a moment of silence, his face blanched. "No, sorry, actually"—he shook his head vigorously—"I said I am looking for some books." She noticed him clutching a little canvas bag tightly to his side, as though clinging on for dear life.

"You're in the right place." She smirked.

"No, miss, I need your help. Please do help me."

She sighed. "What do you need help with?"

"I . . ." His voice quivered, almost inaudibly. His cheeks had adopted a faint pink glow, and she could see his ears turning a fluorescent red. "I'm not sure . . . what . . . books—can I get some stories?"

"You can use the self-service machines for that." She pointed to the computer desks.

He looked at the computers, and down at his hands. "I don't think I will know how to use them," he said.

"Do you know what books you're looking for?" She sighed, turning to her screen, minimizing Facebook, briefly glimpsing the new photo her ex Rahul had posted, and opening up the correct database.

"No, that's where I need some help too."

She was trying so hard not to lose her patience.

"I'm afraid I can't help you if you don't know what books you want. I've just got a search engine."

"But don't you have knowledge of books? Librarians know what people want to read. I know the *sort* of thing. I want books to read that I will enjoy. Maybe even something I could share with my granddaughter too . . . Like, something classic, maybe? Novels, I think. I have read *The Time Traveler's Wife*." His hand flew to his bag and he clasped it tightly. "Yes, I *really* liked that one. It helped me a lot, that book did."

"Never heard of it. I'm really sorry, but I'm better with nonfiction, books for school and things. Things that *teach* me stuff. I don't read novels."

The man looked horrified, his jaw dropped. "You *should* know novels. It is your job. Can you point me in any direction? Any direction at all?"

"No, I think you might need to use Google or something."

"I—"

She stood up from her chair, an aching throb in her temples. She thought back to last night—to her mum, shut in her room, her brother pacing the hallway outside, listening out, checking in on her. Worry written on his face. Aleisha's eyes felt sore, tired, her head heavy. "Please, sir," she snapped through gritted teeth. "*Do* feel free to browse the shelves if you want to find something to read. The novels are over there." She waved her arm in the general direction.

And with that, she sat down and watched as the man made his way over to the shelves, slowly but surely. He glanced back at her a few times, his brow furrowed. She glared at her screen, determined to ignore him. She could feel something that might have been guilt start to bubble up in her throat, making her cough. What had come over her? She plugged her headphones in, shoving them firmly into her ears.

She pulled one latex glove farther up her arm, feeling it pull the tiny hairs on her skin. She was ready to forget the last few minutes when someone *else* accosted her. It was one of the five library regulars: Crime Thriller Guy. He was almost always found in the crime/thriller section, sitting at the tables overlooking the park. It was sheltered a little from the rest of the library. Tucked away, quiet. Sometimes, when the library closed, Aleisha liked to sit there herself, looking out. Just for a minute or two. Just for a tiny bit of a break before she went home. A moment to brace herself.

"What?" she snapped. She knew she was being rude but didn't have the energy to care.

"Hey, sorry," he said, mumbling. His hair was long—too long for an adult man, in her opinion—and it covered a lot of his face. He liked bright T-shirts but almost always wore a thick black hoodie over them. Just looking at him, in this sweaty summer weather, made her wilt. "I just wanted to return this book." He held up a copy of *To Kill a Mockingbird*.

She pointed with her latex finger to the returns pile. "Just put it there and I'll get to it," she said.

He nodded. "Not my usual crime book, of course. But it's really good. I've read it a few times now—I keep coming back to it . . . It helps me get out of my head—well, all stories do that, you know? This *place* does that for me."

She frowned—if dark crime was his *escape*, what on earth was he escaping *from*? She nodded in response.

Crime Thriller stumbled on, awkward and shy. "This book . . . you know . . . I'd recommend it." He raised his eyebrows and nodded almost imperceptibly toward the old man framed by the shelves. Aleisha frowned again, and Crime Thriller waved the book once more in the old man's direction. "It's a *classic* . . . a book *everyone* should read." He labored over each word, before carefully placing the book next to the other returns—like it was some sort of precious gift—and turned away from her slowly.

What was his problem? Was he trying to flirt with her?

When he finally left, Aleisha picked up *To Kill a Mockingbird*, scanned it on the system to log it back in, and started to shake it in search of any illegal scraps to be binned. When a piece of paper fell out, she half-expected it to be his phone number or his Instagram handle or something. But as she unfolded it, she saw it was some kind of shopping list. She sighed, she wanted to call him back, tell him off for adding to her workload. But then Aleisha looked closer—the handwriting was nice, curly in all the right places. It wasn't how she imagined Crime Thriller would write. She scanned the words again: it was a list of books.

A reading list.

There were eight titles scribbled there. It began with *To Kill a Mockingbird*, the book she was holding in her latexed hands.

Just in case you need it:

To Kill a Mockingbird

Rebecca

The Kite Runner

Life of Pi

Pride and Prejudice

Little Women

Beloved

A Suitable Boy

At first, she dropped it on the chuck pile. But as she went to dump the whole lot in the bin, something stopped her. She took one of her gloves off and carefully ran her fingers over the delicate words *To Kill a Mockingbird*, before stuffing the scrap of paper into the back of her phone case, along with the chicken-shop stamp card.

She held up the book, taking in the cover and feeling the weight of the pages in her hands.

Then she got up and headed over to the old man, her heart pounding in her chest, *a book* everyone *should read* ringing in her mind. Here it was, her olive branch.

CHAPTER 3

MUKESH

Mukesh had felt the girl's eyes boring into the back of his head as he stomped toward the shelves. He had no idea where to begin in his "search for a novel"—the colors of the books all blurred into one. He ran his hands over the spines, feeling the different textures—mostly shiny and soft, silky. He thought of Naina's neat saris piled up at home. The words written down the spines washed over him, ran away from him, laughed at him, as though they knew he didn't really belong here. Was the girl still watching him? He wandered between shelves, trying to get out of her eyeline.

He heard someone whispering. He didn't know where the sound was coming from, but it felt as if they were whispering about *him*. His cheeks grew hot. Desperate to hide himself away, he quickly grabbed a book, any book at all, from the shelf.

The Highway Code and Theory Test for Car Drivers. Well, he certainly hadn't been looking for *that*. It wasn't even a novel, though it might come in handy for his granddaughter Priya's driving theory test in six years' time. Reluctant to admit defeat, determined to pretend he didn't need the librarian's guidance anyway, he sat down at a table and started to read: *Introduction:* The Highway Code *is essential reading for everyone.*

"Oh, Naina," he said out loud. "What am I doing here?"

Someone, hidden away in the corner, *shush*ed him quite aggressively and his head jumped up in fright. How long did he need to wait here for it not to look as though he'd made a silly mistake? It was obvious he wouldn't be taking a driving test anytime soon! What would people think of him, panicking like that? He read the entire contents page, and then some of the introduction, which was interesting, though entirely irrelevant to his day-to-day life. He'd long since given up driving. His daughters had seen to that.

As he sat there, he could feel *The Time Traveler's Wife* burning a hole through his canvas bag, drawing his attention. He'd been unable to give the book back at the crucial moment. He knew, if he gave it back now, he'd get into so much trouble for keeping it so long. Maybe he could escape into its pages, to take his mind off this terrible, awkward, embarrassing trip . . .

He heard footsteps behind him, the only sound breaking the silence, and, with no time to pull out *The Time Traveler's Wife*, he delved back into *The Highway Code*. Something was *clack*, *clack*, *clack*ing—he glanced over his shoulder, trying to be as inconspicuous as possible. His eyes opened wide in horror as he saw it was the girl. She was holding a book between her hands—probably to *mock* him. Her nails, long and pointy, were doing the *clack*, *clack*, *clack*ing on the cover.

"Sir?" she said. She sounded polite this time, but he couldn't trust her. His head snapped back to the pages. He wanted to read this fascinating book in peace.

"Sir?" she repeated. "Is that what you were looking for?" She pointed down at *The Highway Code*. "I could have found that for you if you had told me."

"Don't call me 'sir,' I am not your 'sir'!" Mukesh stood up, bristling with anger and embarrassment.

With that, he picked up *The Highway Code* and marched toward the door as quickly as he could manage, pressing the automatic-open button (hardly automatic open!) to let himself out. His head held high, he ignored the beeps from the detectors, forgetting the stolen book in his hands.

Arriving home, Mukesh opened the door to emptiness; he was calmer now but his eyes were prickling with tears, his ears burning with shame. Slipping off his shoes at the door, he threw his canvas bag down onto his chair in the living room with unexpected force before checking his landline for messages. There was another from Rohini, ending with "Papa, call me when you get this. We need to know what to cook when we visit on Friday, I'll need to do the shopping tomorrow. I hope you've been eating properly."

He slumped down onto his sofa. Rohini's message only served to increase the pounding of his heart. Last week Priya had begged him for something to read. She'd left her own book at home and had nothing with which to pass the time. He'd suggested watching *Blue Planet*. She'd groaned at him.

"I wish Ba was here! She had *so* many books."

Priya and Naina had been forever wrapped up in books. Naina would hole up with Priya in their downstairs bedroom—they'd make a fort out of sheets and cushions and sit together and read. He would hear them talking about characters as though they were real-life people. He thought it fanciful, but completely lovely. He watched his documentaries with the same passion instead. Just as educational, but easier on the eyes. He really wanted Priya to love David Attenborough as much as he did.

"I *have* a book," Mukesh had said to his granddaughter, as he hurried upstairs to his spare room. The bookshelf now showcased only the dusty plastic-jacketed copy of *The Time Traveler's Wife*.

When he brought it down to her, held out in his hands, Priya's face showed nothing but outrage. "Here, Priya. Even *I* have read this one, it is the most beautiful story." Priya had slapped it out of his hands and commenced an uncharacteristic temper tantrum.

"Dada, this is too grown-up for me!" Her face fell, and he could see her cheeks start to glow red with frustration. "I wish Ba was here. She would know. You don't *get* books, Dada." Her bottom lip began to quiver, and then, eventually, she sniffed. "You just don't *care*!"

His heart crashed, a punch to the chest. He let his eyes glaze over, wishing to be spirited away, desperate to hear Naina's voice once more, to feel her sitting beside him.

No. He couldn't *bear* a repeat of that. He'd felt so ashamed, so *useless* . . . Naina would be so disappointed in him. "What can I do?" he called out to the silent house.

Now is not the time to give up, Mukesh.

Mukesh stopped in his tracks, knowing his mind, his disappointment, was playing tricks on him, but it felt like Naina had said that to him.

Everyone needs to ask for help sometimes, Mukesh. Her voice came to him once more, and he felt the hairs stand up on the back of his neck. She was right, she was always right.

His heart sank at the thought of Priya sitting in an armchair, or tucked up on Ba's side of the bed, with a book—miles and miles, and worlds and worlds away from him.

"Does she enjoy coming to visit me?" Mukesh asked out loud.

He waited, hoping for Naina to come back to him, to tell him it was all going to be okay—but there was only silence.

He picked up the remote, turning on *Blue Planet*. Usually David Attenborough's voice, the deep blues of the sea, the funny noises from the creatures, helped him to focus and to relax. But today, he let David Attenborough's voice fall on deaf ears and wandered back over to his canvas bag, pulled *The Time Traveler's Wife* out, and clutched it to his chest. He shuffled to his bedroom and flumped onto the bed. He let the novel fall open in his hands and allowed himself to be transported back to the world of Clare and Henry; they had been warned in advance—a blessing and a curse—about Henry's death. That was the starkest warning anyone could be given. They knew their days together were limited—they were waiting for the end to come.

But from Mukesh's own experience, he knew that a warning, no matter how stark, how clear, was never a comfort; it was only the slow drip of fear through all the good and all the bad times. A ticking time bomb. He remembered when the doctor had sat him and Naina down after her last scan.

"I'm sorry, Mrs. Patel," the doctor had said, his voice solid; yet under the surface Mukesh heard a quiver. He wore glasses, which sat neatly on the bridge of his nose. He looked how Mukesh imagined his own son might have, had they had one. That familiarity, it made it worse somehow. They'd always wanted a doctor in the family, for moments like this, for an expert to say to them, "Don't worry, Papa, often doctors get these things wrong."

Naina and Mukesh had both known this doctor was not wrong.

Rohini came to collect them both from the hospital; she'd bombarded them with interesting facts from the news, trying to deflate the sadness in the car, while Mukesh and Naina sat in silence. This was *their* moment—the moment equivalent to when Henry traveled into the future and watched himself die—wondering how long they had until that day finally arrived.

For weeks after, in the pitch-black of the night, as Naina lay asleep beside him, Mukesh's mind replayed those words: *I'm sorry, Mrs. Patel.*

"Naina," he'd whisper to her, "how can I swap places with you? How can I tell God to take me instead?" Mukesh knew what was coming, just like Henry, just like Clare. But he refused to admit it to himself.

"Mukesh," Naina said to him one morning. "We should talk about arrangements, for after . . ." She'd said it softly yet so matter-of-factly. She was hurting him. Henry never let Clare dwell on that moment, on his death, did he? Mukesh wasn't sure anymore; his memory of the story had merged with his own life. Henry was Naina, and Mukesh was Clare. The one left behind.

"Naina," he would say, smiling. "Don't you worry about any of that, let's just enjoy this beautiful day." He said the same thing, whether it was stormy outside or brilliant sunshine.

"We should talk about the girls, what they will need. Priya, and Jaya, and Jayesh too. I have things I want to give to them, for when they are older. I should show you."

Mukesh just shook his head, sipped his tea. "Naina, it is okay. You need to rest, we can do *all* that another day. Let's watch something, one of those films, a nice one." The words tumbled from his mouth like a waterfall, trying to wash away Naina's practicality.

"Mukesh." Naina's voice had been stern. Every few days she tried to speak to him, and every few days he dismissed her. "We've been given time, we should use it."

Despite it all, she had never once tried to talk to him about how he should *feel* when she was gone, what he should do for himself, to bring her back. That was all he had ever wanted to know.

Now here he was, alone, still without any clue as to what he should do now she was gone, left in a lifeless, soulless, bookless house that had once been their home. Naina had once given her personality to this house, her heart hung up among her saris, her possessions decorating every surface—fabric and cardigans draped over every chair, books stacked in every corner, and jewelry hung from the bedposts.

He lay the book down, hopped off the bed, and opened some of Naina's cupboards, pulling out infinite saris, more roughly than he wanted to. He told himself he was looking for books, for something to give Priya to read, but really he was hoping it might bring Naina back to him. As sari after sari tumbled to the floor, he could smell the warm, musty tang of Naina's perfume. It surrounded him like a cloud. For a moment, she was here again. She was everywhere.

He was wallowing for no reason—Rohini would want to give him a firm shake when she got here, saying, "Papa, life must go on. Mummy would have wanted that for you."

He lay back on the bed, looking up at the ceiling, and immediately regretted his decision. Would he ever be able to stand up again? He watched as the cracks in the ceiling grew before his eyes, as cobwebs began to overwhelm every corner of the room, as the shadows cast by the windowpane developed into thick inky-black lines, and he waited, waited for the ink to drip on him, obscuring him completely. He thought back to Henry, to Clare, to a time when his wife lying next to him wasn't just the wish of a grief-stricken man.

CHRIS

2017

He forced himself out of bed, his head heavy with sleep. But this was progress: it was the first time he'd been awake before midday in *weeks.* He felt the empty space beside him—Melanie's side of the bed—and he immediately wanted the ground, the mattress, to swallow him whole and take the pain away. On the floor, a pile of crime books sat staring up at him, taunting him, a thin layer of dust collecting on the top.

Usually, Chris's books were all he needed to get himself out of a funk. But when he'd first picked up a novel after the breakup and encountered a detective who was smart, tall, elegant, and beautiful—all he could think about was Melanie. She was smart, tall, elegant, and beautiful too. He'd shut the book in frustration, hearing the pages slam together. He'd stared up at the ceiling, his eyes unfocused, and stayed like that for the rest of the night, images of her running through his mind. Melanie . . . happy. Melanie . . . sad. *Melanie, Melanie, Melanie.*

Today, however, he was determined to put Melanie from his mind; his embarrassment, his weakness, his inability to "emotionally connect" to people. He needed to tuck it into a little box, with a tiny wooden lid. He hoped and prayed that something would keep that box shut. He just needed a few hours to forget, to be another version of himself.

So, he pulled on his trousers, freshly washed ones today, and a new T-shirt, also just out of the cupboard, and headed for Harrow Road. He was in a reading slump, but every day he'd still taken himself to the library: a little sanctuary in this lonely city. Since the breakup, his phone had been buzzing with messages from friends: "Hey, do you and Melanie want to join us for dinner tonight?" "Hi, Chris, let's go for a walk. Joanna is missing Melanie and you!" "How are you? How's Melanie's new job going? Hope you're both good. Miss you guys x." *Melanie, Melanie, Melanie.* Everyone loved Melanie; *he* loved Melanie. But in the library at least he could breathe, he could escape the onslaught of messages, just *be* for a little while.

Today, as he sat down in his usual spot, he saw something—a book, just sitting there. Some people were careless, stacking up books to "peruse," never returning the discarded ones to their rightful places, leaving it all down to the library staff. He would do the good deed and return it to the shelves.

But, as he picked the book up, he saw a Post-it note stuck to the table in its place. He peeled it off, carefully, and brought it close to his face. His eyesight wasn't as it had once been, before the hours and hours of reading in his dimly lit flat. The Post-it note was covered in handwriting, an elaborate scrawl of letters.

> I know this isn't your usual thing, but I read *To Kill a Mockingbird* when I was twenty-one and going through a hard time—it taught me a lot back then, and I got to see the world through the eyes of a child once more, the good and the bad. It was an escape for me; I threw myself into the world, into the injustices, into the characters, and it was the respite I needed from my own life—for it helped me care deeply about someone else's. I hope it can be an escape, a bit of respite, for you too. Some-

times, books just take us away for a little while, and return us to our place with a new perspective.

He brushed the hair out of his eyes. There was no name on the note, no "to" and no "from"—it could be for anyone. But then how could he explain that sudden feeling of being *seen*? As though someone had read his mind? He looked at the book afresh, his eyes taking in the title: *To Kill a Mockingbird*. Whoever had written this little Post-it note—had they known he sat here, day after day, wasting his hours wallowing?

He held the book tightly in his hands, as though imagining it might spring to life and explain it all to him. Nothing happened. No one jumped out from behind the shelves revealing that he was on some comedy show, a "Chris, this is your shitty life" episode. But someone, somewhere, was telling him they'd understood what he was going through.

He thought about waiting, of saving this book for a rainy day . . . but today was the day he had vowed to distract himself.

To Kill a Mockingbird was burning in his hand: *read me, read me, read me*. There was no other explanation for it—this book, it was a sign. He turned to the first page, forgetting the gentle hum of the library around him, and was amazed how the words didn't jump around and run away from him. They stayed firmly in place, and soon became nothing but images. As the narrator, "Scout" Finch, introduced Chris to her childhood home, to the town of Maycomb, Alabama, he felt a laugh bubble up in his throat—the quaint quirks of the townspeople, the childlike resilience of Scout's brother, Jem, and their friend Dill . . . it was another world, and he was so glad of it. When he reached page twenty-seven, which arrived sooner than he could have imagined, he found another note settled there. A whole reading list, of which *To Kill a Mockingbird* was the very first. This book had kept Melanie from his mind—kept her in that little box, with a tiny wooden lid—so he didn't have to feel his pain and doubt fizzing through his veins every minute. Those first twenty-seven pages had given him something he hadn't felt since the breakup: hope.

The list was for him—he knew it.

He thought of that scripted message at the top: *Just in case you need it.* He felt like he'd never needed anything more.

To Kill a Mockingbird

by

HARPER LEE

CHAPTER 4

ALEISHA

Aleisha's walk home from the library was accompanied by the sounds of the park—kids playing and crowds of people her age laughing, smoking. She wondered if it was anyone she knew. She wanted desperately to go to the park, have a cigarette, but she'd agreed to be home for Mum, to cook the dinner tonight. She knew she would want spaghetti hoops on toast—her mum's favorite. But she'd asked for that every day for two weeks and Aleisha was *sick* of spaghetti hoops. *She* wanted lamb stew with dumplings now, her uncle Jeremy's specialty, even though it was the middle of summer and blisteringly hot.

She sent a text to Rachel, her cousin, for the recipe (Uncle Jeremy was completely useless with his phone) and got a message back almost immediately—a picture of Uncle Jeremy's recipe scrawled on the pages of a Delia Smith cookbook. **Dad knows better than Delia, for sure**, said Rachel. Aleisha's mum *loved* her brother, Jeremy, and she *loved* his cooking, so Aleisha hoped and prayed this recipe might be the spaghetti-hoop breakthrough they needed this week. Nerves bubbled in her chest as thoughts flashed through her mind of the best- and worst-case scenarios. Burning the stew—setting off the fire alarm—triggering Leilah's anger, her upset, her anxiety. Cooking the stew to Uncle Jeremy perfection too had its drawbacks. What if Leilah couldn't stand anyone else cooking her brother's stew? What if she shut herself off for even longer? Aleisha drew a deep breath, feeling the hot summer air fill her lungs, and focused on the recipe instead—one step at a time.

Aleisha zoomed in on Uncle Jeremy's messy handwriting, and found the list of ingredients, before popping into Variety Foods. She wandered around, picking up the veg she needed, checking, double-checking, then triple-checking them against the list, trying to decipher Uncle Jeremy's handwriting.

She handed over the money to the guy behind the till and walked out, tapping out a message to Rachel: Thanks so much, Mum's gonna love this, I'm sure—better than spaghetti hoops.

Rachel started typing back, then stopped, then started again, but no new message appeared on Aleisha's screen. Aleisha kept staring, waiting. She began typing a message back—How are you?—and let the words linger before hitting delete, delete, delete. Her cousin was probably busy. She didn't have time for casual chitchat. She shoved the phone back in her pocket.

Once she'd picked up the frozen meat from Iceland Foods, she followed the busy bustling high road for five minutes longer than she needed. Partly because she hated the shortcut, lined with huge commercial dustbins always overflowing with rubbish, probably sickly sweet and stinking after the hot day. But, mostly, she was just trying to delay getting home. *Home.* She wondered what that word meant to everyone else.

As she turned the corner, she saw that, as expected, every window of their house was pulled shut. Every other window on the street was as wide as it could go, letting out the sounds of the TV, of kids playing Xbox, or a shouting match in full swing. Her mum, Leilah, would be boiling, but she couldn't stand the outside air leaking in, the inside air leaking out.

Aleisha unlocked the door cautiously, like one wrong move would set everything on fire. Aidan was already out, gone as soon as that clock struck six—announcing the end of his Mum-shift. Sometimes, when he was at home, he'd spend his time outside on the street in his convertible, which he borrowed their mum's money to buy in the first place years ago, listening to music blaring through the car's speakers. Their mum never minded. She barely noticed. Aidan was her golden boy. People in the street would sometimes shout out of their windows to tell him to *Shut the fuck up*, and he'd shout back and say it was a free country, though usually only when his friends were around watching, expecting something from him. Other times he'd turn the music down to a reasonable level of his own accord and continue with his day.

Aleisha left the shopping bag on the kitchen counter and wandered upstairs to find her mum, knowing she'd be in the same room, in the same position, as she'd left her in the morning. She braced herself as she turned the doorknob.

Leilah was curled up on her bed, enveloped by a thick winter duvet. Aleisha started sweating just looking at her. Leilah's eyes were closed and her breathing was deep, but she wasn't asleep. It was still a bad day for Leilah, but they'd had worse days in the past.

"Mum, I'm going to make lamb stew for tea, 'kay? Just how Uncle Jeremy likes to make it."

"Fine, hun." Leilah's eyes remained closed.

"You wanna open a window?"

Leilah shrank smaller, disappearing into the bed, as though Aleisha's words themselves had stuck burning-hot pokers into her skin.

"Guess that's a no." Aleisha slammed the door behind her as she left, that ache in her temples suddenly back. The room had already started to take its hold over her; she stomped downstairs to shake it off. She wanted to storm out of the house. She wanted to shut herself in Aidan's convertible, and blare music at full volume. She wanted the neighbors to scream at her, to yell at her. She wanted to scream back.

Instead, she slumped into the kitchen, tipped the plastic bag of ingredients onto the countertop, and began to organize everything with a practiced calm. She thought of how Rachel and Jeremy always prepared their ingredients before they started cooking—like they were TV chefs or something. Aleisha got into a rhythm of slicing, chopping, measuring—it allowed her something to focus on. She looked up at the clock—seven thirty already. Just under the clock, she caught sight of the ceramic Beatrix Potter Peter Rabbit plate in pride of place on the kitchen wall. Aidan had won it when he was about ten for painting a (not-so-great) picture of Peter Rabbit for the school fair. It had been up there ever since.

She tapped her phone, her fingers sticky with onion, wondering if Aidan might have sent her a message, updating her on when he might be home later. No new messages.

She tipped her head back in frustration, her eyes back on the smiling, carefree Peter Rabbit. His little bum shaking his little fluffy tail.

"Aleisha!" Leilah's voice was coarse, pleading. Aleisha felt the familiar build of fear charge through her gut.

"What is it, Mum?"

"I need you to come. My feet are cramping."

"You need to move them," Aleisha whispered to herself.

"Please, come here *now*."

Aleisha made her way up the stairs. "Mum, you just need to stretch your feet." She spoke softly, trying to keep the impatience out of her voice.

"I can't do that on my own. How can I stretch anything myself right now?"

"This is how," Aleisha said, tiptoeing into her mother's room. She sat on the floor and demonstrated stretching out her feet and her legs. Leilah watched her, moved her limbs gently to imitate the action before sighing audibly and collapsing her hands beside her on the bed.

"I can't *do* that."

Aleisha stood up. "You can. Everyone can do that." She smiled, her voice encouraging. "That's like *beginner* yoga." She held her breath for a moment, worried she'd taken it too far . . . too soon for a joke.

Leilah frowned at her.

"Maybe you should try a yoga class," Aleisha said lightly. She got down on the floor again and tried the pose once more. "Limber you up."

Leilah let out a single strained, breathy "ha," raising her eyebrows;

Aleisha felt the pumping of her heart soften. Leilah mimicked her daughter's pose once more, her limbs suddenly coming alive. Aleisha spotted a flinch on Leilah's face as the cramp shot through her leg, but she continued to stretch. Leilah put her thumb and forefinger together in an O shape, "Aum," and she began to hum.

Aleisha closed her eyes, brought her palms together, and spoke in an airy-fairy yoga voice. "I hope you enjoyed your practice today." Aleisha slapped her own knee, laughing at her mother, at herself. Her mum wouldn't be caught dead in a yoga class. She perched on the end of Leilah's bed as her mother let her stretch go and Leilah exhaled a sincere "Namaste."

"Hope that cleared up your chakras for you."

Leilah grabbed her left foot. She prodded the ball a few times. "Yeah, my chakras are doing okay now."

"No need for a downward dog then."

Leilah began to giggle, her eyes scrunched shut—Aleisha's eyes were wide, and she laughed too, to cover her surprise. Then, within moments, they were both in hysterics. Leilah's head lolled back on her neck, her mouth open, a schoolgirl kind of glee ringing outward. Aleisha watched her. Sun from a gap in the curtain illuminated a stripe of her face. Her skin looked bright, gently glowing. She looked happy. Aleisha took a mental snapshot. She wanted to stall this moment here, forever. When they were done with their giggling, they sat beside each other in relative peace, a hiccup of laughter escaping here and there.

When everything was calm, she moved her hand toward her mother's face instinctively, but with a jolt Leilah moved away before Aleisha's skin met hers.

The next morning, Aleisha could hear her brother in the kitchen, frying something. The smell of the oil drifted under the gap in the doorway to her room. She shimmied herself out of bed, rubbing her eyes. Her head ached, and she could feel the oppressive heat of the day closing in already. She glanced at her phone, trying to ignore the many notifications from her school group chat, which would just be filled with photos of them sipping cocktails on the beach on holiday. She thought about texting Rachel again, to say thanks for the recipe—Leilah had eaten more than she'd expected in the end—but she left it. Rachel didn't need thanks. They were family.

She joined Aidan in the kitchen, her slippered feet *click-clacking* on the lino.

"Hey, Leish, didn't see you last night. How was work?"

"Really shit, to be honest."

Aidan looked at her, his eyebrows raised slightly, meaning: *Go on, tell me.*

"I just . . ." Aleisha sighed, really not wanting to relive it all. "This old guy came into the library—he was literally about ninety, I swear—and he was asking for book recommendations and . . . you *know* I don't care about books." Aleisha looked up at him, but Aidan didn't give anything away. "I just snapped at him."

"Aleisha!"

"I *know*. You don't have to make me feel worse about it."

"Look, it's fine. When I worked there, I'm sure I pissed loads of people off . . . probably not in the way *you* did . . . but just take it as a lesson. Like Uncle Jeremy always used to say, just do better next time."

"Come on, you're not Mum . . . or Uncle Jeremy. I don't need a lecture from you. You gonna be home today?" Aleisha asked, unsure, registering his apron, dressing gown, and slippers.

"Yeah, it's your day off. Go see your friends. I'll stay here with Mum. Think she had a bad night again—woke up quite a few times."

Aleisha walked toward the plate of food next to Aidan. There sat three fat, oily sausages, cooling. She picked one up with her long nails, trying to keep the sausage away from her skin. She dangled it above her mouth.

"Watch it, Leish! You're dripping oil on the floor." Aidan dropped to the ground with a paper towel, wiping up the yellow globs, his apron ballooning out with a whoosh. "Look, get out of the house today. Get some air."

"It's okay, I've not got any plans. I'm just going to hang out here and watch TV."

"No, Leish, Mum won't want any loud noises today. She's got a migraine." Aidan looked at her with a serious frown; there were deep purple shadows under his eyes. "I'll be here, don't worry."

With a shrug, Aleisha ate the sausage as quickly as she could; Aidan watched her with disgust. "It's fine," she said, her mouth still full. "Really. I've got no one to see, I'll stay here. I'll sit quietly in my room—it'll be like I don't even exist."

Leilah suddenly shouted from upstairs, "Shut up! Aleisha, shut up!" Aleisha and Aidan looked at each other, their faces blank, their smiles gone. She wasn't surprised. Last night, the giggling, the yoga . . . but nothing had changed. Nothing would ever change. That thick black curtain would always be there, shrouding the whole house, holding Aidan down with it this time. After a moment of silence, the two of them barely drawing a breath, Aidan finally shook his head to say, *She doesn't mean it*. He didn't say it out loud because he couldn't know it was true.

"So, I'm just going to have to leave?" Her voice was sharp—but she was whispering. She didn't want to make a sound.

"Leish, you can stay, but you know it's going to be like walking on eggshells here."

Aleisha shrugged. "Literally no one else has to put up with this crap. Don't you hate it?" She was exhausted—exhausted from being alert, exhausted from listening to her mum cry at night, pretending she couldn't hear a thing and letting Aidan sort it all out, exhausted from never being needed, and always being a trigger. She was tired.

Aidan stayed silent. He was wiping down the surfaces, but they were already spotless.

As the front door slammed shut behind her, Leilah's voice rang out in Aleisha's head: *This is my house, not yours!* Her standard comeback.

She had nowhere to go, but nowhere was better than home.

Without thinking too much, she just let her feet lead her. She walked, slowly, past the market stalls being set up, ignoring the fruit sellers shouting things at her, prices, unbelievable prices, that never sucked her in. She wandered past kids already out on their bikes, cycling across the road without looking, shouting at their friends behind them, turning their heads a full 180 degrees to see their mates, wobbling on the handlebars.

With each step down Ealing Road, then along the high road, she edged farther and farther away from home. With each step, she felt her heartbeat slow. She didn't know where she was going, not really, until the bend in the road straightened, and there it was, like a little Tudor cottage, looking thoroughly out of place.

Of *course* her subconscious would bring her here: the library. The only place where she knew she could just be quiet, alone, for a little while. Maybe it *wasn't* the worst idea. If books actually could let her escape, reading was at least cheaper than getting shit-faced.

Goody-two-shoes Kyle was on the front desk today. Aleisha nodded to him in greeting as she walked through the library doors, ignored the surprise written all over his face, and started to wander the aisles. She went to the crime/thriller section, wondering if Crime Thriller Guy's words would impart some kind of inspiration. She watched the spines, sparkling in the sunlight, shimmering in their plastic covers. She let her fingertips graze each book, but she didn't pull anything from the shelves. Eventually, the reds, blues, yellows of the spines merged into one big book mass, and nothing made sense to her. The library was silent, but it rang in her ears. The words jumped out—"Death," "Murder," "Killer"—as well as softer, creepier titles like "Watching You" . . . It was all getting a bit much. How did he do this? How did he feel chilled here, in this space, with these words bearing down on him? She tapped her finger on the side of her leg, trying to look calm, trying to look as if she knew what the hell she was doing.

Her phone buzzed.

It was the WhatsApp group again—they had set it up when they were fourteen, but Aleisha hadn't spoken in the group in weeks. No one had noticed. Three of them were tagged in the last message from Mia. Once upon a time, Mia had been Aleisha's very best friend.

@Beth @Lola @Kacey you at home? Wna do something tonight?

The other two girls, Jenna and Shreya, were on holiday—they'd been relentlessly sending poolside pictures from Ayia Napa and Croatia.

The rejection still stung Aleisha, even after months and months of her making up excuses to her friends. She was known to bow out at the last minute due to illness, food poisoning, migraines—missing birthday dinners or gatherings in the park. But being flaky was easier than telling the truth: she didn't want them to know her mum was mad. They'd never understand.

Beth, Lola, Kacey, even Jenna, all responded immediately.

Ping. Buzz. I'm around, let's do something

Ping. Buzz. Missing u girls, have fun without me. 😘 Ill b there in spirit 🍸 vodka 🍸

Ping. Buzz. Yh where shall we go?

As Aleisha stood in the library, the walls of books began to close in on her, the spines growing larger, heavier. She watched her friends continue their lives without her. Message after message. Book after book. She didn't exist anymore. Emojis, dancing girl, high fives, a thumbs-up. *Happy.* They were all happy. They didn't have anything else to worry about. It was summer, after all. The future stretched ahead. The best time of their lives.

She pushed herself through the stacks of shelves into the clearing beyond. She needed to breathe again, to draw oxygen deep into her lungs. She turned her phone over in her palm and her eyes blurred at her watermelon phone case.

Between the melons, she spotted the reading list poking through.

There it was again. That book. The first book on the list. *To Kill a Mockingbird.* The image of Leilah throwing her head back in glee rushed in, her screams and shouts this morning, her sobbing through the night. Aidan's eyes, dark rims, unable to give her any words of comfort. Her head was driving her crazy and she needed to get away, leave Wembley, leave her family, leave everything. But still, could a book work those kinds of miracles? At least it was a place to start.

She found a chair—Crime Thriller Guy's chair, actually—and sank into it, shoving her phone into her bag. The chair was worn in places, the arms had started to fray, but it was comfortable. The sun illuminated the pages of *To Kill a Mockingbird*. If she was going to do this, it felt like the right kind of position, the right view, the right environment, to turn to chapter one and begin. But just as she was about to settle in, psyching herself for full immersion, Kyle's very loud, very patronizing tone pierced her silence. He was dealing with another irrational, irrelevant, and annoying customer who had phoned in—but at least that was better than dealing with the irrational, irrelevant, annoying customers in real life. What *had* Aidan loved about this job so much?

"No, sir. I think I *will* have to charge you for the book if you removed it from the premises without checking it out."

Kyle's brows knotted into a frown.

"Sorry, sir, could you repeat that just a little more slowly for me please?" And after a beat: "Do you have a library card?"

Aleisha couldn't tune out of the conversation, Kyle was so sodding loud.

"I'm so sorry, sir, I didn't realize. When was this? Yesterday? Hmm, yes, thank you, sir. Thank you for letting me know. I'll investigate and see what I can do . . . Yes, well, if you don't have a library card, how about I set one up for you today and take the book out for you, and you can return it when you can? That way I'll make sure my colleagues can't charge you when it is returned."

Aleisha hid herself behind the wing of the chair, frozen, ashamed. She pictured the old man from yesterday, standing in front of her, asking for help. She heard her own voice, harsh, telling him that no, she couldn't be arsed. Aleisha wanted the chair to eat her whole.

The moment Kyle shoved the handset back onto the desk, he jumped up and turned his head on his neck like a meerkat. Searching for something . . . for her.

Aleisha kept as low as she could. But it was useless, Kyle knew exactly where she was.

"Hey, Kyle, what's up?" she said as he arrived at her side.

"You were on shift yesterday, right?" he asked.

"Yeah."

"I've just had a lovely elderly gentleman on the phone, rather *distressed*, to put it lightly, saying you forced him out of the library. Is that true?" He was putting on his "authoritative" voice. When Thermos wasn't around, Kyle took it upon himself to step up to the plate.

"That's not exactly what happened. He wanted book recommendations. I don't *do* book recommendations."

"You need to. Do you want this job?"

She didn't *want* it, she needed it. She needed to help Aidan out. Leilah was an artist and a designer—usually she worked with ad agencies around the world and often she was swamped with work. But it came in waves. And her income was sometimes irregular, especially when she was going through one of her bad patches. Aleisha couldn't lose this job. There'd be nothing else to go to. And, for all its faults, this place was becoming her silent retreat from the chaos that was her home, she knew that much.

She nodded.

"Do you know how many people could work here, how many people actually *wanted* to work here?"

Aleisha shook her head.

Kyle continued, his chest expanding. "*Loads*, quite frankly. Dev is *always* saying we need to do our best to keep people happy, provide a friendly place with *book recommendations*, the full service, otherwise we'll lose regulars. If you don't start actually doing your job, you'll get sacked, or worse, we'll just get shut down—and we'll *all* lose our jobs."

Aleisha didn't believe it. It had been *so* easy to get in. But she really couldn't lose her job, and she couldn't face it if she was responsible for the volunteers, Lucy and Benny, losing their favorite place.

Or for Kyle, as much as he annoyed her, losing the only place he could ever be bossy and get away with it, and for Dev, who would literally do anything to keep the Harrow Road Library up and running. She pictured this cute building with its windows blocked out, a sign from the council on the door directing people to the Civic Center instead. It wouldn't be right. Even though they were never completely crammed with customers, people loved this place. She imagined Aidan in her mind, parroting Uncle Jeremy: *Do better.*

"If that man makes a formal complaint about you to Dev, you're out."

Aleisha shifted in her seat. "Look, I'm actually here for *pleasure* today, not work, so can you save it for—"

"And it's pretty horrible being nasty to like an eighty-year-old man. I don't know what you're going through, Aleisha"—Kyle's tone had softened now—"but try to be nice to people. Just a smile or a friendly face can make someone's day a bit better. You might have ruined his. Was it worth it? Did you feel *satisfied*?"

Aleisha shook her head again, unable to speak, feeling like a toddler being told off for fighting.

"Right. If you see him again, give him a blooming book recommendation—"

"I did try, he ran off!" Aleisha interjected, but Kyle ignored her, continuing his pre-rehearsed speech.

"Read some stuff," he said, pointing to *To Kill a Mockingbird* in her hand. "If you *like* that, then tell him to read it. It's simple. Read a book. Recommend a book. You know what, even if you really hate it, recommend it to him anyway. Everyone has different tastes and beggars can't be choosers, as my nan says."

Aleisha sighed and watched Kyle strut off back to the desk, feeling like a boss, probably.

She reached for the book again and opened it somewhere in the middle. The spine was broken in so many places, but she wanted to make her own mark on it, and bent it in two. It wasn't as satisfying as she'd suspected. The book was soft, supple . . . the warmth of the library had turned the glue to jelly.

She rewound to the first page. She started to fiddle, with her nose, with the pages, with a few straggly bits of hair that were falling over her face. She couldn't take in anything. She was forcing her eyes to focus on the words in front of her, but she couldn't settle.

She was stupid, a fraud. Giving up, slouching back into the fading salmon-pink chair, she surveyed the room. A few people were reading and browsing. *They* were proper readers, people who belonged here. Bookworms. Book nerds.

"Ef this," she hissed to herself. She gathered up her stuff and shoved it into her tote. The book was still on the table. She didn't know whether to take it or just leave it here. She glanced around again before shoving that into her tote too.

The beeps from the library alarm ushered her out, her own stolen library book nestled in her bag.

CHAPTER 5

MUKESH

Mukesh was lying on his back when the doorbell rang. Had he fallen asleep? Rohini and Priya weren't due to be here for hours, or so he thought. He gradually hauled himself up, groaning and creaking on the way, his back stiffer than he'd expected. He wanted to swear, but that wasn't the sort of thing Mukesh did.

He was looking forward to seeing his granddaughter, his daughter too. But he knew the Rohini whirlwind was about to hit . . . And no matter how many times he'd survived it, he wasn't sure he was ready for it after the aimless, lonely day he'd had. Once upon a time, Fridays were his and Naina's relaxing day, the day they spent for themselves. These days, on Fridays, he usually did nothing.

He plodded down the stairs very slowly, holding on to the handrails on either side. Rohini's handyman friend had fitted the rail on the other side of the stairs, to give him more stability. He was embarrassed about it. On the rare occasions he had nonfamilial visitors, he would joke about it before they mentioned it first.

He spotted the head and shoulders of a woman, obscured by the frosted glass in the center of his front door. He would recognize her anywhere.

He took a deep breath and pulled it open. "Rohini, beti!" he called, arms wide open in a welcoming gesture, forcing his voice to sound cheerful and bright.

"Papa," she replied, walking straight in, avoiding his open arms. Behind her came Priya, a book held tight in her little palms.

"Priya, come in, darling."

Without wasting any time on greetings, Rohini stomped through to the kitchen and began rummaging in the cupboards. She tutted a few times. Mukesh glanced at Priya, hoping to exchange an *oh dear* moment, but she had already tucked herself up with her book on Naina's living-room chair.

"Papa? What is this?" Rohini called, holding up a Tupperware of rice he'd had sitting in the fridge for a few days . . . maybe a little longer. "This is disgusting!"

"Sorry, beta, I promise I wasn't going to eat it."

"Never eat rice left longer than a day, Papa! You should have at least let me fry it up for you."

"Beta, don't worry." He shuffled forward, grabbing the Tupperware from her and emptying it into his food bin. "Gone! Out of sight, out of mind." But Rohini had already started making her way over to the sink.

"Uh-ruh-ruh!" She vocalized her disgust, just as Naina used to do. "How long have these plates been sitting here, Papa? This is *so* unhygienic! You'll get all those ants back again—they love this hot, hot weather."

"Rohini, please, beta, just go and sit down and I will make you chai."

"Papa, no! I need to wash this all up. You think I come here just for chai? I come here to look after you. If only Mummy could see you now."

Mukesh knew that last sentence came only from her frustration, but nonetheless it hurt. He'd noticed how over the past year, Rohini only ever mentioned "Mummy" to berate him, to tell him he was living in a pigsty.

He was too tired for this, too tired to argue back. Instead, he wandered to the living room and slumped himself down, trying to tune out Rohini's frequent grunts and groans as she found cracks in the cupboard door ("I told you I could get someone round to fix this! This is almost a brand-new kitchen; you can't have it looking scruffy like this, Papa!") and boxes and boxes of mung beans in the fridge ("Papa, this is very unhealthy if this is all you eat! I know Mummy always used to say good for fiber, but you must eat a balanced diet, Papa, like the doctor told you!") and three empty cartons of his favorite packet chai in the recycling ("Papa! You'll rot what's left of your teeth, and these are not good for your diabetes! Mummy said only for special occasions, Papa; I have shown you how to make it from scratch.").

He wished more than anything that—rather than suffering creaking joints and ailing eyesight—he'd started losing his hearing first. In his family, where each of his daughters liked to talk a thousand decibels louder than the average human, that would have been particularly useful.

"What are you reading, darling?" Mukesh asked Priya, as Rohini roamed the house, searching from top to bottom, like a sniffer dog, on the lookout for the next thing to complain about. The living room was deadly silent.

"*Little Women*, Dada," she replied, her eyes remaining fixed on the page. "It was one Ba recommended to me. She said she read it when she was a very little girl. Dad bought it for me last week."

"I haven't heard of it," Mukesh said honestly, but he made a mental note—now that he was a library member, he could and *should* pay attention to these things . . .

"It's a *very* famous book, Dada. Everyone knows it," she said, still not looking up, but her eyebrows were arched in a mock-accusatory, surprised frown.

"What is it about?" Mukesh asked, a little nervously—remembering her words from the other day: *You don't* get *books, Dada . . . You just don't* care*!*

"Shhh, Dada, I'm trying to read it. I'll tell you another day," Priya snapped in a sweet kind of way, and Mukesh did as he was told. Naina used to be a bit like that when she was reading too—maybe one day he'd understand.

He remembered evenings, when the children had gone to bed, he'd be reading the newspaper beside Naina, who was leafing through the pages of her book at breakneck speed. He'd try to engage her in conversation, looking over, waiting for her to realize he was watching her.

"Mukesh, what are you *doing*? You know I am concentrating," she would reprimand, smiling all the same.

"I just wanted to read something to you from the paper. It is very interesting."

"Mukesh, I am just getting to the good bit. Shh," she would say. She was *always* getting to the good bit. At first, Mukesh thought that perhaps books had good bits every two or three pages, and then he started to wonder whether it was just an excuse.

He would watch her, tucked up in her blue-and-white nightie, her reading glasses with large frames resting neatly on her nose, and her black hair pulled back into a small bun at the back of her head. He could see her in his mind's eye at twenty, at thirty, at forty, fifty, sixty, seventy too. The same ritual, the same response. For a moment, he felt like Henry from *The Time Traveler's Wife*, flying through the decades to visit Naina in all those moments of her life.

At the time, he had never wondered where she went when she was within the pages of her book. He just loved seeing the concentration on her face. Sometimes she would smile, just slightly, from the corner of her mouth. Other times she would throw her head back and chuckle, creasing her eyes, and tapping Mukesh on the shoulder as though he was in on the joke. At the time, seeing how happy she was had been enough. But now she was gone, he wished he'd tried harder to be with her in every single moment.

"Papa," Rohini called. Her voice was close, in his ground-floor bedroom next door. "Can you come here?"

Mukesh looked at Priya, hoping she would give him some excuse to stay exactly where he was, but she was lost in the pages of *Little Women*. Her expression was so very *Naina*.

"Okay, coming," he mumbled, scooping himself up from the chair, both arms pushing.

He stood in the doorway; Rohini was standing by a cupboard, one hand on her hip, the other hand pointing toward a trickle of sari flowing from a closed cupboard door onto the floor.

"What has happened here?" Rohini asked as she opened the door. She gasped theatrically. Everything was a bit of a mess, folded but out of shape.

"Vritti and I folded this all *perfectly* after Mummy . . ." She paused.

"For Mummy. What happened? Have more people come round to take something to *remember her by*?" Rohini's voice went high and squeaky on the final three words.

"No, I was just looking through because—"

"All those masis, her *friends*, they were always jealous of Mummy, always wanted her saris. No wonder they used the excuse of giving condolences to come round like vultures . . . Good friends, ha, but they still want her stuff . . ."

A memory of Naina—dressed up for the mandir—flashed into Mukesh's mind. *What do you think? Effortless chic?* She'd pronounced it "shick."

"Well," Mukesh said to his daughter, "your mummy always had the nicest saris."

"Yep, and luckily an eye for a bargain—otherwise these masis would be robbing us blind. So, Papa, you're telling me *you* did this? Help me tidy this up, can you?" Rohini said, not unkindly, and Mukesh wandered in as told. He sat on the bed, waiting for Rohini to pass him something to fold, but instead she just got on with it, admonishing him every so often for making such a mess.

As Rohini pulled out each garment, even the ones that were actually fine and didn't need refolding, he caught the familiar whiff of Naina once more. Good whiffs. He could smell her perfume again, and this time her shampoo. Forgetting, for a moment, he looked over his shoulder, hoping and praying Naina had come to say hello.

These were the saris Naina had worn regularly, for the mandir or a trip to the shop—they were saris people came to associate with Naina: patterns, brocade, paisley. Others had jewels, sequins. They were beautiful, often simple. As Rohini tucked the last sari away, she ran her hand across the fabric, feeling the detail with her fingertips.

"I wonder when Mummy last wore this?" she said out loud. Her voice had softened, no longer Admonishing Inspector Whirlwind. Mukesh didn't reply. He knew what she really meant was "Had Mummy known she was dying when she last wore this? Had she known it was going to kill her sooner than they all expected? Too soon."

Mukesh watched in silence as a small tear, almost imperceptible, ran down his daughter's face. He sat where he was, wanting to reach out to her, knowing she would shrug him off if he did. "I'm sorry, Rohini. I was going through her things. I think I was looking for her books. I wanted to read to Priya. I'm so sorry for making a mess."

Rohini looked at her father, her eyes brightened up as she wiped away her tears, pretending they'd never been there at all. "Papa, that's okay. But you know Mummy always got books from the library. She didn't own any. There's no space here." She gestured around the room, the whole house. It was strange how now it felt as though there was no room, but all five of them had lived here once, living busy, bustling lives. Now it was just him, and there was no space at all. Every corner was full to the brim with memories.

Mukesh nodded. "I know, I thought that. But I just . . . I wanted to find a book for Priya. She's very quiet, and she doesn't like the television. My David Attenborough documentaries . . . they are very educational, you know."

Rohini stood up and shuffled over to her papa, tapping his shoulder gently. Mukesh was grateful Rohini knew that if she gave him a hug he would burst into tears. He hated to cry in front of his girls. She left him in the room, the door wide open. In Rohini language, he knew that meant: "I'll give you some space, but just call me if you need me." She might have been his bossy daughter, but she could be kind too.

Rohini insisted on making a full thali (she'd conveniently brought her own ingredients, even though Mukesh had insisted she didn't need to) and the three of them were now tucking into badh and kadhi, Priya's favorite.

"Rohini, beta, you treat me so well." Mukesh scooped some up with his fingers. Rohini never made food quite as thiki as Naina had, which was perhaps a good thing as he couldn't deal with the spice so much now anyway.

As soon as she'd finished eating, Priya wasted no time in jumping up from the kitchen table and heading back to the living room, to dive back into her book.

"Rohini," Mukesh said, "is Priya always this quiet? Her head always in books?"

"She just likes to read, Papa, it's fine. Mummy did that all the time, and she definitely wasn't quiet."

"But I never hear her talk about her friends, things she likes to do other than reading. Your mummy liked books, but she always had friends over too."

"Yes, Papa, Priya does other things. Have you ever asked her?" Rohini wasn't looking at him when she said this, but he felt the sting as though her eyes were boring right through him.

"Well, no, but . . ." Mukesh stammered.

"She has two best friends, Papa, Christie and James," Rohini continued. "They're very nice, and quiet like her."

"She has those two friends to visit?"

"Papa, kids don't do that these days. They play together at school. In the break times."

Mukesh wondered whether "these days" was a thinly veiled way of saying "You're so old, Papa!" He thought of the group of boys who were often out playing on his road, laughing and shouting and sometimes saying bad words with the kind of enjoyment you only get when they're new to you, recently learned. Those boys were out there almost every day, when it was sunny, even in *this* day and age when people were scared of letting their children live lives at all. Rohini, this time, was wrong.

He thought of Priya, sitting in the living room.

She *was* lonely. Her ba had died when she was nine; she had been old enough to really feel her loss. He knew what it was like to lose your best friend, your life partner, but he'd never allowed himself to wonder how Priya would have felt losing her best friend too. Naina understood her—when Priya was quiet, Naina had helped her open up. How did Priya feel now that she was gone?

Rohini shuffled to the living room; he followed behind, until the phone trilled. Mukesh diverted his path, slowly, creakily, trying to prove to his daughter he didn't need to be completely looked after.

"Hello?" he said, not recognizing the number as he picked up the phone.

On the other end of the line, he heard his friend Harishbhai yapping away without even uttering a greeting.

"Bhai! You must help me. Something very, very urgent has come up. Sahilbhai has dropped out of the mandir's sponsored walk. You must step in. I told them immediately I knew Mukeshbhai would do it, he is a good man, his Naina would have put him forward in a moment. You are going to help, yes?"

Rohini was watching intently, her brow furrowed. Mukesh's first instinct was to put the phone down immediately—to tell Rohini it was telesales—but no matter how annoying Harish was, he couldn't be so rude.

"Harishbhai, please, what do you mean?"

"Mukeshbhai, my friend, Sahilbhai has sprained his ankle. The walk is coming up soon, he cannot take part, and we do not want to lose any of his sponsorship."

"But no one will ask for their money back, surely? It is charity."

"You never know, bhai, not everyone is so generous like you, me, Naina, ne?"

"So, you need someone to fill his spot . . ."

"Ha, precisely. You can do it?" Harish asked, but they both knew that this was not a question.

"Bhai, my back. You know. Bad back."

Harish continued talking, as though Mukesh hadn't spoken at all. He signed off with "Back, schmack. Thank you—we meet at the temple at eight in the morning. Thank you, bhai. Thank you."

Mukesh looked at his daughter, who had now turned to Zee TV and was bopping her head in time with the theme music.

"Who was that?" she asked absently.

"Your fua, Harishfua."

"What does he want?" Rohini looked up at her father now, disdain on her face. She disliked Harish as much as Mukesh did.

"He wants me to fill in for Sahilfua in the mandir-sponsored walk."

Rohini laughed. Mukesh remained straight-faced. Rohini stopped laughing.

"You know it's ten kilometers this year?"

Mukesh gulped: he hated walking for anyone other than Naina. She used to have a little book about the best walks in London. She would always complain that they lived in the capital city of England and had barely ventured outside Brent in all their years. Besides, on weekends he usually took things slowly, called up his daughters one at a time, spoke to his grandchildren, and caught up on *Gardener's World* (even though his garden was nothing more than paving slabs—he liked how nice and easy it was to maintain), and then *Blue Planet*, again. He didn't know if he was up to breaking his routine quite so drastically. He'd already ventured out to the library . . . throwing the sponsored walk in the mix was bound to be one step too far.

"Papa, it's nice really. They want to get you involved."

"Why would they want me involved in anything? In ten kilometers? Why not wait for the five one?"

"Maybe because they think you need cheering up."

"Very funny!"

"Do you?"

"No. I'm a widower. Lots of widowers are lonely, bored, boring. I've got you and Priya, the girls, and the twins. I have my routines. I'm fine."

"Papa, just go. Don't go too far if you can't handle it. You're not too *old*, are you?"

Mukesh straightened himself up, pulled back his shoulders, puffed up his chest. He'd once seen his son-in-law do this before a jog. "I can *do* the walk. I just don't want to—I don't have *time*!"

Rohini tried to hide a smile.

"I *can*!" Mukesh tried not to look offended.

"Right . . ." Rohini said, giving her daughter, now snoring gently in the armchair, the once-over. "I think it's best we head back. It will take us a couple of hours. And Priya has some summer homework to do." She gently shook Priya awake—she rubbed her sleepy eyes, and for a moment, she was the little girl Mukesh had taken to the park on Fridays after nursery, the little girl who had sat on his lap and watched Christmas films, the little girl who had fallen asleep reading a picture book in her ba's arms. He knew, as she grew up, she wouldn't want to spend any time with her old dada. Especially if they had nothing in common. Time was running out, wasn't it?

"You can both stay here if you want," Mukesh said. "I don't want you driving back too late, not if you are sleepy."

"No, Papa, it's nicer to be home."

Her words stung—he hadn't expected it. It had been years since Rohini moved out, but he still thought of this house as her home.

"Good luck for your walk—have *fun*," Rohini continued, as she flung her bag over her shoulder. "Do you have everything?" she asked Priya, sweeping her palm over the girl's forehead, removing some straggly hair from her eyes. Priya nodded.

As they wandered toward the door, Mukesh knelt down with difficulty to say goodbye to Priya, his little girl who was not so little after all, but she walked straight past him and jumped into the car, ready to go home. He held a smile that he didn't feel as he waved them off, and as he closed the door, he felt more alone than ever.

Mukesh shuffled into bed that evening, in the bedroom he had once shared with Naina, mattress and bones creaking. He whispered, "Jai Swaminarayan," and rested his head in the very center of his pillow, looking up at the ceiling, the dying sunlight creeping in through the cracks in the curtains, casting an orange glow on the paintwork. He closed his eyes for the night, praying and hoping he would wake up with Naina next to him. He knew, if he was going to finally get to know his granddaughter, to earn her trust and her respect, he might have to start making some changes. The library was the key, he just knew it . . . but the sponsored walk, it couldn't hurt to have a go, could it?

CHAPTER 6

ALEISHA

It was a relief to be out of the house today, even if Leilah was acting as if she was totally okay—scrubbing the already spotless kitchen from top to bottom. Aleisha walked along the high road, weaving in and out of people wandering every which way, ignoring men selling knock-off phones, past the stadium, almost empty at this time of day with no match, concert, or anything else going on. The traffic, like always, was heavy here. Cars tooted. She could smell the fumes; the taste made bile rise to her throat.

She wandered past the terraced houses, once white but now gray with pollution, and the Hindu temple, in all its marble grandeur—a huddle of people, young and old, congregated in the forecourt, speaking passionately, joy and sincerity combined. She sat on a wall opposite and watched for a while, picking her nails. A few of the men here, chatting away, were wearing a red-and-yellow string around their wrists. She thought of the old man from the library. He had been wearing a bracelet just like that, she remembered. The huddle dispersed and she trudged to Stonebridge Park station, the heat sending prickles over her skin.

It was the middle of the day. Everyone on the platform seemed aimless. Some would be going to their jobs, shift workers, something she could sympathize with. Others would be doing what she was doing—wandering with no agenda, no destination, because there was nothing else to do on this too-hot, sticky day.

Then someone caught her eye—a guy. He had a beanie on his head . . . in this heat? He must be sweltering. He had a wash of carefully curated stubble on his face. His eyes were a sharp, vibrant green. She watched him for a while. His bright-colored T-shirt was too big, hanging over his jeans. He stepped onto the train coolly, like he had nothing to prove and no one to prove anything to. Aleisha couldn't say why, but she was interested in him, intrigued. She stepped onto the train too, without registering where it was going until the loudspeaker announced the final destination: Elephant and Castle. The guy was sitting, his knees far apart, in the middle of two seats, just because he could.

He pulled out his phone, scrolled, slouching into the train seat. He would have signal for a little while now until the Bakerloo line train went underground. She pulled out her own phone and swiped without looking at the screen. Her eyes were directed above the phone to her left, to the man, the boy.

She ran one hand over her hair, and shuffled deeper into her seat, eyes still on him. He glanced up for a moment, just a moment, and their eyes made contact—small and insubstantial.

She hurriedly looked down at her phone again, nervous—unsure what to do. She opened up Tinder. She'd never used Tinder properly. Unlike all her friends, who seemed to be on Tinder all the time, with dates every other night of the week, she didn't have the time to be meeting guys, for dates or hookups. But sometimes, when she wanted to pretend that her life was something else, that she had some kind of freedom, she just swiped for the sake of swiping.

Was this guy on Tinder too? What if she'd just mindlessly swiped left to him? Worse . . . what if she'd swiped right?

She pressed the home button hurriedly, minimizing the app, then stuffed her phone into her pocket, panicking. But he was scrolling on his phone again and wouldn't even have noticed. He wasn't paying attention to her. She smoothed over the pocket of her jeans, feeling the warmth from her phone radiating through the fabric.

She looked up again and let her eyes roam slowly around the carriage before they came to rest on the Tube map above her, as though she hadn't been looking at anything in particular at all. In a final attempt to *really* look like she wasn't interested, she pulled the copy of *To Kill a Mockingbird* out of her bag . . .

They were already at Queen's Park and no one in her carriage had left yet. All five of them still there, waiting for their stop. She started to read, her eyes darting over the page, racking her brain to recall where she'd left off earlier, just as her phone buzzed.

It was Aidan.

"Hello?" she said, self-conscious, trying to whisper. The boy-man looked up at her, and she hoped her cheeks hadn't flushed.

"Come back, Leish," he said.

"What?"

"Can you get back home within the next hour or so?"

"Why? Are you home?"

"Yes, just come back if you can. I . . ." He paused.

"What, Aidan?"

"I need you," he said quietly.

And then he hung up. Aleisha felt an immediate tightening in her chest. Leilah had seemed okay this morning, hadn't she? Okay in the circumstances.

Aidan hadn't said *I need you* to his little sister since their father had left the house, and Aidan had been desperately trying to clear out all his stuff. She hadn't known at the time why he needed to eradicate every little detail of their father from their home.

That had been the summer when Aidan gave up his place to study business at uni, just until things "settled" again. When they were kids, they'd always played pretend that she was a particularly grumpy customer at his bike shop. For years, she'd never doubted that her brother would make that pretend bike shop (with the cutlery from the cutlery drawer as all the tools and bits and pieces for sale) into a reality. But things hadn't settled again. Aleisha wasn't sure if they ever would.

I need you rang in her head. The train came to a stop, and she looked at the boy-man one last time, before stepping onto the platform toward the Tube train ready and waiting to take her home. She dropped one hip and looked at her phone, trying to pretend to the whole world that this was her intention, that she had a plan. That she had a life.

She glanced behind her, hoping to catch a glimpse of him again. The train had gone.

She stood on her doorstep, looking up at the windows, listening hard, hoping for a clue, the tiniest clue, of what to expect inside. All she could hear was a helicopter hovering a few streets away, the wind gently buffeting her hair.

Before she could pluck up the courage to take the keys out of her pocket and put them into the lock, her ringtone made her jump. Then the door flew open to reveal her brother standing in the doorway, his mobile to his ear.

"Aleisha, there you are," he said quickly, putting his phone down by his side. "Why are you just waiting here?"

"I don't know. I just got here. What's going on?"

"Erm, I've got to go out . . ." He was looking beyond her, down at his feet, up at the sky, anywhere but in her eyes.

"Where are you going?" Aleisha kept her eyes trained on him, trying to work out what was going on.

"I'm going to work. Can you stay in?" His feet were rooted to the spot.

"What for? Mum?" Aleisha watched his face carefully, searching for any hint about what state Leilah might be in, what she was walking into. "I thought you had the afternoon off."

Aidan was now staring at his car keys. "Yeah, I . . . I've been called in last minute. Look, I'm really sorry to do this but I don't want to leave her on her own today and I've got to get out."

Aleisha stepped forward, but Aidan made no move to get out of her way. There was something he wasn't telling her. "Is she okay?" Aleisha was trying to keep the panic out of her voice, the words "I need you" flashing up in her mind again.

"Yeah, Leish, yeah, I'm sorry, she's totally fine. I just, you know, it's been up and down, and I've got some stuff to do and I didn't know where you were, you didn't leave a note." For a moment, Aleisha saw panic, stress, hurt in her brother's eyes, but dismissed the thought. Aidan was *never* panicked, right? He had so much going on, but out of the three of them, he was the one who had it all together. Uncle Jeremy always said, "That boy, he carries the world on his shoulders with so much grace." He was right.

"So, you going to let me in then? Or do I need a secret password or something?"

"Yeah, sorry." He stepped aside, grabbing his bag from the step, and headed out. He plastered a smile on his face, but there was still something else behind his eyes, lingering just for a moment.

Aleisha dumped her bag in the hallway. "Fine. See you later." She heard the calmness of her own words, when really she just wanted to shout after him: *Don't pull the "I need you" card when everything's fine.* She wanted to tell him how much he'd scared her. She wanted to shout at him, to scream.

"I've got a slightly shorter shift today," he said now. His voice was immediately lighter, his eyes brighter now his feet were on the pavement, now he was out of the house—she'd never noticed such a stark reaction before. "Finish at eight. See you then. Call me if you need anything, okay?"

"Whatever."

"I'll get you a pizza or something, to make this up to you. Sorry if we ruined plans," he shouted over his shoulder, climbing into his car.

She knew he was using the "we" to mean "me and Mum" because she couldn't be angry with him when he was "just thinking of Mum."

"I *hate* pizza!" she shouted back.

Aleisha waved to her brother and walked inside, carefully placing one foot in front of the other, hoping her mum was still in bed. But Leilah was sitting on the sofa, watching an international channel where everyone on it was speaking a different language.

"Mum," Aleisha said, trying to keep her tone soft, "why're you watching this?"

Leilah said nothing, seemed unable to reply. Eventually she shrugged, and murmured: "It's calming."

Aleisha looked at the TV—it was some over-the-top drama, thunderous music, intense stares. One woman's venomous glare shot straight through the screen. "Calming how?"

Leilah's eyes were glazed over, as though they weren't taking anything in at all.

"Cup of tea?"

"No, I'm okay." Her lips looked dry, slightly gray. There was a soft film of sweat on her forehead, the down on her upper lip collected tiny droplets of water.

She could tell today was a spiral.

There hadn't been a proper spiral for a while. Aidan always knew what to look out for and now she wished she hadn't left this morning. But Aidan had insisted, because *he* could cope with this—and he knew she couldn't. She felt his absence now, she was flailing, she didn't know how to make Leilah feel safe today, she didn't know what to say to her or do for her own mother. No matter how many years they'd been through it, when Leilah felt like this she was nothing but a stranger to her.

In the kitchen, she steadied herself with both hands on the countertop before pulling out her favorite mug. Her dad had bought it for her from a Christmas market. It was hand-painted, according to the note on its underside. It had an angel on it. Blond. Blue-eyed. The angel was definitely not her. When she was younger, she liked to pretend that that's how her dad saw her, as his little angel with the blond hair and the blue eyes and the pale, peachy skin.

As the kettle fired up, Leilah called out, "Tea, please." Aleisha rolled her eyes and hastily cleaned her mum's favorite *Star Wars* mug. It had been sitting in the sink for days, stained with dark, thick coffee rings.

Once the kettle was boiled, she poured hot water over fresh tea bags and enjoyed watching the water turn brown, color emerging from the bags as she added a dash of milk in each.

She carried them through to the living room gingerly, keeping her eyes on the liquid, careful not to spill any. She wouldn't hear the end of it if she made a mess.

She quietly set the mug down on the table next to Leilah and turned the television off. Leilah was, impossibly, fast asleep and snoring ever so quietly.

Aleisha sat in a chair opposite her mother and watched her for a while. She heard kids cycling past on their bikes, she heard swear words on the street, mothers laughing together, the cruising of stroller wheels in front of them. She sighed and then jumped when she saw her phone was flashing with an incoming call: *Dad*. She picked it up and shuffled out of the room, closing the door gently behind her.

This was the first time Dean had called in three weeks. She hovered her finger over the green button, and then the red button. Talking to Dean, when Leilah was only in the other room . . . it felt like a betrayal. But if she hit the red button, Dean might not call again. He had a new life now, new kids, a new wife. He had excuses not to call back. He was "so busy, darling."

"Hello?" she whispered, her hand covering her mouth. She was trying so hard to keep the hope out of her voice. She just wanted a conversation, an ordinary conversation.

"Hey, sweetheart!" His voice was upbeat, deafeningly happy—she could hear chatter in the background.

"Hey, Dad, where are you?"

"I'm just at home—the kids are watching a film. Where are you? Why are you whispering?"

"I'm just at home. Mum's asleep."

"Is . . . is everything okay, with you all? How's Aidan?"

"He's busy, working. Mum's not too good right now. She's stopped taking on any new design work for a bit, so we're doing the best we can."

Aleisha loved seeing her mum designing, painting too sometimes. But when she was feeling this way, she stopped everything.

She packed away her computer, she put away any materials, and she stopped accepting commissions. It was always the first sign, for Aleisha and Aidan, that things weren't right.

"Aleisha, you know if ever you want to get away, you can come and spend some time here. We'd love to see you. Are you on your summer holidays now?"

"I've finished my exams, yeah. But . . . I'm working. Maybe another time? When things are quieter. Anyway, I'm going to try and get loads of reading done—prepare for uni applications and things. Law . . . it's gonna be competitive. Aidan wants me to work hard." She stared at the wall, imagining her father sitting in his house, always spotless, with his perfect kids sitting in front of the TV, laughing, joking. She wondered how heavy the air in his new house was.

"Of course, I understand. That's good, sweetie, I'm glad you're taking it so seriously." He paused—Aleisha heard a cackling in the background. Someone calling after him. "Dad?"

"I'm really sorry, Aleisha, I have to go. I'm sorry—I'll call you again soon. But I mean it, okay? If you ever want to visit, you are always welcome."

"I know," Aleisha said.

"Okay, bye, darling, love you." He rang off without waiting for her reply.

"Bye," she said to her empty phone. Desperate to keep her brain working, to avoid the silence of the house around her, she began to scroll through her call log.

Aidan. Aidan. Aidan. Home. Home. Kyle. Dev. Kyle. Home. Aidan.

She went straight to her address book and hit "Call" next to Rachel's name. She listened to the dial tone, almost hoping Rachel wouldn't pick up. She didn't really know what to say. But speaking to her father, hearing his voice, hearing how *relaxed* it was, it made her feel more useless than ever.

"Hey, little cousin!" Rachel's voice chirruped.

"Hey," Aleisha responded, unable to keep the gloom out of her voice. "You all right?"

"I'm so sorry, babe, but I'm just out with friends at the moment. Can I call you later?"

"Don't worry, don't worry," Aleisha replied with a lightness she didn't feel, not wanting to make Rachel feel guilty for living a normal life. "We'll speak this week, yeah? Have a good night!" She hung up the phone with a sigh, the only company she had for the foreseeable future: her mum's gentle snores.

Leilah sat beside her, her head slumped against her own shoulder, sleeping peacefully. Aleisha, for one moment, had a desperate urge to shake her, to wake her up, and shout, "Mum, talk to me! Let's talk!" But just as quickly as the urge had arrived, it dissipated.

She pulled out the reading list from her phone case, unfolded it and folded it in her hands, and then she slowly took *To Kill a Mockingbird* out of her bag. Someone had taken care with this list—they'd curated it. What was in these books? Why had they chosen these ones? Had the reading-list author known their scrap of paper would become someone else's reading list too?

She looked at *To Kill a Mockingbird* and felt a drop of awkwardness, remembering how flustered she'd been when she first opened it—as though everyone in the library had been scrutinizing her, wondering what she was doing, acting like some kind of bookworm. But here it was just her, alone. No one here could judge her.

She bent the pages back over the spine and began to read, self-conscious at first, whispering each word cautiously, as if she was reading out loud in an English class, until she allowed herself to enjoy her own gentle rhythm, letting each word linger. Every few lines, she looked over to see if Leilah showed any signs of waking: but her mum didn't move at all. She noticed how this book was allowing her to step into two worlds: the world she was in right now, beside her mum, in her house, the air muggy from the heat of the day, and another world, the world of two children, Scout and her older brother, Jem, who lived somewhere called Maycomb, a small town in Alabama, where they'd play outside, being foolish, being . . . *children*. She would do anything to see life through a child's eyes again; a time when life wasn't so serious, and scary neighbors were nothing more than a fun pastime, and family just meant home. From the first few pages, she could tell that Scout definitely cramped Jem's style, but he put up with her all the same.

"Mum." Aleisha turned to Leilah, whose eyes were still shut tight. "What do you reckon about Scout and Jem? Remind you of anyone?" Aleisha smiled, not expecting a reply, as she caught sight of the photo displayed on the mantelpiece: Aleisha and Aidan, aged seven and fifteen, embracing each other (forced to by Leilah, who was directing from behind the camera), with their faces screwed up in mock disgust. She smiled to herself.

Then Aleisha met Scout and Jem's father. The narrator, Scout, just called him *Atticus* . . . it made sense only because he was important. "Dad" seemed too generic for Atticus. He was a lawyer. Wise, kind, fair . . . She turned to Leilah, her face pulled into a grin. "Mum! He's a lawyer!" she whispered. "A bigshot one in their little town, it sounds like." She could see Atticus through Scout's eyes—a large man, powerful, someone to be respected. She remembered thinking of her own dad in that way before, a long time ago. It was strange how, once childhood left, your parents became simply human, with fears and worries just like your own.

"Mum," she said in hushed tones. "I think I'm getting the hang of this." For one small moment, she thought she saw Leilah stir, saw her eyes open just a bit, and she wondered if she was about to say something to her after all. When she said nothing, Aleisha curled up on the sofa, tucking herself around her mother, in the way she used to when she was a kid. She held the book in her arms, and allowed her eyes to close.

When Aleisha woke up the next morning, the book was cradled in her hands, its soft plastic jacket sticking to her slightly clammy skin. She looked around the room, and for a second, she thought she saw a small child sitting in the chair opposite her: scabby knees, shorts, legs a bit dirty from the Alabama dust—Scout. For that first waking moment, she wasn't in Wembley any longer, she was in Maycomb. She looked to the other end of the sofa, expecting to see Leilah, wondering if Leilah was sharing this moment too. Leilah wasn't there, and Aleisha was all alone. But, for the first time in a while, the silence in the house wasn't so cloying; she could breathe.

CHAPTER 7

MUKESH

Beep. "Papa, it's Rohini, I have to go into the office today, so I'm going to drop Priya off with you for a few hours. I've done her a packed lunch because she's being a bit fussy today and she'll have a book, so don't worry about entertaining her. I've booked her in for a hair appointment on Wembley High Road at five, so can you drop her back with me there? Will be good for you to get a walk in today if you can. See you later, Papa. I'll be round at elevenish."

Beep. "Hi, Papa, Rohini just called me, wanted to check you'd gotten her message? She texted me to say she's on her way to yours."

Beep. "Hi, Dad, it's Deepali. Rohini told me you have signed up for the sponsored walk this year! Brilliant. I am going to come round soon with my fitness DVDs for you. Mummy used to love them. Kept her very healthy. Might be good for you to start looking after yourself too."

It was ten minutes to eleven, and Mukesh was listening to Rohini's message for the fourth time, just to check he'd gotten all the details right. Elevenish arrival. Five o'clock hair appointment. No need to feed Priya. Phew. He ignored Vritti's message, knowing she didn't need or want a reply; Vritti always played the role of Rohini's messenger. And he did not like the sound of Deepali's fitness DVDs one bit. As far as he could remember, Naina only *pretended* to like them, so Deepali didn't feel she had wasted her money.

As he scrawled all the specifics on a pad of Post-it notes, left here by Rohini for this precise reason (*Papa, you never seem to listen to the details of my telephone messages; how about I keep this next to the phone so you can write things down?*), the phone trilled again and his heart began to race. He pulled out more Post-it notes in case Rohini had any more instructions ahead of her impending arrival.

"Ha—I am nearly ready, I promise. Eleven A.M.," Mukesh garbled, jumping into action.

"Hello, is that Mr. Patel?" said a male voice.

"Yes," Mukesh responded, cautiously this time. "It is Mr. Patel. Who is speaking?"

"Hi, Mr. Patel, this is Kyle from the Harrow Road Library. We spoke the other day. We have a book on request for you that has just become available."

"But, but I haven't put a request in for anything. I don't know how to do that."

"Are you sure? We have *To Kill a Mockingbird* on file."

"I didn't order it, I promise. I am so sorry for wasting your time." Mukesh rushed through his apology.

"Oh, that is odd. Maybe it's a technical error. Would you like me to cancel the request? I have it here for you, but I can put it back on the shelf."

Mukesh was about to reply, when a thought struck him. He saw his scribbled handwriting on the Post-it note: *Priya . . . no need to entertain or feed.* A book was a book, after all . . . and if the librarian couldn't recommend one, maybe this technical error was the closest he'd get. He didn't have any time to waste. Maybe this could entertain Priya after all! It could be the start, to show her that he was trying to understand. "I will come and get it today, if that is okay?"

"Of course, Mr. Patel."

"Thank you, young man, thank you. How do I collect?"

"You just give your new library card to the person at the desk along with your request. Simple as that!"

Mukesh wasn't sure it sounded simple, but he'd have to work it out. He felt a flutter of butterflies in his stomach. "Thank you, thank you, young man."

As he put the phone down, the clock struck eleven and there was a knock on the door. "Rohini! Priya!" Mukesh opened the door, a smile plastered across his face. "How lovely you both look!" Rohini was in her work attire, a linen trouser suit and very trendy spectacles. She nodded toward him, her business face on too.

"Thanks for doing this so last minute, Papa. I'm sure you two will have lots to catch up on," Rohini said, and Priya and Mukesh looked at each other—clearly both thinking, *When have we ever had lots to catch up on?*

For a moment, Mukesh felt his heart drop. "We're going to the library today, actually!"

Priya looked up at him, confusion written all over her face.

"Great," Rohini said, trying to hide her surprise. She headed toward her car as Priya hurried into the house, resuming her usual position, book in hand.

"Rohini," Mukesh called to his daughter, and she stopped in her tracks. "What's *To Kill a Mockingbird* about?"

"Huh?"

"The book, what's it about?"

"Oh, Papa. It's so long ago I read it. I don't really remember—I can just about remember it made me cry once. I think Mummy comforted me. She thought I was stressed about my exams, but it was just the book." Rohini's mind had jumped back to that day, he could see it in her eyes. "You're not going to get it out for Priya, are you? From the library? I think it might be a bit grown-up for her right now."

"No, no, just for myself."

"Really?" She looked at him properly for the first time. "Well, that's great, Papa. Mummy would be proud."

He couldn't help it, but his chest puffed up with pride. Rohini hopped in her car and waved him goodbye, and as her car disappeared out of view, he heard Naina whisper in his ear: *Thank you, Mukesh. Thank you for trying again.*

CHAPTER 8

ALEISHA

"Aleisha?" Kyle was using his "professional" phone voice this morning, which told her that he was already in the library.

"Yeah?" Aleisha replied.

"That old man, the one you upset . . ." Kyle loved a guilt trip. "Well, he's coming in today sometime to pick up the book you've reserved for him. Your 'trick' seems to have worked . . . Did you want to be here to recommend it to him? I'm happy to do it, I know the book really well."

Aleisha rolled her eyes. Of *course* he did. Kyle knew everything. She wasn't quite sure what made her put the reservation in, but as soon as she'd turned the final page of *To Kill a Mockingbird*, she had wanted to talk to someone about it, and the man had wanted a book. And, she wondered now, perhaps he'd come to the library in search of more than just a story. What if he had wanted a friend, someone to talk to too? For a little while, Scout and her brother, Jem . . . they had felt like friends to Aleisha. She wondered if this man, if he read it, might discover that too.

"Actually, yeah, I want to be there. I'll be there in like an hour. I'm just waiting for my brother to get home."

"All right, well, make sure you have some interesting things to say to him about it, really *sell* it to him. Every customer counts, remember?"

She hung up and groaned inwardly. What had Crime Thriller Guy said to her about the book? Had he mentioned anything interesting she could say to the old man in turn? The only thing that had stayed with her was that it wasn't his usual read but had gotten him out of his weird, creepy, crime-filled head.

She googled "Themes in *To Kill a Mockingbird*," followed by "Discussion points in *To Kill a Mockingbird*," bringing up a list of questions her English teacher could probably have written. She flicked through the book, and her fingers rushed over pages and pages she'd already enjoyed, when she'd watched Jem and Scout and their friend Dill mess with the old man who lived in the spooky house down the road. She landed on a page with Atticus, preparing for a court case, and his defense of innocent Tom Robinson. She'd subconsciously been taking notes, wondering if this was what law was really like. She'd ripped through the pages, enraged at the townspeople's treatment of Tom, and Atticus too.

"Aidan," she'd shouted a couple of nights ago, storming into his room. He'd been sitting on his bed absentmindedly scrolling on his laptop.

"Leish, what's up?"

She'd waved the book at him. "This! The people of Maycomb—this little fictional town. They're *so* awful—there's this man, he's been accused of attacking this white woman, and just because she's white everyone believes *her*. Atticus—he's like a lawyer, a really good lawyer—he's defending Tom. But everyone . . . everyone else. They're so awful."

"*To Kill a Mockingbird*?" Aidan eyed the cover appraisingly. "It's a good one," he said, and winked. "I know, it gets deep—but when it stresses you out, you've just got to remember, it's *only* a book, you know?"

"That's rich, coming from you—you're the one who dressed up as book characters at Halloween. But you know what I mean . . . it feels real. I'm sure it *has been* real. It's a proper fight for justice."

"It's really gotten to you, this book, hasn't it?" he teased kindly.

It *had* really gotten to her. But now—now she needed to say something *interesting* about it, she literally had no clue if her thoughts were valid. The book had made her feel things, but was any of it worth sharing?

She leaned against the worktop in the kitchen, waiting for the kettle to boil. The edge dug into the small of her back, reminding her of the time when she was little and Aidan had been chasing her through the house, when she'd tumbled. It had felt like flying for a moment. Until she'd hit her head, just above her left eye, and caught her skin on the sharp worktop.

Aidan had come to her rescue, as always. Dean had told him off, for running in the house, but he hadn't had to ask Aidan to collect a bandage, a cold damp cloth, to help stem her bleeding forehead as well as he could. Aidan had taken it upon himself to look after her. Leilah had called him "our little doctor" for a long time after that—Aidan was perfect, as always.

Settling herself down in the living room with her mug clasped between her hands, she gazed out of the window, watching people wander by. Taking a sip, sometimes two, every time she saw someone. Her very own boring, solo drinking game. She was starting to panic—if Aidan took any longer, she might not get to the library in time to see the old man.

And that's when it happened—as if lifted straight from the pages of a novel. Through the window, she spotted the guy from the train. Without his beanie, this time. Was her mind playing tricks on her? No, she told herself, it was him. Definitely him.

She slowly moved closer to the glass, her breath misting against it, and watched as he walked from one corner of her vision to the other. Just at that moment, Aidan's car pulled up on the opposite side of the road, his usual parking spot. Her heart rate slowed. Her brother, silhouetted through the glass, leaned over to the passenger seat, probably putting his driving glasses away—he hated to admit he needed driving glasses—before leaning his head back and staring up at the sky. Aleisha waited, expecting him to step out of his car, but he sat there for minutes.

Time stood still as she watched, waiting for Aidan to move. She felt like an intruder, spying on him. What was going on?

And then came a whisper behind her.

"What are we looking at?"

It was Leilah, dressed already in jeans and a T-shirt—a good day, maybe. Aleisha tried to wipe the surprise from her face.

"You're up!"

"Of course I'm up."

Aleisha frowned.

"What are you looking at?" Leilah continued.

"Nothing." Aleisha turned around, trying to hide Aidan's car from Leilah's view, wanting to give Aidan a moment to himself. "Just spotted some guy I saw on the train once," she said, to distract her.

"Gripping." Leilah smiled. Her eyes looked less tired this morning.

Aleisha stole one last look at Aidan. He knew she was waiting for him; she'd texted him to say she needed to go to work. Why wasn't he coming inside yet? What was he doing? Inside his car, her brother brought both his hands to his face, his shoulders dropping; he stayed like that for a few moments—and then looked toward the house, toward her.

"Mum?" Aleisha jolted into action, but when she turned around Leilah was gone.

"I'm up here!" Leilah called from her room. Aleisha got up from the sofa quickly, pretending she hadn't been watching at all, and stomped upstairs. Outside Leilah's bedroom, she could hear the tinny voices of the radio. She walked in.

"Come in, darling," Leilah said, her voice light. "Come and sit with me." Aleisha tried to suppress her jittery panic about the library, tried to focus on her mother in this moment. Right now, she wanted a hug. She wanted Leilah to tell her that it would all be okay.

Leilah was sitting upright at the foot of the bed—Aleisha was so used to seeing her curled up—and her legs were dangling over the edge, her toes not quite touching the floor. The radio sat beside Leilah, headphones connected to her as though injecting her with life.

She tapped the bed on the other side of the radio. Aleisha sat down as instructed. Leilah unplugged the headphones. She curled them around and around, before placing them neatly next to the radio. Aleisha noticed the lines. Her mother's feet and the floor. Her mother's back and the bed. The radio, perpendicular, the headphones too. She felt as though invisible boundaries were being drawn through her, over her, around her. She recognized her own lines: Her back (curved slightly, slouching) and the bed, her own legs and the floor. Her feet (toes pointing down rather than straight forward like her mother's). Her mum was smiling at her, but Aleisha didn't know how to act right now; all she could think about was how she was ruining the pattern. She didn't belong.

Aleisha was frozen to the spot, scared of making any movement, in case it knocked Leilah's mood back, in case it drew Leilah's attention to how out of place Aleisha was. But minutes later, they both heard the jangle of keys in the door, the turning of the lock. Leilah hopped up from the bed, and Aleisha was forgotten. Their spell, whatever it had been, was broken.

"Aidan!" Leilah called as she made her way to the front door. Aleisha stooped over the banister, watching as Leilah embraced her son. Aleisha inspected Aidan's face, wedged between his mother's shoulder and her head. He was smiling. His eyes were bright, weren't they?

"Come with me to the kitchen," Leilah said, dragging her son. "I might do some cooking!"

Aleisha remained where she was, feeling like a useless spare part.

Then, speeding back into gear, she picked up her bag from her bedroom, pulling her shoes on at the door. Aidan approached her, already in his apron.

"You off to the library now?"

"Yeah, that old man, you know the one, well, he's coming in to pick up the book I recommended."

"That's great, Leish! And you're going to do better this time?"

"Obviously. That book I've been reading—"

"*To Kill a Mockingbird*?"

"Yeah, you remembered."

"Of course, you didn't stop banging on about it."

"Funny . . . I don't know if I'm going to be able to say anything decent."

"He'll love it. You said loads of cool things to me about it."

Aleisha felt her face go warm, feeling as if she'd been put on the spot. Besides know-it-all Kyle and Dev, her brother was the only other person she knew who understood books. "Yeah?"

"Yeah. But I'm not gonna lie, when I saw you fast asleep with it in your hands, I literally thought it had bored you to sleep."

Aleisha rolled her eyes at him, and punched him lightly on the arm. "Shut up. I *can* actually concentrate on things. Remember, I'm the one who gets the good grades."

"What have you been waiting for then?"

"You!" Aleisha grabbed her bag and ran out.

"It's like a scene from *Love Actually* or something," Aidan shouted down the road, while Leilah's voice traveled outside the front door. "Aidan, love, please come help me with this!"

Aleisha returned his comment with a middle finger.

INDIRA

2017

Indira was late for today's satsang because Dial-a-Ride had mixed up her booking. When she arrived at the mandir, she was flustered and panicked. She knew that Naina was leading the satsang today, though she hadn't been able to for a very long time because of her treatment, and she'd promised Naina she'd be there. She wanted to see her, to support her. She prayed for Naina every day. They weren't particularly close friends—Indira wasn't particularly close friends with anyone—but Naina was there for everyone, and Indira firmly believed in repaying those favors when people needed it most.

Of all the days to be late, it had to be today, didn't it?

Indira sat on the chairs by the shoe racks, and slipped off her chappal, strapped tightly with Velcro. She left her socks on, though her doctor recommended she tread carefully. "If you have to, walk barefoot, as it's much better for you, Ms. Patel. Much less slippy." Indira never liked listening to the doctor anyway.

She placed her shoes carefully in a plastic bag and selected her favorite shoe shelf. Number 89, in Shoe Rack D. It was a ritual. Sometimes when there was a school trip, the rack would be taken, but everyone else knew that was Indira's spot.

She checked the shelf for other shoes—nothing in sight but a crumpled bit of paper pushed toward the back. Indira pulled it out, and, because she was a curious type, she unfolded it to see if she might be able to return it to the original owner, or the litterer. (Who would dare litter in *her* shoe spot?!)

Just in case you need it:

To Kill a Mockingbird

Rebecca

The Kite Runner

Life of Pi

Pride and Prejudice

Little Women

Beloved

A Suitable Boy

Indira furrowed her brow. What was this? Some kind of list, written in neat English handwriting she didn't recognize. With this as the only evidence, it'd be impossible to name and shame the litterer.

Her eyes flew to the clock. It was already five past two, and she hadn't gotten to the hall yet! She knew she should put the piece of paper in the bin, be the responsible one, but it was a bit of a walk away and in completely the wrong direction. To save herself time, and because there was some niggling thought at the back of her mind that "Just in case you need it" was a message to someone, maybe even a message to *her*, she folded it up neatly and popped it into her mandir plastic bag with Swami Bapa's face staring up at her, safe and sound.

She spotted Naina's husband, Mukesh, peering through one of the windows of the wooden doors, separating the main hallway from the hall itself.

"Eh, what are you looking at? This is ladies only! Shoo!" Indira joked.

"Kemcho, Indiraben. I'm just watching, making sure she is okay. I promised I would stay." His voice was shaking slightly, his eyes were red, tired.

"You'll do your back in peering like that!"

"Indiraben, you understand. Look." He gestured into the hall and Indira's gaze followed, her elbows resting on her mandir-branded walker. "I must look after her."

Naina looked so different. Her hair, usually jet black and plaited, was today covered completely by an old sari that didn't match the rest of her outfit. That was very unlike Naina, but Indira didn't say anything to Mukesh. He was watching his wife so intently, as though if he were to look away, she might disappear entirely.

Naina's face was shrunken, but her expression was the same as always—vibrant, animated. Indira could sense a heaviness in Naina's eyelids, even from here, but her arms were gesticulating in time with the music and her mouth was open wide: she was putting all her energy into the song. Perhaps this song was giving her life right back. The women, seated in chairs or on the floor, were all clapping in time, their saris and Punjabi dresses a sea of color.

If it wasn't for Naina's shrunken stature, a stoop in her shoulders that Indira had never noticed before, her slender face, the scarf over her head, Indira would have never believed that Naina had cancer. But there *were* all those things, clear to see, and Indira wondered why God had chosen her. Why Naina? Naina had a family. Loved ones. Indira—Indira was as healthy as anything, and she barely had a soul left to love her.

"I must go in," Indira said to Mukesh, who nodded, his mouth turned downward. He held the door open for her as she wheeled herself in.

Naina beamed and beckoned her forward to a seat. She didn't stop singing for a minute.

In that room, Indira could sense the love and respect everyone had for this woman standing in front of them. If Indira was going through the same thing, would people be here for her, watching with the same look in their eyes? She doubted it—she knew why, she knew that she and Naina were different kinds of women. But Indira was always searching for connection; it was just that, quite often, no one was searching with her.

After the satsang ended, Indira huddled against the far wall, pretending to make sure she had all her things, feeling awkward and alone, not knowing whom to talk to. Naina approached her. Everyone else was focused on chatting with their own friends, their sisters, their cousins, their neighbors.

"Indiraben, so lovely of you to come. It has been a long time, ne?"

"Ha, Nainaben. You did wonderfully today; your daughters, they are very proud." Indira gestured to the three women sitting right at the front, now engaged in conversation. "Clapping and cheering all the way through!"

Naina looked toward her daughters, Deepali, Rohini, and Vritti. "Ha, they are wonderful."

Indira nodded, held her hands to Naina's face, felt her warm, soft skin. "Jai Swaminarayan," Indira whispered to her.

Naina's hands clasped hers. "Thank you, ben," she said, her smile gentle, a sparkle in her eyes.

That day was the last day Indira saw Naina. The reading list remained screwed up and forgotten in the plastic bag for a long time, taken to and from the mandir every week. But, at just the right time, it would find its way out.

CHAPTER 9

MUKESH

"Hurry up, Dada! I want to get to the library."

Mukesh enjoyed the walk up to the high road, but the air hurt his lungs as he struggled to keep up with Priya, skipping along ahead of him. Just watching her somehow made him feel even older, frailer. Once upon a time, he'd held Priya as a newborn. All eyes and ears, and a tiny button nose. How small and breakable she had seemed then. And now look: their roles had already reversed. He was the breakable one now.

The Harrow Road Library was an old building, completely different from the modern Civic Center; it looked as if it had been someone's house once, with big white walls and timber framing, black and bold. Behind it was the park, so it was quiet and peaceful despite being on the main road. There were lots of windows, some were definitely new and modern, along with those terrifying "automatic-open" glass doors. He spotted a sign on the door that he hadn't noticed before: SAVE OUR LIBRARIES, it said. SPREAD THE WORD.

"Wow," Priya whispered as she approached. "Ba took me here once, when I was little. I don't really remember it though."

Mukesh nodded; he was nervous, embarrassed after last time, but Priya's excitement was spurring him on. Keeping hold of Priya's shoulder, to prevent her from running off again, he took a moment, before approaching the door, to check who was there. He peered through to see dark hair, pulled back into a bun, surfacing above the desk. It was *her*, the rude girl. He sighed and squared his shoulders.

The doors parted for them as if by some sort of miracle and, as soon as they were inside, Priya shot off in the direction of the children's area. He knew she was a little too old now for those books, but she probably knew what she was looking for.

He watched as Priya dipped in and out of the shelves, already browsing, completely unperturbed by this strange new world. How did she find it so easy? Looking around, *everyone* knew what they were doing. Everyone but him.

Some shelves were brimming with books, whereas others were sparse, with barely four or five volumes spread along the whole row. There were tables and modern-looking computers lined up against one wall, and chairs dotted around, some scruffy, some that looked brand-new. There was even an upstairs area, but there was a chain hanging from the banister with a sign clearly stating it was for STAFF ONLY. This library was on the small side, but he felt sure he might be able to find *something* here—and his mind returned to why he was back again so soon; this mystery book reservation could be his *first* step to becoming a "library person," just like everyone else here.

He took a deep breath and walked toward the girl at the desk. He was surprised to see that she was smiling at him.

"Hello," he said warily as he approached, one eye catching sight of Priya, assuming her usual pose on a beanbag: book held open between her hands.

"Hello, can I help you?" the girl asked. He looked around for her phone, for her headphones, for a sign that she wasn't really paying attention, but there was nothing. How odd.

"I'm here to pick up a book I have reserved. Except I have a question."

"Oh, okay?"

"You see, *I* didn't reserve a book. I only just joined the library. Is this a welcome book or something?"

"Mr. Mukesh Patel?"

"Yes? That . . . that's me." Either she knew too much, or this was excellent library service.

She typed something into the computer. Her nails made that *clack-clack-clack*ing sound. It forced Mukesh's teeth to grit together.

"Yes, *To Kill a Mockingbird*. That's right." Her eyes were still on the screen. Mukesh didn't know what was meant to happen next.

Then she pulled something out from under her desk. A book. She handed it to him. He didn't like the feel of its laminated cover very much, but he could get used to it.

"I, erm, *I* reserved this for you. You asked the other day for a recommendation; I thought this one might work." She hesitated. "Erm . . . it's good."

Mukesh held the book in his hands as though he'd never held a book before. He wanted to ask the young lady what it was about, but he didn't know if that was a stupid question. Maybe he was meant to know already.

"Dada, can I get this one please?" Priya had appeared by his side, holding up *A Wizard of Earthsea*. Mukesh shrugged, looking to the girl behind the desk for some kind of guidance. She nodded.

"Of course, you can take up to"—she paused for a moment—"six books out at a time on each card."

Priya looked at her dada, nodding vigorously. He'd never seen her so animated. She swung from side to side, the book clutched to her chest.

"You know, that book you've got, *To Kill a Mockingbird*, your granddaughter could read that too." The girl looked at him knowingly. Mukesh pondered this for a moment—remembering Rohini's words that it was *a bit grown-up* for her.

"So, this *isn't* an introductory welcome book?"

"Yeah, maybe, something like that. If you don't wanna read it, that's fine. But I thought it was good." She seemed suddenly unsure of herself, cautious.

"I've heard of that book, Dada; it's a film and everything," Priya jumped in.

"Ha, beta? What is it about?"

Priya shrugged, a frown clouding her face. "I don't know, I don't know *every*thing."

Mukesh chuckled. The girl behind the desk breathed in, as though she was about to embark on a long speech, but all she said was "It's a good *introductory* novel, you know? A classic."

"Do you think I'll like it, this book?" Mukesh didn't know whom to look at—the girl, or Priya. He had liked *The Time Traveler's Wife* but mainly because it had fallen into his lap at the right time and brought him closer to Naina.

The girl nodded.

Mukesh looked at the book cover. The title was scrawled like handwriting; he had to squint to make out the words. *To. Kill. A. Mockingbird.* "Why does it have that title?" he asked.

"There's a line in it . . ." The girl's voice jumped. "Sorry, I won't spoil it. You'll have to read to find out. If you want to. No pressure at all."

"Yeah, Dada!" Priya said, smiling at the girl, as though they were in on this together. Mukesh could see admiration in Priya's eyes—the kind of look his daughters used to get when they met their older cousins, whom they always looked up to as "cool young women."

"Can you recommend me any other books too? If I can take out six?" Mukesh asked. "Including this one." He pointed to Priya's book.

The girl stopped for a second, her eyes wide. "No, no, I think start with this. Trust me. It could, erm, give me an idea of what you should read next. If you like it."

"I'll try it," he said, smiling at her. She smiled back. He looked down at Priya and smiled at her too. "I'm getting a book!"

"I know, Dada, that's cool," Priya said, handing over her *Wizard* book to the girl behind the desk. Mukesh followed suit.

"Dada," Priya whispered. "And your library card." She nudged him gently in the ribs, and Mukesh did as he was told.

He watched as the girl scanned the card's barcode. *Beep.* As she scanned each book in. *Beep. Beep.*

"When should we give them back?" he asked.

"In three weeks. You can renew it on the phone or online if you need to."

"No, I will finish, and I *know* she will finish too."

"Would you like a stamp reminder in the front of the book, just in case?"

Mukesh turned to the front page of *To Kill a Mockingbird* and noticed the Brent Council Libraries sheet, full of black, splotchy dates. So many! It was strange, the idea that this book wasn't just for him, it was for everyone. All these people who had taken it out before him, people who would take it out after him. They might have read it on a beach, on the train, on the bus, in the park, in their living room. On the toilet? He hoped not! Every reader, unknowingly connected in some small way. He was about to be a part of this too. "Yes, please." He handed both books back to the girl, stamp at the ready, and as he watched, he wondered, had Naina ever held either of these books? She'd been here all the time, she'd read hundreds of books. Had *To Kill a Mockingbird* been one of them?

Mukesh put the book in his canvas shopping bag.

"Sir, if you would both like to sit and read here, we even have a coffee machine and some juices. And what's your name?" she asked Priya.

"Hello, I am Priya. What's your name?" Priya responded boldly, unexpectedly confident.

"Aleisha, nice to meet you. Would you and your granddad like to sit here and read?"

Priya looked up at Mukesh, hopeful, but he shook his head—it was nearly five o'clock—time for Priya's haircut! He felt both sets of eyes boring into him. Could they tell he was relieved? He didn't want to sit here and read . . . he'd feel too self-conscious. He was glad for the excuse—and besides, there was no time to waste, or he'd never hear the end of it from Rohini.

"Can I help you with anything else today?" the girl asked them.

"No, thank you. You have been very helpful. I have to drop my granddaughter off somewhere."

She beamed, running her hand over her hair, smoothing one flyaway down.

"I will go now and enjoy reading *To Kill a Hummingbird*. I will make sure to read some this evening," he said.

"*Mockingbird*," the girl said pointedly, and he just smiled, unsure as to why she'd repeated him.

Priya waved goodbye to the girl, who waved back, kindly, as Mukesh wandered out. Today he was taller. He could see farther afield now, to the end of the car park, beyond the trees, beyond the buildings; he could see past Wembley Stadium. He could see the whole of London from here, standing just that little bit taller. It's amazing what posture can do for you, he thought.

Well done, Mukesh, you faced a fear. It was Naina, speaking in his ear. He could hear her. Louder than ever before—like she was standing right beside him.

"Thank you," Mukesh whispered back.

"What, Dada?" Priya said.

"Sorry, nothing, beti. Let's get you to your hairdresser's!"

"Dada, *no*! I don't want to. Mum always wants to cut my hair, but I want it long."

"Sometimes you just have to listen to your mum. It makes her feel good! But you can sit and read there. How does that sound?"

"That's true." Priya shrugged, and followed her dada, letting him, slowly, lead the way.

Today he had borrowed a book from the library, legitimately, and the girl behind the desk had even been *helpful*. He felt a little bad for complaining about her but, then again, if he hadn't, she might not have been so polite today. When he worked at the Wembley Central ticket office, everyone loved giving customer feedback—good, honest customer feedback was the only surefire way to improve a service—and now, years later, he enjoyed it as well.

Today too he had taken his granddaughter to the library. For the first time in ages, Priya had looked excited or at least content in her grandfather's company. Perhaps today marked a new chapter.

LEONORA

2017

Leonora namaste'd her instructor and went to pick up her shoes from the hallway. Everyone was in a rush to get away, pulling their shoes on without undoing laces, and running out through the door, immediately forgetting the peace of the yoga class. But Leonora always took her time over this bit. She didn't mind if she got in people's way. She savored the dreamlike calm of this moment as she gradually adjusted to reality.

When people asked her why she'd moved back to Wembley, she always said it was to be closer to her parents—she never mentioned her divorce, she never mentioned her sister, Helena, who was slowly fading away; Helena was the real reason she had left Manchester for London. As soon as her divorce was announced, Leonora's parents had jumped on her, begging her to move in with her sister, to help her out, to put their minds at ease. She'd reluctantly agreed, but Helena didn't really want help, so now they lived side by side in awkward silence—Leonora an unwanted stranger in her own sister's home. And she had no one to talk to about it. No friends in this familiar but unwelcoming place. She was struggling.

Being back was a weird experience. Her parents and Helena had seen Wembley evolve—they'd been a *part* of that change—so the contrast wasn't so apparent to them. But Leonora had barely seen beyond the North Circular on her trips back home, for Easter and Christmas, bank holidays too, so to her, everything, the place she'd grown up, felt different. There were new high-rises everywhere; the residential streets had turned grayer with dust and age, whereas the shopping malls, the station, the stadium had all been polished to shiny perfection for the benefit of tourists alone.

Flailing in this lonely, changed city, Leonora had hoped this yoga class would help her meet new people. But beyond the occasional "hi," no one seemed that interested in chatting. People filtered out, while Leonora lingered, not wanting to go home.

There was one lady who always gave her a warm smile, but she felt too awkward to make conversation. She knew she should just suck it up and introduce herself, but everyone here was so self-contained. It felt strange, alien, to even try to say hello.

Today, she pulled on her shoes, slowly tying the laces. As she did every week, she read the notice board right in front of her, loitering long enough in the hope that someone else might say hi to her first . . . She wanted that meet-cute moment, like in the Hollywood films. Well, if she was really honest, she just wanted a friend.

Yoga retreats at £500 per week—no thank you. Cat-sitting opportunities—with her allergies? No thanks to that either. A book club at the local library on Harrow Road . . . She hadn't been there since she was a kid. Beside the poster was a handwritten list; she presumed these were the book club titles.

To Kill a Mockingbird

Rebecca

The Kite Runner

Life of Pi

Pride and Prejudice

Little Women

Beloved

A Suitable Boy

Maybe *this* would be a chance to meet people. If it was a book club, they had to *speak*. And she remembered the place fondly. Harrow Road had been her library of choice as a teenager. She remembered the librarians—they'd probably be long gone now—and the young manager, Dev, who always had a good book recommendation up his sleeve, tailored to the tastes and interests of each and every cherished library-goer.

She looked down the list, taking in one title at a time. She had read some of these already, including *To Kill a Mockingbird*, when she was a teenager. She didn't remember the story, she was terrible with details, but she remembered the way it made her *feel*. It had this kind of warm, magical quality about it. The title brought memories of eating breakfast outside on a wooden bench—and it was so long ago she couldn't recall whether the memory was her own or a scene from the book itself.

When she reached the seventh title on the list, she pulled out the book from her yoga bag, a copy of *Beloved*. She held it up. Well, it looked as if she already had a head start.

She turned the book over in her hands. She'd only just started reading it, after years and years of her friends recommending it. In the afternoons, when Helena took her long nap, Leonora had started to read, sitting just beside her sister, listening to her breathing, and allowing her mind to escape elsewhere. Her heart was in it already.

She wondered when the *Beloved* date for the book club might be. There was no more information on the notice board. Would she be ready to discuss it in time? The book was about a mother, Sethe, and her daughter Denver, left alone in a house haunted by the ghost of Sethe's first daughter, Beloved, who had brought heartache to the family for years. It reminded her of Helena's house. That too was filled with a ghost; a ghost of Helena's past, of Helena's happiness, of the future Helena might not get to see.

Leonora took a deep breath, wiping away a mist of tears on her cheeks. She tucked the book back into her bag. A book club. It might be a good idea. A chance for her to talk, to make friends. She took a picture of the reading list and the sign about the book club too; she'd have a look for it, tomorrow, when Helena took her nap. She'd go tomorrow.

CHAPTER 10

MUKESH

Beep. "Dada? It's me!" Priya's voice was gleeful. "I'm really enjoying *A Wizard of Earthsea*, but I have been reading quite a few at once, so I won't be able to return it to the library with you. Mummy said you were going back today already, so I wanted to call to say I'm very sorry if it will be late, and I can't come over today because Mum got me some extra math work to do for the holidays and I have to do that."

She said all the words in quite a hurry, so Mukesh had to rewind and replay slowly to check he'd caught every detail, his pad of Post-it notes at the ready.

He'd been looking forward to seeing Priya; he'd gotten himself up and dressed earlier than usual because he was eager to talk to her about their books. He had even noted down a few key phrases. He wanted to "impart" some wisdom from *Hummingbird*, just like Atticus, even if the wisdom wasn't really his to impart.

Don't take it personally, he heard Naina say, her voice jumping out from the pages. *She's young, she doesn't want to hurt you.*

He knew Naina was probably right. But going to the library with Priya had been easier. And it had felt as though he'd finally made a breakthrough with his granddaughter.

Mukesh sighed. He knew he had to go back to the library. He wanted to return the book and get another. But deep down, he wasn't totally sure if he could manage it all on his own. He flicked through the book one more time, searching for a piece of Atticus's wisdom to help him through this little moment.

As he approached the library an hour or so later, the book in his hands, Scout was running ahead of him dressed as a ham, taking

Priya's place, cheering him on, and wise old Atticus was striding beside him. As Mukesh walked through the glass doors, emboldened by his fictional companions, the first person he saw was the girl, Aleisha. She was hard at work, with headphones stuck in her ears again. He wandered up to her desk, Scout and Atticus now gone. A cough caught her attention, and he placed his book in front of his face, proudly peeping over her desk.

"Hello? Mr. Patel? You finished already?"

Once he had gotten into it, and gotten over himself, more importantly, he had finished it quickly. He was very proud of his achievement: he'd only watched one episode of *Blue Planet* in that time.

When he was nearly thirteen, my brother Jem got his arm badly broken at the elbow. He'd started slowly, wincing as he'd read that first line of *To Kill a Mockingbird*, for he'd felt Naina watching his every move.

It's a good one, Mukesh, it won't take you long. Her voice rang loud and clear in his ear. He'd looked around, expecting her to be there. After trying to get comfortable in the living room, and then the kitchen, and then the garden, he had finally settled on Naina's spot in their bed—it was perfect. There he could feel, just for a moment, what it was like, to be her, tucked up with a book. But that niggling thought at the back of his mind had squeaked, *Fraud, fraud, fraud.*

He'd tried to adjust his focus to the feel of the pages.

The softness.

The *whoosh* as they glided across each other.

The gentle snap of the gluey spine from time to time.

Trying to get back to the book, and away from his nagging imposter syndrome, Mukesh pictured tall, broad, authoritarian Atticus in his small bedroom on his IKEA rug (selected by Vritti). Within a few pages, Mukesh learned that Scout and Jem's "courteously detached" father was a widower, and he had raised his children alone, with the help of Calpurnia their cook. As his eyes ran over the words, he could feel a lump begin to rise in his throat.

Mukesh wasn't a lawyer, wasn't a pillar of the community, didn't bless his children with his wisdom. He wasn't tall, broad, and authoritarian like Atticus. But Mukesh knew what losing your wife felt like too. Mukesh sat up straight, his attention now firmly focused on this man, this powerful, kind, and fair man. As the story went on, Mukesh wondered how Atticus could continue with his life so boldly. Was any part of him stuck in the past, hiding from his wife's death? He could feel his self-consciousness lift, and he continued, intent on discovering Atticus's secret to success. How had Atticus moved on with his life seemingly unscathed?

After a slow start, Naina was proved right later that same evening. Mukesh hadn't been able to tear himself away—he had felt himself taking on Atticus's life lessons, putting himself in Scout's shoes, seeing the world through her eyes. The *fraud, fraud, fraud* was nagging at the back of his mind, but the story had well and truly taken over.

Mukesh lowered the book to reveal his face to the librarian—a huge grin brightening it, the memories of turning the final page, the sense of pride he'd felt then, returned to him. He took off his hat, and rearranged his hair, all blustered and flustered from the wind. "Yes! I finished it!"

"Would you like to return it?" the librarian asked, and he handed the book over, nervously. He didn't want to let go of it, but he allowed her to ring it through her system.

"That's all sorted for you." She smiled back at him. He waited, not sure what to do next. He wanted to talk to her about it, but he didn't know what to say, or where to start. He could feel his cheeks starting to blush—what if he said something stupid?

"Erm," he started. "Walking in someone else's skin." His voice came out all croaky and quivery.

"I'm sorry, what was that?"

"Walking in someone else's skin, you know—that's what Atticus says," he stammered.

"Oh yes, I remember," she said, her eyes brightening.

"I think that's what stayed with me most. It is very wise. Atticus—*he's* very wise."

Aleisha nodded. "Definitely."

They looked at each other awkwardly. The silence hung between them.

"When I finished it," the girl started, "I was so enraged, and so desperate to talk to someone about it."

"Me too." Mukesh nodded vigorously.

"Well . . ." The girl looked at her phone on the table. "I've still got some of my lunch break left, shall we have a chat about it?"

Mukesh could feel Naina prodding him, and he nodded again, warily. She led him over to a table by the window. "Feel free to sit here, Mr. Patel," she said very kindly.

"Mukesh, please," he whispered back. He didn't know where to start, but she was watching him, waiting for him to go first.

"That line about stepping into someone else's skin . . . Well, we were in Scout's skin—the little girl in the story," he said slowly. He thought it sounded like something someone would say in a book group, or in an English class: "We see Atticus through her eyes, don't we?"

The young lady smiled, and Mukesh couldn't tell if she agreed or if she was pandering to him.

"I think that one line is very interesting—because if people could step into Tom Robinson's skin, maybe they wouldn't be so awful to him, accusing him of something he never did, when that lie could have ruined his whole life. And not as awful, but what if Scout and Jem could see what it was like to be the old neighbor Boo Radley, maybe they would have been kinder to him as well. He was a lovely soul . . . maybe just lonely. People don't always understand lonely people." The words rushed out of him, like he wanted to get them out of the way. Maybe, if he spoke quickly enough, she wouldn't notice him saying silly, stupid things.

Aleisha nodded again. "You're right, but . . . it's literally impossible, that's the thing. People just live their lives, they can't ever fully *get* . . . you know . . . understand someone else or what they're going through." She spoke slowly, as though trying to put her own thoughts together. He wondered if she was just trying to make him feel less of an idiot.

"I always used to think that when I was a young man, when I first moved here . . ." He took a deep breath. The book had made him think of it, how out of place he felt in Wembley when he first arrived, how everyone looked at him and his family differently for a while, forever. "I moved here from Kenya, you see. With my wife and our little girls. We wanted to start a brand-new life here—we had family here, always talking about all the opportunities, the jobs. But when I got here, it just felt lonely. I wondered why people were so unkind to me. I thought to myself, why didn't they know who I was, that I was just like them? No matter what I did, what I said, no one even *tried* to understand me. Some of our neighbors were really lovely—but other than that, everyone else saw us as just different from them, impossible to understand. So they didn't even try.

"I'm sorry." Mukesh shook his head, trying to banish his thoughts. "This isn't anything to do with the book. What am I babbling on about? My wife always told me I was a babbler."

"No, no, you're not babbling. I think you're right," Aleisha said, smiling kindly. "No one can ever really understand what other people have gone through. But people should try."

For a moment, it was hard for Mukesh to align the grumpy person he had met a week or so ago with the young lady sitting in front of him today. He wondered whether, if he'd walked around in *her* skin that day, he might have understood her behavior a little better.

"So when I read this book . . . er, ages ago . . ." She hesitated for a moment, her eyes darting around the room. She reminded him of his youngest, Deepali, who did the same thing whenever she was nervous, or fibbing. "Ages ago now . . . Well, it makes you feel things. I've got a big brother, and we're really different from Scout and Jem, but like reading about them as kids made me think of me and Aidan as children. Being silly. Seeing the neighbor as like a figure of fun and stuff. I'm sure we did stupid stuff like that when I was young, like the whole world was a big game to us."

"It's true! I liked them both. I liked the story very, very much." Mukesh nodded emphatically. "I like Atticus a lot too! He was a very clever man."

"He was *so* good!" Aleisha lit up. "I just . . . All the court-case stuff with Tom Robinson, like it was so emotional and mega-tense, but I loved it. I'm applying to do law at uni—"

"*Law?*" Mukesh gasped, looking utterly delighted. "You are very, very clever! No wonder you are such a big reader."

Aleisha laughed uneasily. She shrugged her shoulders, immediately shy again. "Not that clever, I just work hard."

"Well, Atticus is a very good lawyer, but you, you'll be even better!" Mukesh clapped his hands together and they laughed at each other.

Their chatter petered out to silence, an edge of awkwardness creeping in. "Well, thank you for all your help," Mukesh said again. "I liked that one, so what do you recommend next? You said you could tell me which one!"

The girl paused. He noticed her hands crunching into each other, one finger twisting around and around the other.

"Erm, maybe you might like *Rebecca*—it's by Daphne du Maurier."

"Whatever you recommend I am sure I will like!"

She hopped up from her chair and headed to the shelves—she found the copy immediately. He thought it was very clever, how Aleisha knew where every book in the library was placed. She took it over to her desk, and Mukesh clambered out of his very comfy armchair to meet her there.

"My wife loved to read," he said, filling the silence, as she tapped in the code.

"What did she like?"

"I don't really know. She always had a book with her. I never knew what. She died, you see. A couple of years ago. I . . . She was the reader. I have never really read much, until now."

"I'm so sorry." Her voice was just louder than a whisper. She looked at him, gave him room to continue.

"She was my *wife*, I should have paid attention to the books she liked. I liked to watch her read, but never asked her what was happening in her books. I feel silly starting to read storybooks at my age."

"It's never too late to read stories."

"Stories feel so weird. Like seeing someone else's life that you are not meant to. Being nosy!"

Aleisha scanned his library card in. "I'm sure your wife would be so impressed with how quickly you read *To Kill a Mockingbird*!"

"I think she would be too." He nodded, solemnly.

"What job did you used to do? Or what do you do now?" She looked up sharply, probably hoping she hadn't offended him.

"Oh, dear, I definitely do not do anything now. Too old and creaky! I *was* a ticket master at Wembley Central. Now I don't really do anything."

"A ticket master?"

"Yes, I sold people tickets. I knew people, I knew their faces, and I would always try to ask their names—I knew who had to get what train and when. People were less grumpy then. People weren't so busy. There were very few mobile phones, not like today, so people looked up when they walked around instead of down at their hands." He nodded toward Aleisha's iPhone, facedown on the table. "Speaking was all you could do then. I would call out to some people if I knew they might be late for their train." He raised his hand. "'Your train is here, miss!' I would say. People always thanked me then."

"Literally can't imagine people speaking to each other in London. Not sure I've ever said more than a few words to people on the Tube."

"I know, I find it sad. Often I say hello to people and they just look at me like I am crazy."

Aleisha nodded knowingly. "That man over there," she whispered under her breath, and pointed to a young gentleman sitting in a thick black hoodie. "We call him Crime Thriller Guy, it's all he reads. He came and spoke to me a while ago, like just making conversation. I found it *so* strange. And this is actually my job. I *work* here."

They giggled together then, and Crime Thriller looked up for a moment; they both quickly averted their gazes. Mukesh felt as if he had been let in on a secret.

"My wife, she would have liked you," he said once he'd gotten his breath back. "She likes young women who are kind, clever, and focused. And readers! Just like her."

He noticed he had switched into present tense; the girl had noticed too.

"Here's your next book, Mr. Patel!" She handed *Rebecca* to him before he could say anything else. Mukesh clasped it in both hands, placed it in his shopping bag slung over his shoulder, and wandered outside. He didn't turn around to say goodbye until he was already out of the door. Framed by the doorway, cut in two by the divide in the glass, he waved with one hand. The girl waved back, just as enthusiastically.

The girl was right—Naina *would* be proud, not just because he'd read a book quickly . . . but because today he took himself out of his comfort zone, and for a few moments of his day, he'd made a brand-new friend. He looked at his feet, to check he was still fixed firmly on the ground and he wasn't just daydreaming. Satisfied this was all very real, he turned back around and shuffled away.

Rebecca

by

DAPHNE DU MAURIER

CHAPTER 11

ALEISHA

A few days later, Aleisha jumped at the sound of her phone ringing. It was seven in the morning . . .

"Aleisha," Thermos Flask's morning voice croaked. "Any chance you'd be free to cover for Benny today? He's been taken ill after a stag do last night. Kyle will be in too."

"You mean Benny's hungover?" She yawned.

"Probably—still, best he stays away. I don't want any dodgy moments in the aisles."

Aleisha glanced wearily over to her bedside table, where *Rebecca* sat, waiting for her. "All right, yeah. Let me check with my brother, otherwise I'll be there." She was grateful for the opportunity to just sit in the library today, put some books back on the shelves. Last night had been a bad one for Leilah. Aleisha had woken several times in the night to hear her mum shouting out, and then to the sound of Aidan trudging back and forth to her room; his footsteps slow, soft. Exhausted.

When she arrived at the library, it was quiet, with only two regulars, including Crime Thriller Guy in his usual spot, and the elderly Indian lady who loved to chat, but there was no one demanding her attention. As the glass doors closed behind her, the sounds and smells of Wembley, and the memories of Leilah's fractious night, all disappeared.

But as she was walking up and down the fiction aisles, putting the returns back on the shelf, she saw a figure hiding around the corner. It brought her back to earth with a thump. Mia. Aleisha would recognize the back of her head anywhere, with the slightly sloppy undercut, one long earring in her left ear, a short stud in the other.

She hurried past, ducking behind the sparse *W* fiction shelf, keeping her eyes trained on her feet, trying to be as inconspicuous as possible.

"Aleisha?"

Oh fuck.

Aleisha turned around slowly, trying to be casual, trying to plaster a natural smile on her face. Really, she just wanted the ground below her to open up and suck her in.

"You *actually* work here?" Mia's face communicated her confusion, but her tone made it doubly clear.

"Hey, Mia! How are you? Yeah, what you doing here?"

"Just studying for my last exam next week. I know you told us girls you were working here since your exams ended, but I didn't actually believe it." Mia smirked, like Aleisha's job was the funniest joke in the world. In that moment, Aleisha hated her.

But she giggled awkwardly, acting as though she was in on the same joke, laughing at her own expense. She hadn't seen Mia since her own last exam in the middle of May, over two months ago—they'd not exchanged a word after. She certainly didn't think of herself as one of "us girls" anymore. The WhatsApp group was now the only sign that they'd ever been connected to each other. She wondered what it would be like in September, thrown back at school. Would they be the "best of friends" again? Would they never speak again?

Mia's textbooks were scattered all over the desk.

"That looks like more than one exam's worth of stuff." Aleisha nodded her head toward the table: a distraction technique.

"I want a head start too. Not long before uni applications, I don't want to be playing catch-up."

"Yeah, I get you." Aleisha nodded, her eyes darting around the library, looking for an excuse to leave. "I'd better go. It looks like someone needs me." She bobbed her head in the direction of the front desk where a kid of about ten was preparing to ring the bell. Kyle was making his way over too—Aleisha caught his eye and shooed him back.

"Hey." Aleisha waved her arms at the kid. "I'm here." She marched to the desk, settled herself into her chair, and put on her game face. "How can I help?"

"I want to take a book out."

"Any one in particular?"

"I don't know. Can you recommend me one?"

Aleisha rolled her eyes. Here we go again. But she could feel Mia watching her, and she kept a wide smile: Good Librarian Mode in full force.

Mia didn't leave quickly. She stayed for *hours*. Long enough to see Aidan walk in with a Tesco carrier bag of lunch for Aleisha. She spotted her friend's ears prick up at her brother's voice. Mia had always had a crush on Aidan; all Aleisha's friends did.

"Hey, Leish," Aidan said, wandering up to her. "What you doing?" He pointed his carrier bag at her as she leaned back in her seat, reading *Rebecca*. Seeing as Mr. Patel had read *To Kill a Mockingbird* in two days flat, she'd had to recommend *Rebecca* before she'd even finished it herself. In a panic, not wanting to be caught out again, she'd called up during Lucy's shift later the next day to reserve *The Kite Runner*, *Life of Pi*, *Pride and Prejudice*, *Little Women*, *Beloved*, and *A Suitable Boy*. The whole list. The books were piled up on her desk, ready to be taken home.

Lucy had squealed down the phone. "Aleisha! You're reading a big old load of books, are you?!" And right on cue, the library assistant embarked on her favorite story about her kids becoming readers. "Honestly, trust me, even if you think storybooks can do nothing for you, it just really opens up your world a little bit, my dear. Look at my Hannah, she's a big business lady now and she always says she got her focus from this place. Those textbooks you read for school and stuff can teach you a fair amount, but novels teach you so much more! My little ones became readers here, babe," she said for the trillionth time. "So happy you're doing it too! Especially after all your whingeing."

She was pleased for the protection the book gave her today, something to hide behind. But she still felt stupid, with Mia there glancing around every so often, despite the fact that reading felt a smidge more natural to her now. She'd been drawn in at first by Mr. de Winter, charming, attractive, as well as by his new wife, nervous, so obviously in love. And Aleisha couldn't shake that ominous feeling of the past coming back to haunt them, captured by the description of that grand, overgrown, overbearing, and creepy house, Manderley, a secret festering between the newlyweds.

Aleisha had jumped out of her skin earlier. A line in the story mentioned a pile of books from the library. It had haunted her; it felt as though the author had suddenly turned her gaze outward, on Aleisha.

She didn't yet know where this story might go, but she wanted to find out.

"I'm just reading," she replied to Aidan.

"I can see that, I'm just . . . pleased you're so keen. Remember when Nan got you that Lemony Snicket book and you ended up using it as a stage for your Kinder egg toys?"

Aleisha rolled her eyes.

"How'd it go with the old guy in the end? You're still reading these for him?"

"Not just for him," she replied. "Helps pass the time too, I guess."

He pulled the book out of her hands to scrutinize the cover. "*Rebecca*? Careful you don't scare the old guy to death with this one. You could get fired for that."

"Shhh!" Aleisha hissed, looking over at Mia. "Give that back!" She snatched the book from his hand.

"Sorry, sorry, don't want to ruin your street cred in front of all your friends." He waved his arms around dramatically at the library buzzing with imaginary people. Then Aidan's eye caught the back of Mia's head. "*Mia?*" he mouthed, in an over-the-top, typical Aidan kind of way.

Aleisha nodded and pulled a face that only Aidan would understand to mean, *Yep. Fuck my actual life.*

"Want me to hang out here to, you know, protect you? Why aren't you mates anymore, anyway?"

"Shush! We're all right. Plus you only want to stay 'cause you know she fancies you."

"Well, who can blame her?" Aidan winked, and Aleisha got up from her chair to punch her brother on his shoulder. "Hey! That's not how you treat everyone here, is it? No wonder you're getting a rep as the world's worst librarian. I'll go then . . ."

"Wait! Seeing as you've come all the way here . . ." she shout-whispered. "I feel like this is the first time I've seen you in ages, we've been ships in the night. What you been up to?"

They both knew that managing Leilah's spiral was taking over everything else at the moment, their mother's need hanging unspoken between them.

"Yeah, it's okay, they're thinking of promoting me to manager at the warehouse, which would be good . . . finally."

Aidan worked at a biscuit warehouse, which wasn't quite the job of his dreams. He'd taken on the evening shift in his summer just after sixth form, intending to find something else, but after seven years he was still there. Aleisha knew he liked the stability, the familiarity . . . and probably the biscuits too. "That's so great!"

"But it would mean spending more time there and potentially giving up the job at Elliot's." Elliot's was the car mechanic's Aidan had been working at for the past few months, covering the odd shift here and there. Aleisha saw it as another avoidance technique of his—trying to be practical, putting his own ambitions of setting up his own shop on hold. He'd spoken about doing an Open University business course before, but every time Leilah was unwell, he acted as though he'd never suggested anything of the sort, and threw himself into something else.

"Would that be the end of the world?"

"Leish, you know I like mechanics, like I think it could be a good career for me in the short term. Might give me some hands-on insight into running a business too. Elliot's really nice, he said he'd let me help out on that side of things if I wanted."

"Right, but other than that, are you actually interested in it?"

"I don't know." He suddenly looked a little stony-faced.

"What's the money for a manager position at the warehouse?"

"It's more than I expected. It's not loads. Not as much as you're gonna get as a lawyer."

Aleisha laughed, but it was tinged with sadness. Aleisha had always been allowed to dream, had always been pushed to do more. Aidan had never had that same opportunity. She'd decided on becoming a lawyer when she was thirteen, mainly because she *loved* to argue, and from that moment Aidan had never let her drop it, planning his own life to support hers.

She wished she could say to Aidan that he could be anything he wanted too, he could follow whatever dream he had, but he'd never take advice from his younger sister. Aidan didn't take advice from anyone.

"What's your dream?" she asked, unable to stop herself.

Aidan just let out a low, guttural laugh. "What are you, my career adviser?"

"I'm your sister, and I don't think I know what it is."

"That's because I'm not like you, Leish. Some people don't have dreams."

"Everyone has *something*."

"In that case, if you really want an answer, I have you guys. You and Mum. You're it."

Something caught in Aleisha's throat and she couldn't reply. The silence of the library echoed around them. What had they done to this young man? What had they done to his dreams?

He launched the meal-deal bag at her, which broke the tension with a clatter, the juice and sandwich meal deal rolling out onto the floor.

"Shit!" Aidan shouted, and all four people in the library, including Mia, turned around to frown. When Mia spotted that Aidan was the source of the disruption, her face changed, and she beamed at him, doing one of those cutesy little waves. Aidan raised his eyebrows, waving back, picking up the sandwich and juice with his other hand and placing them carefully on Aleisha's desk.

Mia started to approach, and Aidan smirked at his sister, mouthed, "I'm sorry," and rushed out at breakneck speed. On cue, Mia slowed down, diverting her path ever so slightly away from Aidan's ghost and toward Aleisha.

"Oh, you dropped this," Mia said, bending down to pick something up from the floor. A little orange Post-it note. She presented it as though it was some kind of precious gift.

Enjoy your lunch. Pick up some stuff for dinner tonight—I'll cook. A x

Classic Aidan.

"From your brother? *Awwww*, super cute," Mia said, reading it for herself.

Aleisha snatched it back. "Thanks."

"Erm, I was just coming over to say I'm going to head out now, but see you soon. Enjoy your *book*. And your meal deal. Good to see you, yeah?"

At seven o'clock, closing time was fast approaching. Aleisha was the only person left in the whole library. This was just the kind of peace she wanted. The perfect environment to spend some quality time with *Rebecca*. When she'd first flicked through the pages a few days ago, she'd known she'd give the book a decent chance. The first sign was *My Cousin Rachel* on the list of other books written by Daphne du Maurier. Aleisha missed her *own* cousin Rachel. They used to be inseparable, but Rachel now lived over a hundred miles away . . .

The beautiful, isolated mansion—Manderley—pulled her right into the book, taking her somewhere else altogether. She was slowly learning about Rebecca herself . . . Rebecca was actually Mr. de Winter's *late* wife, yet her presence was so overbearing in the house, so all-consuming in the new Mrs. de Winter's life, she deserved to be the title character. Manderley's location was never mentioned precisely, but all the descriptions reminded her of Cornwall . . . Well, it reminded her of the photographs she'd seen of the beautiful Cornish coastline plastered all over her Year 9 Classroom wall after all her friends had gone on a school trip to Bude. Aleisha hadn't been able to go. Aidan, who had been just twenty-one at the time, had rearranged his work shifts to try to make it work, but ultimately she had to stay back because Leilah wasn't well. She'd hated seeing those beautiful pictures at school, hearing the stories from her friends, learning about everything she'd missed.

Aleisha had always wanted to see Cornwall in real life, but she had still never had the chance. She *loved* the look of its rugged cliffs, dramatic crashing waves—so different from the wide sands and pine trees of North Norfolk, the only seaside Dean and Leilah had ever taken them to as kids.

But now, through *Rebecca* and Mrs. de Winter, Aleisha was experiencing Cornwall from a totally different perspective. And she could go as far away from Wembley, from Mia, from Leilah, as possible, one page at a time.

Rebecca skulked about Manderley like a ghost and, a chill running down her spine, Aleisha dropped the book down onto her desk suddenly. Bloody creepy. After a breath, to calm herself, she tucked the novel under her arm and grabbed her bag, overloaded with books. When she stood up, a big, dark shadow was looming over her, slicing through the waning light of the summer evening.

"Shit!" Aleisha yelped, clutching the book to her chest for protection. As her eyes readjusted, she realized it was just the vacuum cleaner, left out by Kyle as a reminder to "keep this place looking sharp." This bloody book—it was still basically daylight and it was already scaring her half to death.

As she locked the library up for the night, kicking a grand total of zero readers out into the summer evening air, she tucked the reading list into *Rebecca* to mark her spot.

Once again, she found her mind lingering on the curator of the list. She pictured someone fairly young, younger than her mum probably but older than her, judging from the super-neat and kind of fancy handwriting, not like Aleisha's bubble handwriting. They could be a student, but she doubted it. All school reading lists were typed out and just handed out to people. This was one the person had put together themselves, or copied out of a newspaper or off the internet or something. Like off the lists that say "Twenty books to read before you die." In the case of *Rebecca*, she wondered if it was "the one book to read before you get married in case you discover his ex-wife is going to haunt you and the housekeeper is going to be a right bitch through your whole marriage and maybe you can't trust your new hubby either."

Aleisha had no idea what it was like to be haunted by a dead woman or to live in a mansion, but the way Manderley was described, the atmosphere, sharp, heavy, and suffocating . . . she got that. She knew exactly what that felt like. She wished she'd never made the comparison. Maybe it wasn't the best book choice for her after all. But it was already too late.

She let herself out of the library, locking the doors behind her. She looked back through the windows. It had been unsettling seeing Mia here today—an intruder in the space that was starting to feel different to her. More like a refuge than a prison sentence. More like somewhere she could, one day, actually belong. She watched as the last beam of evening sun shone on her desk, her spot. Even if she'd never admit it to Mia, maybe she was starting to like working here.

It was the little things.

IZZY

2017

Izzy saw it there, lying on the pavement in front of her. She had a look around, wondering if someone had dropped it, where it had come from. It had a piece of sticky tape at the top, now lacking any adhesive. It was just dry and dirty from the London smog.

She hadn't found a list in a long time. It was a bit of a weird habit of hers, collecting lists. She'd started when she first moved to London, when she'd found one abandoned in a shopping cart in Sainsbury's. The city had been so large, so vast and lonely sometimes, finding lists was like finding tiny moments of human connection, where she could prove that the silent strangers who walked past her, avoiding eye contact, were people too. They wrote shopping lists, they planned their dinners, they added some treats in every so often—the lists grounded her.

Every list she'd ever found was now stuffed into a little box in her hallway dresser drawer. She knew that one day she'd upgrade them, put them in a folder or a photo album or something, but for now, that's where they lived. Most of the lists were from supermarkets, found in baskets, on the floor, by the cash register, left at the self-service checkout. Sometimes she discovered them floating down the street outside a shop. Almost *all* the lists were shopping lists, once useful then suddenly discarded. Apart from one, which was an invite list—a small dinner party, maybe. There were names scribbled out—and some responses too: *doesn't eat eggs* or *allergic to chicken but fine with other birds.* For days she'd wondered how the dinner party had turned out—whether the people who were crossed off had RSVP'd no, or were dumped by the host.

Every list gave her some kind of insight into the person—she loved trying to work out what meal someone might be cooking, whether they were meal planning for the whole week or just for one special dinner, maybe a date, a meet-the-parents lunch, or just a cozy night in.

Sometimes she wished she was all right at art, because the images of these people were so vivid in her mind, she wanted to draw them, immortalize them in some way. She could work out if someone had kids, was vegetarian, was cooking for one or two, even what their skincare regime was or how smelly they were (deciphered by their choice of deodorant).

But this list, floating down Wembley High Road, was a bit different.

Just in case you need it:

To Kill a Mockingbird

Rebecca

The Kite Runner

Life of Pi

Pride and Prejudice

Little Women

Beloved

A Suitable Boy

She knew what it was. She'd written loads herself when she was at uni and had to get a pile of books out of the library. It was a reading list. It might even have been someone's university reading list, if it weren't for the line at the top: *Just in case you need it.*

She recognized some of the books, had read them years ago, but, as she stood in the middle of the busy pavement, scrutinizing the handwriting, she struggled to find the connections between each title. What, and, more importantly, *who* had brought all these books together?

Looking down at this smudgy list, her fingers brushed over the words. Silently, it began to rain. She didn't notice until the drops fell on the words, and the ink, once dry, was suddenly fresh and running into a puddle. She tucked it up her sleeve in a hurry and sprinted to the nearest bus stop. Here she stood looking down at the words, the handwriting, the gentle curl of the *J*, the *d*. The titles were written less floridly, as though whoever wrote the list wanted the books themselves to be as legible as possible. Yet they couldn't resist adding a flourish to the *g* and the *R*, and eliding the *B* and *e* of *Beloved*.

That evening, as Izzy was tucking the list away with the others (the one underneath said simply, *Baked beans (lo salt), ice cream, sausages, sausages veggie, cat food*), she glimpsed a title that stirred something: *Rebecca*. Her dad had had a *Reader's Digest* copy bound in red leather with gold lettering that he'd inherited from his own mother—he read it every year because it was his mother's favorite book.

"This book reminds me of her, Izzy," he'd said to her, when she asked him why he was reading the same story again and again. "You like to reread your books, and I do too."

It was beautiful, the book—and she'd loved seeing her dad pick it up so often. He turned each page so carefully. He never opened it wide enough to bend the spine. It was precious to him. The day he'd finally given it to her, she knew that she was old enough and trusted enough to read it; she'd felt like a grown-up that day. But, for fear of damaging it, of getting her sticky fingerprints on it, of ruining her father's precious copy, she'd never passed the first page.

She wandered to her kitchen, where her only bookshelf was kept (she'd never asked her landlord why the shelf was screwed to the wall, here of all places), and began to rummage through the books. This time, she couldn't quite picture the list writer, and it niggled at her, this unknowing . . . But perhaps reading the books themselves—some again, some for the first time—would help her to get a clearer picture of who they might be?

She was sure she, or her flatmate, Sage, had another paperback copy of *Rebecca* somewhere. She'd seen it. A black cover, with gold writing, all curly, and a rose. Red and bright, luxurious. But she couldn't find it anywhere. She turned the list over, about to give up, when she spotted HARROW ROAD LIBRARY emblazoned on the back. The books had been scrawled on the back of a renewals slip: "Return date 11/03/2016." The pixelated text had almost faded to nothing. Aha, she thought to herself, as though she was an evil villain or successful detective from a TV show. She knew that library, and she knew one university student who used it quite a lot. She pulled out her phone, dropped a WhatsApp to Sage, Hey, can you get me Rebecca by Daphne du Maurier from your library plz?

Sage's reply was almost instantaneous: Get it yourself, lazy bones. Come see the banging library vibes your missing out on.

Izzy read each title on the list once more and took in that line: *Just in case you need it.* Unlike every other list she'd found, this felt as though it was intended to be discovered. This list was a letter from a stranger—and Izzy wanted to find out what it meant.

CHAPTER 12

MUKESH

Beep. "Dad, good luck today! You'll be good, and remember to stretch properly. I hope those fitness DVDs arrived in the post for you—I didn't hear back from you. Sorry we didn't drop them round, we've just been so busy; the twins are on the go all the time and it's hard to find a spare moment. Twins, say good luck to your dada." "*Good luck, Dada! Don't fall over!*" the twins chorused in the background.

Beep. "Hi, Papa, it's Rohini, remember to eat properly before you go and keep your blood sugar up. Have one of those packet chais or something, yeah? And enjoy it—the walk, not just the chai. Remember to wear an undershirt too, it will help with the sweat patches."

Beep. "Hi, Papa, it's Vritti. Good luck today. Sending you loads of love. Hopefully see you soon, yeah? Anyway . . . I'm really proud of you. For doing this. Seriously."

Today was the day he'd been dreading: the day of the sponsored walk. Mukesh stared at his book, the voicemails from his daughters ringing in his ears. His heart was pounding. He couldn't be sure it was because of his own nerves, or whether he'd become jittery because of *Rebecca*. He'd been lost in its pages late last night and it was haunting . . . scary. It was about a woman, in love with a wonderful man, just married. The start of a happy story, Mukesh had thought at first, until it became clear that the ex-wife, the *dead* wife, Rebecca . . . she would never be forgotten, and this new lady would forever live with the ghost of the past. It was terrifying.

Mukesh gulped loudly—swallowing his fears. He was clutching his canvas bag with his Canderel sweetener, a spare sachet of chai just in case, and a water bottle. *Mukesh.* Naina's voice filtered through the air. *You can do this, okay? It is good, it is for charity. Just imagine I'm there walking beside you.* He clutched his book to his side; Naina used to carry a book with her wherever she was, in case she got stuck in a lift on her own, or if there was a queue at a supermarket with no one to chat with. For Mukesh, having the book with him today was a method of avoiding chatty conversations with mandir volunteers, and it felt like Naina, a small part of her, was with him. A lucky talisman.

Getting off the bus at the mandir, he saw the group of people outside in the courtyard, all wearing matching T-shirts. He'd have to wear one too. On cue, the ever-annoying Harish strode over to him at the bus stop, a neatly folded T-shirt in his hands.

"Kemcho, Mukeshbhai," Harish said. "Please, this is for you. Are you ready for the walk?"

Mukesh nodded, meaning, *Absolutely not*. In the temple forecourt, he was surrounded by many of the people he usually tried to avoid. Not because he didn't like them. Most of them were perfectly nice people, though a handful of them had rather odd, harsh views about politics, immigration, the National Health Service, and who was deserving of certain privileges and who was not, which he always felt was rather hypocritical and un-Hindu of them, but these were the ones who delighted in sharing their thoughts with anyone who would listen (he thought of the people of Maycomb)—while others seemed happy to simply boast about their children, or even their friends' children . . . Mukesh felt strongly that unless they were blood relatives in some way, there was absolutely no boasting potential.

"Mukesh!" Chirag called over to him. Chirag was another youngster who didn't address his elders formally and politely. Respect for your elders seemed to have vanished, for him anyway.

"Hello, Chirag," Mukesh replied. "How are you? How is your papa?"

"Papa is fine, he's not coming today any longer. He has a bit of a cold."

Mukesh cursed under his breath—why had he not thought of something like that? Anything to get out of this walk.

"That is a shame. Would have been nice to see him. It has been a while. A good long while."

"You don't come to the mandir much anymore?"

He tried to respond with "Yes," but what came out instead was "Yes, I come on special occasions with my daughters, but I pray at home a lot as well. I do not need to be at mandir to pray and be faithful to God."

Chirag's eyes widened. "Mukeshfua, no," he said. "Please, I didn't mean that at all."

Mukesh saw the horror in the boy's eyes. "I *should* come more," he babbled hurriedly, trying to ease the awkwardness. Mukesh clutched the book for dear life, hoping it might help him channel Naina. "Enjoy the walk." He waved at Chirag and walked away toward the entrance of the mandir, wondering what uncomfortable conversation he would find there. Naina would have known what to do, what to say, in any and every moment. Everyone loved her—the women at the mandir, the men, all the volunteers. She had been the community-minded one, and she had done this walk every single year. Now, being here, surrounded by people . . . he could feel her, couldn't he? He could feel her spirit.

"Excuse me, sir," a small boy in an oversize reflective vest said as Mukesh tried to enter the mandir. "The queue for the walk is back there." He pointed back toward the crowd of people he had just tried to escape from.

"I want to go into the mandir."

"Are you not here for the walk?"

Mukesh really wanted to say no. Right on cue, again, Harish appeared, out of nowhere.

"Get in line, my friend," he said to Mukesh. "You will walk with me, no?"

Mukesh nodded and followed Harish, looking back at the boy, pleading. The boy shrugged.

They reached a woman with a clipboard. "This is my friend

Mukeshbhai—bhai is going to be Sahilbhai today." She ticked Sahil's name off the list without a second thought. *Here we go*, Mukesh thought to himself, taking a deep breath.

As everyone got ready, and once the sadhus had performed the ceremonial prayers and rituals, the ribbon was cut and the walk officially began. Harish's best friend, Vivek, was at the front, holding up a red umbrella to lead the way.

Mukesh squeezed his book, for good luck, and Naina's voice came to him. His talisman was working! *Well done, you did this. You're* actually *here!* She was laughing. He felt his body flood with energy, and that optimistic spirit Naina always had too. She'd be happy he was out "meeting" people—he hadn't done this kind of thing for years. Maybe the library had been the first step out of his comfort zone. For a little moment, he held himself taller, prouder. He even felt a little invincible.

That was, until he tried to make conversation with Harish—always a thankless task, even for the invincible. Mukesh desperately hoped if he pelted him with questions, Harish would eventually get bored and walk faster to get away. "Harishbhai, how is your eldest grandchild doing applying for university?"

"Ah, Bhagwan." Harish waved his arms melodramatically. "It has been a nightmare, bhai—but I am still hoping he will get into Bristol or Bath. Very good universities. He did not get into Cambridge. We believe he is just *too* bright, also much too sociable and well rounded. He would not be suited to the purely academic lifestyle there."

"Ah, yes, I can only imagine how stressful. It was not like this when my girls were young."

"No, no it was not. Parents all care too much now. My son is constantly googling chances and predictions based on his son's estimated grades and to see which university is best. When he was going, we let him make the decisions—we just said work hard, do what is best."

"Yes, that is what we told my girls too—they all turned out brilliantly."

"I never even went to parents' meeting. Now, when my son was on a business trip, he video-called his wife so he could be there at the same time and hear what was happening. He bought extra data especially."

"Is that a bit over the top, bhai?"

"No, Mukeshbhai." Harish looked horrified. "Not anymore. This all means so much for our future—for our *country's* future now. Our children and grandchildren have more chances now. We have given them that. Neel is going to be a lawyer, you know. He will be the first lawyer in the family. I have high hopes for my granddaughter too. She likes medicine. I hope she will be pharmacist. Probably not doctor. She is very squeamish."

"A lawyer—very exciting! We must keep in contact. Never know when you need a lawyer." He thought of the only other soon-to-be lawyer he knew, Aleisha, and felt a smidge of pride.

"I imagine your Priya will be one, ne? Always with her head in a book. If she can read lots, she can be a lawyer."

"She is young still."

"But she is thinking now about the future, ne?"

"Priya wants to be a writer or a bookshop worker."

"But for a real job, I mean. Not hobby."

"They *are* real jobs."

"But I mean what about lawyer? Neel can tell her about the course when it is time for her to study."

"She doesn't want to be a lawyer."

"Doctor? Businesswoman? Na?"

Mukesh shook his head.

"Don't worry, my friend. My Neel wanted to be a football player and a fireman at her age. They grow out of these things. I'm sure you do not have to worry."

"I am *not* worrying," Mukesh said firmly.

They both fell silent, not knowing where to go next with the conversation. Harish rolled his eyes. If he was trying to be discreet, he wasn't trying very hard. Harish waited a polite three minutes before breaking off to join another group, talking excitedly and loudly about the cricket.

Mukesh was pleased to be alone, and could feel his energy cascading back to him, ready to keep going, to do Naina proud. Before he could speed off, Naina's closest friend at the mandir, Nilakshiben, trundled over to join him. Naina and Nilakshiben, once upon a time, had been inseparable.

A year ago, Nilakshi had lost both her husband and son in a car accident. Nilakshi's husband, Prabhand, had been a kind but reserved man. He kept himself to himself, but Mukesh always remembered his smile—it would light up a room. His son, Aakash, had inherited that same smile but used it all the time—he was a charmer, so intelligent too. Losing both of them, in one go, it had devastated the whole community. The sadhus had known Prabhand very well and led the temple in prayer for him after his death. Mukesh had attended, because Naina would have wanted him to, and because Mukesh missed Prabhand's smiling face already. Nilakshiben had cried, sitting far back, while men who had never even known her husband or her son sat right at the front, under the gaze of the sadhus. He had felt sad for her, but had never known what to say. When Naina had passed away, Nilakshi and Prabhand had both been a great comfort and support to Mukesh. Mukesh felt ashamed, knowing he had never been as much of a comfort for Nilakshi when she needed it most.

"Mukeshbhai." She walked next to him, smiling—she was keeping a very brisk pace for someone so small.

"Nilakshiben." He smiled back. "It is lovely to see you."

"Yes, what a surprise! I didn't expect *you* to come to this."

"Harishbhai persuaded me to walk in Sahil's place. He has hurt himself somehow."

"Ah. Of course. Harish is very persuasive! And persistent." She gave him a look that said, *You know what I mean*. "I missed a few satsangs recently. Meenaben is upset with me. So, if it's okay, can I walk with you? She wouldn't dare venture up here."

"Sure. But remember Harish is still very close by. Meena tells him everything."

"I expect she does. But *he* is easier to handle."

The sponsored walk took in the sights and sounds of Neasden and Wembley, plodding through residential streets full of houses once painted a maroon red, now a dusty brown, huffing and puffing up and back down the footbridge that crossed the North Circular, allowing them to enjoy the beautiful view of its everlasting traffic jam, with the stadium's halo floating in the distance, and past rows and rows of shops, fruit and vegetable stalls, money-exchange shops, and chicken shops already crowded with people. Mukesh took the walk slowly, but surely. At one point Nilakshi had to clutch his hand and pull him gently along. But the view, of the stadium, of the Wembley skyline—it felt as if he was discovering Wembley anew. Naina had always *loved* to walk. Now, despite the dull ache in his calf muscles, he could see why. He was in pain, he was not fit enough for another three kilometers, but he was so proud he'd even gotten this far.

Nilakshi was encouraging, kind, chatting away as they walked. She made him feel as though he might be in some way capable of finishing. With each step, he felt the book in his bag spurring him on. And he kept listening out for Naina too, telling him he was doing well. But Nilakshi was here walking beside him, and Naina was nowhere to be found. Suddenly, Mukesh's mind flew to *Rebecca*—the story of the new wife coming in to replace the old, living forever in the dead wife's shadow . . . He shook the thought from his mind. These books . . . they were playing havoc with his imagination.

He tried to keep his mind one step ahead. He tried to channel his positivity into moving each limb, one at a time. He tried to hold on to this feeling of being alive. Until reality, and his breathlessness, soon caught up with him. "Nilakshiben," he said, bending down, his hands on his knees, "I think I will have to stop here and get the bus home."

"You will miss out on the certificates. And most importantly, the prasad!"

Mukesh shook his head. "I think prasad is the last thing I need right now—all that sugar might give me a heart attack." He looked to the floor. His legs were on fire. He was breathing as deeply as he could, but the air filtered into his lungs in rasps. He couldn't finish the walk, but he had *walked* . . . farther than he'd been in a long time, and he'd been around people, so many people, for longer than he had in years. This was progress, wasn't it?

"Mukeshbhai," she said, "I will go and talk to Harish and let him know. He will understand."

She wandered off. Mukesh watched as people slower than he was overtook him, smiling and waving. The majority were men, now lagging behind, where once they had been at the front, separated from the women. They were wearing cotton linen trousers, sandals with Velcro straps and good soles. The outlines of their undershirts were visible under their bright temple T-shirts. Mukesh knew this look well—it was a look he liked to sport himself—the accepted uniform of the over-sixties Hindu male.

He watched for Nilakshi's light-blue Punjabi trousers in the sea of white and cream and navy. He couldn't see her. She was too far away now. Unable to take another step, he sat himself down on the wall of someone's house, separating their unkempt front garden from the busy road in front. Mukesh felt every car pass—a brush, a whoosh of air, of wind, hot and sticky and stale: polluted. He hadn't really believed it until now, but he could taste every bit of smoke, every fume, as it entered his lungs.

He thought of Naina again. Is this what had killed her? Dirty air? He'd heard somewhere that bad air had carcinogens. Cancer-causing things.

He remembered her booming laugh when he'd come downstairs with a T-shirt on back to front. Suddenly, the memory was replaced by an image of her in the hospital, a ghost of the woman she had been.

A second later, Nilakshi returned with a bottle of water.

"Harish says go home. He gave me this to pass on." She presented him with the water. "Sounds like an achievement to me—a bit of fresh air, and no need to talk to Harish after this is all over! It's like you planned it. How will you get home?"

Mukesh took the bottle, hastily unscrewed the cap, and drank. He hadn't even said thank you. He closed his eyes, took a deep gulp of putrid air, and stood up. "I will get the bus."

"I'll come with you." He began to shake his head but she stopped him with: "Mukeshbhai, Naina would never forgive me if I let her husband go home on his own when he can barely walk."

And then, in an instant, with the flick of a switch, Mukesh felt stupid—he felt frail. What if the young men could see him now? The ones who drove fast cars and never called him masa or fua. They would call him dada instead.

He clutched the bag again, for strength, for something. "Nilakshiben?" he said as they began to walk (he, hobble) toward the nearest bus stop, which was still too far away.

"Yes, Mukeshbhai," she replied.

"Thank you for helping me."

"As I said, Naina would never forgive me."

"Would you like to come in?" Mukesh asked tentatively, standing on his doorstep, nervous. Nilakshi looked up at the house, her eyes wide.

"No." She gave two small shakes of her head. "I shouldn't, I'd better get back. But I am glad you are okay. You *are* okay now, yes?"

"I'm doing much better, Nilakshiben." Mukesh smiled, pleased his heart rate had returned to normal during the bus ride.

"Well, I hope to see you again soon. Very nice to see you after so long, Mukeshbhai." Nilakshi gave a small wave with her hand. "As I said, I can pop round soon and teach you how to make a proper brinjal bhaji. Just let me know."

"Naina used to make the best brinjal bhaji," Mukesh said absently, the book weighing heavily in his bag.

"Ha, I remember. Well, this might not be quite as good, but better than nothing!" Nilakshi's voice went up a decibel or so, and she nodded her head by way of goodbye.

Mukesh felt all stiff and awkward, and couldn't quite work out whether it was because of the situation, or his muscles seizing up after the walk.

Shutting his front door behind him, from the hallway he spotted the photograph of Naina above the television, with a garland hanging across the top. He looked intently at her face. Had it changed? He thought her eyes were less carefree, now hiding something: disappointment, even anger?

His mind careened to *Rebecca*, imagining a portrait of her hanging in the hall at Manderley, always there, always watching.

He *was* being silly. If Naina were here she'd ask how Nilakshiben was, how she was coping. She'd probably ask him to take her a Tupperware of tepla. Naina had never been a jealous person. But Mukesh felt a stab of guilt anyway. The first thing he did was pull his book out of his bag, showing it to the photograph of Naina, secretly hoping it might bring her voice back to him, just for a moment, to reassure him, before placing it on his newly christened reading chair.

After all his exertions, Mukesh needed an afternoon nap. He turned the radio on—he often liked to listen to something as he fell asleep—and lay down heavily on his bed. He would be achy when he woke up. He had a moment of panic, wondering if he would even be able to get himself out of bed later, but decided that wasn't something to worry about just yet. He'd cross that bridge when he came to it.

As he lay his head on the pillow, his thoughts began to drift. Today he had felt vibrant, alive, despite the muscle pain. He had felt seen, by Nilakshi, even by Harish for a bit, as a person in his own right, rather than just a burden, an elderly father to be checked in on every morning via a voicemail, as a human being with feelings and emotions and likes and dislikes, rather than just as a patient number on his GP's register, or an item on each of his daughters' to-do lists.

Moments later, feeling sated, resting his bones, Mukesh was asleep.

When Mukesh woke up again it was just turning dark, day was becoming night, the shadows stretching, and the light in the room was warm but slowly getting colder, emptier.

He looked automatically to his left, to Naina's side. He hadn't done that for a while now. But today, in the confusion after his unplanned nap, it could be any time. When they'd first moved here, in 1985, with the three girls sleeping in the one room next door on mattresses laid on the floor. When two of the three daughters had moved out in 1998 and Rohini had insisted she sleep in the downstairs room for some privacy—though the downstairs room had nothing but a screen of beads separating it from the kitchen. Or it could have been 2010, when Naina and Mukesh had adopted that same downstairs room for themselves, having just gotten used to being the only two in the house, finally enjoying being alone. Though Naina still loved company. Craved the days their only granddaughter, at the time, would visit, filling the house with life.

But it was 2019. The year Mukesh least hoped it would be. The second year of his life since Naina, the year that began without Naina and would end without Naina too. He opened his copy of *Rebecca*. Even though the book had scared him half to death, he needed to be somewhere else for a while, beyond the confines of his little Wembley home, walking in someone else's skin.

As he turned the pages, Mukesh met Mrs. Danvers, the housekeeper, who so loved the first wife, Rebecca, and so *hated* the second wife, constantly reminding her and Mr. de Winter that she would never fill her beloved Rebecca's shoes. In an instant, Mrs. Danvers took on a new life, a new meaning, for Mukesh. She was his own internal guilt. He stopped reading midsentence, and sat in deathly silence. Books were an escape. But Mukesh was learning that they weren't always an escape in a good way. "I'm not forgetting Naina!" he said out loud, to himself, to the judgmental Mrs. Danvers. "I'm sorry, Naina," he said. "I am such an idiot. This book, it doesn't mean anything."

In response, he thought he heard Naina's words through the still evening air: *I know, Mukesh.* But he couldn't be sure if he was just hearing things, his imagination heightened by the story, telling him what he needed to hear after all.

The Kite Runner

by

KHALED HOSSEINI

CHAPTER 13

ALEISHA

"Aleisha," Benny called as he wiped down the tables. "What you up to this evening?"

"Just going to the shops to get stuff for dinner," she replied, one foot already out the door. "But then literally no plans, Benny—what about you?"

Aleisha thought of the book stuffed in her bag—*The Kite Runner*. She didn't want to admit it to him, but she was excited to have no plans, so she could just curl up with her book. To her, it was the closest thing she'd had to a plan in ages. Now, every morning, she read a chapter or two—every lunchtime she read some more—and she couldn't sleep until she'd turned the pages, revisited the characters who were becoming more real with every passing chapter.

"I'm going on holiday!" Benny did a little dance. Aleisha liked Benny—she never got to see him much, because their shifts rarely crossed over, but he was always so joyful.

"All right for some! Where to?"

"Ayia Napa!"

Benny was forty, and every summer he went on a lad's holiday with his friends. Thermos Flask loved to mention it whenever Benny came up in conversation.

"With my boys!" Benny finished.

Aleisha giggled to herself.

"You going away this summer?"

Aleisha shook her head. "Although you know, Benny," she said, pulling out her book. "Actually . . . I'm going to Kabul tonight." She waved *The Kite Runner* at him.

"Oh, Aleisha! That book . . . it's devastating, you know."

"Well, Benny, my life's devastating. I'm seventeen and my forty-year-old colleague is going to Ayia Napa instead of me."

"Soz, hun. You win some, you lose some," Benny said as he trotted out through the doors with a spring in his step.

The Kite Runner by Khaled Hosseini—she liked the cover: two boys, arms around each other, a bright blue sky, a kite. From the back cover, Aleisha had learned it was about two best friends, Amir and Hassan, who want to win the local kite-flying competition, but something will change both their lives forever. Years later, Amir, who has moved from Afghanistan to America, realizes he must return to Kabul, for forgiveness, and for redemption.

Looking at that cover, it made her wonder—what happens to Hassan? What did Amir do? Benny's words rang in her mind, *It's devastating, you know*, and she braced herself. She was putting a lot of trust into whoever had collated this list—but she'd loved *To Kill a Mockingbird*, and *Rebecca* too: they'd been so different, one so easy to read but with heartbreaking moments, the other dark and brooding, atmospheric. *Rebecca* had been one she read under the covers, terrified for young Mrs. de Winter, the new wife at Manderley.

At first, she'd been blindly following the list, accepting the books without question. And now, she realized, reading them made every day go a bit quicker than the last. She had stopped using the list as a bookmark, and had replaced it in her phone case, to keep it as safe as possible. She didn't want to lose it—she knew the books by heart, even without her iPhone photo of it, but the physical list . . . it felt like some kind of lucky charm.

Aleisha took the book out of her tote bag in the corner shop, imaginatively named Corner Shop, and started to shove her ingredients in. She'd bought more than she needed because she couldn't make up her mind. If the reading list had shown her anything, it was that she was shit at making decisions for herself.

"No!" the woman at the register said. "No, seriously, don't show me that again."

"What?" Aleisha looked up from her packing, confused.

"That!" the woman exclaimed, holding onions in one hand, pointing to *The Kite Runner* with the other.

Aleisha frowned. "What are you talking about?" she said flatly.

"That book *killed* me! It's so hard to read. Honestly, do you want your mascara all down your face? It's *harrowing*."

Aleisha shrugged.

"Honestly, it's even worse than that film they made. The book . . . wow. I'm not going to tell you any more, your life is your life. But seriously, you better be in a super happy place before you pick it up."

Aleisha gulped. How sad *was* this book? The onions rolled down the counter toward her; she grabbed the label with her nails and plonked them into her bag. "If you say so, thanks for the tip!" She stuck a smile back on her face.

The lady continued to scan the rest of her shopping in silence.

"Good to see a young girl reading," the woman muttered, a few moments later, as she threw two plastic bags toward Aleisha.

"Lots of young people read," Aleisha replied, sharply. She thought of the teenagers she always saw in the library, the girl with the pink hair who came in sometimes, the student with the untied shoelaces, even Mia.

"I know, but . . . it's just nice to see it." The woman shrugged. "All these mod cons, mobile phones, video games . . . it's been ages since I've seen someone your age with a *book*."

Aleisha thought of herself—just a few weeks ago—never carrying a book unless it was a textbook. She had been one of those teenagers—always on her phone, barely looking where she was going, her face always down at the screen.

"You're right. But you know, books are cool again now." She smiled at the cashier, and packed up the other two bags, before waving goodbye and heading out. After just a few paces, she dropped the bags down and readjusted, using the time to get her strength back. God, she needed a granny cart! She rolled her eyes at herself. The person this library was turning her into . . . seriously.

She drew in a breath and tried again just as someone jumped in front of her, blocking her way. A man, wearing a beanie, holding a fresh pack of cigarettes in one hand and a receipt in the other.

She looked at him as if to say, "I don't want your cigarettes, and I don't know what you're doing, get out of my way," but she said nothing. She looked at his face.

It was *the guy*. The guy she'd seen on the train.

"Can I help you?"

"Can I help *you*?" he replied.

She looked back blankly. Her shoulders ached.

"Here, you dropped this." He bent down to the concrete at her feet, where *The Kite Runner* was lying faceup.

"Thanks." She went to snatch it from him, but he pulled it just out of reach and turned the cover over in his hands. He turned to the first page, nodding his head.

"Harrow Road Library?" he asked, almost to himself. "Is that place still open? I thought they closed it down years ago."

"It's still open," Aleisha snapped. "I work there." She felt defensive; she didn't know why.

"Wow, you don't look like a librarian to me." He laughed to himself shyly. "Sorry, I don't even know what I mean." He pushed the book toward her; she grabbed it from him as swiftly as she could. "I think your bags are heavy. I can help."

"No, I'm fine," she said; her fingers screamed in pain. She rolled her eyes, trying to hide the nervousness bubbling in her chest. She forced her feet to walk, step by step.

"Honestly, I can help."

"I said I'm *fine*." Aleisha grimaced, the handles tearing through her skin.

"Right, well, looks like you're going in my direction anyway," he teased, half a step behind her. "So, if you're actually a librarian, tell me . . . what's that book about?"

Aleisha stopped, putting the bags on the ground once more to readjust. But before she could pick them up again, the boy-man swooped in and grabbed two of them.

"Oh, great," Aleisha hissed under her breath.

"Look, I just want to hear about the book. I'll just carry these some of the way for you and then leave you alone forever."

Aleisha slung the final bag over her shoulder. "I'm sorry to disappoint you," she said, "but I actually haven't even started reading it. I only know what it says on the back of the book."

"That's all right. What's your name?" he asked.

"Aleisha."

"Nice to meet you, Aleisha," he said. "I'm Zac, by the way."

Aleisha thought to herself, *I didn't ask*, but said out loud, "Nice to meet you," feigning a casual air.

"You too," he said, smiling awkwardly. Was he as nervous as Aleisha? As he struggled with her bags, lagging slightly behind, she couldn't help but hide a smile under her hand.

"So," he said, catching up with her, trying to hide the fact he was out of breath. "You a big reader then?"

She took a moment before replying, thinking of the old man, Mr. Patel, thinking of their chats about the books so far. She felt the list burning in her phone case. "Not really," she said honestly. "It's a new thing for me. But, yeah, I'm liking it."

"*The Kite Runner* . . . you think you're ready for it?"

"I thought you didn't know anything about it."

"I've seen the film. It's literally the saddest thing ever."

"That's what the woman at the counter said."

"Well, we're right. Sad ending too—"

"Seriously! Don't tell me! Why is everyone intent on spoiling it?" she cut in, her eyes wide, surprised at her reaction. She felt relaxed now—this felt *normal* for a moment, walking side by side with a stranger, talking about a book.

He laughed. "Don't worry, I'm not gonna spoil it for you. So . . ." His eyes stayed locked on her. "What do you do when you're not at the library?"

"What is this? *Married at First Sight* or something?"

"Sorry, I'm kind of intense."

"Yeah, you don't say."

"So?"

She shrugged. "Why's it any of your business?"

"I mean, it's not . . . I'm just making conversation." He shrugged, hobbling with the bags at his side. "What on earth is in these?" he wheezed.

When they reached the end of her road, she stopped. "I'll take them from here." She nodded down the road. "I'm just down there."

"It's all right, I can take them all the way; it's fine."

"No," Aleisha said sharply, taken aback by her tone. "I'll take them from here."

He nodded, placed the bags gently on the sidewalk, and stepped back, as though passing over a highly dangerous package.

"Thanks, Zac," she said breezily.

"No problem, Aleisha. Hopefully I'll see you again. Summers always feel a bit lonely for me, so, yeah, this has been nice."

The boy-man headed off as she picked her bags up and started to shuffle them down the road to her house. She took one last look at him, taking in the shape of him—the guy from the train. She couldn't quite believe her luck.

As she approached her house, she could see the windows shut, the darkness within, like Manderley, or Boo Radley's house. But for this moment, it didn't feel so daunting. She dropped the bags at her door as she fumbled for her keys, and saw *The Kite Runner* staring up at her from one of the bags, with the boy-man's final words hanging in her mind. Summers always felt lonely for her too—but this one, this one felt a little less lonely than usual.

CHAPTER 14

MUKESH

Beep. "Papa, it's Rohini. Harishfua has been calling me, and he'd like you to go to the mandir with him. No need to return my call, but just give him a ring, okay? I know you haven't been for ages, and not on your own, but it'll be good for you. Deepali, Vritti, and I have all discussed it and think you should go. Okay? Priya told me to tell you she loved the book, *Wizard of Earthsea*, I think it was called. She sends her love! Bye, Papa. Speak soon."

Beep. "Hi, Dad, it's Deepali. Rohini said Harishfua has been trying to get in touch? Why don't you just go to the mandir? It'll be nice, and a chance for you to eat a proper balanced meal for once. Okay? See you soon."

Mukesh had pulled his book out, settling himself on his seat, when the phone started to trill again. He looked up at it, and down at his book. "If they want me, they will leave a message, ne?" he said to himself.

Beep. "Good morning, Mukeshbhai. It is Nilakshiben." Mukesh nearly jumped out of his seat, his eyes automatically flying up to the photograph of Naina on the wall. "I have bought some ingredients for brinjal bhaji, so I can come round maybe one day next week? Maybe Saturday? Teach you! Hope you have a lovely weekend."

He hadn't expected to hear from Nilakshi. He looked up at his photograph of Naina once more, looking for a sign as to what to do. Was she upset? Angry?

He sighed and tried to settle back into *Rebecca*. He was in his own armchair, with four and a half lamps around him, taken from different rooms in the house, all placed at various heights. The half a lamp was a USB-powered book light he could clip onto the book itself—it was Priya's, a gift from Naina. This corner of his living room currently looked like it was one of those ironic, trying-to-be-cool hipster bars that Vritti was always showing him on Instagrab, which she called "eenspo" for her own small chain of cafés.

It was no use, Nilakshi's call had unsettled him; how was he supposed to read about an intruding new wife right now? He flung down *Rebecca* and called Harish back in a bid to distract himself, agreeing to go to the temple this evening, for Abhishek, puja, and food. It had been so long since he'd done this—he only ever went to the temple with Rohini or Deepali, or sometimes Vritti, just because they made him go. He didn't like being there. Because being there reminded him of Naina, of how he was only half a person without her.

"Looking forward to seeing you this evening, bhai!" Harish bellowed. Either he was deaf or still unsure of how modern telephones worked. Mukesh forgave him anyway. He'd done that too until Vritti and Rohini had complained and said the volume on their handsets didn't go down low enough for a conversation with him.

"Ha, yes, thank you for convincing me. It will be good for me." Mukesh tried to sound like he believed it.

"Fantastic, my friend. I see you later, bhai!" Harish shouted.

Mukesh held the phone away from his ear and said goodbye.

After a few hours of reading, Mukesh looked up and gave a little jump when he saw the four main characters from *Rebecca* sitting opposite him on the sofa. Mrs. de Winter, the new wife and narrator, who was *completely* blurry because she was never really described. Could he trust her? Mr. de Winter, the very wealthy young gentleman who seemed charming at first but had an edge . . . No, he didn't like him. Then there was Mrs. Danvers, that nosy, distrustful, judgmental lady who *hated* Mrs. de Winter just because she didn't compare to Rebecca, dead . . . but far from forgotten. And there was Rebecca herself—a ghost, sitting on Mukesh's sofa, staring at the portrait of Naina above the television.

Mukesh inhaled sharply, rubbing his eyes, but just as Rebecca stood up, looking as though she was reaching out toward him, a car horn tooted and all four characters vanished into thin air. Mukesh took a deep breath, holding himself as still as possible. He hadn't imagined that a book, set so far away, could affect him so much, could feel so *real*—it was chilling.

The car tooted once more. Harish. Mukesh looked at his watch. Right on time.

The car horn tooted again thirty seconds later.

Impatient, as always.

Sometimes Harish thought he was a cool, swish forty-year-old in a cool, swish car, with places to be, people to see, too important to wait a few minutes for his friend to shuffle his slippers off, collect his shoe bag for the temple, and slip his Velcro trainers on his feet. But Mukesh let him wait and moved extra slowly. Or at least, that's the excuse he gave himself. Really his stiff legs wouldn't let him go much faster than this anyway . . . The sponsored walk had proved that to him.

Harish's car was big, and always shining, even in the smoggy, dirty London air.

"Mukeshbhai!" Harish shouted through the car window, leaning over the passenger seat and pushing the door open to welcome Mukesh inside.

Before saying anything, Mukesh slammed the door shut behind him. He sighed. His back ached. His legs felt cramped in this car. "Bhai, lovely to see you."

When they parked up at the mandir, Harish tapped his dashboard lovingly, and got out of the car much more swiftly than Mukesh could manage.

They wandered to the building side by side, but Mukesh fell behind. It looked glorious in the light, with the sun bouncing off the domes, revealing the intricate carvings in its shadows. It was beautiful, and he didn't often appreciate it from this angle. It was surprising, seeing this masterpiece of a building nestled among houses, a school, a few car parks here and there, and the North Circular with all its tooting cars and angry drivers, oblivious to the peace that lay just behind.

It was lovely, unexpected, and it was what he loved so much about London. Variety. Contradictions and contrasts.

Harish was far ahead of him now, and he didn't turn around, didn't even notice Mukesh's absence. So caught up in his own little world.

Mukesh took his time. At moments, he felt as if his legs might give way—being here, without his daughters, without Naina, felt like a different experience altogether. At the entrance, he passed through the body scanner. He always wondered whether the security person could actually see his nude bits. He hoped not. He blushed at the thought. It wouldn't be very Hindu of them to do that, would it?

He was given the all clear, his keys and his belt, and he turned to the left. He imagined Naina by his side, turning to the right, to the ladies' shoe racks. As he glanced over, he spotted Indira. Indira was *always* on her own, he'd never seen many people speak to her. Everyone knew that once Indira started talking, it was almost impossible to stop her. Other than that, he didn't know her very well, but Naina had always insisted they make an effort with her. He waved, but he let his hand fall to his side quite quickly when she just nodded back in response.

After Abhishek, where Mukesh and Harish poured holy water over a brass statue of Swaminarayan to collect their blessings, they quickly left the peace and tranquility of the ritual behind, and headed straight to the noisy sports hall where the food was served. The men's and women's sides were separated by a net partition. Harish raced to get his food and grab them a table, while Mukesh took his time, said hello to everyone serving ("Mukesh, it's so lovely to see you here to eat after so long!"), but he joined Harish soon after, his plastic plate teeming with delicious food and bright colors—khichdi kadhi, jalebi, puri, buttata nu shaak, papdi. They ate in silence; Mukesh noticed himself trying to peer around the curtain to catch a glimpse of Nilakshi, whom he'd seen a few moments earlier—he used to peer around the curtain to get a glimpse of Naina and his girls. That's when the grumpy, stern, judgmental housekeeper Mrs. Danvers came into his mind once again. She appeared opposite him, next to Harish, wearing, strangely, a sari and chanlo, her hair pulled back into a tight bun. She was frowning, shaking her head, eating her food with her hands just like he was.

Mukesh blinked several times, trying to banish the image of this strange lady who didn't exist, but nothing was working.

"Bhai," Mukesh said to Harish, desperately trying to keep a grip on reality, his eyes running from Harish to a scowling Mrs. Danvers. "How is Meenaben?"

"Oh, she is very good. Very good. Of course, tonight is her night off from me, so I am sure she is happier than ever. Happy to be apart from me!" Harish chuckled to himself, with a mouth full of food. The imaginary Mrs. Danvers looked over at her neighbor and pulled a face of disgust. Mukesh thought this might be the only thing he had in common with the horrible housekeeper of Manderley.

He pictured Naina on the other side of the curtain, serving food to Mrs. Danvers herself. "I have not forgotten her," Mukesh said to himself, but he didn't know if it was for his own benefit or Mrs. Danvers's, to tell her that he was not ever going to forget Naina; no one, not even Nilakshi, could replace his wife. Suddenly, Mrs. Danvers picked up her plate and wandered away to the other side of the hall.

Harish was still talking. Mukesh didn't have a clue what he'd just said, but his response of "My God, ne?" was apparently just what Harish had been hoping for.

"Meena wondered if you want to come for dinner. It has been ages, bhai." Harish seemed to have noticed that Mukesh was elsewhere. He clapped a hand on his shoulder. Mukesh responded with a shake-nod of the head.

"Of course. Whenever!"

"Saturday? My eldest is home too so that will be nice. He will like to see you."

Saturday was no good. It was the day Nilakshi was going to come over. "I am busy."

"Seeing Rohini?"

Mukesh shook his head.

"Priya or Deepali's twins? I haven't seen those little ones in ages. Not since—"

Mukesh shook his head.

"Vritti? Has she found a husband yet?"

Mukesh shook his head. He didn't want to lie, but he was very grateful for the double questions. Perhaps Harish wouldn't know which one he was answering.

"Ah, I am so surprised. She is such a *lovely*, pretty woman. She reminds me so much of your Naina. What are you doing, then? Have you joined a chess club? Cricket club?" Harish chortled, slapping his stomach. "Imagine! Mukesh, doing cricket!"

"I am having dinner with Nilakshiben." Mukesh said it quickly, matter-of-factly, making sure to enunciate the "ben" clearly, to prove there was nothing more than a brotherly-sisterly friendship between them, uttering it loudly so even Harish's patchy hearing could pick it up.

"Who is Ben?"

Mukesh blushed. "No, bhai. Nee-lak-shee-*ben*."

Harish frowned for a moment, and then his eyes widened. "Oh, Bhagwan! You are *dating*? But Naina?"

Mukesh went fuchsia-pink. "No, bhai, bhai. You totally misunderstand."

At that moment, that gruesome Mrs. Danvers skulked back from the other side of the hall, her eyes boring into Mukesh.

"But she is Naina's friend! You are a widower!"

"No, Harish!" Mukesh held his hands up in defense, a warning, to him, to Harish. A pleading—please, please listen. "We are just friends, catching up. Nothing like that at all."

And he meant it. It *was* nothing like that. But *this* is why he felt so weird about it. They hadn't even spent more than a few hours together and people were already putting them down as widow-adulterers. Adulterants? Adulterists? Mukesh shook his head, it didn't matter either way, because that was *not* what they were.

Mukesh picked his plate up and scraped the leftovers into the bin. He could feel Mrs. Danvers following him every step of the way as he stormed out of the hall, and then out of the mandir into the open air of Neasden. He pulled the book out of his tote bag. *Rebecca*. For a moment, he thought the name *Naina* was emblazoned on the front instead. Why was this book doing this to him? What did it want from him?

JOSEPH

2017

Joseph had been coming to the library since he was little. When his mum had to work during school holidays, she'd drop him off here, encouraging him to finish his homework or read ahead for the following year. Now he came to the library after school on Mondays, Wednesdays, and Fridays, even though he was old enough to be at home by himself. He had his favorite table, which was mostly unoccupied because it wasn't quite as tucked away as the others. It was close to the librarian's desk. Joseph enjoyed the gentle murmuring from the few people who would come and take books out. It helped him concentrate. He liked the library. It was peaceful. And no one from school *ever* came here.

One day, he was sitting in this exact spot when someone actually sat down opposite. He didn't look up—he'd made that mistake before when a youngish man had started asking him questions about his schoolwork, and Joseph hadn't known how to make it clear that he wanted to get on with his work in peace. As usual, he kept his head down, his eyes on his page.

He noticed from the person's hands, as they placed a book on the table, that they were older. The skin was a little bit looser, a little like his mum's hands. He glanced up to see what the book was, trying to get a glimpse of the cover, but he was too late, the hands had whipped the book open. He turned back to his homework.

Bullying and Peer Pressure. He hated PSHE homework, but it had to be done. He hated the lessons too, mainly because he had to sit next to Moe Johnson, who *despised* Joseph. "What are you meant to do when someone is bullying you, eh, Joey boy?" he'd sneer. "Tell someone?" He taunted Joseph for going to the library after school. Once, he'd followed him all the way there, calling him a wuss, a sissy, a loser, a nerd, a geek, a suck-up. As soon as Joseph was inside the doors, though, he was safe. Moe would never be caught dead in here.

Bullying and Peer Pressure. Where was he meant to start? The first question was "What is the definition of bullying?" and he felt as if Moe Johnson had put the question there specially to mock him. If Moe didn't lay a hand on Joseph, it wasn't *actual* bullying, was it?

Then there was the second question: "How do you know if someone is being bullied?" People covered up so many things.

Joseph put his head on the table. When he looked up, he noticed his paper was a mash of wet, soggy circles.

The stranger opposite him, with the slightly wrinkly, not-very-wrinkly hands, took a piece of paper out and began rummaging through their own book, running their fingers over the words. They stopped, tucked the piece of paper inside, and pushed the book across the table toward him. Joseph raised his gaze just slightly, so he was looking at the book, but he didn't make eye contact with the mysterious stranger. He didn't want to talk right now, not when he had silent tears streaming down his face.

Life of Pi. The cover was a sea of blue and one giant tiger, colorful and bright. He could see the dog-eared note peeking out between the pages.

Joseph didn't pick up the book. He left it on the table, as though he hadn't even noticed it, and moments later the stranger opposite put on their jacket, packed their stuff away, and off they went. Joseph never saw their face.

Joseph had never been a super-bookish person; he hadn't really read *reading* books since he was small, he had too much schoolwork these days. But as Joseph pulled the book toward him, turning it over in his hands, he ran his eyes down the words on the back cover. It was about a boy—sixteen years old—stranded on a boat with a tiger, a hyena, an orangutan, and a zebra. *How strange.* He turned the cover back over—he saw the boy, curled up at one end of the boat, hugging his knees tightly. Joseph had never been on a boat with a tiger before. But Joseph knew that feeling, the feeling of wanting, *needing,* to be as small as possible, invisible. He laid the book on the table. Somehow, he knew this book had been left here deliberately: for him.

In a heartbeat, he shoved his PSHE homework into his bag, and slung it over his shoulder. He marched the book over to the self-service machines. He desperately wanted to be at home now, so he could curl up with the book and find out what the stranger intended for him to discover.

At home, Joseph opened then slammed his front door, and ran upstairs to his bedroom. He tucked himself under the covers, the duvet resting on his head as he sat cross-legged on his bed, and opened the book to where the scrappy bit of paper had been left.

He pulled it out—being as gentle as he could with the paper—and scanned it. It was a list. One, two, three, four, five, six, seven, eight books. With one of them circled.

Life of Pi.

His book.

CHAPTER 15

ALEISHA

She turned the final page and took a deep inhale. She hadn't noticed the hours passing as she sat in the deserted library, her head between the pages. It was the first time she'd read freely, without doubting herself, without wondering if she was taking the story in properly, without thinking about the outside world at all.

Putting *The Kite Runner* back on her desk, Aleisha covered her face in her hands. She could feel her pulse racing; she could feel her heart beating as though it was going to blast out of her chest, and her head hurt—she was so glad the library was empty. If anyone spoke to her in real life, she might just burst into tears.

She picked up her phone, wanting desperately to message someone instead, to talk without actually talking, to tell someone about what she'd read. She wondered if Rachel would know the book, but she hadn't messaged her for a few weeks and texting out of the blue about a book would be weird. Then she thought of the woman in the shop, and then that guy, Zac . . . Had he said he'd read it? She was surprised to find her mind wander to him again.

She pictured Amir and Hassan, two best friends, as close as brothers, running around Kabul flying their kites—Hassan, who was so kind, and so loyal to his friend, who would do anything to protect him, and to make him happy; and Amir, who enjoyed Hassan's friendship and his loyalty, yet still treated him unkindly in the small ways that children do, without thinking. Amir spent the rest of his life regretting what he did to his best friend, finally understanding everything Hassan had sacrificed for him when they were both just children. But Amir spent the rest of his life trying to be good again. And, if Amir's story showed Aleisha one thing, it was that—no matter how terribly you have behaved in the past—you should do everything you can to be good. Amir and Hassan's friendship had literally broken Aleisha's heart; she hadn't known she could feel this bereft from a story, some words on a page.

To Kill a Mockingbird and *Rebecca* had been good, but at points she'd felt as though she was reading them maybe more like schoolbooks. She was reading them looking for a message, searching for what she could talk to Mr. Patel about.

But *The Kite Runner*—she'd lived and breathed this book for days. When she was at home with Aidan, and he'd been asking her how her day was, her day was *nothing* outside of the world of the book.

"I'm reading *The Kite Runner*," she'd told him. "It's literally all I can think about."

"I've seen the film," Aidan said. "It's so fucking sad, how are you coping?"

"No one warned me!" Aleisha said, waving the book at him, knowing it was a lie. Everyone had warned her—but even then, she hadn't been prepared for this. "Why did no one tell me this was literally going to shatter my heart into a million billion pieces? Hassan, he is so, so kind. And Amir just walks all over him."

"Well, they're both just kids, aren't they?"

"Yeah, but still—stuff you do when you're kids can really affect everything, can't it? Like Amir, he spends the rest of his life with regret."

"There's a lot in that book. Making amends and *meaning it* before it's too late." Aidan paused for a moment, and Aleisha's eyes shot to the photograph of Aidan, Aleisha, Leilah, and Dean. "Not taking people for granted," Aidan finished, keeping his eyes firmly fixed on his phone.

A lump formed in her throat. Amir wasn't able to fix things with Hassan, but he was able to make amends *some*how. She thought of Dean, she thought of everything he'd done in his past, and how now, he did all he could to *appear* the concerned parent—texting, calling, leaving voice notes, dropping random sums of money into their bank account. But unlike Amir, Aleisha wasn't sure Dean *really* regretted anything.

Back in the library, Aleisha wiped a tear from her cheek. *Crap*, she said to herself, as she spotted Mr. P wandering in. He was smiling so widely. She wasn't sure she'd be able to be chirpy right now. Hassan, so young and kind, and his friend Amir were running around in her mind—but there was Dean too, encroaching, bringing her back to her own life.

"Hello!" he said, wandering up to her desk. "I've finished this one too!" He held *Rebecca* aloft.

Aleisha tried to force a smile onto her face, but she felt her bottom lip drop and knew there was nothing she could do about it. "Hi, Mr. P!"

"Aleisha," he said softly. "Are you okay, beta?"

Aleisha felt the lump rise up in her throat again. *Don't cry, don't cry, don't cry*, she thought to herself.

"Yeah, absolutely. Just finished reading a book, a sad one. I'm all right." She cleared her throat, tried to deepen her voice.

Mr. P leaned awkwardly over the desk and tapped her gently on the shoulder. "There, there, it's okay, beta," he said, his voice soft and soothing. "My daughter Deepali looks *just* like that when she's trying to pretend she's okay but she isn't! She was always like that as a teenager. 'I'm okay. Leave me alone, Dad. I'm fine!'" Mr. P chuckled. "It is okay to say you are sad when you are. These books can be very sad, can't they? I once read a book that made me cry lots and lots."

"What was it?" Aleisha was doing all she could to keep her voice even.

"*The Time Traveler's Wife*," he said, his voice catching. "We found it under my wife's bed after she passed away. Reading it made me feel closer to her; it made me realize my loss as well." His eyes drifted away for a moment, and his melancholy only added to the pain in her throbbing forehead. "I . . . I wanted to talk to you about *Rebecca* but maybe we save it for another day? I would like to pick up another book though. What is this book that has upset you?"

Aleisha held it up.

"*The. Kite. Runner*," Mr. P read slowly, squinting.

Aleisha nodded her head frantically. "I mean, yeah, I would so love you to read it. I need to talk to someone about it!"

His eyes lit up. "You want to talk to *me* about it?" he asked quietly. "Let me take that one out in that case. I would love to. And thank you for *Rebecca*. It has made me think a lot about things, although I don't know if I liked it."

"You didn't like it? Too spooky? I found it pretty creepy. That big old house, that ghost. Terrifying!"

"No . . . it—it was more that it was a little unkind. I don't believe in remarrying, not really. So *modern*."

She laughed aloud. "Mr. P, I don't think the book was about *remarrying*, you know? And I think this book was written *years* ago."

"It seemed to be all about remarrying to me." He looked down at his shoes.

"Hmm," Aleisha said, checking *The Kite Runner* out with Mr. P's library card. "I guess books say different things to different people."

"You know, Miss Aleisha." Mr. P stood up tall. "I would *never*, *ever* remarry."

Aleisha tried to hide a smile. "But what if you found the right lady, Mr. P?" She quite enjoyed teasing him, until his eyes visibly widened and his jaw dropped a little; he wasn't taking this well.

"What on earth do you mean, young lady!" Mr. P's voice jumped two octaves higher. "There is only *ever* one true love for a person."

"Right, if you say so," Aleisha said, plonking *The Kite Runner* on the desk in front of her. Her mind flew back to Hassan and Amir. It felt weird, handing it over . . . She felt possessive, protective, over it. But when she looked up at Mr. P's face, now slightly less outraged, she could see the eagerness in his eyes. "Look," she said to him. "I've got to be straight with you—this is really, really hard to read, like, not difficult, but it's deep. So, so deep, okay?"

"Okay," he said. "I've had deep in my life, I think I can do it." He smiled broadly. She could tell he was waiting for her to ask a question, so he could impart some Atticus wisdom.

"Like what, Mr. P?" she said, indulging him.

"Well." His eyes looked up to the ceiling. "I wasn't born here, you know? I left my home, Kenya, behind to come here, to raise my children, to bring them opportunities. It was hard, settling in, always being different."

"Well," she said, "this book's about moving away from your home. The main character, Amir, he leaves Afghanistan, where he grows up, for America."

"Really?" Mr. P brushed his hand over the cover.

"I know you'll love it! But trust me, this literally makes *Rebecca* seem like child's play. Like that's an awesome book, really atmospheric, but this is like an emotional roller coaster that just keeps going and going and going . . ."

"Okay, Miss Aleisha," he said. "I understand you very well. I will read and report back!"

With almost a skip in his step, he headed toward a seat in the library, and just before he sat down she said, "Don't cry, okay?"

"Yes, boss!" he called back.

He sat down in his favorite chair next to a little alcove of bookshelves with a tall reading lamp.

"From here I can see you, Aleisha, or the other librarians, Lucy, Benny, and the other young man," he'd told her once. "Or that student dumping their books in front of them and pulling out a scraggly notebook, or the young mums and dads reading to their children. I like this spot; it is becoming like a new routine when I read here. These strangers, they are my silent companions."

Aleisha had been pleased that Mr. P was opening up, little by little, not just to her, but also to the other people who worked here. A few days ago, Lucy had said, "That old man you're becoming mates with, he's rather sweet, isn't he?"

She thought of the first time she was rude to Mr. P, and how

Aidan, and Kyle, had convinced her to right her wrong—just like Amir had done in *The Kite Runner*. It was true—it wasn't too late to be a good person. Never. Aleisha now felt a strange sense of pride for the old man—she knew that Mr. P was lonely, but he was starting to do things to help himself. He was doing *so* well.

CHAPTER 16

MUKESH

Mukesh hadn't told his daughters that he was planning on seeing Nilakshi today. She was Nilakshimasi to them, she was like family, always had been. He suspected—hoped—that Vritti would think it was nice that he'd finally found someone who could be a good friend, a companion. But Rohini and Deepali would get the wrong idea, *modern* ideas. They would read into it, mutter things like "Papa is getting serious with this woman, why would he do that to Mummy?" to each other behind his back. He couldn't face being talked about.

When the doorbell rang, Mukesh's heart almost leaped out of his chest. He stared up at Naina, hoping for some kind of message. Silence.

"Nilakshiben!" Mukesh held his arms open wide in greeting at the door, sounding more confident and comfortable than he felt.

Nilakshi held up a blue plastic bag of vegetables. "Ready to learn how to cook brinjal bhaji?"

Mukesh nodded hurriedly and stepped aside to let her in.

"Sit down, Nilakshiben," he said politely, nodding his head formally, suddenly realizing he was standing uncomfortably straight. They both stood side by side in his hallway, beside the doorway to the living room. Naina, in her photo frame above the television, was staring down at them.

"Thank you, bhai," Nilakshi said. He noticed she gave Naina's chair a wide berth, leaving a space for her memory to be. "I can sit here?" She pointed to the sofa, the bag still in her hand.

"Ha," he replied, leaning forward to take the bag from her. "Anywhere you like." On the sofa, Nilakshi clasped her hands together, shrugging her shoulders as though she wanted to take up as little room as possible.

"Please," he said, "make yourself at home."

Nilakshi didn't move, she just smiled and nodded.

A few minutes later, Nilakshi joined him in the kitchen as he was straining the chai. He'd made it from scratch this time—he knew that's what Naina would have wanted for a guest.

"I thought I better join you," Nilakshi said. Her face looked as though she had seen a ghost. "Shall I start chopping for the brinjal bhaji?" He could tell she didn't know what to do with herself, drifting around her late best friend's house.

"Ha," he said. "But tell me what you are doing step by step or I will never keep up!"

"Of course!" She pulled out the eggplant, and began cubing it, as Mukesh added Canderel sweetener to the tea. They skipped around each other, searching for utensils, and awkwardly knocking into each other at annoying moments. "I am *so* sorry" was always followed by "No, no, I am *so* sorry, bhai! Clumsy, clumsy me!"

"Look at us," Mukesh said. "We are being very silly. I shall just stay over that side and you let me know if you need to get anything."

"Ha. Thank you. Oil please?"

Mukesh passed the oil, and Nilakshi made sure to take it by the lid, keeping her fingers as far away from Mukesh's as possible.

He felt he was holding his breath for the whole of the brinjal bhaji tutorial and he hadn't taken a word in.

"Please could you maybe write me some notes for this recipe too?" he asked as he tried the first fried spicy piece of eggplant.

"Of course," Nilakshi said, about a foot away from the plate, observing Mukesh tucking in.

"Do you want some?"

"No, thank you, bhai. I hate eggplant."

"What?" Mukesh laughed, his eyes creasing. "How come you wanted to make this?"

"Well, Naina always used to tell me it was your favorite, and we are always hearing from Harish how you are never making it; even your daughters tell us at the temple. They say your diet is not great! I thought you might want to learn."

Mukesh gulped. His cheeks flushed red. Of *course* his daughters, probably Rohini, had loved to spread the news that Mukesh Patel was stuck in his ways.

Nilakshi's face blanched slightly, and he could see her mind whirring, looking for something else to say. "It is nice, people care about you! How are your grandchildren? And little Priya?"

"They're doing okay, having their summer holidays now. Priya and I went to the library the other day."

"The library?" Nilakshi asked. "Is it the one Naina went to?"

"Yes! I've been reading—for Priya, and for me. There's a librarian there. She helps me, picks out books for me."

"That's wonderful, Mukeshbhai! What you are reading? What is it like?"

"I'm reading a lovely book called *The Kite Runner*. It's about Amir and Hassan," he began, and told her everything that had happened so far. Amir was now living in America, his best friend all but forgotten—now just a moment of severe guilt and regret in Amir's mind.

"That sounds so terribly sad," Nilakshi said. They were sitting in the living room now, and he noticed how she was leaning back, her hands by her sides. She was taking up more room. She was settling in.

"It is. The lady at the library who recommended it for me, I saw she was so sad at the end when she finished it. Hassan, he is such a lovely boy and he is treated so horribly."

"Ha." Nilakshi nodded, knowingly. "It's so often the way, isn't it? My son . . ." Mukesh saw Nilakshi's head bow slightly. He hadn't heard her talk about Aakash. "When he was younger, he was so gentle, so calm, always with his head in books, always loyal to his friends, and they would pick on him. Bully him. When he came home to me, I would ask him about his day. I just wanted to make him feel better."

Mukesh's brow furrowed. Nilakshi's eyes glistened. He didn't know what to say—his mind ran through all the books. Was there anything he could take from them? Any wisdom from Atticus to help in this moment? But then he realized, someone to talk to, to listen to her, was probably all she needed. Mukesh could offer her that.

"I just wanted to make him happy." Nilakshi's voice caught in her throat. "But there's only so much a mother can do. That's what I realized."

"He had a wonderful family," Mukesh said quietly. "Children can be so mean sometimes, but your son, he was mature, he was bright—he would have known it was never about him. It wasn't a reflection on him."

Nilakshi cleared her throat and dabbed her eye with the back of her hand. She smiled. "He loved brinjal bhaji too. He loved *Naina's* brinjal bhaji most of all."

When Mukesh's house was bathed in silence once again, the smell of brinjal and oil and mustard seeds filling the air, he relaxed into his armchair, his belly full, his mind content. He hadn't had company, *real* company, just for him, in months, maybe even years. But as he allowed himself to settle, another niggling part of him forced him to look up at the portrait of Naina, and in a flash, he was in Manderley, with Rebecca following him everywhere he went.

Life of Pi

by

YANN MARTEL

CHAPTER 17

ALEISHA

She waited four minutes for a bus, and a bus never came, so she legged it down the road, stopping at every bus stop on the way to check the waiting time. Still, too long. She kept running. Aidan had called to say he urgently needed to head to work, and it had taken Aleisha so long to pack all her things up at the library and get Kyle to come and cover the rest of her shift, she was going to be an hour late if she didn't move quickly.

Her shins were tight. Her chest was hurting; she hadn't done this kind of cardio for years. Every pore was stinging as sweat tried to seep out from behind her makeup.

As she rounded the corner onto her street, her heart began to buzz with apprehension. The closed windows of home; they were as ominous to her as the gates of Manderley. She spotted Aidan leaning on his convertible BMW, music still blaring, talking to someone whom she recognized immediately. Mia: it was the undercut again. Aleisha stopped, wished she hadn't run all the way home, now looking like a mess. She pictured mascara trailing down her face.

Aidan waved frantically, his teeth gritted together, but his eyes were pretending to be carefree. "Leish," he shouted, a smile plastered on his face. Aleisha's heart started beating double time as she soaked up Aidan's nervous energy—he kept tapping his feet constantly, as though he was trying to hold his energy at bay. "It's Mia! She asked if you want to hang out."

"Yeah, nice idea, would love to," she garbled, trying to catch her breath. "Although I've got to help Mum with some stuff."

She shot a look at Aidan. His eyes were red-rimmed, as if he hadn't slept in weeks. They were darting everywhere—at his watch;

at his steering wheel; at his sister, her friend; and back up at the house too.

"Okay, cool, yeah, cool," Mia said casually, completely oblivious to the fact that both Aidan and Aleisha had other places to be. She was tilting her hips slightly, probably for Aidan's benefit. "Just, I haven't heard from you since the library day a couple weeks ago and wondered if you wanted to catch up, Leish. You didn't message again in the group."

That WhatsApp group.

"Yeah, I'm so sorry." She wasn't. "Really sorry, Mia. I can't right now but thanks *so* much for coming by."

Mia turned on her heel, heading off.

"We're doing a barbecue in the park. Seven. Come along. Rahul will be there too," Mia called back to her.

"Thanks!" Aleisha waved at her retreating friend, before turning her eyes on her brother.

"You've been avoiding her," Aidan said when Mia was almost out of sight, jumping back into the car.

"Yeah, we don't really talk anyway. You know that day when she saw me in the library? Must've reminded her I exist."

"You used to be tight though. It's sad."

"Do you like her or something?" Aleisha let her gaze linger on Aidan, who didn't return it.

Aidan laughed, his voice heavier than usual. "Look, I don't have time for this. I've got to be at work. Go be with Mum." He turned away from her, put his key in the ignition, and sped off without a second look.

The house was quiet; Aleisha wanted to call out to her mum, find out where she was, but she didn't dare make any loud sounds. She peered around the doorway into the living room. There she was, her legs crossed, on the sofa. Aleisha tiptoed in, moving slowly. She sat down on the opposite side of the room, and pulled her next book, *Life of Pi*, from her bag.

"Mum?" Aleisha whispered. "Want to hear a story?"

Leilah didn't look up.

Right now, all Aleisha wanted was to replicate that day she'd read *To Kill a Mockingbird* out loud to Leilah. Her mother had been fast asleep, but still, that was the most peaceful the house had been in weeks. One wrong move might ruin it all, but she was desperate to avoid an evening of stony silence.

Eventually Leilah nodded; Aleisha allowed herself a deep exhale. Feeling thoroughly exposed, she cleared her throat and began. Leilah didn't take her eyes off her daughter.

"Wait," Leilah said, after Aleisha had been reading for ten minutes. "I've missed something. What's this about?"

Aleisha stopped. She hadn't expected her mum to *follow* the story. She'd just been expecting her to listen, letting the words wash over her. "Erm . . . well, it's about this boy, Pi Patel . . ." Whenever Aleisha thought of Pi, she imagined a young Mr. P, with a thicker head of hair, but the same beaming, smiling face. "He's just escaped a shipwreck that was transporting his whole family and their zoo animals to Canada. Now he's stuck on a boat with a tiger and some other animals . . . in the middle of the Pacific Ocean."

"What the . . . That's not likely, is it?"

"Er, probably not. But I think that's kind of the whole point of the book—like truth, and what's true and what's imagined."

"Ah, that's clever," Leilah said. Aleisha smiled, suddenly shy, a tiny bit of pride creeping through her veins. "Okay. Who's the Richard Parker he keeps going on about?"

"Mum, that's the tiger."

"Called Richard Parker?" Leilah's eyes were wide, disbelieving.

"Yeah! A clerical error that stuck—it was actually the name of the person who *captured* the tiger, but the paperwork swapped their names round."

"Okay, I'm caught up—go on."

Aleisha continued, picking up with Pi leaning over the boat trying to catch some food, in a desperate attempt to feed Richard and keep himself alive. Pi was almost entirely alone in the middle of the ocean, with nothing but animals, a volatile tiger, for company. Aleisha tried to squash down the rise of a familiar feeling—the survival mode that kicked in every time she heard Leilah shout out at night. It was with a stab of guilt that she realized, yes, she knew a thing or two about volatility. Like Pi, Aleisha was constantly watching for a shift, a change, that could come at any moment. But on the other hand, the tiger, despite everything, was the one thing saving Pi from his own loneliness. When she looked up from the page, she saw that Leilah was in Pi's world too, her eyes were focused on the ceiling, painting the images before her eyes. Aleisha wondered how Leilah's artistic eye was visualizing this story. She pictured some of Leilah's recent designs, the ones she did for herself, rather than for ad agencies, printed as postcards and stuck to the wall in her bedroom. Were the colors vibrant? The sea, a deep blue, the orange of the tiger bold, burning. And, Aleisha allowed herself to wonder, to Leilah, was she Pi, or the tiger? Or no one at all?

She put the book down for a moment. "Do you want a drink?"

Leilah nodded. "Water, please. Cold as you can."

The water from the tap streamed into the glass; Aleisha stared straight ahead. She could see an outline of herself reflected in the tiles: her hair, pulled back into a bun on the top of her head. She looked like her mother, in the pictures from back when Leilah had still been married to Dean. Her smile then was ever-present, it seemed. But people *always* smiled for photos. From those pictures, she couldn't ever really tell what was going on in her mum's mind. She wondered if Dean ever knew either.

She smacked some ice cubes out of the tray onto the countertop, before plonking, plinking them into each glass. "So loud, Aleisha!" Leilah called from the other room.

"Sorry, Mum," Aleisha called back, wincing. The spell cast from the book was starting to wear off.

Condensation was already forming on the outside of the glasses when she handed one to her mum. "Okay, Mum," Aleisha said softly, "I'm going to finish reading in my room. Will you be okay?"

"No," Leilah said. "Sit next to me and read again." Her voice was hopeful, like a plea.

"Okay." Aleisha collected her book, trying to keep the surprise from her face.

They sat close to each other, but not too close. Her fingers trembled almost imperceptibly as she started to turn the pages once more.

For a moment, Aleisha was a child again, curled up under the covers, resting against her mother, who was holding a huge schoolbook open in front of them. The letters were large, and Aleisha formed the words timidly—one by one. Leilah would stroke her hair, kiss her forehead, every time she said something right, and if she got it wrong, she'd just whisper gently, "Do you want to try that again?" Aidan would poke his head around the door and beam at his sister, a goofy gap between his front teeth. He stuck his thumb up and mouthed, exaggeratedly, "Good girl!"

She remembered snuggling up with Leilah, the two of them falling asleep, and then young Aidan's whispers rousing her: "Aleisha did loads of good reading," he said to Dean, a lisp muffling his words. "My little sister is so clever." Dean mumbled something and Aidan replied, "I love her millions." Aleisha had felt proud of herself then. She wished Aidan could see her now; she wanted to share this moment with him, to show him that she was finally getting through to Leilah. She knew Aidan had always been able to do that, but it was her chance to say to him, "I can help you out more now, because I know what to do. I know how I can help."

By the time Aleisha had read another chapter—Pi had just "marked" his territory in the lifeboat after five days at sea—Leilah and Aleisha were both laughing. When she finally started to read again, through cry-laughing eyes, her mother had pulled her hand out from under her legs and placed it gently on Aleisha's knee. Aleisha froze. Her every nerve stilled, a shot of ice piercing straight through her skin, her bone, and into the sofa. Aleisha placed her own hand gently on Leilah's, and turned the page with the other.

She kept reading; she heard the words of the story, but she didn't take them in. The voice no longer felt like her own; she was alone, trapped inside her own body with no control. The only part of her body she belonged to was her hand, the hand connected to Leilah's hand, connected to Aleisha's knee, which didn't feel like Aleisha's knee at all.

Leilah's voice then. "The characters feel *so alive*. The animal, that tiger, it feels so . . . human."

"They do, don't they?"

"Who gave you this book?" Leilah asked, stroking the cover.

"The library."

"Who recommended it? I've never heard of it before."

"I found it on this." She pulled out the list from her phone, unfolded it, passed it to Leilah. Suddenly, to Leilah, it was the most precious thing in the world.

"Oh, Aleisha! I remember *Rebecca*. I loved that book." Leilah ran her fingers over the words, lingering for a moment in the folds. "I read it in one day, when I was pregnant with you, actually. I couldn't sleep. You never let me sleep. So I read this—it was perfect. Wow," was all she said for a moment. "Someone *curated* this list. It's lovely. So simple. Who wrote it?"

Aleisha shook her head. "It was just left in one of the books. I also found this—not in the same book though." She held up the chicken-shop stamp card, her first thoughts on *To Kill a Mockingbird* scrawled in tiny handwriting on the back after Kyle had told her to "say something interesting" to Mr. P.

"You're going to keep reading them? The books?"

Was she going to carry on? She'd felt so unsure at first—it had just been a tick-box exercise, so she'd have enough to say to pretend to Mr. P that she knew all about books, that she was a good librarian. But *Rebecca* . . . it had scared her half to death. She could picture Manderley so clearly in her mind; the house itself, Rebecca's room, left almost untouched. And then *The Kite Runner*. She'd never forget that book. And she thought of Atticus, his kick-ass lawyer skills, how much she *admired* him, even though he was literally made up. And, right now, she felt Leilah's hand still resting on her knee as Pi and Richard Parker drifted across the ocean.

"Yes," Aleisha said with conviction. "All of them. This is the fourth."

"Were the others good?"

"Yeah." She wanted to say more, but she stopped herself. She thought of *The Kite Runner*—it was so sad, there was so much grief there, she was scared of how that might make Leilah feel.

Leilah brought the piece of paper close to her face, squinting. "Could be a student, like a uni reading list or something?"

"Maybe."

"*A Suitable Boy*. Dean read that when we were on holiday once. He ended up using it as a doorstop. It's fat. I don't think he got very far."

She hadn't heard her mother mention Dean in months; she hadn't used his name in years. Usually it was "your dad" or sometimes just "him." But she laughed anyway. Of course her dad would use a fat book as a doorstop.

"When was that?"

"You must have been just five or six, we left you with his parents. We went on a cycling holiday, just the two of us. The first holiday just us in ages. It was nice, not having to look after you guys." Leilah paused. Aleisha frowned at her. "As much as we *loved* you, we could just be *us* for a little while again. He kept forgetting things in his saddlebags when we were at the villa, and every time he went to get one thing, he'd lock himself out. Finally, he caught on"—Leilah smiled—"and stuck that bloody book there to keep the door open. But he'd only ever remember to bring one thing in at a time, so the door was almost permanently wedged open. He's so forgetful."

After a moment, Leilah said, "Keep reading?"

Aleisha continued, until the sunlight vanished from the room, and Leilah mentioned dinner, vaguely, noncommittally, before deciding instead that it was too late, it was time to go to bed. Aleisha should have fed Leilah. Aidan would be upset that she hadn't. But for the first time since Leilah's dark days, weeks, and months had begun, she had let her daughter in, even if just for a moment. All thanks to a boy, a tiger, an orangutan, a zebra, and a hyena stuck on a boat.

Leilah kissed Aleisha gently on her face and wandered upstairs without looking back. The book was still open in Aleisha's hands, but she couldn't read the words any longer. The plastic cover was hot and soft under her fingertips. She wanted to remember this moment, the warmth of it, and how a terrifyingly unpredictable tiger and a boy could create this magic beyond the pages. She didn't want to think about whether this moment, this feeling, her own and Leilah's, would last until the morning. She knew she might never recreate this moment again, but she hoped she could. She believed the book . . . and the list . . . they might bring her mother back to her.

She collected the glass of water; Leilah hadn't even taken a sip.

GIGI

2018

Gigi spotted Samuel running up ahead. Her son loved supermarkets. He just ran, and ran, and ran. That's why she always took him to the Tesco Express now, because there wasn't so much space, it was harder to lose him.

As Samuel charged into the shop, he ran past a man perusing his shopping list, and an opportune gust of wind from the automatic doors, combined with Samuel running at the speed of light, sent the piece of paper flying out of his hands. Samuel, spotting this opportunity to play a new game, followed the piece of paper, dodging through people's feet, ducking and diving around small shopping carts and baskets.

Eventually, Gigi caught up with him in the fruit aisle, where she spotted his little fingers reaching for the grapes—his new favorite. A week ago, she'd have had to smash grapes up with a banana or something before he'd touch them.

She knew he'd lost interest in the shopping list, wherever it was. He loved rummaging in the fruit at the moment. He'd pick something up and show her, then name it, confidently. Mostly he was right, "nana" and "gwape," but often he was wrong with the trickier fruit—mango was often "apple," pineapple was "bababa," which was his made-up word for "I have not a fricking clue," and orange was "ball." But she so loved watching him change, watching him turn into a little person.

She tried to get to him before his sticky fingers made contact, but, as she approached, his hand wasn't going for the "gwape" but for a piece of paper tucked under them. The man's shopping list. He pulled it out and started waving it, triumphant, looking around for applause from his fellow shoppers.

She grabbed it gently so he wouldn't start wailing about having been "fiefted." "Samuel," she said calmly. "We should return this to the man it belongs to."

She looked down at the list and frowned. It wasn't a shopping list after all. It was a book list, a film list, or something like that.

She held Samuel's hand in one of hers, and wandered toward the front entrance, hoping to find the man again. He was nowhere to be seen. She hurried around the shop once, with no clue what he really looked like.

After a minute or so, Samuel grew restless. "Mummy, slow down, slow down!" Gigi gave in. The best place for this list would be on the community board, which was right next to the spot where the man had been standing, in case he came back to find it. She placed it gently on one of the sticky pads, faceup. Maybe he wouldn't mind that it was gone—she imagined he had the list on his phone or something anyway; everyone did these days. She looked at it one last time, trying to work out why someone had been perusing this kind of list in a supermarket.

To Kill a Mockingbird—that was one of those black-and-white films, wasn't it? Based on a classic book.

The Kite Runner. This was another film that she'd seen with her ex, at the point they'd been close to breaking up. It was really way too much of an emotional film to see with someone you weren't totally comfortable around anymore. She'd tried to hide her ugly crying but had ended up giving herself hiccups—twice as embarrassing.

Pride and Prejudice—also a classic book turned film; she'd watched it with her mum because her mum *loved* Keira Knightley. She called her "the English Rose." She missed her mum, she hadn't spoken to her in ages—both busy with their lives, living far away. Now, whenever she called, they ran out of things to talk about beyond the usual life updates. Once upon a time, they'd spoken for hours—about everything and anything.

Life of Pi—the one with the special-effects tiger. She'd seen it in the cinema, in 3-D. A date, again. A better one, the guy was her guy now. But she couldn't wait until Samuel was old enough to watch it with him—he *loved* tigers. He would love that film. And the boy, Pi, she imagined Samuel might look a bit like him when he grew up.

She didn't know all the other titles, but she brushed her hand down the list, securing it in place, as Samuel pulled at her free hand. These titles, they pulled her away from the person she was right now, back to a previous Gigi. Those films she'd seen on dates—that was her *go-to date night*. She hadn't seen a film in the cinema for ages now. Samuel didn't have the attention span for it, not just yet.

She missed it; she missed sitting in those fluffy, worn cinema chairs, eating popcorn, with either her mum or a guy beside her. She missed that feeling, as the lights went dark and the credits started to roll. If it was something she loved so much, why hadn't she done something about it?

"Mumma, I want gwape." Samuel's voice pulled her back to the present.

"Yes, sweetie, we'll get them. Just putting this up for someone who lost it."

"It's mine!"

"It's not yours, but you nicely found it for them. Isn't that nice of you?"

"Mine!"

"Okay, come on then, let's get some grapes."

But, just before Gigi turned around, she pulled out her phone and took a quick snapshot of the list. She would call her mum, her mum knew *everything*—she'd know every title, every film, every book. Maybe they could go see some of these together. To make up for lost time.

CHAPTER 18

MUKESH

"Why don't you take her somewhere *outside* of Wembley for once?" Aleisha said politely as Mukesh sat in his favorite library armchair.

"I never take Priya outside of Wembley. Why would I?"

Mukesh had asked Aleisha for advice about bonding with Priya—she was the only *young* person he knew, so he thought she might understand Priya better than he did. But he was now starting to regret bringing the topic up at all.

"Because she's a kid. When I was her age, I was always out, on the road playing or something. Being at home is boring."

"You don't find home boring. You're *always* at home! Or here!"

"Ouch, Mr. P. You know, that kinda hurts." Aleisha held her hand up in front of her face and turned to the side, as if upset.

"Have I really offended you?" he asked, panicked.

"No! Mr. P, I'm kidding. But you know, I don't *always* want to be at home."

"Why not? Home is nice. Especially as you have your family."

"Yeah, but . . ." He saw her eyes drift away for a moment. "Well, family's not always easy. My mum, she's sometimes . . . You see, she's not very well."

"What do you mean? Naina always told me to take my vitamin C and zinc tablets. I would recommend."

"No, not that. Sorry . . . I never talk about this, to anyone." She looked at her hands, anywhere but at him. "Just, she doesn't look after herself, so I have to do it for her. Since my dad went to live somewhere else, me and Aidan are all she has."

Mukesh was silent; he didn't know what to say.

She'd never spoken about her father before. He'd never come up, not when they'd spoken about Scout and Jem's father or Amir's father too.

He wracked his brain for words of comfort. Naina would know exactly what to say. He kept as quiet as possible, hoping she might come to his rescue—but it had been weeks since he'd last heard her voice. He was on his own here.

"I don't know what to say," Mukesh admitted, finally. "So you *don't* like being at home? But you don't like being in the library either?"

"I don't mind the library now. It's all right."

"And what does your brother do?" He remembered her talking fondly about her brother, whenever they discussed Scout and Jem.

Aleisha fiddled with her long fingernails. "He's working *all* the time, these days. I think he's stressed a lot now . . ." Aleisha paused then, almost surprised at her own words. "He never really gives himself a break." Then she took a deep breath, and kept her eyes fixed on her hands. Mukesh had the sense that she'd never said this out loud before. "But we *used* to hang out, he loved going into Central London on summer holidays—we never did anything. Sometimes we just got on Tube trains and would see where we ended up."

"I used to like doing that after work. It can be very peaceful."

Aleisha nodded. "Totally. Aidan usually loves it, just being among people but sitting quietly, everyone minding their own business. When I first got my Oyster card, he begged Mum to let him take me on trips. She wasn't sure about allowing us both to go on our own, but she said yes. Mum's an artist, well, a graphic designer, so he took me to some galleries because I never really understood what she did. We didn't see the exhibitions, but Aidan picked up some postcards for her. She gave us the biggest hug when we got back, like we'd been gone years."

Mukesh watched as Aleisha's mind wandered, her eyes giving the same telltale expressions as Naina's when she was buried in a book.

"You love your family, ne?" Mukesh asked.

Aleisha shrugged, her reverie halted.

"Families aren't perfect, but we love them." He held up his book,

The Kite Runner, as if to illustrate his point. Aleisha rolled her eyes, but in a kind way. He was thinking about Amir, Hassan, Amir's father—the small family they'd created for themselves, the hurt they'd caused one another as a result.

"Are you still trying to do your Atticus words of wisdom thing?"

"My friend, I have my own words of wisdom, thank you very much!"

"What do you think of *The Kite Runner*?"

"Good question. It has made me very sad. I think we have all been a bit of Amir in our lives—self-centered, focused only on ourselves—and we have all been a bit of Hassan too, forgotten by the people we love the most. But in the end, the book was as happy as it could be. Amir made the right choice, to do the right thing. I couldn't help thinking what a selfish boy he was though. Ne?"

"Oh, Mr. P—I know. But he was only a child too—he wasn't thinking."

"Yes, that is true, you're right." He took a deep breath, feeling the sadness of the novel sink in before trying desperately to distract himself, to distract Aleisha. "So, you really think I should take Priya *outside* of Wembley?" He wouldn't admit it to Aleisha, but he was nervous. He had routines; he never ventured very far.

"Yes! Take her into London—Wembley's boring for her. It's boring for *us*. Surely you're fed up of this library!"

"Boring for you, maybe! This library is still my adventure." Mukesh clapped his hands together. "Wembley, it's big enough for me, and always changing."

"Mr. P, you deserve to get out a bit more."

"I know I should, but . . ." He paused, looked down at the desk. "The truth is it *frightens* me a little bit. My wife, Naina, she was the brave one, she—" He came to a halt, a lump forming in his throat.

He could feel Aleisha staring at him, *pitying* him.

"Look, Mr. P," she said softly. "You know that journey Amir took back to Kabul, not knowing what the city he'd grown up in would look like now?"

Mukesh gulped back the lump.

"That was a big journey," Aleisha coaxed. "And well, no offense, Mr. P, but it was way more of a big deal than you stepping out of HA9 for an afternoon. If he can do that, you can certainly do this. And Priya, she might see you in a different light. She might think you're less of an old man, stuck in his ways, and more like her . . ."

Mukesh nodded, trying hard not to be a little offended by that last bit. He looked down at *The Kite Runner*, sitting on Aleisha's desk, ready to be put back on the shelf for someone else to read and weep at.

As he headed to the door, Aleisha caught up with him. "Hey, Mr. P, you forgot your next book. It's got a tiger in it. One of my mum's new favorites." She handed him *Life of Pi* and Mukesh pulled a face of mock horror at the tiger on the front. "Yet again, a story of someone being *forced* out of their comfort zone, onto a lifeboat with a fierce animal," Aleisha said with a wink.

"Thank you, I can tell you're choosing these books just for me. I'm just sorry I can't give you anything useful in return!"

Aleisha smiled shyly. "Mr. P, don't worry, it's my job, remember?"

With that, he wandered out with a spring in his step, trying hard not to let the SAVE OUR LIBRARIES sign on the door dampen this small moment of joy.

Think of positive things. Think of positive things, Mukesh chanted to himself silently, trying to allay his nerves. It had been a long time since he'd gotten on the Tube, and he felt as if he was learning to walk all over again.

He'd decided on the destination for his and Priya's trip today: Central London, where the sounds were louder, the people were grumpier—the thought terrified him a little. It was a big step, a big change. He hoped Aleisha was right about this.

When he'd worked on the Tube, many years ago, this had been his life. Back then he had loved the Bakerloo line trains best. They were still old-fashioned, almost exactly the same as they were when he would explore the area with nothing but a ticket and a watch to get him back home on time, ready for dinner with Naina and the girls. It was rare that he'd have an evening after work with an hour or so to spare to sit on the Tube for a little while, but if he did, that's what he liked to do.

The train pulled up; a handful of people stepped up and off and onto the platform. Mukesh held on to the rubber on the edge of the door as he took a big step onto the train. Priya hopped on easily, and offered her hand to her dada. He declined. He could do this by himself. Priya ran ahead to save them seats, and all of a sudden Mukesh could feel himself weakening with the distance. Until a woman came close behind him and said, "I gotcha," taking a firm hold of his arm.

He was a little wobbly as he set both feet on the floor of the train carriage, no longer light enough to float away, but found his seat next to Priya, who was already reading her book. He realized his opportunity. He had *Life of Pi* with him, he could read alongside his granddaughter. Suddenly his heart rate started pulsing. Priya hadn't *seen* him reading, and he'd never read on a train before—he didn't want to make himself queasy. He decided against it. The tiger and the boat could wait. Instead, he watched Wembley go by.

Sixteen stops.

A family of four got on. Two little girls, a mum, and a dad. They got off again at Maida Vale. He hadn't been to Maida Vale for years.

Then another man hobbled onto the train, in the same style as Mukesh. He tried to avoid eye contact, but couldn't help looking out of the corner of his eye, wondering what was going to happen next. Mukesh knew how he felt, unsure if the floor beneath you could hold you, whether it would stay firm or quickly turn to jelly. It was *always* jelly these days. The man grabbed hold of the maroon bars, his knuckles a purplish-white with effort, and he lowered himself onto a seat.

The man looked Mukesh dead-on and he couldn't hide anymore,

so he smiled. The man simply nodded back. Priya was oblivious to it all, her face pulled in the same look of concentration that defined Naina's reading state. She was somewhere else.

"Where are we going, Dada?" Priya asked, holding Mukesh's hand tightly as they pushed their way through the streets of Charing Cross. Mukesh wished his palm wasn't so clammy.

The signs were brighter in Central London, the traffic louder, faster, than he had remembered. He couldn't see more than a few paces in front of him because of all the people blocking his way.

"Well, I think you'll like it. Your ba took me to this place once, to pick up presents for your mum and your masis one day, when they were very young. I thought it might be nice to get you a present too."

Since Naina had died, Mukesh had failed to buy Priya presents she actually liked. Last year, he'd bought her a pink, fluffy, sequined purse. She'd passed it straight to her little cousin Jaya, who had used it as a musical instrument for a few hours before leaving it in a corner of Mukesh's house for him to find weeks later, covered in dust, with a dead ant lying on top of it.

"Mum says she *never* got presents." Priya frowned.

"She did!" Mukesh tried to hide his shock. "On special occasions," he qualified. "Usually a new dress that your ba made. And I remember coming here around Christmas, you see, all those years ago. We said we'd do Christmas, but we agreed we'd still do Diwali. *Double* presents, *and* a Christmas tree *and* Christmas cards, barfi and gulab jamun. We did it all. Your mum wanted to be like her school friends, who got gifts all wrapped up in glitzy paper."

Naina had bought books for Rohini, Vritti, and Deepali. He could tell the girls hadn't been impressed. He remembered, clearly, Rohini saying, "Mummy, I thought I was getting a new dress this year?" While Deepali and Vritti worked hard to feign gratitude as they opened them, their smiles plastered on their faces, two unconvincing toothy grins.

The two of them stopped as they entered the bookshop, their

eyes caught by the books in the windows—a whole scene was captured on the glass itself, a sea and an orange-pink sunset showcasing books, all different sizes and colors. The waves, the deep blue of the sea, reminded Mukesh of Pi, his ocean, his lifeboat, and his tiger.

"Wow!" Priya gasped quietly. She quickly shook off her awe, trying to play it cool. Mukesh felt the same. He'd seen books now, but the library was sparse compared to this. Shelves and shelves. Floors and floors. Tables and tables. Piles and piles of books. It was as though they were floating all around him, lifted up by some kind of magic, offering up new worlds, new experiences. It was beautiful.

"Follow me," he said to Priya, leading her toward the tills.

As he reached the desk, he paused, bracing himself, that first day in the library flashing in his memory. "Excuse me," he said to a woman behind the desk, wanting to look bold in front of his granddaughter, who was peering excitedly over the counter.

"How can I help?" she said, smiling at him.

He relaxed. This was *so* very different from his first meeting with Aleisha. "I want three books please. *Rebecca*," he said, smiling down at Priya, "*The Kite Runner*, and *To Kill a Hummingbird*." He said the last two so quickly, she, "Louisa" judging by her name badge, asked him to repeat himself.

"*Re-bec-ca*," he enunciated quietly, "*The Kite Runner*, and *To Kill a Hum-ming-bird* by Lee Harper."

"Thank you, sir. Let me check for you."

Her fingers moved at the speed of light on the keyboard. "Ah, yes, we have all of these. Let me show you."

She stepped out from behind the desk. There were a lot of other people browsing, and he wondered if she had time to show them where to go, and still make it back to serve someone else. He looked around. All he could see were books, tables, and staircases. Behind one table, piled high with paperbacks, was a young woman he felt sure could be Scout all grown up. He stopped in his tracks. Her face was exactly how he'd imagined it. She had short, messy blond hair too. *Was* it Scout? How could it be? Scout didn't *really* exist, no matter how much he wished she did. Priya tugged at her dada's sleeve and pointed him toward the woman, a few paces in front. Her eyes wandered the bookshop, taking in every inch.

"Isn't this exciting?" he whispered, more to himself than to Priya.

When he looked back at Louisa, she was far ahead of him, heading up the staircase. He shuffled to catch up, dragging Priya with him. He wondered why all the other browsers couldn't see the characters walking among them, the ghost of Rebecca lurking in the corner, picking out the novel she was going to read on her beach holiday this year, and Atticus, holed up in the reference section, surrounded by big, fat, chunky books—Mukesh wouldn't have expected any less of him! Why was no one else as giddy with elation as he was?

Eventually, they tracked down all the books. Louisa fetched them from the shelves one at a time, checking they were the editions he wanted. He nodded. He didn't really know what that meant but as long as it was the right book, he was happy.

He passed each one to Priya. "What do you think? What covers do you prefer?"

"What?" Her eyes shot up at him, disbelieving. "These are for *me*?"

"Yes!"

Within moments, Mukesh felt breathless, all the air squeezed out of him by Priya's arms, hugging him tightly at the waist. The woman watched them, smiling, and Mukesh didn't mind that he could barely breathe. He couldn't remember the last time Priya had hugged him without her mum instructing her to.

When she finally let go, her eyes shot down to the books. "I like *these* ones," she said, running her fingers over the bumps and gloss of the covers, before clutching them to her chest.

"Wonderful, young lady. Anything else at all I can help you with?" Louisa asked.

"Why these books, Dada? Were they Ba's favorites?" Priya said between mouthfuls of cheesecake from the bookshop café.

He shrugged, shoveling down his chocolate muffin—a small drop of shame coming over him. He *didn't* know. He'd never asked.

Naina had always looked so preoccupied when she was reading. He'd never stopped to think that sometimes the book she was reading might reveal more to him than anything else. Only now that he'd started reading himself, now that he saw Rebecca browsing the shelves, Mrs. Danvers sitting beside him in the Foyles café, eating a cream-cheese bagel, or Amir and Hassan running up and down between the tables, only *now* did he realize how lovely it would have been to learn a little more about the world Naina had been occupying, the characters she'd been walking with.

He didn't want to show his regret to Priya, when she finally seemed excited to hang out with him, so instead he said, "I think your ba read *every* book. She loved reading!"

"I know that, Dada," she said, scrutinizing him. "But did she read *these* ones? Were they her favorites?" She'd laid out her three new books in front of her like playing cards. Wiping her hand first so as not to get any cheesecake on her books, she stroked the covers again. Naina would always wipe her hands on a tea towel before picking a book up.

"I'm not sure. But they are *my* favorites." He waited to see if that held any resonance for her, if she even cared at all. His little girl gave nothing away. She shrugged.

"Can you tell me what they are about then? Just a little so I have the *flavor*, you know."

He nodded. He'd never had to do this before—it felt a bit like a test. He remembered Aleisha's face after she finished *The Kite Runner*—how her recommendation had been filled with so much emotion and enthusiasm. He tried to channel her energy as he summarized each novel.

"So, *To Kill a Mockingbird*." Mukesh glanced over to Atticus Finch in the reference section, just about in view from the café. Priya's eyes were wide, totally engaged, focused on her grandfather's face. "It's about brother and sister, Jem and Scout, learning some crucial life lessons. Their father, Atticus Finch, is a big, important lawyer—he's *really* good, and *very* wise and fair—he's defending a man called Tom Robinson, accused of attacking a white woman just because he's black. It's her word against his. Now, these are things quite *big* for young Scout and young Jem to understand—so we see them coming to terms with what's going on, seeing injustice for themselves in their own childlike ways. So, what happens—"

"Stop, Dada!" Priya held up her hands. "I'm going to read it for myself. I just want the *flavor*."

"Yes, yes, you are right. Well, then that is a little *flavor*." He moved on to the next one: *Rebecca*. He began describing Rebecca by going "Ooo," in what he hoped was an atmospheric, spooky way, but actually he sounded like an old grandfather with some joint pain.

"Are you okay, Dada? Do you want to sit on this seat, it has more padding?" Priya stood up and pointed to the cushion underneath her.

"Na, beta, it's okay; I am okay, just a little twinge," he said, embarrassed. "Where was I? . . . Oh, yes. Do you remember your summer holidays to Cornwall?"

"Yes, Dada, of course."

"Well, you know all those cliffs, the rough waves."

"Yes, Dada."

"Well, imagine a large house not far from there, and a ghost of a woman walking the halls . . . That's how *Rebecca* really *builds* the atmosphere, spooky and eerie, and I think the landscape is a person in itself! I don't know if it really *is* Cornwall in the book, but it sounds like it. Did Cornwall ever feel like that to you?"

For a split second, Mukesh was watching himself—and he couldn't quite believe it. He was discussing books as if he *knew* what he was talking about. He sounded like an English teacher, maybe even a librarian. He felt himself sit up an inch or so taller, pride sending pinpricks over his skin.

"Not really, we usually go surfing and it's very beautiful when it's sunny. But windy and scary when it's not."

"Exactly! It's got that beautiful side, and the dark side . . . like *Rebecca*."

Eventually, he moved on to *The Kite Runner*. He didn't know how to begin describing it to Priya. "This book might be a little sad, and a little grown-up, for you."

Priya shook her head. "One of my friends read it at school. She's a bit older than me, but I'm a better reader than her," she said matter-of-factly.

"All right, well, it's the story of two friends—they're like brothers, Amir and Hassan." Mukesh pointed to the two little boys on the front cover. "Except Amir is from a wealthy family, and Hassan is not. Hassan is the son of Amir's family's servant."

He held *The Kite Runner* in his hands. While this story was so different from his own, and that of his friends, something about the kinship between Amir and Hassan always reminded him of his good childhood friend in Kenya, Umang. They were so alike in so many ways, but the two boys had different pasts and different futures—Mukesh always knew he'd have opportunities, but Umang . . . Umang didn't.

He hoped Umang was well—he was a boy with a big heart, a clever mind, wise beyond his years. Mukesh had loved playing with Umang—he was someone Mukesh could always be himself around. "Two peas in a pod," his mother always said to them in English.

They'd drifted apart in their teenage years—but still saw each other walking the roads, at the beach—but Mukesh hadn't thought of Umang for years now. Until *The Kite Runner.*

"When I was a boy, I had a best friend," Mukesh started, not quite knowing how to phrase it without making himself look like a villain. He noticed Mrs. Danvers had stopped eating her cream-cheese bagel to watch him. "He always wanted to spend time with me. One day, I shut Umang out of my house because I didn't want to play, I just wanted to be alone. But my friend, well, he was just here for some company, for some peace and quiet, and probably for some of my mummy's dosa—everyone in our village *loved* my mum's dosa."

"Is it as good as Ba's used to be?"

"You know, my mum actually gave your ba her recipe! I did other things I wasn't proud of—now I look back and can see how terrible I was as a friend to Umang, playing with him only when I wanted to. When some of the older boys asked me to play, I abandoned Umang, not wanting the boys to know that we were the best of friends, worried about what they might think. We were from quite different families, you see." He took a deep breath. How would Atticus find the meaning in this story? "It's good to be kind to people, especially the people you love, because you never know what it's like to walk in their shoes until one day you do. And by then, it's often too late to make a real difference. But yes"—he tapped the book again—"maybe save this one until you're a teeny bit older. Ha?"

"Okay, Dada, if you say so . . ."

Suddenly, sitting beside him was Naina. She was back. She had come back to him, for the briefest of moments. Her face was aglow, her smile iridescent. Today was a milestone, and he couldn't wait to tell Aleisha what a good job he had done.

THE READING LIST

INDIRA

2017

Indira stood outside the library, peering through the doors, with the list held in her hands. She looked at it, as though it might give her direction. This morning, her next-door neighbor's daughter had posted a note through the letterbox: *Dear Indira, I wanted to let you know that my mother, Linda, will be moving away from Wembley. She is coming to live with me—we're all keen to have her closer to us. Her memory is not what it once was and we feel the time has come to have her near. Please do keep in touch. All best, Olivia x*

Linda had been Indira's neighbor for the last twenty years. They weren't best friends, but they spoke almost every day, at ten o'clock in the morning when they both sat out in the garden for a few minutes before they got on with the rest of their day. They were both lonely; they both filled their days with crosswords, and tea and chai breaks. They both had routines that meant nothing. But today, Indira realized there was a difference. Linda had people there for her, and now she wouldn't be lonely again. Indira . . . she had no one. Her daughter, Maya, was living in Australia—she saw her every few years. Not once had Maya and her husband ever suggested she move there with them. She read Olivia's note once, twice, three times, folded it up and unfolded it again and again.

Upset, but unable to explain why, she hopped over to her coat on the coat rack and pulled it over her shoulders—she needed to get out even though she had nowhere to go. She pulled her plastic mandir bag out from her pocket, and out came a note. The *other* note. The one she'd found weeks ago in her shoe rack at the mandir, with the list.

She turned it over. HARROW ROAD LIBRARY.

Right, Indira had thought to herself. That's *where I'm going to go.*

Throughout Indira's life, she'd always looked for signs. While the list of books hadn't felt like one at first, her mind had kept being drawn back to it, like a siren in the night. And today, it had found her just when she needed a distraction. The library was only a few streets away from her house. She might as well go; she had nothing else to do—she never had anything to do. She hadn't been to the library since her Maya had been little—and they'd curled up in the children's corner reading books.

To Kill a Mockingbird—Harper Lee. It would be under *L,* she kept telling herself over and over again.

After a deep breath, she walked through the doors. Immediately, she was greeted by an Indian man behind the desk, wearing a sweater-cardigan-waistcoat-type thing.

"Hello, madam!" he said, smiling broadly. "How may I help you?"

His smile was infectious; she couldn't help but beam back at him.

"Oh, hello! I am looking for some books." She passed him the list. "Any one of these would be good, but is there one you'd recommend reading first? Perhaps I should just start with the first one?" She couldn't stop herself from talking. The man didn't respond for a while, as his eyes scrolled down the piece of paper, then up again.

"You could start anywhere, of course. But *The Kite Runner,* eh?" he said. "You know, our volunteer-run book group is actually reading that one together. There's one of them over there." He pointed to a white woman, about twenty years younger than Indira, with her white hair pulled back into a bun, half her face hidden behind the book.

"Lucy," he called over, and the woman looked up. She smiled big too. Everyone here was a smiler. "I've got a lady looking for *The Kite Runner*!"

The woman hurried over, holding her own copy—"Oh my, yes, you're in for a treat! We've got a couple of copies on the shelf. If you *are* interested, you could come along to our book group."

"What day is it?" Indira asked, cautiously, not quite sure what she was signing up for. She only came here for a few books.

"We meet every second Thursday of the month."

Indira knew she was free then—Indira was always free.

"Yes, okay—I will . . . I will read the book, and then, if I like it, I can come?"

"Of course," the woman, Lucy, said. "But if you don't like it, that's fine too! We like a good discussion, we do! We have a young woman called Leonora who joined the library specially because of the book club. And we have a girl called Izzy; she's such a voracious reader, always in here with a long list of books, a bit like yours actually, but she's already read *The Kite Runner*—she's got *so* many little sticky notes on it—the rest of us aren't like that! She's like a detective or something . . . Anyway, she's already told us she isn't a fan. So, whether you like the book or not, you'll always have *someone* on your wavelength. It's a good way of connecting with people."

The librarian lady smiled warmly, but she lingered on that last sentence, staring straight into Indira's eyes. Or was it just Indira's imagination?

"Lucy is one of our volunteers, so she knows this place like the back of her hand. Would you like me to grab the rest of these books for you?" The Indian librarian was looking Indira up and down, her walker his obvious concern.

"Erm, no, actually—maybe I will take this one, first of all. See how I get on." She looked at the book in the woman's hand and wondered whether she would be able to manage concentrating on a whole book. It had been a long time since she had read that much in English. "Do you have this one in Gujarati?" she asked the Indian man, hoping he might understand.

"Not this one, but we do have quite a few books in Gujarati," he said, and he led her toward the shelf. There were about fifty books there. Enough to keep her going for a good long time. "Wow," she exclaimed. "Well, I will start with *The Kite Runner,* but then, I think I will need to come back for this."

"And the other books on your list?"

She looked down. "Oh, yes, of course. I *will* come back."

"It's been really nice to meet you . . . Sorry, what's your name?" the white woman said to her.

"Indira," Indira replied. "Nice to meet you also, Lucy. I am looking forward to the book group."

"Oh, we're a lovely bunch of people, if I do say so myself! You'll love it. We bring cakes and snacks too, so if you ever fancy sharing anything, you would of course be more than welcome to."

"Thank you!"

"We're a little community, we are," Lucy said, beaming still. Indira wondered whether her cheeks were hurting from all her happiness.

As Indira left the library that day, she knew she'd be back—that shelf of books was so exciting to see. She liked reading English, and she could read it well, but she missed reading Gujarati novels.

The list was still held in her hands, tucked into *The Kite Runner.* "Thank you," she muttered to it. "Thank you for bringing me here."

Pride and Prejudice

by

JANE AUSTEN

CHAPTER 19

ALEISHA

She glanced over to her bedside table. *Pride and Prejudice* was staring back at her. It *really* wasn't her kind of thing. She'd picked it up twice now and couldn't get into the early nineteenth-century world of dances, of balls, of marriage matches, of interfering mothers. But at the pace Mr. P was reading, he'd have caught up with her in no time, so she forced her eyes to focus on the words, on the images of the Bennet family house, Mrs. Bennet, bossy, overbearing. Elizabeth, pretty uppity herself actually, and Mr. Darcy, the love interest, the Colin Firth character in the BBC series . . . pretty uppity too. She tried not to, but she couldn't help comparing him with Zac. He'd been popping up in her head ever since she'd started reading this cheese-fest of a book. She couldn't work out why, but he kept appearing on her mind's horizon, wearing period costume, his face brooding and moody, just like Mr. Darcy. She imagined Leilah in Mrs. Bennet's place . . . Would she approve of him? She caught herself, her imagination already wandering too far. What was she doing, thinking of Zac, and Leilah, in this way?

She heard the floorboards above her room creak. Aidan's room was directly above hers, but she was sure he'd be fast asleep by now. He had an early shift tomorrow, according to the Post-it notes stuck on the fridge. It sounded as if he was pacing his room, frantic. She'd lived in the ground-floor bedroom long enough to work out what every creak meant. Usually, it was the ones from Leilah's room that she was most attuned to. She sneaked out of her bedroom, leaving the book facedown on her bed, and wandered upstairs, trying to be as quiet as possible. She didn't want to be the one to wake up Leilah. She stood outside his bedroom door. She put one hand out, ready to knock, but she could hear the pacing clearly now, as well as a soft, choked sobbing. Her heart crashed to the pit of her stomach. Part of her wanted to rush in, envelop her brother in a hug. But the other part of her, the cowardly part, told her that he'd hate that, that he'd just want to be left alone. She let that second part win, and she tiptoed back down the stairs.

She shut the door to her room. She tried shoving her headphones in, forcing herself to listen to her music, to forget about her brother, but it was futile. Her mind was still on him.

She opened up *Pride and Prejudice* once more, wishing for some connection to the old-school characters, their frills and dresses, even wishing Zac would pop up in his period outfit and whisk her imagination away, but her mind was still with Aidan, in his room. She shut the book with force and dumped it back beside her bed. It didn't matter what she did, her house had become Manderley again, with ghosts creeping in the corners. She squeezed her eyes shut, the darkness swirling behind her eyes.

"Hey, Leish." Her brother's head popped around her bedroom door the next morning. The light was shining through the curtains already, but she could tell from the stillness of the house that it was early. She grumbled in response, rubbing her eyes awake.

"I've swapped some shifts around, so I'm working today but will be back home tonight." He paused. "So I'll be here in time for you to go out. You know—for your barbecue." Aleisha desperately searched her brother's face for stress, tension. But she only saw a brightness; his eyes had a twinkle to them, as if he was plotting something. It was the face he used to make when he was a child, planning to make her a mud pie in the garden for her birthday, or when he'd put clingfilm over the toilet seat . . . and then planted the clingfilm box in Aleisha's room for Dean to find. She wondered how last night, whatever had been going on with him, was already forgotten this morning. Had she dreamed it all?

"Aidan, all okay with you? Do you—"

"Yeah, good!" he cut in. "So that barbecue, the one Mia mentioned. You should go, get out of here and enjoy the last few weeks of summer."

"No." Aleisha laughed, hollow. "I'm not going. I'll stay here. I mean, you've not had a night off in ages." Aleisha swung her legs over the bed, sliding her feet into slippers. "We could chill."

"No, you're going. I haven't seen you hanging out with your mates for weeks. Mum and me think it'll be good for you."

"You told Mum?"

"Yeah."

There it was again. Aidan and Leilah: the joint parental unit, dictating how Aleisha should live her life. It made her laugh how she was a child when they wanted her to be one, yet when Leilah needed her to be a grown-up, there was no room for Aleisha to even be a teenager.

"Promise me you'll think about it?" Aidan asked, putting his little finger up in the air.

"I promise," Aleisha grunted, watching his face for a momentary lapse, for anything. Aidan waggled his little finger so only his face and his hand were visible, the rest of his body was tucked behind the door. "Yeah, I promise!" Aleisha snapped, waggling her little finger back.

"Great. See you later. I've left some reminders on the fridge too."

She observed Aidan's every move as he marched off with his usual energy. She shook her mind free of the image, the story, she'd invented last night, the scene she'd pictured through his bedroom door.

If Aidan hadn't made a special effort and swapped shifts just so she could go out, she would have been typing her excuse on WhatsApp right now. Saying she was sick. Feeling nauseous. Migraine. But his Post-it notes on the fridge saying *Go out* and *Have fun* and *I'll be here, so you don't have to be* made her feel guilty. So here she was, putting on shorts and a top she only really wore on nights out. She put her "going out" pack of cigarettes in her back pocket. Her mum and Aidan didn't know about those.

She called to Aidan from the bottom of the stairs, "Aidan, can you let me in when I'm back later? I'll give you a ring. I haven't got space for my keys." Aidan and Aleisha both knew that the real reason she was leaving her keys behind was her drunken tendency to leave them in random places. Aidan had already had to pay for the locks to be changed twice.

"Yeah, sure," he called back down. "Now go have fun!"

The air was cooler this evening, refreshing, and the sky had turned to candyfloss. She picked up a six-pack of beer using the ID she'd doctored with the Wite-Out and pen skills that Rahul had taught her. When she reached the park, she heard them before she saw them. She knew it well: an illegal barbecue, laughter fueled by booze and cigarettes—what friendships are made of. The park was almost deserted, though there were a few dog walkers and a couple of groups of teenagers. (Aleisha's friends never considered themselves actual teenagers. They looked *down* on teenagers.)

She heard Rahul laughing, bellowing as though he really wanted to prove how much fun he was having, what a laugh he was. "You came!" Mia jumped up as soon as she saw Aleisha. "I didn't think you'd come. You know, *flaky*." Aleisha laughed uncomfortably, Mia winked back.

"Kacey and people not here?"

"Nah, they were going to see some gig or something. Last-minute tickets. Bailed. They'll be gutted to miss you though—but you know, they didn't think you'd come." That stung, but Aleisha felt the truth in it. "Anyway, what have you been up to recently? *No one* has seen you."

Aleisha held her breath for a moment. She hadn't been up to *anything*. Her only news was meeting Mr. P, reading the books, reading to her mum. It was all rubbish to them. "Not much really," she said.

"Guys!" Mia called out to everyone. "Aleisha's working in the Harrow Road Library!"

Aleisha felt her face blanch. Some people cackled; mostly, no one looked up.

"I thought they were shutting it down?" Rahul said, winking at her, trying to draw himself into her conversation.

Aleisha didn't say anything. She wanted this to end—she had nothing else to say anyway.

She spent the evening trying to *act* like there wasn't a massive gulf between her and Mia, friends who were now nothing but strangers who moved in the same circles, lived in the same place, yet knew nothing of the details of each other's lives. Rahul kept looking over at her, looking for any opportunity to start chatting, so right now Mia was her only protection. She kept her eyes fixed on Mia as she swigged back the bottle of summer fruit cider, pretending to care about her family summer holiday and the weed she smoked with her dad and brother. Wild.

By eleven P.M., people had already started dropping off. They all wanted to go home early—this was the third night out they'd had this week. It was just a chilled one. Aleisha hadn't left Mia's side all night. Out of nowhere, Mia threw her head back and laughed, toppling over and nearly taking Aleisha with her. Aleisha anchored them to the floor. She had clocked some of the guys looking at Mia, watching her get drunker by the second, louder, happier.

"Mee, shall we go home now?"

Mia shook her head, put her wobbly drunk arm up in the air, singing along to the tinny music playing out of someone's phone. The barbecue was now forgotten, and the group had marked out their territory with a ring of discarded bottles and tin cans.

Aleisha tried to pull Mia to her feet, but she was determined to lie back down on the floor, looking up at the sky, singing into the breeze.

Suddenly, Rahul was by Aleisha's side. "Let me help you," he said.

"No, I'm fine," Mia spoke for Aleisha, from the ground.

"Okay." Aleisha nodded to him. She couldn't do it alone.

Rahul didn't say any more. He bent down to Mia, sitting on his heels. "Mee," he said softly, "I think we should go now. It's late, everyone's going home."

Mia shook her head dramatically. "No one's going home," she said, her words suddenly crisp and clear. "Aleisha's here, we have to make the most of it. We might *never* see her again."

Between the two of them, they had enough strength and determination to lift Mia off the ground, carrying her with an arm on each of their shoulders. Even when Mia picked her feet up, floating between her two friends, they carried on. Mia said her goodbyes, complaining about her shepherd and chaperone, and they wandered out of the park.

Aleisha was pissed off, but tried hard to conceal it. Aidan always said he could read her like a book—she hoped no one else could. She didn't want the night to end this way. She wished her friend wasn't so pissed. She wished Rahul wasn't here.

Mia still lived in the house she'd grown up in, on the other side of Wembley from Aleisha. She hoped she'd be able to get a bus back. It was still early, so she knew Aidan would be up. He'd probably be watching something on YouTube, which was how she usually found him at this time in the evening, in the dark living room, the computer screen illuminating his face, giving him a deathly-green glow. She should text him. But she knew it would be like admitting defeat—that she couldn't have fun, no matter how much she forced it. It would prove to him that she wasn't as good as her big brother. She kept her phone firmly in her pocket.

On Mia's road, Aleisha recognized the houses and muscle memory took her the rest of the way.

When they got to the door, all the curtains were closed, the windows black. It was midnight, the street was quiet, Aleisha didn't dare ring the doorbell. Rahul shrugged. Mia wasn't sober enough to find her keys in her bag, so Aleisha went to help, following the sound of the jangling. Finally, she opened the door for her friend, who waltzed over the step and shut the door on Aleisha and Rahul without a word. They heard a few more clatters, crashes, and bangs. They shouldn't have worried about waking up the house—Mia was doing the job anyway.

"So," Rahul whispered. "I'll walk you to yours, yeah?"

Aleisha shook her head. "No, it's fine."

Rahul insisted, but Aleisha got her phone out. It was time to put up that white flag. She called Aidan.

They waited outside Mia's house; Aleisha was freezing cold, suddenly aware she was wearing shorts and a stupid strappy top. She hugged herself, avoiding Rahul's eye in case he offered her something to keep her warm. The wait felt like forever. She wanted to talk to Rahul, tell him what had been going on at home, about the old man she'd made friends with at the library. Would he laugh, or think it was stupid, or maybe tell her it was a nice thing to do, to keep a lonely old man company? She wanted someone to talk to, someone who wasn't Aidan, who didn't know what it was like to look after your mum when she couldn't look after herself, but who might try to understand.

At one point, she opened her mouth to start talking. But she stopped herself. There was no point. It was probably the little bit she told Rahul about her mum that ended up scaring him away in the first place. It wasn't something teenagers were used to talking about. She'd told Mr. P some stuff, that was enough. She had Aidan, they were in this together.

Then, through the silence, Aidan's car pulled up, music playing more softly than usual through his stereo, and he called out through the window: "Get in, you two."

No matter how much she'd been dreading this evening, her heart was a hollow pit. She'd wanted to be the carefree teenage binge-drinking liability for once. Instead, she'd been the sensible one, doing the right thing, looking after others. Nothing had changed.

CHAPTER 20

MUKESH

Beep. "Hi, Papa, it's Rohini, thank you so much for looking after Priya." "Yes, *thank you, Dada!*" "She said she had a really great time in London with you. I hope you were careful. For your sake, more than anything."

Beep. "Hi, Dad, it's Vritti. Sorry for ringing earlier than usual—I've just gotten off the phone to Rohini. Would you like to come round next week for lunch or something? I can pick you up so you don't need to get the train. Would really love to see you!"

Beep. "Hi, Mr. P, it's Aleisha. Sorry for calling, it's so quiet at the library here today, so I thought I'd check in on how you were getting on with *Life of Pi*. I've got another book for you when you're ready. Anyway, I'll maybe call again later."

Call again later? Mukesh felt an unexpected panic rise to his throat. He hadn't spoken to Aleisha on the phone before. What would they talk about? He hadn't checked his messages this morning because Nilakshi had popped around early to spend the day with him, so she was bound to call any moment now and he'd barely prepared!

"Who was that on the answer machine?" Nilakshi asked from the living room, sitting in her usual spot. (Yes, she had a usual spot now . . .) Her eyes were trained on a Hindi soap opera on Zee TV.

"Oh," Mukesh said. "Just—erm—my librarian." He wondered if that was the right way to describe her.

"Ah! That nice girl," she said, not taking her eyes off the television for a minute. "You've told me so much about her—she sounds like she's read a ton of books. Naina would have loved that job, wouldn't she?"

"She would," Mukesh said, his legs shaking a little as he settled himself back down in his chair. He just had a few pages left of *Life of Pi*, so he put on his noise-canceling headphones (Nilakshi had brought them for him; they had been her husband's) to block out the deafeningly loud music and chatter from the Zee TV program, and dived straight back in. Zee TV was now the most-watched TV channel in his house—he was strangely pleased about it. It had replaced Netflix and the refrain of David Attenborough on the National Geographic channel.

As he turned the final page of the book, leaving Pi and his unbelievable story behind, he kept his headphones on, hoping for a lasting moment of silence so he could gather his thoughts, not wanting the book to end but needing to know what Pi's journey meant—was it real, was it imagined? This story had clutched him in the heart and mind—it had been a long, arduous journey for Pi, but an awe-inspiring, revelatory one for Mukesh.

Then, breaking him from his pondering, he spotted out of the corner of his eye Nilakshi, shuffling off the sofa and into the hallway.

A moment later, she was back, her mouth moving, but he couldn't hear a word she was saying. She was waving the phone in front of his face.

"What is it?" Mukesh said, pulling the headphones to rest around his neck.

"For you! The librarian!"

"Ah," Mukesh said, his heart rate picking up once more. Nilakshi had answered his phone, but what if it had been one of his daughters? He grabbed the receiver, held his hand over the mouthpiece, and moved quickly out of the room and into his bedroom next door.

"Hello?" he said.

"Mr. Patel! Mr. P! Sorry, I hope I'm not disturbing you at home. It's as crammed as Manderley here today. I like the silence but time's dragging a bit. Who was that anyway?"

"Who was who?"

"The woman who answered the phone."

Mukesh took a deep breath for a moment. "My . . . erm . . . I have a . . . It was my daughter; she sometimes answers the phone for me. I was reading, you see."

"*Life of Pi*? Have you finished yet?"

"Just now!" Mukesh said, pleased she didn't pry further. He could feel the guilt creeping over him. Guilt about the lie; guilt about why he was lying too.

He imagined Aleisha sitting at her desk, watching over the library. He wondered who was there today. Was the other elderly gentleman there, the one who liked to help himself to a cup of machine-made coffee and sit by the window, with a newspaper on his lap? Or maybe Chris, delving into another crime thriller? Or perhaps it was the book club—he'd never actually *seen* the book-clubbers, so far, but he imagined what they might be like: big glasses, huge carrier bags full of books, neat clothes.

"So what did you think?"

"Hmm?" Mukesh said, his mind still on the library.

"Of the book!"

"Oh, yes, silly me! It's wonderful," Mukesh said. "It's unbelievable—I can't imagine it could ever really happen. How Pi lost everything on a sunken ship yet survived on a lifeboat with tigers and monkeys and hyenas for two hundred days!"

"Well, it *is* only a book," Aleisha said. "But, I mean, the way the story is written, it's—everything that happens is mad."

"At the end, it says a little thing that made me wonder if it was all Pi's imagination. Is it true?"

"I don't know what the author wanted us to think, but . . . I believe Pi. Don't you?"

"Yes, but it's so sad. How does he do it? He is so alone and lonely and yet . . . he is so brave!"

"I reckon it all means something else—you know, like those biblical stories, which all have different meanings. My teachers were *always* talking about the Bible when we were kids—I never understood it. I had to ask my dad what they all meant. He didn't have a clue either."

She was talking about her father again. Was it just his imagination or did Aleisha seem slightly less guarded these days?

"But I don't know," Aleisha continued. "I wondered if the tiger meant something like resilience or whatever."

"Maybe, I didn't think that deeply about it. I'm not as clever as you. Or my wife, Naina," he said, the reprimanding image of Mrs. Danvers popping into his head again. "Have I told you how Naina's the reason I came to your library in the first place? And the books, the books you've been giving me, have helped me feel like I might be making her proud. Naina and my little granddaughter Priya—they always had such a lovely connection with each other because of books. But still, I'm not as clever as you with all the deep meanings."

Aleisha laughed softly. "I'm not sure that's true. That's really lovely, though, Mr. P. Your wife would be really proud of you. Especially if you really had just read one book before all of this. I don't believe you, though—you're getting through the books like a machine."

Mukesh let that thought rest with him, pride inflating his chest, his head, just as Mrs. Danvers fled the scene. Then the *ding-dong, ding-dong* of the doorbell rang.

"Oh no!" Mukesh said. Who could it be?

"Wait! How was your day with Priya?" And suddenly Mukesh forgot about the doorbell, about Nilakshi and her Zee TV dramas.

"Aleisha, it was magical!" he exclaimed. He heard Aleisha giggle in the distance. "I took her to a bookshop—in Central London. I took your advice. There were *so* many people there, all browsing, or drinking in the café . . . it was so full! I'm sorry, I don't mean to be rude to the library, but, you know . . . it was busier than the library. I wish people loved the library as much as we do, Miss Aleisha."

Ding-dong, ding-dong.

"Mukeshbhai! I'll get it!"

"No!" Mukesh shouted, as Aleisha started to say, "That's so brilliant, Mr. P—" He dropped the phone on his bed, forgotten, and trotted as fast as his slippers allowed to the front door. But, as he entered the small hallway, he already saw Deepali standing on the welcome mat, Nilakshi with a smile plastered on her face, beckoning her in.

"Hi, Dad," Deepali said. "I . . . I was just popping in to say hi. But . . . I should have called. I, er, didn't realize you'd have company. I'd better go." She turned to Nilakshi once more. "Goodbye, Nilakshimasi. Nice to see you."

Before Mukesh could get to the doorstep, Deepali was already in her car, the engine started, ready to drive away.

The excitement he had felt at his conversation with Aleisha had vanished completely. He watched his daughter drive away. Nilakshi clamped a hand on his shoulder. "Mukesh, we are just friends. We both know this, your daughters—of course they'll understand."

But Mukesh knew they wouldn't. He had disappointed them—he had seen Deepali's face drop. Speaking to Aleisha might have made Mrs. Danvers disappear, but Deepali had brought her flying back again and Naina was nowhere to be seen, felt, or heard.

THE READING LIST

IZZY

2019

"Hello?" Izzy said, peering over the library's front desk. "You all right there?"

The man behind the desk was covered in dust, with piles of boxes all around him. "Yeah," he puffed. "I'm all right, I'm just clearing some stuff out. My boss says we need to make this place spotless in case *they* try to shut us down. I don't actually know who this mysterious 'they' is, but there you go . . ."

Izzy stared at him, remembering the SAVE OUR LIBRARIES sign that had been stuck to the door for the two years she'd been coming here, ever since she'd found the reading list. Every time the words became illegible, bleached by the sun, someone—the save-our-libraries elf—replaced it with a new sheet of paper. The library, to her and Sage's relief, was still going—though perhaps not going strong. Now that she'd found it, she couldn't really imagine it not being here.

"Sorry." The man brushed dust off his corduroy trousers, and his T-shirt. "Sorry. Hello, I'm Kyle. How can I help you?"

She'd seen Kyle several times before over the years, and he always had this distinct air of being completely frazzled yet absolutely serene at the same time. Izzy paused for a moment. Was this the right thing to do? She held the list in her hands—she'd kept it pristine, tucked away in her box of lists for ages, for safekeeping.

She'd spent the last two years hiding away from the world in the library, joining the library book club every so often, chatting to anyone she could find, just in case they were the curator of the list. But she'd had no luck yet. She'd read each book again and again, writing notes on them, sticking little sticky tabs on crucial scenes, momentous lines, in case the books themselves, and their messages, were a kind of jigsaw. But she'd tried everything and still, after two years, she couldn't shake her fascination.

"You need to get over this, you'll drive yourself mad," Sage had said to her one night, when Izzy was flicking through *Little Women* for the umpteenth time. It was the third library copy she'd taken out; she wondered if something, a clue, a message, had been marked in certain copies of each of the books on the list—so she was trying every single one. But, again, this copy of *Little Women* told her nothing new.

"I've already driven myself mad," Izzy had said back. "I just need to know now."

So, here she was, exposing her peculiarities to Kyle. A last resort.

"Erm, so, this sounds a bit strange—but I have this reading list," Izzy started. The boy's eyes were wide, a smile plastered on his face, eager to please. "I don't know who wrote it, but I'm . . . I just need to know."

"All riiight," Kyle said, a little unsure.

"Well, I know that whoever used the list came to this library. I sort of wondered if you'd be able to tell me *who* took these books out. I guess, either over several years, or all in one go."

Kyle stood up straight—his smile vanished. "No, no, sorry. That's against privacy; I can't give you that information, even if I could find it."

For a minute, there was silence between them.

"Can I have a look?" Kyle asked, holding his hand out. She popped the list gently in his palm. He held it like an historic artifact.

"You see, I collect lists," she said tentatively. "I know it's a bit of an odd habit, but I just love it. My dad used to call me his little magpie."

"That's cool," he said, but she knew he wasn't sure if it was. "I mean, we see lists like that all the time, obviously. So it feels a bit less special to us."

"Yeah, I guess that makes sense. I just think a list gives you a little look into someone's soul—like books, like art . . . It's silly, I know."

"No," he said, "I think it's nice."

He muttered each of the titles under his breath. Izzy looked around the room, hoping for another clue. She saw Indira; she'd met her at the book club a few times. She really liked Indira, but she *loved* to chat, so whenever she was around, Izzy had to make sure only to approach if she was in a really chatty mood too. The rest of the library was almost empty.

"That's strange, I'm sure it's completely random, but I've got a friend who's reading these books in almost the same order."

"Right now?" Izzy's eyes shot open.

"Yeah, I think so."

"You reckon *they* wrote this list?"

"Noooooo, she hates books," he said matter-of-factly. "But . . . I'm wondering if she's seen your list. Have you left it hanging around here at all?"

"Never." Izzy shook her head.

"Well, I'm really sorry, but I don't know how I can help. But my friend, she's a librarian too. She works here. Maybe come see her? She's often in on Wednesdays." The man smiled, but Izzy could sense he was a little weirded out by her. She *could* get obsessive, she had to admit.

"I'm sorry, is there anything else I can help you with today?"

Izzy shrugged, smiling. "Just this please." She dumped *A Suitable Boy* on his table with her library card balanced precariously on top.

"And how many times have you read this?"

"I've *never* read this copy, if that helps." Izzy laughed. "It's a huge book—I've got to make sure I don't miss anything."

"This list," Kyle said. "It makes sense now, why you always take out the same books again and again. We just thought you were too nervous to ask for recommendations." Kyle passed the book over to her, and she hugged it, comforted by its heft.

"Thank you!"

As Izzy wandered out of the library, she looked around her, wondering—as she always did—whether the list writer was hiding in the bookshelves. Or, could they be sitting behind the library desk? What had this person wanted from the list?

Even after all her reading, all her snooping, she wasn't sure she was any closer to the person who had written it, but she was enjoying the journey. She'd appreciated reading again—before the list, it had been so long since she'd sat down and just allowed herself to get lost in a book. Life felt too busy, it had felt like an indulgence she couldn't afford.

But the list had given her so much—she enjoyed speaking to people here, and in this new city, where life never seemed to stand still, it had given her a place just to be.

CHAPTER 21

ALEISHA

"So, Mr. Darcy, he likes Elizabeth Bennet, and she clearly likes him, but she spends most of her time being rude to him and vice versa," Aleisha said to the silence in her house. She'd been reading to Leilah again, doing everything she could to re-create the calm they'd found this way before.

But Leilah was distracted, her eyes wandering the living room. She nodded when Aleisha explained bits, but then got lost quickly.

"Sorry, sorry," Leilah said drowsily. "So it's a love story?"

Aleisha had gotten lost trying to explain all the different characters. She'd tried to map out who was related to whom, who fancied whom, who wanted to be married to whom, as she went along . . . and now she'd skipped back to the moment when Elizabeth and Darcy had first been thrown into each other's company, hoping it would prompt some interest from Leilah. Aleisha also secretly hoped it might prompt Leilah to ask her about her love life. But of course, why would she? Aleisha didn't have a love life. Even Leilah knew that.

But as she was reading, listening to Elizabeth use her smart-arse comebacks to rebut Mr. Darcy, Darcy doing the same back, her mind was occupied by Zac, and that walk home. Except, unlike Darcy, Zac hadn't been sullen and dull and boring—he'd been overly chatty. He'd made her laugh; he'd been trying to get her to let her guard down. But this was London, not nineteenth-century wherever, and *no* one spoke to strangers.

She looked over to Leilah, and for a split second she saw her dressed from head to toe in one of Mrs. Bennet's best gowns. She blamed it on the story. On her overactive imagination. It was ridiculous—

Mrs. Bennet was nothing like Leilah. She was snobby, loud, brash, and scheming, interested in everyone else's business. Whereas Leilah was reserved, too lost in her own world to be interested in others'.

"Okay, so that's Elizabeth and Mr. Darcy," Leilah said, her eyes waking up. "But you also mentioned a Lydia. Who's Lydia?"

"Elizabeth's younger sister."

"Okay. And who's Wickham?"

"I think he's meant to be the villain, isn't he?"

"I can't concentrate on this," Leilah said. Aleisha felt herself deflate, the book open in her lap, the words tiny and hard to read. Leilah got up from the sofa and wandered out, and Aleisha tried to focus on the page.

Aidan poked his head around, holding up a Post-it note Aleisha had left for him. *Picnic?* it said, with a smiley face emblazoned on it.

"Seriously don't think this is the right time to be getting Mum outside, Aleisha," Aidan said sternly.

Aleisha was so set on the idea, especially now she'd seen *Pride and Prejudice* hadn't done the trick in pulling her mother out of the fog. This time last year, Aleisha and Aidan had laid out a picnic in their garden when Leilah had been having a bad time, and it had helped her. She'd laughed so much.

"It's a beautiful day—you know she liked it last time. We'd be outside but still close to home."

"I just think you're setting yourself up for failure," he said with a deep sigh.

"But last year, it was *your* suggestion and it really worked!"

"Yeah, well, maybe now I'm just not sure it's going to work, not this time," he said. "I'm *fed* up of failing," he muttered then, under his breath.

A heavy silence hung in the air. Aleisha studied the frown on her brother's forehead, the shadows under his eyes.

"Look, I'll do the bulk of it, all right? I'll sort everything out, you just have to be there."

Aidan shrugged, unconvinced. "I've got to pick something up

from the chemist's—come with me. Mum'll be okay for a bit, and we can get stuff on the way back."

She grinned at her brother. "Thanks, Aidan."

Aleisha sat on a bench in the park, basking in the sunshine, waiting for Aidan to get back from the chemist's. She pulled *Pride and Prejudice* out of her bag once more. It had been okay reading it in the privacy of her own home, to her mum, who couldn't care less about it . . . But now, she felt self-conscious, exposed, worried that someone would be watching her, someone she knew.

A stranger sat down on the bench beside her, and as quickly as she could, she swapped *Pride and Prejudice* for the next book on the list, *Little Women*, which she'd been carrying with her in preparation for the moment she finished the Jane Austen. She turned to a random page.

She stole a glance, trying to be super subtle.

For a minute, she thought her *Pride and Prejudice*–addled brain was playing tricks on her. She blinked once, twice. But there he was: Zac, just looking at her.

"Hey, kid," he said.

She shifted uncomfortably, aware of the blush in her cheeks. *Kid.* Great. She tried to think of an Elizabeth Bennet–style comeback—but nothing came to her at all.

"Hi," she said, allowing a drop of ice into her voice; it was the best she could manage.

"*Little Women* . . . I read that *years* ago. With my little sister. It's her favorite. Always made her want sisters rather than brothers though. But who'd want a sister like Amy?"

She had no idea who Amy was . . . she hadn't read a page, so, just to be contrary, she said, "I like Amy. She's misunderstood." Aleisha kept flicking through the pages, trying to act aloof. "How many books *have* you read?"

"Thousands, probably. You seem to be sticking with the *obvious* ones for now." At first, it felt as if he was doing a sharp, disinterested, Darcy-style response. But, when she looked up at him, a generous grin decorated his face; he was teasing. "Do you have time to get a coffee?"

"Bit harsh." Aleisha smiled, looking down at her book. She refused to reveal the reading list to him. It felt like something sacred, just for her (and sort of for Mr. P, though he didn't know it).

"No, sorry, I'm waiting for my brother," Aleisha said sharply, putting her book down and looking straight at him. "I can't."

"Okay, well, why don't we put a date in the diary?"

"Who *says* that?" Aleisha cringed. "Actually, probably someone from here," she said, slapping her hand on *Little Women*, "or *Pride and Prejudice*. That must be where you get your lines . . ."

"Very funny. There are worse places to get lines from."

"Look, I've got five minutes now. If you want to talk, please be my guest," she said sweetly.

"Oh, right, okay." She watched in surprise as his face went pink. He started scuffing his sneakers uncomfortably. "I don't know where to start." He laughed, a tremor lingering in his voice. The pink turned into bright red blotches that began to spread across his neck, crawl up to his chin, and creep onto his face—he had none of that casual nonchalance of Mr. Darcy after all. In that moment, she felt bad for putting him on the spot, exposing him. So, after letting him suffer for a few more moments of silence, just because she could, she gave him a little help. "You at uni then?"

"Yeah, Birmingham."

"Cool. What are you studying?"

"Law."

Aleisha turned to look at him. "That's what I want to do."

"Really?" His eyes brightened. "Think you're up for it?"

She frowned at him. "Yeah, I'm serious."

"What are you doing with all these stories, then? You gotta read some real books." He pointed toward the rucksack at his feet. "Pick it up. Try it."

She shook her head.

"Go on."

She shook her head again, but then made a lunge for it. "Fucking hell. You got a dead body in there?"

She was leaning back into the bench, leaving the bag on the floor, when she spotted Aidan walking toward them. Zac followed her gaze.

"Your brother?"

"Yeah."

"You look alike."

Zac started to get up, but before he could pick his bag up too, Aidan was right beside him.

"Hey, Leish, this guy bothering you?"

"No," she said more coolly than she felt. "He's just a friend. Zac, meet my brother, Aidan."

"Hey, mate." Zac put his hand out to Aidan. Aidan didn't reciprocate.

"Not heard of you before. You a mate from school?"

"Just . . . around," Zac replied. He looked suddenly young, awkward again, like a rabbit in headlights.

"I'm joking, man." Aidan cracked into a smile and Zac instantly released the breath he was holding captive.

"Hey, that's okay, I'm heading off now. Aleisha"—he turned to her—"really nice to see you. Let's not bump into each other next time, and just put a date in the diary. Here"—he passed her a card—"I can talk to you about being a lonely hermit, or even law, if you want to know what you're getting yourself in for." He winked at her.

She took the card, rolling her eyes. Who their age had business cards?

ZAC LOWE—LAW STUDENT/FREELANCE GRAPHIC DESIGN, it said, his mobile phone number bold and bright in the center of the card. Graphic design too, like her mum, she noted.

Aidan sat down beside her.

"What took you so long?" she asked.

"Just picking up a prescription. Really long queue at the pharmacy."

"For Mum?"

"No, no, just something for me. For my headaches. Let's get food then, yeah? If you still want to. The picnic?" he said, ruffling her hair.

Stepping through the doors of Tesco, they regretted it instantly. It was crammed. They rushed through the aisles to find their sandwich fillings of choice. Aleisha chose pâté, because she loved it. Aidan got himself corned beef, because it reminded him of sandwiches that Dean used to make, though he'd never admit the association. They bought prawn cocktail for Leilah, hoping she hadn't gone off it.

They wandered past Creams, the ice-cream parlor, on the way back. She peered in, wondering if anyone she knew was in there. It had once been a regular haunt for Aleisha, because it was one of the only indoor places under-eighteens could loiter for hours, stuffing their faces with sugar. But the black and purple chairs and tables were riddled with a new generation of teenagers wearing Adidas sliders and socks. Aleisha's friends had grown up and grown out of it—they'd moved on to the next stage of their social lives: getting fake IDs and befriending bouncers to get into proper bars. She didn't miss it. Did she?

An hour later, the sandwiches were made; some were cut into triangles, others into fingers. They sat on Leilah's serving platter—white with a gold rim. Already they were getting stale. Aleisha prodded one with her finger, and felt the bread, dry, against her fingertip.

Aidan was sitting outside. Leilah was seated in a kitchen chair, looking out of the open back door into the garden. She was smiling, although Aleisha could see her face was pale. Her eyes dark and unseeing. The skin on her forehead dry. She was tired again.

Aidan laid an old picnic blanket down. "Mum," he called, smoothing out the wrinkles. "Come outside!" He tried to sound upbeat, but Aleisha heard his voice shaking. He was nervous, he was shit scared. She hadn't noticed it so clearly before.

Aleisha shot a look at Leilah—this was the moment of truth.

Leilah stayed stock-still. Then, gradually, she began to shake her head. Slowly at first. One, two, three.

Then frantically. Onetwothreefourfivesix.

Her breathing became deeper, then shallow all of a sudden.

Her eyes closed. Her hands flew to her face, then she hugged herself. Her fingers digging deep into her arms. Locking herself away.

Aleisha put the sandwiches down. Aidan forgot the final wrinkles in the blanket. They rushed toward her.

Instinctively, Leilah turned to Aidan first. Aleisha knew she couldn't reach either of them now. Aidan started humming softly, a chorus of "It's okay, Mum," and "You're safe, Mum," and "We can eat in here, we don't have to go outside."

Aleisha was forgotten. Redundant.

She walked back to the kitchen counter and watched from a distance, her worries bunched up inside her, forming a stone in the pit of her stomach. Heavy. Hurting. Aidan was kneeling in front of his mother. Both his hands clasped around one of hers. Praying. Begging her to be okay again. Leilah only ever wanted Aidan. The air was thick. Aleisha could barely breathe. Her brother looked at her, for help, to check she was okay, and she could see the air was suffocating him too. At least, she thought for the tiniest of moments, she wasn't the only one.

"It's okay, it's going to be okay," he told Leilah. Aidan slammed the garden door shut, keeping the outside world firmly out, locking the three of them in. He walked Leilah upstairs to her room.

"Can I help?" Aleisha shouted.

"No, it's fine. Just give us a minute," Aidan called down.

Although she tried to swallow it, Aleisha could feel herself getting angry. Her mind started to race. She leaned against the counter, staring at Aidan's fucking Peter Rabbit plate. Always so happy. Always reminding her that Aidan was the best one here. Before she could register what she was doing, she grabbed the plate from the shelf, and let it slip out of her hand. It crashed on the floor, smashing in slow motion, letting Aleisha feel every microsecond of her selfishness.

"Leish?" Aidan came rushing down to find her picking up the first shard, pushing the sharp edge into the tip of her finger, watching as a bead of blood blossomed in front of her eyes. "Are you okay?" He grabbed a tea towel, wrapping it tightly around her finger as if it was the biggest injury in the world. "I'm so sorry, I should have helped you clear up."

"Is Mum okay?" Aleisha asked, not wanting to know the answer.

"She'll be okay."

He said nothing about the fact it was his plate, his special display plate. The sandwiches were still sitting on the kitchen counter, untouched, as he swept up Peter Rabbit's cotton tail.

A few hours later, Aleisha was curled up on the sofa, trying to disappear. Aidan walked into the living room. He stood, just looking at her for a while, a beer clasped in his hands. "Aleisha?" he said softly.

"What?" She didn't want to look at him.

He took a deep breath. "I really think we should get Mum to speak to someone," he said, his voice harboring a tremor for the second time that evening.

The silence in the room echoed in Aleisha's ears. Aidan had tiptoed around the subject before, but he'd never said it so clearly. They'd both believed "next time, it would be different." Now his words told her that he wasn't sure it would be.

She could feel his eyes focused on her. Aleisha didn't reply. She didn't want to talk right now.

He stood where he was for a while, and then sighed deeply again. He sat down, stared blindly at the TV adverts. Comparing the meerkats. Should have gone to the optician. Every little bit is useful.

"I'm going back to the warehouse for my night shift later," Aidan said eventually.

"You can't drink that then," she snapped. She could smell the beer through the cap of the can. "Look, Aid. Call in sick. Go to bed. It's been a long day."

Aidan didn't say anything at first. Then: "One can is fine."

She looked at him. She could tell from his tone, from the droop in his eyes, he had had more than one already.

"Who was that guy earlier, in the park? Boyfriend?" She watched him trying to conjure up an expression of interest on his face.

"Between the library and being here, I've got no time for a boyfriend, do I?"

"You're not always here," Aidan said.

"Feel like I am."

"Mum said you've been reading to her. The books from the library."

"I think she likes it."

"Just be careful, okay? Nothing triggering."

"She likes it. It helps her relax."

"She's probably not even concentrating."

"That's fine. She's listening. She doesn't need to concentrate."

"Okay, okay. And look, invite that guy round. I want to meet him properly."

"*I've* not even met him properly," Aleisha said, turning back to the television.

"Why'd he look so friendly then?"

"Guess I just invite people to open up." Aleisha laughed. Although she hated to admit it, the thought of Zac made her want to throw herself into *Pride and Prejudice*, to spend time going to dances, to be carefree for a moment, to live life as a normal nineteenth-century teenager, occupied with flirting, boys, marriage. Turning herself to her real life, away from her make-believe, she wondered what it would be like if she actually had time to hang out with Zac, if he could actually become a friend, more than a friend.

She was flicking aimlessly through the channels now. She turned the TV off. "Night, Aidan. Go to bed. Don't go to work, you won't be doing anyone a favor."

She walked away as Aidan took another gulp from his can. She could hear him tapping on his phone, leaving a ghostly glow as the screen illuminated his face. She wished she knew what he was thinking.

In her room, she pulled out her phone and started typing a message out to her cousin Rachel, the only person who might understand. But then Rachel was busy—always busy, studying, working—and as soon as she'd typed her message out, she regretted it. She didn't need to worry her cousin about all this now. She'd call her another time.

Instead, she pulled out Zac's business card—she got the sense that sometimes he was as lonely as her. She wanted to talk to someone, someone who might not judge her for feeling lost and alone. She typed his number in, followed by a short message: Hey, it's Aleisha—the library girl—how are you?

CHAPTER 22

MUKESH

The phone trilled and trilled, once, then again, then a third time. He was confused, and then a little panicked. It was eight in the morning, usually his daughters called at this time but only once, waiting for it to go to voicemail. They didn't call again and again. He shuffled out of bed, just in case it was an emergency.

"Hello?" His voice was shaky as he answered.

"Papa? Hi!" Vritti said, a little too loudly for the morning. She sounded bright, chirpy.

"Good morning, beta."

"Are you still coming by today? For lunch?"

"Oh, yes." Mukesh had completely forgotten. "Yes, I am looking forward to it! Are we going to one of your cafés?"

"No, I thought it would be easier for you to come to mine. Deepali and the twins are coming too."

"What about Rohini and Priya?"

"Papa, you know my flat's not big enough. Rohini is at work, anyway." Mukesh was relieved that Rohini wouldn't be there—he could just about deal with the impending Nilakshi conversation with Vritti and Deepali, but adding Rohini to the mix would make it much harder. "I can come and pick you up if that's easiest?"

Mukesh shook his head. He thought of the demons he'd conquered during the trip with Priya to Central London—he could do this.

"Papa?"

"No, no. I will get the Tube."

"It's a long way . . . You sure?"

"Totally sure! I know the Tube. I used to know the timetables and the routes off by heart. I will be fine."

"Okay, I know. See you later, Papa! Jai Swaminarayan."

Mukesh was looking forward to going farther afield today, looking forward to seeing his daughters—despite the impending doom about the Nilakshi situation. He might even try reading some more of *Pride and Prejudice* on the train. But the font was so much smaller than the other books and he worried it would make him feel twice as queasy. It was funny, so far he'd discovered that Mr. and Mrs. Bennet have five daughters—a gaggle of strong-minded and exuberant women that reminded him more than a little of his own three—and Deepali was *so* much like Lydia Bennet. He knew he was being cruel, but it was true! Gossipy and self-involved, Lydia shared a fair few character traits with the youngest Patel sister. The shock on her face when she'd seen Nilakshi open the door; yes, shock, but there was a hint of glee too, wasn't there? He could tell Deepali had already been imagining herself disclosing the scandal to Rohini and Vritti when she got home. He thought about Rohini then—was she most like the main Bennet sister, Elizabeth? Queen Elizabeth! Bright, intelligent, but always one to judge someone straightaway—that was *quite* like Rohini. And Vritti—was she Jane, who always gave people the benefit of the doubt, or was she Mary? He didn't really know much about Mary—she was plain. And he didn't think Vritti was plain at all. And finally, there was Kitty—quite cheeky and silly, always getting into trouble and mischief. Mukesh was glad none of his daughters was like Kitty—she would have run Mukesh and Naina ragged.

He thought again of gossipy Lydia-esque Deepali. What was he letting himself in for? He took a deep breath, needing to prepare, and he tapped his pocket. He had his keys, and crucially his sixty-plus Oyster card—Harish always called it the "old person's" Oyster, but Mukesh knew to give it its proper name, as Transport for London would want him to. He was ready to go.

Apart from the swish new bathroom, Vritti's flat hadn't changed much since he had last been here. It was a fairly modern block of flats, with a lift up. "*So* good that she has a lift, Dad!" Deepali had said. It was bright to make up for the fact that it wasn't spacious; and it was airy to make up for the fact that there wasn't a garden, though there was a small balcony covered with plants—all green, no flowers.

The flat itself was minimal, with lots of art on the walls. Vritti had never had much stuff. She'd never wanted much stuff, unlike the other two. But Mukesh wondered if this flat really felt like a home. Could it feel like a home without piles of merchandise from the mandir in every corner, the pink Tupperware used for prasad recycled as candle holders, pots for safety pins, and a salt shaker and a jeeru container? Without the family photos and pictures of Swami Bapa haphazardly framed and hung on every wall? Without Naina's saris everywhere?

Naina had always loved this flat though—it represented a life she just couldn't have because instead she'd raised three children, and three grandchildren, and kept a home as well as a job too. She loved this flat because her daughter had made it her own, and Naina had always prided herself on letting her daughters do what felt best for them, and making a space in the world for themselves. "Because if you don't, who will?" she used to say.

Vritti was standing at the door ready to greet him as he came out of the lift. Her arms were open wide, as they always were whenever she was greeting family, friends. Ever since she was a little girl, she'd loved to play the host.

"Dada!" Jaya and Jayesh, Deepali's twins, chimed in unison from behind the door. Mukesh clamped his hands over his ears, hoping he wouldn't end the day with an earache as the two little ones hugged his legs.

Deepali stepped toward him as he headed for the kitchen. "Hi, Dad. Ooh, nice T-shirt. But aren't the sleeves a little short for you at your age?"

Mukesh only saw Lydia Bennet, in her fancy frock, staring out at him from Deepali's eyes.

"Hello, Deepali. No, I had a fashion adviser pick it out and this is exactly the right length."

Aleisha had helped him to pick out some new T-shirts and ordered them on the library computers. She had told him which arm length would suit him best. She chose the colors for him too. She selected one in an olive green that he wasn't sure would suit him; she said it was a "wicked" color at the moment. "Wicked" wasn't necessarily something he'd consider for himself, but he went with it. She was young, she'd nearly gotten a job in Topshop, so she *definitely* knew what she was talking about. She picked a navy blue one too—"Because you can never have too much navy blue," she'd said—and a white one as well. She called it the "summer staple."

Dressed like this, like a trendy person, he felt as though he fit in. In this sporty top, he was suddenly ageless, invincible. He thought of Nilakshi as she waited in the living room while he tried his new purchases on in his bedroom, walking out to show her—he called it a "fashion show" because Naina used to. "Ooh," Nilakshi had said, right on cue. "Very snazzy."

"Looks great, Papa!" Vritti said. "Come sit down!"

The table was set already. It was clear and white with a lovely bouquet of flowers set in the middle—Mukesh just knew Vritti had nipped out and picked them up that morning. They were fresh and colorful. It was a habit she'd picked up from Naina, and their first neighbor in London, who had turned up on their first day in their new home with a bunch of big daisies, greeting them with "Flowers for you! Lovely fresh blooms make a home." Vritti would beg and beg Naina to go and fetch some new flowers whenever the old ones were on their last legs.

Deepali sat down immediately, sighing, exhausted after constantly running around after her twins—he felt a quick pang of guilt for his Lydia Bennet comparison. His daughters weren't little horrors as children, were they? He always remembered that time so fondly—they were angels, that's what Naina said, always helping around the house, and they would sit nicely when they were meant to and eat whatever they were given.

The twins, Jaya and Jayesh, on the other hand, *looked* like angels, but instead liked to spend their time running up and down the house, crawling up and down the walls, and on rainy days they would get their felt-tip pens and draw on any surface they could find. Deepali's once perfectly decorated house had suffered because of it. She always said as long as they were happy that's all that really mattered.

As soon as the kids got their plates, they inhaled their chips and chicken nuggets. Pranav, Deepali's husband, was not a vegetarian and therefore the kids weren't either. Naina had been upset that Deepali hadn't convinced her entire nuclear family to follow their vegetarian Swaminarayan beliefs, but Mukesh didn't mind so much. Chicken nuggets would be much easier to make than mung beans, he thought, though he had just discovered halloumi fries, which were pretty easy too.

"How have you been, Papa?" Vritti asked, fetching some cutlery.

"Fine, yes, same same as always," he said. "What about you both?"

"Ah, Dad," Deepali said. "Rohini said you've been going to the library?"

"Yes! I have read so many books." He whipped out *Pride and Prejudice* from his jacket pocket—he hadn't read it on the Tube, but he liked carrying it with him, just as Naina always used to. "It's very good."

"*Pride and Prejudice*?" Deepali giggled. "I can't imagine you like it!"

"It isn't maybe my cup of chai, but the cover is nice." He held it up. "Your mummy always liked paintings like this—it feels very proper, like a good old book."

"Isn't it basically nineteenth-century smut?" Vritti laughed, sitting down at the table.

Mukesh's face blanched. "Smut? Really? I am only a quarter of the way through. I haven't seen smut yet."

"Just you wait." Vritti winked.

"How is Nilakshimasi?" Deepali asked, passing Vritti's colorful salad around. The question smashed into the table like a grenade. Vritti fell silent. Mukesh didn't move an inch. Even the twins seemed to freeze, their chicken nuggets in midair.

The reason he was really here, of course. Mukesh looked around the room, hoping that some invisible person might be able to answer for him. Vritti's eyes were fixed firmly on her plate.

"She is good, yes," he murmured.

"Lovely to see her the other day," Deepali said. "I didn't want to ask, but how is she after you know . . . what happened to her husband and son? So tragic. Mummy would have been devastated if she knew."

Mukesh took a deep breath. Typical *Lydia* Patel, he thought to himself. How would Mr. Bennet deal with his daughter talking to him like this? Lydia was always causing all kinds of fuss, ruining the family name on a whim. He wracked his brain. Mr. Bennet would *never* get into this situation in the first place, would he? He was always so stern—he commanded respect in a way that Mukesh probably didn't.

"I've heard she's getting over it rather quickly!" Deepali exchanged a glance with Vritti, but Vritti frowned at her in response, shaking her head slightly.

Deepali was talking as though Nilakshi was just *anyone*, not their mother's *best* friend. She had looked after them when they had been little, she had been by their side when Naina was ill, and she had driven them to and from Northwick Park Hospital when they were too tired to drive themselves. And now all Deepali cared about was the gossip.

"You have to move on with life," Mukesh said, more sharply than he had expected. "Grief can trap you for a while, and you have to be bold to step out of your comfort zone."

Vritti stepped in, trying to draw a line under the conversation. "Now, pile up your plates please!" she chirped. "Hope you like it."

Mukesh did as instructed, but as soon as he picked up the salad bowl, Deepali pulled it out of his hands. "I'll do that, Dad." When he reached for the bottle of water to pour into his stainless-steel cup, especially for him, Vritti took it out of his hands, and said, "Let me help you, Papa." He gave in.

When his plate was fully loaded, and his cup was up to the brim, he picked up his knife and fork, feeling slightly awkward holding them between his fingers, knowing he was being watched, but slowly he began to eat. And within moments, his two daughters had almost forgotten that he was there, as though he was a ghost at the table. "Papa's boiler is sometimes not working, we should get someone to look at it." "I don't think it's healthy the amount of mung he eats. I hope he is getting the chance to eat something else too." "I want him to start cooking new things—I just don't have the time to teach him." "He doesn't go to the mandir to eat a lot anymore, he should. They give balanced meals." "He seems all right most of the time."

"Talking of Nilakshimasi," Deepali said, even though they all knew that Vritti had put a stop to this line of inquiry, "Pranav's friend is also Swaminarayan and he heard that there is a lot of gossip about Nilakshimasi, spending time with men. You don't want to be the reason she gets a *reputation*, do you?"

Mukesh froze.

"Hold on," Vritti said. "Let it rest, Deeps."

"Papa, is Nilakshimasi looking to *re*marry?" Deepali smiled sweetly.

"Nilakshimasi is about Papa's age—she's not going to be remarrying," Vritti said matter-of-factly. "Now just move on, Deeps."

"I should hope not! That's not our way," Deepali huffed.

Mukesh looked at Vritti, and she rolled her eyes for his benefit. Deepali missed it entirely.

"Dad," Deepali said. "How often *do* you see her? When I saw her in your house, was that the first time?"

Mr. Bennet would never put up with this. Mr. Patel just gulped. "She is my friend. I see her every week, every few days. We keep each other company. What is your problem with that?" There, he'd said it, and now he waited for the chair to eat him alive, salad and all.

Deepali didn't respond.

Mukesh suddenly wished he could be at home with Nilakshi, telling her about how awkward this all was, and wondering whether she might teach him some more recipes, because Deepali and Vritti were probably right—he did eat mung too often.

The phone rang then, cutting through the tension.

"Hello?" Vritti said, picking up the handset. "Oh, it's Rohini," Vritti said to the room, as though she was in some kind of pantomime, but her face flushed and she looked embarrassed. "Ha, Papa and Deeps. And the twins." She nodded a little bit more. "Papa, Rohini wants to speak to you," she said, and handed the phone over.

Rohini spoke extra loudly just for him; he could see Deepali and Vritti and even the twins listening to every word.

"Dada is going to be told off by Rohinimasi!" Jayesh stage-whispered to his sister. "Mum told me she was going to call!"

Mukesh gulped again. He was being cornered.

"Papa, have you been spending much more time with Nilakshimasi than you should have been?"

"Hello, Rohini, lovely to speak to you too," he said sarcastically, his eyes jumping from Vritti, looking uncomfortable, to Deepali, triumphant.

"I bumped into Hetalmasi on the way to work, and she asked me if you two were now a couple."

"That is *not* true, and why would Hetalben know?" Mukesh was outraged. He was being spied on—he hadn't seen Hetal from the temple for months!

"I want you to be careful, Papa. We all know that Nilakshimasi is lovely, and kind, but we don't know what she wants from you. And it is important that people don't think that you are being disrespectful to Mummy in any way!"

Vritti stood up. "No one would ever think Papa is being disrespectful to Mummy," she said forcefully.

In the earpiece of the phone, Rohini's voice came again: "I'm not saying *we* would but some people have funny ideas. Not everything always seems so innocent."

Everyone was quiet for a little while.

"Papa, you love Mummy. We all know that. And you're allowed to be happy, but I'm worried some people will talk, say shameful things. And Nilakshimasi, I don't know if she can make you happy."

Mukesh stood up, still holding the phone to his ear.

"I am lonely, Rohini," he said, looking Vritti and Deepali in the eyes. "My wife died. My wife is gone. Her memory is still in here, and here"—he touched his heart, and his head—"but she is gone. You all have your own lives, you are busy. You have no time for me unless I can be useful. And when you do, you just fuss and fuss and fuss. And you don't listen to me! You don't actually have conversations! You just leave me voicemail messages and never expect me to call you back. You used to speak to your mother, you used to care for her. If you care for me too, and if you understood that I want a friend . . . Well, Nilakshi has been kind to me."

His heart was pounding. He could feel the skin on his head prickling with sweat. His hand holding the phone was moist; he held it tighter, hoping it wouldn't slip and fall. His ears thudded with his own blood. Vritti and Deepali looked at him. Vritti seemed pleased, trying hard not to let a smile curl the corners of her mouth, but Deepali looked sad, pitying.

Mukesh shrank back into his seat. He had enjoyed feeling big, vast, powerful, for that moment. And now, with one look from his youngest daughter, and hearing a sigh through the phone from his middle daughter, he felt small again, like a child.

He passed the phone back to Vritti, who held it at arm's length. "Vritti, thank you for a lovely lunch. I must go now. Goodbye. Jaya, Jayesh, bye!"

Jaya and Jayesh were watching TV now, chicken nuggets decimated in front of them; they weren't listening.

"Deepali, bye," Mukesh continued. He collected his hat, shaking. He shuffled his way out of the door and shut it behind him.

He stood in the corridor a moment, trying to get his breath back, find his bearings, hoping that one of his daughters would come after him. They didn't. On the other side of the door, their conversation continued without him.

"He felt ambushed. It was clearly a setup," Vritti hissed. "He's not an idiot. Who calls up their sister randomly to ask to speak to their father to see if he's in a relationship? I *knew* it was a stupid idea, but you never listen to me! Why can't you let him enjoy his life?"

"Don't go pretending *we* are the bad ones. It is probably you who has put these silly ideas into his head in the first place. This independent, do-what-you-want mentality you have. At least we got it out in the open rather than just talking about it in the family WhatsApp!"

Mukesh didn't want to hear any more. He made his way into the lift, and before he knew it, he was back on the street, back on the train, and, eventually, back home.

CHAPTER 23

ALEISHA

The credits were rolling, and Leilah hadn't fallen asleep. She hadn't sat down to watch a film with *anyone* in years. It was a Disney film, so nothing that required concentration, but it was an achievement enough. Aleisha was half-baffled, half-waiting for the spell to break—it had been days since their failed picnic, but for Leilah, that all seemed to be forgotten.

Aleisha had watched as her mum beamed, showing off the gap between her front teeth. Her mother's smile always took her back to long-ago family trips to the beach, like a photograph imprinted on her memory.

She wished Aidan were here to see it. He'd tell her to be careful, to not get her hopes up—he'd remind her that there may still be a few more weeks, even months, to go until Leilah was "totally herself" again.

Right now, though, that didn't matter. They had been a dull, boring, ordinary family for an hour and a half. It was all Aleisha wanted.

She remembered film nights with Leilah when she and Aidan were little, usually when Dean was working late. They'd curl up together under a blanket if it was winter, tuck into a bowl of Tesco's own vanilla ice cream if it was summer. Aidan usually insisted on sprinkles—chocolate sprinkles, hundreds and thousands. Aleisha preferred syrup. Sometimes Leilah allowed both. They'd dubbed these their film critic nights, because they'd watch the film and then talk for ages afterward—discussing different characters, funny bits, the sad bits too. Leilah would ask probing questions like "What did that character learn from what he did?" Aleisha recognized herself doing this in her conversations with Mr. P, trying to find out a little more about his views on each book. Leilah did it to spark conversation, to help their favorite moment last longer. To keep them in the bubble, the bubble that would burst as soon as Dean came home and everything had to go back to boring reality—getting ready for bed, then for school, so Dean could settle down in front of the TV himself and unwind with the ten o'clock news. She missed the three of them just being in one another's company with nothing else to worry about but the character motivations and the theme music.

"What did you think?" Aleisha asked as Leilah watched the screen, her mother's palms held together as if in prayer.

"It was quite *emotional*!" Leilah said softly, still staring at the credits. Her face was illuminated by the television in all its different colors: reds, blues, greens. All the creases in her mother's face were clear: the expressions, the sadness. She was lovely.

"Thank you," Leilah said, still staring, gently squeezing Aleisha's hand as her daughter stood beside her.

"You're welcome," Aleisha replied, unsure of what she was being thanked for.

"Come sit with me?" Leilah slapped the cushion of the seat beside her.

Aleisha did as she was told, not wanting to break the spell again.

"How are you?" Leilah looked at her.

Aleisha let the question hang in the silence between them for a moment, not wanting to say the wrong thing.

"Yeah, I'm okay." She opened her mouth to continue, but her mind was a blank.

"Who's that person you *keep* texting?" Leilah asked as Aleisha's phone buzzed.

"What?" Aleisha flushed.

"That person—the one you're messaging now. Someone you're always on your phone to when you're here. Who?"

Aleisha looked at the message from Zac: Hey, you all right? How was the film? Fancy that coffee sometime soon?

"Oh, no one," she mumbled. "A friend."

"A *boy*friend! Do you have a boyfriend?!" Leilah's eyes glinted with girlish glee. Aleisha couldn't help but smile for a moment.

"No, no, no. It's no one." An image of Zac dressed in Jane Austen–style clothes, a formal, frilly white shirt, popped up in her mind. She covered her face with her hands.

"Someone you work with? You mentioned someone called Kyle before?"

"No!" She was horrified at the suggestion.

"You have to tell me."

Aleisha laughed. She hated this. But her mother actually gave a shit if she was seeing a guy. *That* was new.

"Are you going to invite him round?"

It was like Leilah believed they were living a different life at times like this, as if she and Aidan could invite friends around at the drop of a hat.

"So, come on, spill, who's the guy?"

"Why do you think it's a guy?"

"Look, I might be old but I know it's a guy and I want to know everything. Not because I'm your mum, just because. Why can't I know something fun and exciting? Look at me!" Leilah held her arms out to the side. She looked small. Her T-shirt was sagging around her waist, and her legs were crossed tightly in front of her.

"But I mean, what if it was a girl? Not a guy."

"I don't mind either way. You'll tell me!"

Aleisha sighed. "His name's Zac. I saw him on the train once. And then he helped me home from the shop with my bags and he lives not far from here. And I saw him at the park and he insisted on giving me his number and we've been talking."

"Love at first sight."

"Mum!"

"Okay, that's fine. Just tell me more!"

"He studies law—"

"That's it. Marry him!" Leilah put her hands in the air, theatrically.

"I've always said you were going to study law! We could soon have two lawyers in the family!"

"No! Chill out." Aleisha was staring straight ahead at the wall, embarrassed. "But he's being really helpful and said he'll show me some of his uni prospectuses. He's kept them all."

"What a line." Leilah winked. "No, no. I'm kidding. He sounds like a good guy. He's how old?"

"Twenty. Not too old."

"That's *okay*. I dated a few twenty-six-year-olds when I was your age."

"Mum!"

"Not at the same time. And does he know about your other love?"

"What other love?"

"The list. That reading list you showed me."

Aleisha was startled that she had even remembered.

"No, that's nothing."

"*That* could be the start of a love affair. What if the list curator is your perfect guy or girl? It could be a Richard Curtis movie."

Aleisha didn't reply.

"Well . . . something about this list has really hooked you. You're still reading, yes? This boy hasn't distracted you?"

Aleisha contemplated this for a moment. "Yes, Mum. I'm still reading. I'm enjoying them, and I'm interested. Besides, it gives me something to do while everyone else is going to Reading Festival, or whatever. Or they're on holidays or working somewhere decent. I've not seen anyone in ages, and no one chats to me. It's like I'm not even around."

Aleisha took a deep breath. The list wasn't just a distraction for her anymore. She'd learned how to fight for something you believe in from Atticus Finch; she'd learned how to survive with a tiger like Pi; she'd learned never to stay in a creepy house in Cornwall, maybe just go to a B&B or something instead; and from Amir in *The Kite Runner* she'd discovered it was never too late to do the right thing. *Pride and Prejudice* . . . that was more like a guilty pleasure read, but she liked aspects of it—especially the parts that reminded her of Zac.

She thought of Mukesh now—her new, unlikely friend. He'd been a good companion for her at the library. The last time he'd been in, she'd seen him sitting up very straight, with his reading glasses pulled halfway down his nose, focusing on *Pride and Prejudice*.

"Hey, Mr. P," Crime Thriller Guy (Chris) had said to him, wandering past. "Enjoying that?"

Mr. P had shrugged. "Not right now . . ."

Aleisha had laughed to herself—she didn't expect Mr. P, usually so polite, to be so honest.

"I liked the characters—they were very, very funny. All sorts of characters. But the story line, I don't think it is very . . . what's the word . . . *relatable* for me, Aleisha?" Mr. P had said. She wasn't sure it was very relatable for her either. According to the internet, though, people loved this book—thought of it as some kind of feminist bible.

"What do you think of Darcy and Elizabeth? Did it take you back to your wooing days?" she teased.

"No, no. This is not at all how my marriage started," Mr. P said to her, almost looking for a reason to put the book down.

"What do you mean?" she'd asked.

"There was none of this prolonged courtship. We were thrown into it—like those marriage matches Mrs. Bennet loves to set up. We had an arranged marriage—the first time I met Naina was a little before our wedding—but it was the most special moment of my life. My wife—she was *perfect*. I was so lucky." For a moment, his mind drifted off. "You see, just because we didn't spend months chasing after each other, like Elizabeth and Mr. Darcy, it doesn't mean it wasn't meant to be. We didn't know each other at all, but it felt like I'd known her my whole life. I could open up to her. And I did; it was the best decision I'd made."

Aleisha had thought of Zac then—of the first time she'd seen him; wondering whether she'd known then that they might become friends.

"From the first moment you meet Mr. Darcy and Miss Elizabeth, you know that they're meant to be together. The rest of the book is just the author trying to keep them apart for our entertainment."

Mr. P was right—she wondered if her own reluctance to be honest and open with Zac, who was trying so *desperately* to help her open up, was actually the main thing keeping Aleisha shut off and alone . . . just for the sake of it, for the entertainment of her imaginary readers.

Leilah shuffled herself closer to Aleisha, snapping her out of her daze.

"Have you told your brother about the list? He loves that library."

"If he loves the library so much, why doesn't he go anymore?"

"He's busy, he's working a lot. He doesn't have the time that you have."

Leilah's words had their unintended sting. "Look, I'm sorry, I didn't mean that. I know I'm not easy to talk to, I know how much you two do for me, and how hard everything has been. I really wish I could help you out more, but I want you to feel you can tell me anything. And Aidan. You both come first for me."

Aleisha tried to keep her surprise out of her voice, and said, cautiously, "Mum, that's nice." She then took a deep breath, worried about how her next few words might land. "But I want you to be here for yourself too."

A cloud settled on Leilah's features for a moment before being banished away by her false cheery tone: "I bet she's a teacher. I'm so sure of it. Who writes reading lists other than teachers?"

"Why are you so sure it's a woman?"

"I'm not, but feels like it could be?"

"I guess *all* women write lists, do they?"

"Maybe it's Aidan. He loves the library, and I *know* Aidan writes you lists all the time."

"Yeah, but I really cannot imagine Aidan *ever* reading *Pride and Prejudice* . . . or *Little Women*." Aleisha pulled out another list—this one in Aidan's WhatsApp messages to her. "'Sugar. Lamb. Get washing-up liquid. Order food recycling bags from council. Take out bins tonight. PUT NEW BIN BAG IN EMPTY BIN.'" Aleisha read it out loud, enunciating the words in capital letters. "Now, that bin-bag stuff . . . *that's* the true beginning of a love story."

The two women burst into fits of laughter and soon found they couldn't stop. They held on to each other for dear life as they heard Aidan's key turn in the lock.

"Oh, hey." His voice drifted into the living room.

"Hey!" Aleisha said, jolting herself away from her mother as though she'd just been scalded.

"What's going on, guys?" His eyes were tired, but he held himself up tall, a smile stuck on his face, as though he was trying to inject some kind of energy into himself.

"We just watched that Disney film *Up*."

"It. Was. Great!" Leilah enunciated, illustrating each full stop with a poke of her finger into her thigh.

Aidan nodded. "All right, sounds okay." Leilah and Aleisha both smiled at each other, and glanced back at Aidan, who'd already turned away and was walking up the stairs. "Cool, well, I'm shattered."

"Why the long face, Aidan?" Leilah asked, giggling away to herself.

Aidan shot a soft glance at his sister, avoiding his mother's gaze. "Long shift." He yawned. "Going to bed. See you in the morning, guys." From halfway up the stairs, he boomed, "Aleisha, don't forget to do the bins!"

Leilah brushed her hand over Aleisha's hair. "He's good to us, isn't he?"

She nodded. Leilah pushed herself up from the sofa and left the room. Then, alone in the living room, Aleisha felt a chill. It was noticeable, in a house that had recently only ever been stifling hot, and she suddenly realized the windows were wide open. She couldn't remember opening them herself.

CHAPTER 24

MUKESH

Beep. You have no new messages.

Mukesh felt a lump in his throat build. He slumped down on the sofa, staring straight ahead. He hadn't seen Nilakshi in days, he hadn't returned her phone calls. He hadn't been to the library either. *Pride and Prejudice* was still sitting on his bedside table. He'd tried, he'd tried so hard, but whenever he started to read, his mind just wandered. He'd just think back to Vritti's house, and everything his daughters had said, and hadn't said too.

He'd failed—himself, Aleisha, his girls. And Naina. Naina—she'd been silent for so long. Despite everything he was doing, trying to let her spirit live on in him, through the books, it felt as if she was lost to him.

Reputation. That word pulsated in his mind—Deepali's face, the disappointment in her eyes, it still stung.

He lay back on his bed, staring up at the ceiling. The last few weeks, all those moments when he'd felt like he was *achieving* things—it meant nothing in the end. Because here he was, back at square one.

An hour later, there was a knock on the door. Mukesh hauled himself up from the bed, his head heavy and sore, slipped his slippers on, and slid his way across the hallway.

"Vritti?" he said as he pulled the door wide.

"Hi, Papa." Vritti's voice was soft. "I just wanted to pop in for a chai. Are you free?"

Mukesh felt his eyes sting with tears, but he blinked them away as he stepped aside to let his daughter through.

"Sachet chai?" Vritti asked, wandering straight to the kitchen.

"Yes, okay, but please add Canderel. Rohini bought the unsweetened ones last time." Mukesh hovered in the kitchen doorway, watching Vritti make her way around the kitchen like it was her home.

"Fine by me, but don't tell *her* I'm doing that!" Vritti called back. "I'd never hear the end of it. You go sit down, Papa, put your feet up."

He did as he was told, unsure what to say.

Moments later, Vritti walked in, balancing two chais on Naina's little tea tray with some extra tablets of Canderel sweetener scattered all over, between the mugs. She placed it down gently on the table next to Mukesh, but still managed to spill some tea onto the tray. The Canderel began to float, and some began to swim as fast as they could to reach the shore. Some survived, others slowly disintegrated. Vritti and Mukesh just watched for a moment, until Rohini's scolding came to them through the inertia: *Get some kitchen towels. Clean that up!*

"I got this!" Mukesh looked at Vritti, his eyes bright. His arm reached down beside his armchair and he brought a handheld vacuum with a squeegee top into view. "It cleans up water!"

Vritti laughed. "Where on earth did you get that, and why?"

"Those television programs. It was *so* easy! This is the second time I have used it for a proper reason. Most of the time I just use it for condensation on the shower."

Vritti laughed again, and Mukesh suddenly saw how ridiculous it was, how mundane, and he started to chuckle too.

"How long have you had it?"

"About three months. You know, when my Netflix wasn't working, so I got very hooked on those shopping channels. Silly stuff, but *this is* useful!"

The doorbell punctuated their afternoon once more, and Mukesh felt the blood drain from his face. Vritti was here . . . What if, could this be another cornering? He looked up at the portrait of Naina, hoping for a sign, a warning.

"Do *you* know who that might be?" Mukesh asked Vritti, who shrugged casually.

He shuffled into the hallway and cautiously opened the door.

"Dada!" came two squealing voices. Within seconds, two little pairs of arms had clasped themselves around Mukesh's legs, and Deepalydia Bennet was standing in front of him, but without the bonnet he'd imagined all the Bennet sisters would wear.

"Hi, Dad," she said tentatively.

"Deepali," he said, smiling. Just behind her masi was Priya, smiling from ear to ear.

"Rohini just called me, asked me to pick up Priya so she could spend some time with you, and these two wanted to see you as well." Deepali nudged the twins inside and looked down at her hands. He had known Deepali all her life, and imagined her to be bubbling with awkwardness inside. "I just—I just wanted to say sorry, for the other day. It was unfair of me. I could just hear Mummy telling me off, she's been in my head ever since . . ." She *hated* apologizing . . .

Mukesh thought of good old Atticus Finch from *To Kill a Mockingbird*—old enough and wise enough to rise above any personal falling-outs. And this was his *daughter*—while he didn't always understand her, he knew she didn't want to hurt him. Jaya and Jayesh rushed into the living room to pester Vritti, as Deepali leaned forward and clutched her father.

"Oih," Mukesh grunted. "Don't squeeze too hard, I am an old man now."

Deepali didn't move. "I miss her," Deepali said, into his shoulder. "I just miss her."

Mukesh felt a frog jump in his throat. "I know, beti, I miss her too. Every day." He saw his daughter, years younger, a little older than Priya perhaps, coming home from school crying. He had been able to understand how she felt then, when he'd seen the tears streaming down her face. But the other day, at Vritti's house, he hadn't seen the hurt behind the anger, he hadn't seen how much she was missing her mother. She was always so brave, so bold. As Atticus said, the only way he could see what it was really like for Deepali would be to walk around in her skin.

"Come in, beta," he said, leading his family to the living room. Deepali settled herself in her mother's favorite chair, and Jaya and Jayesh crowded at her feet. Priya wandered straight over to her dada, holding her book up to him, excited. "I have only just started reading, but it is *lovely*. I know about Atticus Finch now." He beamed. For a moment, Mukesh couldn't quite believe his luck. He couldn't wait to tell Aleisha that the books she'd recommended were, so far, a big success with Priya. She had found him books he could read with his granddaughter after all.

"Dada," Priya chirped. "What's *this* book about?" She held up *Pride and Prejudice*. He could tell she was trying to take her Deepali-masi's mind off everything and anything.

"It's a love story, isn't it?" Vritti volunteered.

"Ha, in some ways," Mukesh said. "Bossy Mrs. Bennet wants to marry her daughters off to rich men. But one of her daughters, Elizabeth Bennet, she wants to marry for love, not money," he explained to Priya.

"Dada," Priya said. "Do you think Ba read this book?"

Deepali looked up at her father. "I bet she did, even I've read it."

"Are you her Mr. Darcy, Papa?" Vritti and Deepali chuckled; Priya looked completely blank, but she smiled anyway.

"I don't think so! I've never been that suave. Besides, your mummy had no choice with me," he said self-deprecatingly. "But, she was my entire world." In his mind's eye, he saw Naina on their wedding day—the first moment they'd met. He had been scared; he hadn't known this woman at all but she was about to become his family. "She always knew how to make people feel comfortable, didn't she?"

"Why do you think the temple made her come to every event?" Deepali said, rolling her eyes.

"I remember my mother taking me aside the day before my wedding," Mukesh continued, "telling me what a lovely girl she was, intelligent, kind. I didn't want to believe her—she just sounded too good to be true. And I felt so strongly that if I'd been given the time and freedom, I could have chosen someone better for me. But then I met her and, instantly, I knew . . ."

"What, Dada?" Priya asked.

"I knew your ba was the *only* person right for me!"

Their courtship began after the wedding. Every day with Naina brought surprises. The first was what Naina looked like in the morning—remarkably, no one had braced him for the fact that she might look the same as any other time of the day. But even years down the line the surprises continued: when his father was dying of a slow illness, Naina knew what to say.

"Mukesh?" She'd appeared in the doorway one morning, a huge book clutched in her hands. She'd brought it toward him—a family album that she had put together. "It's for you."

He'd only had a few photos in there of his childhood, but there was one of him, sitting on his father's knee—their faces were stern, but immediately Mukesh's father had come to life for him. He didn't know where that album was now. Tucked away somewhere safe, he supposed.

"What was he like? When you were young?" Naina had asked.

"He could be scary, I remember that. He was always telling me off if I ran around in the house, or got my shoes too dusty from outside. But he *loved* playing with me—we played cricket." He laughed.

Naina frowned. "But you're *terrible* at cricket."

"I know—I took after him. He was terrible too." He'd smiled; he'd held the photo album close, peeling off that photo of him and his father, their eyes highlighted by kohl as though they were in some kind of awful Goth band. He hadn't thought anyone would be able to soothe him in those months, but Naina had. Speaking about his boyhood, about his relationship with his father, was one way of coming to terms with the fact that his father wouldn't be around forever.

He only wished that when Naina had gone too, Naina had been there holding his hand. Leading him through his grief step by step.

Though he'd held on to her in his own small ways, it wasn't quite enough.

As Mukesh's mind wandered into the past, Priya wrapped her arms around him the way she used to wrap her arms around Naina, anchoring him in the present with his family.

They love you, he heard in the distance. *They've always loved you.*

He'd know that voice anywhere—it was Naina. She was back once more.

"Papa." Deepali walked toward him. "I'm glad you've found people, people to talk to, you know? At the library. The temple. Nilakshimasi." She pulled him into a hug. "Mummy would be so proud of you."

Little Women

by

LOUISA MAY ALCOTT

CHAPTER 25

ALEISHA

"You all right, Aleisha?"

It was "Call Me Chris"—Crime Thriller—approaching the desk, a heavy-looking rucksack on his back, no doubt laden with books.

"Yeah," Aleisha said, wiping hair out of her tired eyes, her fingers frantically searching for the to-do list she'd left somewhere on her desk. "Just having one of those days."

"I can see. Don't worry, I've seen that woman in here arguing about the same thing when Dev and Kyle have been on duty."

"Really? She does this every time?"

"Yeah, I'm pretty sure she must just click the wrong library when she orders online."

Aleisha had just, quite publicly, been ambushed by a rather disgruntled customer who had come to pick up a book order, only to discover the books had been sent to Hanwell Library instead. As Thermos Flask Dev would have wanted her to, she took full responsibility on behalf of Brent Libraries, and had offered to pick the books up from Hanwell and *home-deliver* them to her, just to get her to go away. The woman had charged out, grumbling: "*This* is why so many libraries are closing down. Useless, poorly run. I bet this place will be the next to go."

"I literally could do without this today. I've got to go pick the books up from Hanwell now."

Crime Thriller Guy pulled a face to show his sympathy, before wandering off to his usual spot, a new hardback thriller, just delivered today, tucked under his arm.

The irate woman had been holding a reading list of her own, written on a scrap of paper, which she'd held aloft in her hand in a gesture of *So there, the customer is always right*. The woman had waved it frantically, so she couldn't make out the handwriting, but Aleisha *hoped* more than anything that that woman hadn't written Aleisha's reading list. That really would ruin the magic, wouldn't it?

One of the books the woman had ordered was *Beloved*, and it *was* in the Harrow Road Library, but tucked safely in Aleisha's bag . . . checked out ready to read weeks ago. She could have given it to her there and then, one small step to placating her. But she wasn't about to give it up. The books, the *list*, it had become too important.

A few nights ago, she'd been reading to Leilah again while they were waiting for Aidan to come home.

"Where is he?" Leilah said. "He's never normally this late."

"Mum, it's all right, he's always late. He'll be home soon." Aleisha had opened the copy of *Little Women*, feeling Leilah's eyes trained on the pages, as if a spell had been cast once more.

"Wait," Leilah said. "What's *Little Women* about then? I've heard of it."

Aleisha turned to the back cover—she scanned the text. "Right, it's about four sisters in New England . . . set in the 1860s." She continued to scan. "It's about their attempts to help their family make more money, their friendship with a family living close by . . . and their later 'love affairs,' apparently. There's Meg, who dreams of being a *lady*; Jo . . . it says she's based on the author herself—she wants to be a writer. Beth is quiet and delicate . . . she likes music, and then there's Amy, she's a 'blond beauty.' The pretty one." Aleisha kept running her eyes over the cover. Leilah was nodding, focused on the middle distance. "Ready?" Aleisha asked.

"Yes, go on."

On the first page, Aleisha had stumbled her way across the line "'We haven't got Father, and shall not have him for a long time.'" Her eyes paid close attention to Leilah's face. The line was about the March sisters' father, he was away at war, but Aleisha couldn't help thinking of Dean. Leilah's eyes were downcast, but there was a faint smile decorating her face. She was already with the March sisters for the moment; she hadn't made the tenuous connection to their own life that Aleisha had.

Mr. P had mentioned this book—apparently it was one of his granddaughter's favorites. As she stepped further into the story, she saw exactly why a young girl might enjoy it—it was joyful, it was different, to learn about all the ways to be a young woman in an ever-changing world. It was an old story, but the March sisters, they were vibrant, gutsy; they followed their dreams, whatever they might be.

Jo, Aleisha liked Jo. Jo was spiky, ambitious, always writing plays and directing her sisters to bring them to life, bringing joy into the family home. She brought a smile to Leilah's face too. "I like her," Leilah said, once they'd been reading together for more than an hour—it was a record, Aleisha was amazed. "She reminds me of you. You were bossy like that when you were little." Aleisha couldn't see the comparison herself, but something in her warmed. "No wonder that boy next door—Laurie, is that his name?"

Aleisha nodded.

"No wonder he loves Jo. She's the best one," Leilah finished. "She knows how to do it—treats him mean, keeps him keen . . ."

"They're friends, Mum, I'm not sure she's *treating him mean*!"

The two of them giggled where they were seated for a moment, before it trickled away to silence. And Aleisha continued to read: "'How happy and good we'd be if we had no worries' . . ."

She sighed and looked up. Leilah's eyes were closed, squeezed tight shut, as though she didn't want to let those words ring out in the real world. They could exist only in the world of the March sisters, and nowhere else.

At that moment, Aidan arrived back home, making a racket as he shoved open the door and dropped his bags on the floor. He shut the door behind him.

"Shh," Aleisha said, tiptoeing into the hall. "Hey, what's all this noise about?"

Aidan just gave her a quick pat on the arm and stomped into the kitchen.

"Mum's resting." Aleisha followed him. "I've been reading to her."

Aidan poured himself a glass of water from the bottle in the fridge. He downed it all before he looked at his sister for the first time.

"Aidan . . . I'm just amazed, you know, it's really working. She's like getting into them."

"That's really good, Leish," Aidan said absently. He was wandering around the kitchen, picking bits from various cupboards: a plate, a fork, and a knife, a Tupperware of leftover curry. He didn't look her in the eyes.

"I'm glad there's something that I can actually do to help. Usually it's only you who can get through to her," Aleisha said, silently begging him to pause for a moment. To allow himself a moment to just stay still.

Aidan looked at her then. "Aleisha, it's not just me who can get through to her. You do it too. You're good at it. Better than me really." His voice was soft, distant. "I'm happy the books are working, for you both."

Aleisha looked down at her feet this time—it was a half-compliment, but it was more than she'd had from anyone in a long time.

"Mum seems to be doing much better now anyway, doesn't she?" Aidan prompted.

Aleisha shrugged.

Aidan started piling his food onto his plate. "I'm sorry we've not seen each other much—work's been busy, and I know I've been focused on having someone at home with Mum all the time, but, I don't know, she's doing better, way better."

Aleisha watched him. She didn't agree—but she didn't want to say that to Aidan. She could see he was trying to convince himself. It wasn't like her brother to be *optimistic* when it came to Leilah. What was on his mind?

"I've got loads of shifts over the next few days, Leish," he continued. "I won't see you much, okay? But Mum'll be fine, you'll be great with her. You *are* great." He turned around then and smiled at her.

"I'll miss you," Aleisha said quietly. "It's been ages since we just spent time together."

"I know, but you'll do fine without me. Whatever you're doing with Mum, it's really working, Leish."

He headed out of the kitchen, his plate in his hand, and gave her shoulder a squeeze. "All right?" he said to her. She nodded. Before she could ask him the same thing in return, he trudged up to his room without turning back around.

Trying to lighten Aidan's mood, Aleisha left a jokey *Welcome Home* Post-it for him on the fridge. But he'd been true to his word—she heard him click the door quietly shut in the morning before she got up, she heard the door squeak open again when he got home, but besides that, there hadn't been any indication as to his presence other than the Post-it notes he'd stuck to the fridge to remind her to do things. They had been, once again, ships in the night. All she really wanted was to hang out with her brother, find out how he was, actually talk to him. She knew there was something on his mind, something he wasn't telling her.

She turned this all over in her mind as she clutched *Beloved* close to her. She wasn't going to give it up to the grumpy woman at the library. If Aidan wasn't around for a few days, working nonstop, the only power Aleisha had to keep Leilah calm was the books. The books filled the space where there had once been silence.

Mr. Patel would be at the library soon. She had checked out another edition of *Little Women* for him already. She imagined he'd be excited to read it—it was the one book he seemed to talk about frequently, without having any idea of what it was about. Though he often called it *Little Ladies*.

Eleven o'clock came and went. Eleven thirty came and went too. Aleisha kept checking the clock, checking the door. No one else bothered her. Everyone opted for the self-service machines today, or just settled themselves down into armchairs to read. She was glad of the peace. But she'd been looking forward to talking to Mr. P. He never gave very much away, but she found it so refreshing to talk to someone who wasn't her brother or her mother, and she wanted to hear more about his trip into London with Priya. For some reason, she'd become invested in this old man's life, maybe as a distraction from her own, but maybe because they were friends now too.

Mr. Patel came with no preconceptions. He didn't look at her as though she was "troubled," though she had told him some things about her "shitty home life." That's how she put it. He had said, "Oh, is your dad not around?" and she'd laughed at how clichéd it was. That it was clichéd, but spot-on.

"He has his own family now."

"You are his family too."

"Not to him."

Mukesh had kissed his teeth then. "Stupid idiot." He had tried to say it quietly, but she had caught it anyway.

"Oh, hai, I am *so* sorry. Bad potty mouth!" Mukesh's hand flew instinctively to his mouth, his eyes wide with surprise.

She laughed.

"No, you're right! Stupid idiot. I wish my mum knew that too. That it was all on him. Not her."

"I am sure she knows. Sometimes men are stupid. I think, anyway. I have three daughters, and none of them are stupid."

Aleisha's phone buzzed next to her, bringing her back to the present.

Hey! How is book life going?

It was Zac—he'd messaged her every day since the park: first a hello, followed by a book meme or a cat meme (turned out he really liked cats—she couldn't imagine Mr. Darcy liking cats particularly). She'd tried to keep her replies short, not giving too much away. Aleisha thought of Leilah's comment: *Treat them mean, keep them keen*. Was Aleisha taking on Leilah's warped *Little Women* life advice? It would be harder than it sounded. Because she *wanted* to talk to him *all* the time.

Nightmare customer just ruined my life! Aleisha texted back.

Do you need anything? Zac's reply came almost instantly.

Talking to Zac was easier—she didn't say "fine" when she really meant "having a shit day," she just said "having a shit day." He didn't know the person she was trying to be with everyone else, so with him she could just be herself.

What you doing later?

No plans! Zac—she knew, deep down—was like her. An outsider, a lonely soul. But Zac wore it well—he never acted as though he wanted to be anything other than himself.

Would be great to see you. I might need your help with something later. If you're up for it? Book business . . . But as soon as she typed it all out, she deleted it and rewrote her message with less eagerness: Might need your help with something—it was the best she could do.

Suddenly her phone started flashing. *Incoming call: Zac.*

Before hitting the green button, she felt her heart pound in the middle of her throat for a moment. She'd never spoken to Zac on the phone before. "Hello?" She heard her voice, higher and squeakier than normal.

"Hi. Want to go for a drive later? If you can. Thinking of going to somewhere like Richmond. Through the park. What do you think?" He sounded his usual cool, calm, collected self.

Aleisha had never been to Richmond. She knew Aidan was in this evening, for the first time this week, so as long as she was back by nine, before he had to head out for his next shift, she was free to do what she liked. But it felt like too much to ask of Zac, to outline a curfew as if she were a twelve-year-old. Her skin started to prickle with nerves, her thoughts darting to Leilah.

"Yeah, that would be nice," she said, shutting down the doubts in her mind. Her voice quivered with awkwardness. "I actually need your car. Happy to help?"

"Obviously, boss. Text me when your shift ends and I'll pick you up. It'll be really nice to see you."

By the time Aleisha was locking up, Zac was already sitting outside in his Vauxhall Corsa, the windows wide open, music softly tinkling out. The complete opposite of Aidan, who was *only* capable of playing music at an antisocial decibel in his car.

He had his forearm resting on the door. He saw her; his face lit up. Aleisha couldn't tell if she was hungry or if her stomach was actually doing somersaults. Elizabeth Bennet and her standoffishness would *not* be impressed with her.

As she opened the car door, she suddenly felt exposed. She shuffled into the seat, scared about hitting her head on the roof, or knocking the gear lever or something stupid like that. She felt as though she'd lost control of her limbs.

"Hi," he said, "ready? Where we going?"

"Absolutely, first stop, Hanwell Library. We need to get there ASAP. Someone's waiting." She used her formal business tone, reserved only for grumpy library customers, to mask the anxiety pumping through her chest.

"Top secret mission. Love it," he joked.

They drove mostly in silence, or more accurately in annoyingly subtle music, for a while. And, eventually, the traffic and the heat got to them. Zac grew steadily frustrated as the temperature ramped up in the car as the traffic crawled along.

"This is meant to be a twenty-minute drive, if that, and I feel like we've been here for an hour."

"It's been half an hour, and we're nearly there," Aleisha said consolingly. She realized she was using the voice Aidan sometimes adopted with Leilah, and her mind flew to the two of them. What were they doing? Was Aidan sitting with Leilah? Were they watching a film? She felt a pang of guilt that she was here, with someone, and they were both at home. She could have been spending the evening with her brother, for the first time in forever.

She gulped the regret down, with no time to waste or wallow, and as they pulled up, Aleisha jumped out of the car and knocked on the Hanwell Library door. The librarian was sitting there, typing something into her computer, the angry customer's books already stacked up next to her, ordered, as suspected, to the wrong library.

After another twenty-six-minute drive, more sassy comments from Zac, through the traffic and damp heat of the high road, Aleisha finally dropped the books off with the woman right on her doorstep.

"Finally," the woman said.

"You're welcome." Aleisha beamed back, hoping the woman could smell the sarcasm.

"Took you long enough." She took the books and shut her door with no whisper of thanks.

Aleisha rolled her eyes—she *so* wanted to say something back, to shout through the letterbox, but she thought of Marmee, the March sisters' mum, who was all about being polite to anyone and everyone. She was fictional, but she was right. It wasn't worth it.

Jumping back in the car, she barked directions off her phone, hoping that Zac was okay with doing one last trip before their evening out.

"Right here—after that sign."

"Okay, boss."

"End of this road, take a left, following the signs to Wembley High Road."

"Got it, boss."

"Then it's the next left, followed by the third right."

"Hold on, hold on, you're going too fast." He switched the radio off, wound up the windows, and turned the AC on. "That's better, finally space to think."

Aleisha rolled her eyes. Zac's gaze was fixed firmly on the road.

"Left onto here!" she called. "Quick, or you'll miss it!"

"What! Where was the advance warning?" He checked his mirrors and took a tight left turn.

They pulled up at the house as her phone told her: "You have now reached your destination." A car was sitting in the drive.

"Just wait here," she told Zac, and grabbed another book from her bag.

Zac kept the car idling. Aleisha felt nervous as she approached the door. She was definitely breaking library rules, using the system to find out his address. She hoped Mr. P wouldn't tell on her.

She rang the doorbell. Aleisha could hear a voice inside, but not Mukesh's. The TV was probably on. One of those Indian channels. A little while later, when Aleisha was about to turn away and give up hope, the door opened to reveal a woman, in her seventies perhaps, wearing a dark blue Punjabi suit with a white contrast scarf around her neck.

"Hello, how may I help?" the lady said. Her voice was quite low but held warmth.

"Hello, I am here to give a book to Mr. Patel. He didn't pick it up from the library today . . . It was on my way home . . . thought I'd drop it off."

"Mukeshbhai!" the woman called into the house. Mr. P shuffled through a doorway. He was wearing jogging bottoms with a few turmeric-colored spillages dotted on the lap area and a T-shirt once white, now a dull gray, again with a ketchup stain on the chest. Aleisha had never seen him in anything other than nice trousers, a shirt, and his trusty cap.

As soon as he saw her, his face dropped. "Miss Aleisha! No, you shouldn't see me like this."

He hurried back the way he had come.

"Hold on, darling. Can you wait?" the woman said. Aleisha nodded. She looked back at Zac in the car. He was resting his head back on his car seat, staring at the ceiling.

She heard their muffled voices coming from what she thought must be the living room, but they were speaking in another language and Aleisha couldn't make out their words.

Just as Aleisha thought she should probably leave, Mr. P came out again, wearing a winter coat covering his spillages; he was sweating.

"Come in. Nilakshiben has made dinner. She would like you to eat with us. I need to get a shirt on."

The woman came back to the door as Mr. Patel made his way to another room, slowly. She could see his hip was causing him pain.

"Is he okay?" Aleisha asked.

"He had a bit of a fall yesterday but he's totally fine. He was running around after his grandchildren, and now feels a little bit useless. I am looking after him today."

"I really don't want to intrude. I just wanted to drop this off." She held the book out to Nilakshiben.

"No, I insist. Come in and eat. It is dinnertime."

"No, it's fine, thank you so much, but my mate is in the car waiting."

"Invite your friend in too."

Their conversation went back and forth like that for a little while, until Aleisha gave in. This lady wasn't taking no for an answer. She checked her watch. Her mind flew to Aidan and Leilah at home—she still had some time, but would Aidan need her much before he went to work? If she stayed for an hour, she'd make it home in plenty of time, she reasoned.

All she needed to do now was convince Zac that this was a good idea.

CHAPTER 26

ALEISHA

"I hate socializing!"

"Zac, he's like eighty years old, just be nice!" Aleisha whispered back, feeling like they were having their first argument. She'd practically had to drag him from his car.

Nilakshiben and Mr. P had been very welcoming, standing in a line from the door like a welcoming party. Zac seemed a bit creeped out by it all, shuffling awkwardly through the hallway; he probably hadn't expected their first date to go anything like this.

Was this a date? Aleisha asked herself. Or would it have been? A drive through Richmond Park seemed pretty datey—the kind of thing Darcy and Elizabeth Bennet might do.

The table had been set for two people, but Nilakshiben was pulling out a couple more spoons, and two more plates. After she brought the big standing fan from the living room into the kitchen, they all sat down, as Nilakshiben dished a roti (Nilakshiben pronounced it "rotli") onto each of their plates and started spooning on different vegetable and dhal dishes.

"Aleisha, do you want some dhal?" she asked, already spooning a huge helping onto her plate.

"Young man, any bhindi nu shaak for you?" she asked Zac, once there was already a pile of okra dished up for him. "Any more?"

After washing their hands, Nilakshiben and Mr. P tucked in immediately. Zac and Aleisha followed suit, observing them to make sure they'd mastered the art of eating with their hands. Their spoons sat forgotten on the table. Zac had ripped off too small a piece of the rotli to scoop up some food. Aleisha noticed Mr. P observing; she could tell he wanted to help Zac, but didn't want to embarrass him either.

After practically demolishing his plate, Mr. P spoke first. "Nilakshiben, this is delicious. Thank you."

"That is quite okay. Get your strength up. Be well," was all Nilakshiben said.

"What happened?" Aleisha asked, concerned.

"Technically, I *took a fall.* But that is not not not true. The fall took me." Mr. P smiled at his joke, but no one smiled back. Nilakshiben patted him on the shoulder with the ball of her hand, her eyebrows puckered in a semi-frown.

"We missed you at the library," Aleisha said.

Mr. P looked up at her, smiling—spinach between his teeth.

"I wanted to bring you your next book. Have you finished *Pride and Prejudice* yet? I know you read quickly."

"I read quickly so I can get to the library and get the next book you recommend me! But, Miss Aleisha, this one has taken me longer to finish. I, er, had a few family dramas of my *own* to contend with." He chuckled, glancing at Nilakshiben, who smiled back warmly. "I couldn't take on the Bennets' soap operas too, but now all is better. And this home service is lovely." He pronounced it "lubly" and Aleisha's heart ached a little bit.

"What do you do, my son?" Mr. P said, turning to Zac, swiftly changing the subject.

Zac stiffened slightly at being addressed. "I am at university. Well, on my university holidays."

"Ah, very good, very good. What you study?"

"I study law," he said, almost mimicking Mr. Patel's way of speaking. They were both nervous, and Aleisha wished the ground would swallow her up. It felt as though her boyfriend was meeting her parents for the first time.

"That is good! Very, very good! I always wanted one of my many, many daughters to study the law, but instead business, which is good too. Very, very good."

"I really enjoy it, Mr. Patel."

"You know, Miss Aleisha is going to be a lawyer too. I remember when we met, and you were so rude and grumpy," he said, turning to Aleisha, pride written all over his face. "Like a proper barrister!" Mr. P laughed, Nilakshiben tutted.

"Mukeshbhai, why do you say that? I cannot imagine this young lady being rude at all."

"I was. I didn't *mean* to be, and I'm very sorry. We're okay now though, right, Mr. P? You've forgiven me."

"Of course! You recommend me top-notch books."

"Ah, of course. It is *you*, the librarian I have heard so much about!" Nilakshiben said.

"I suppose so." Aleisha didn't want to say *And I've heard so much about you*, because she hadn't heard anything at all. "Have you been . . . erm . . . friends a long time?"

"Not really. We are friends now. I was very best friends with his wife, Naina. But Mukeshbhai and I keep each other company. I watch TV; he reads your books."

Aleisha could feel Zac's eyes on her, but she didn't want to look back in case it made her laugh. "That's really lovely."

"Some people think we must be more than friends. At the mandir," Mr. P chipped in. The tips of his ears were a little pink.

"The temple," Aleisha clarified when she saw Zac's confused face.

"As *well* as my interfering daughters," Mr. P continued. "They cannot understand that a man and a woman can just be friends. It's all forgiven now though—family is family. But you two, you are also *just* friends?" He raised an eyebrow, mischievously.

Aleisha and Zac both looked at their plates.

"Oh no! I am so silly, silly!" His eyes were glinting. "You youngsters don't like the 'labels'! You never want to say that you are a couple until you are walking down the aisle, if people still do that these days?"

Zac burst into laughter. "This is really awkward," he said. "I wanted to take her out on a date this evening, so I have no idea *what* is going on."

Aleisha put her face in her hands. Mukesh, Nilakshiben, and Zac giggled.

"That is a good choice. She is a very good, lovely girl," Mr. P said. Nilakshiben nodded too. Aleisha wanted to die.

After their first course, there was another meal of rice, mung beans (which Mr. P said he made himself), and some greenish-yellow sauce, apparently made of yogurt. Zac and Aleisha ate with spoons this time, but Nilakshiben and Mukesh continued to eat with their hands. Aleisha was mesmerized. They managed to do it so effectively, without once looking sloppy or gross.

After dinner, they sat down in the living room. Nilakshiben turned the TV on to one of the Indian channels, but the volume was low, and they just sat for a little while letting their food go down. Mukesh had one foot propped up on a chair, and he kept making "oof" noises every so often.

There was even one tiny toot, but no one owned up to it. Aleisha noticed that Mr. P didn't look embarrassed at all. Zac, on the other hand, certainly did, probably worried that Aleisha might think it was him.

"Usually we sit here in our own little worlds, don't we, Mukeshbhai?" Nilakshiben said.

"Ha, we do!" Mukesh smiled widely. "She gave me some noise-canceling earmuffs so I can read while she watches Zee TV!" He looked so proud of himself. "No more watching documentaries for me!"

"That's dedication to the cause, Mr. P." Aleisha smiled at Zac, who finally seemed less uncomfortable about it all. "Nilakshiben, what do you normally watch on Zee TV?"

"Usually soap operas. My favorite is *Bhabiji Ghar Par Hai*, but recently I've been watching *Sa Re Ga Ma Pa*, like Indian *X Factor*! And beti, you can just call me Nilakshi. *Ben* means sister, and even though I *feel* as young as you, I am not quite your sister!" Mr. P and Nilakshi started chuckling, Aleisha and Zac joined in.

"I think you'll really like the next book, Mr. P. It's *Little Women*."

Mukesh lit up. "My granddaughter Priya has read this! She said my Naina recommended it to her."

Aleisha nodded. "I remember you telling me. It's brilliant, but a little bit sad, just to warn you."

"I can do sad, I read *The Kite Runner*, ne?" he replied.

The sun was shining through the window now, just as it was setting, and the room had a faint orange glow.

"Could someone turn the light on?" Mukesh asked. "Your nice faces are disappearing."

Zac hopped up, switched the light on, and then closed the curtains without being asked.

Aleisha took in the room now, properly. Her eye was drawn to a cushion, adorned with bold, bright paisley. It didn't match the other decorations, but everything fit together in mismatched harmony.

"This is lovely, this cushion," Aleisha said, picking it up. "Where did you get it?"

"My wife's sari. My youngest daughter, Deepali, is very good at sewing. She made it for me. Just after Naina died. I never notice them anymore. You know, when things fade into familiarity," Mukesh said. "I am glad you pointed them out." Then he whispered, almost to himself, "Naina is always here."

Aleisha's eyes moved to a woman's portrait framed on the wall with a garland hanging from the top left corner to the top right, tracing the line of her necklace. She looked young; she was beautiful. Mukesh followed her gaze too. His face dropped, his cheeks soft.

"Are you okay?" Zac asked Mukesh.

"I am. I am okay."

Nilakshi nodded, looking at the photograph. "Naina was amazing. Aleisha, you would have loved her. The most generous."

"More generous than you?" Aleisha asked, and then wished she hadn't, because the air in the room suddenly became a little bit heavier.

"Yes, much more generous than me. She has always been kind. I think it was she who taught me how to be kind. And her daughters.

She always raised them to love others, to think of others before themselves."

"I have never met them. Do you see them often, Mr. P?"

"Sometimes. They are busy girls."

The rest of the evening was peaceful; Aleisha felt almost as though she was someone different, in another world entirely. Everything else beyond these four walls—it simply didn't exist for now. They listened to some music on the television: bhajans, Nilakshi called them. They were gentle, meditative. Aleisha could have sat there all day.

Zac looked at Aleisha. "We'd better get going. To get you back home on time?"

She looked at her watch. Oh God. It was already ten past ten. Aidan would have had to leave the house at nine; Leilah would be waiting. Her heart began to beat frantically.

"I'm so sorry, Mr. P, Nilakshi, I've got to go. I've got to get back to my mum. Thank you!" She rushed out her words in a torrent and pulled her shoes on as quickly as she could. Zac bumbled behind her.

"You all right?" he said when they got outside.

"My mum, she's not meant to be on her own. I promised my brother I'd be back by nine."

"It's okay, don't worry. It's two minutes away."

"No, I'm late. You don't understand!" Aleisha threw herself into the car, and Zac drove her home in silence. All Aleisha could hear was the drumming of her pulse.

Beloved

by

TONI MORRISON

CHAPTER 27

ALEISHA

The whole house was darkness. All the curtains were closed. Aleisha felt her way up the wall and found the light switch. There was no one around.

"Mum!" Aleisha called. Thankfully there was only silence in return. Leilah must be asleep; maybe she hadn't even noticed her lateness.

She dumped her stuff in the living room, pulling the latest library book, *Beloved*, out of her bag and bringing it upstairs with her. She became aware of a noise, a creaking of floorboards. Was Leilah pacing? Her door was ajar.

Aleisha walked cautiously toward it, and she could hear a low groaning, sobbing sound. Her heart sank. She could feel it at the very pit of her stomach.

"Mum?" Aleisha said again, not expecting a reply. She gently pushed the door open. Her eyes adjusted gradually to the darkness and she saw a shadow huddled in the corner of the room, rocking backward and forward. She turned the light on.

Illuminated, Aleisha could see her mother's room had been destroyed. It was as though someone had gone through every drawer searching for something. Her clothes littered every blank space of carpet, her alarm clock, which hadn't been used for years, was on the floor, faceup, glass cracked, and every cupboard door was wide open.

There was Leilah, slumped in the corner, her head in her hands. She was crying; her shoulders moved slightly, shaking.

The room was hot. Filled with stale air. Aleisha could smell Leilah's day. Every moment of it. And she could tell it hadn't been happy.

She stood there, frozen, watching her mother cry, not moving an inch closer, too afraid to find out what it was this time, knowing deep down it was all her fault.

Eventually Leilah spoke. Quietly. So quietly that Aleisha wasn't sure she'd caught every word, until their meaning eventually sank in:

"He never came home."

"Who didn't?" This had happened before. She was talking about Dean. The day he left, with his bags, his things all boxed up, and he never came back. And now Leilah was reliving it all. Remembering it as if it were today.

"Aidan," Leilah whispered. "He didn't come home."

"That's ridiculous," Aleisha snapped. "You were probably asleep. He came home just after I left for the library this morning. I've been out longer than I should have been. It's my fault. I should have been home hours ago."

"No, Aleisha." Leilah looked up now. Her eyes were red, but alert. "After you left, he never came home. I waited. I was awake all day. I couldn't sleep. I tried to pick up the phone to tell you but I didn't want to call. In case he wanted to get hold of me. I couldn't find my mobile. I couldn't. I'm sorry."

"Mum, don't worry," Aleisha said softly, trying to keep the panic out of her voice.

"I don't know what to do."

Aleisha's heart began to race again. Her mind was jumping forward a million steps and she had to pull herself back, had to try to think rationally. Aleisha knew there would be an explanation. There had to be. Aidan wasn't the type to be out of the house for a long time. He always had a reason. Either that, or it was all Aleisha's fault—she'd probably misread his Post-it notes, or misheard what he'd been saying. Did he have an extra shift at the mechanic's? Or maybe there'd been a big delivery at the warehouse?

She had to calm Leilah down, otherwise she'd trick herself into panicking too. This had to be just a stupid misunderstanding.

She pulled her phone out of her pocket and called Aidan. It rang. It rang. It rang. That was a good sign. It was on, and he wasn't rejecting the call as soon as he saw it. The automated voicemail lady said, "Please leave a message after the tone."

"Aidan, where are you? Mum says you haven't been home all day. Call me when you get this."

In the kitchen, she made Leilah a cup of cold water. When Leilah was feeling restless, or scared, or angry, or stressed, a cup of ice-cold water often did the trick.

When she brought the glass up to Leilah, her mother hadn't moved an inch. She didn't take the cup from Aleisha, so she instead rested it carefully on the wooden floor beside her.

Leilah was unreachable.

Aleisha wandered out, needing some air, and went into Aidan's room instead.

It was a complete mess. Aidan usually liked everything so tidy.

On his bedside table: A half-drunk energy drink. A pint of Stella. A pile of Martina Cole novels gathering dust—they had always been his favorites.

Then she spotted his phone, tucked underneath a pile of receipts on his desk. It was charging. She pressed the home button and it illuminated: 100 percent battery, four missed calls from *Al*. Some text messages. Some more missed calls: *Guy*. *Claris*. Whoever that was.

Aidan never left the house without his phone. He always kept it on him on vibrate, even against the regulations at the warehouse, in case Mum called. In case Aleisha called. In case something happened.

She argued with herself, with the booming thought in her head that something wasn't right. She knew Aidan was sensible; Aidan would never have left the house without his phone if he didn't plan on being back soon.

He'd be back soon. Of course he would be back soon.

CHAPTER 28

MUKESH

Mukesh woke with stiff knees, an aching hip, and a stiff back. Today the pain was much worse, like the darkest depths of winter. He should have taken himself to bed at a reasonable time, but he'd become wrapped up in the world of the March sisters, excited to open the book, to step into their world, to find out what all the fuss was about. The warmth of the family—it felt as though they were inviting him in as a beloved guest too. After everything over the past few days, the fallout with his girls, the reconciliation, the tumble that hurt his hip, his confidence taking a knock, that's exactly what he was looking for.

Little Women was undoubtedly *the* book. It was the book he should have asked for at the library when he didn't know what book to read.

As soon as he met the March sisters and Marmee, he knew why Naina and Priya had loved it so much. The girls—Jo, Meg, Beth, and Amy—they were fun, imaginative, they lived in books and outside books. They cared for one another, looked after one another. And everything about *Little Women* spoke of Naina. Every page burned with her legacy, her spirit sprinkled through the sentences. Sadly, the sisters' dad was away at war, and their mother, Marmee, was looking after them all on her own, in America, Massachusetts—and beyond that, she was looking after and caring for so many other people too, helping out with the war effort, treating her neighbors with kindness and warmth, as well as bringing food for families who needed it at Christmas, helping her neighbors and friends. If Naina had still been here, she would have been just like Marmee, so happy to put her own needs and comfort second to that of others. With each page, he just imagined Naina, everywhere, around him.

He wanted to tell her that reading had helped him find something to pass the time, some way to connect with others, a reason to get out of bed and out of the house.

Naina would have gotten on with her life, like the matriarch of the March family, but Mukesh, ever since Naina left, he had shut himself away. He had let his daughters look after him, content with his discontented life. Mukesh took a deep breath. Until *now*, he thought to himself. Was he more like Marmee now than ever before? Yes. He was. He knew he was different. He was doing so much better now.

His stomach rumbled, the words about the Marches' great big Christmas feast running from the pages into his fingertips and spreading through his body. He could smell the food, the piles of roast potatoes, the sweets and cakes too. He was thrown back to the Diwali dinners Naina had used to make: stacks of sweets, gulab jamun, barfi, mithai, everything he could ever want. They hadn't had a Diwali dinner like that since she'd been gone. If they did celebrate together, it was usually just takeaways now. But, he resolved silently, today he *was* going to make a feast for his family—Priya and Rohini were coming over tonight for dinner. He was cooking for *three*. He thought of the March sisters, of Marmee—they oozed positivity, despite everything they were going through; they proved again and again that where there was a will, there was always a way.

He took a deep breath, and pushed himself up from his chair. He was going to make dosa. He could do this.

And the brilliant thing was that now he believed it too.

I'm so proud of you, Mukesh, Naina whispered. *Now, you better get shopping!*

He didn't need telling twice.

Mukesh made his way up the hill—it took him longer than normal, but not as long as he expected, considering his aches and pains. When he reached the high road, there were hordes of football fans with blue-and-white-colored scarves around their necks, and blue football shirts on. He only ever saw this many white faces in Wembley when there was a football match or a concert or something, walking everywhere, cars tooting at them to get out of the way. Mukesh kept as close to the buildings and the shops on his left as he could, trying to keep out of the way so as not to be trampled down, though they just seemed to be singing cheerfully and waving and sploshing beer cans around, signaling a blue-and-white team win. When he finally found refuge in the shop, Nikhil greeted him.

"What do you want today, Mukesh?"

"I'm making something different! Dosa!"

"Dosa! Are you sure you are ready?"

"Mhmm." Mukesh sounded more confident than he felt. Dosa was his favorite meal. Naina used to prepare it for him every other Friday night. And when the girls were teenagers, always out gallivanting in the evenings, she would make it just for the two of them. When she made it for the whole family, she never had a chance to sit down and eat with them, as she could make only one dosa at a time. "Naina used to make the very best dosa you ever tasted, and I really want to make them too. It won't be the very best, but I hope I might make it quite nicely."

"Yes, Nainafoi made me them for my packed lunches sometimes."

"Did she?" Mukesh beamed.

"If she had leftovers. And if Mum needed help when she was working night shifts."

Naina always used to say making dosa was easy, but Mukesh knew she was wrong. Easy for her was like Everest for him.

"Let me get all the ingredients for you. Wait here." Nikhil left his spot behind the counter and began to rummage around the shop at breakneck speed. Just watching him whiz by made Mukesh feel tired and out of breath. His heart was racing and he didn't know if it was because he was stressed watching a youngster move so quickly, or because he was really absolutely completely awfully nervous about making dosa for Priya and Rohini.

He ran through the steps in his mind, as clearly as he could. Did he know how to make dosa? Did he know how to make it properly? As the images in his mind's eye began to whir through his brain, suddenly, looking around the shop, the products shimmied their way off the shelves, closing in on him, the bright colors of the different packets, the reds, the pinks, the blues, all blurred in his vision.

"Nikhil!" Mukesh called.

"Yes, Mukesh?"

"Mane paani joie che?"

"Yes, one second. You need water right now?"

"Ha, please, beta."

Mukesh clasped his hand to his chest, his breathing labored. Nikhil, in a flash, had pulled him up a chair that had been hiding behind the desk, and just as swiftly brought him a stainless-steel cup of cold water.

"Bas."

Mukesh sipped slowly.

He tried some of the yoga breathing that Vritti swore by. In, hold, out, hold, in, hold, out.

And eventually, breath by breath, he began to feel better. He felt a hand on his shoulder. It wasn't Nikhil's. It was Naina's. Reminding him he could do this.

Mukesh watched as the clock turned five. They weren't here yet.

Mukesh watched as the clock ticked to five fifteen. They weren't here yet.

Mukesh watched as the clock ticked . . .

The doorbell rang. Here they were!

Mukesh stood up more quickly than he could physically manage. He'd left his stomach on the chair, and his body walked off without it.

He opened the door, wiping his sweaty-nervous palms on his trousers.

Priya ran in, clasping *To Kill a Mockingbird* to her chest. His heart lifted like it was as light as air.

"I love this book, Dada! I love Scout so much. I wish I could do adventurous things like her sometimes."

"I thought you would, beta." He leaned over to kiss the top of her head as she wrapped her arms about him. "Besides, you have different kinds of adventures. All kinds!"

Priya squeezed him back, before running in to settle herself down on her usual chair, to continue reading. Naina had set this in motion, step by step, in small, intangible ways. Priya was reading a book he knew all about. He knew the world Priya was in right now. There was something magical in that—in sharing a world you have loved; allowing someone to see it through the same pair of spectacles you saw it through yourself.

Rohini put her arm around his shoulders, tentatively, pulling him back to the moment. He could tell with one eye she was scouting out the house, looking for the bits she could quickly tidy, and the bits she could add to her "nag list" too, but as she began to open her mouth to speak, she closed it again with a sigh. "Hi, Papa," she said. "How are you? I have bought some ingredients to make dinner."

Mukesh shook his head. "No. It's fine, Rohini, beti. I am making dinner. I have got all the ingredients."

Rohini raised her eyebrows, visibly impressed.

Nikhil had googled the recipe for him and had written it out on the back of used and forgotten receipts. He'd stapled them in the correct order and they now sat on Mukesh's kitchen counter. He'd already managed to make the filling, potatoes fried with jeera, methi, hing, and raai, so softly cooked they were like a delicious stodgy lovely paste to pop in the middle. He felt like a chef: "Here's some I made earlier."

The sambal (he had cheated and had bought a sachet from Nikhil who said he wouldn't tell anyone) was bubbling away, and the batter for the dosa themselves was already mixed. (He'd used a sachet again, but no one had the time or strength to actually grind the urud themselves. That is what Nikhil had said and Nikhil had let Mukesh in on a secret: even Naina had used the sachets as soon as they had been invented.)

"All I need to do is fry the dosa!"

"Dosa!" Priya jumped up and down. It was like she was a seven-year-old again.

He had managed it; he had achieved the impossible: he had made a dish that *wasn't* comprised of mung beans or okra. It truly was an achievement. Rohini was stunned. She watched, in awe, as Mukesh *almost* successfully made the pancakes (almost, because he was a little impatient with them and they were a bit misshapen, soggy, broken up . . . but they tasted just the same).

"Can I help?" Rohini said, rolling her sleeves up.

"No, no," Mukesh said. Rohini sat on the edge of her chair, as though poised to step in at any moment. But she didn't, and Mukesh was pleased. She had grown too, it seemed. She was trusting him.

The three of them sat down together. Mukesh took his plate last. It was a new thing for him. He was being the mum, he was being Naina, Marmee too, and he loved it.

"This is delicious, Dada," Priya said. "But I think I would have liked it even better if the filling was *in* the pancake and not next to a pancake mound. And also, if you were sitting with us while we ate it!"

"I am your waiter and your chef."

"Papa, this is lovely. Well done, you. The sambal is particularly brilliant. It tastes quite different from Mummy's though."

"Do you remember what Mummy's tasted like?"

"How could I forget? Yours is pretty good though. Better than mine."

He sort of wanted to tell her that he cheated a tiny bit, but it was a secret he would take with him to his grave. It was okay to do that kind of thing now. He didn't have so long to wait.

After dinner, Mukesh expected Priya to take herself off to her favorite reading spot after clearing her plate away, but instead she came back to the table and sat down.

"The mockingbird—you know when Atticus says it is a sin to kill a mockingbird, does he mean it is a sin to kill innocence or innocent people?" Priya asked.

"Erm . . ." Mukesh felt his heart pound—he hadn't actually spoken to Aleisha about this. "I think so." He said it softly, as though saying it too loudly would expose his uncertainty.

"That makes sense! Because *soooo* many innocent people are hurt, or treated wrongly, in this!" Priya's face was defiant. "It made me so angry!"

"Ha, Priya. You are absolutely right."

"Tom Robinson," Priya declared, and Mukesh nodded, his face solemn. "Boo Radley." Mukesh nodded again. "Dill and Jem! It's brilliant, Dada," she said, still clutching the book. "I wish we could both talk to Ba about it too. I wonder if she had read it!"

As Priya continued to effuse about the book, Mukesh realized that Priya had paid a lot more attention to the minor characters, whereas he'd been more swept up in the main part of the story. It reminded him of Aleisha. Youngsters were very observant.

"I think you can read whatever you want to into anything. That is the point of books," Mukesh said hesistantly, hoping he was channeling a little of the Atticus Finch wisdom.

And Priya nodded. "Dada, you're *to*-tally *right*! Ba used to say that too, but these books are more complicated than the ones we used to read together."

"She did? Ba was very wise."

Rohini watched them as she scrolled on her phone, typed out some emails. She smiled.

Mukesh beamed back at her. This was everything he'd wanted. Here his granddaughter was, no longer locked in her own thoughts, in her own little world. He remembered Naina and Priya giggling away at a character, their quirks. He'd never understood. Now he knew that Scout, Atticus, and Jem were as real to Priya, and to him, as her own family. Now he understood.

CHAPTER 29

ALEISHA

She walked beside her dad, her five-year-old hand held loosely in his. She could feel the rough tips of his fingers with her soft ones. She held on tight as she felt the soles of her sneakers slipping ever so slightly on the sand-covered decking. They were walking toward the sea. She couldn't see it yet, she just trusted that that's where they were going.

They were walking through forest. She could see nothing but trees. Tall trees, thin trunks, and long, spiky green leaves. Fir trees, her dad told her. She was in a fir forest. She could hear birds and some dogs barking in the distance, though it sounded as though they might be right beside her. She kept turning around to check. Her dad told her to stop moving, he would lose his footing.

Aleisha didn't want her dad to lose his footing. She didn't want him to fall over. Then she would be all alone, without anyone in the world, without any way to get home. Her mother had taken Aidan to Cromer. He was adamant he didn't want to go to the beach, especially a beach with nothing much on it; he just wanted some food, maybe even an arcade. He wanted to see the pier. His friends had been the summer before and he wanted to be able to say he had seen it too.

Today, it was just Aleisha and Dean. As she felt her small hand in her father's larger one, she squeezed just a little too hard. She had no idea what to expect. She couldn't see very far ahead, but she noticed a glimmer of light breaking through the trees ahead of her. And then she was there, standing on the line that separated forest from beach. Land from sea. Life from what she felt might be heaven.

She looked around. All she could see now was milky, golden sand. Grasses. So tall, maybe even taller than her, reaching up and touching the sky in some places. The sand on the dunes looked warm, the light hitting the beach in patches, leaving everything else in darkness.

They continued walking, and Aleisha finally felt bold enough to let go of her dad's hand. She could feel her feet sink into the damp sand. In some places, the sand was soggy and moist, like treacle. In other places, it was wet but hard, solid, easy to walk on. The wet sand was darker—on a duller, drearier day she might have called it dirty. But not today. Today it was too perfect to be dirty.

She felt crunching under her feet, and when she looked down, she saw shells. Thousands and millions of shells. Normally, she would have picked them up, collected as many as she could. But it was just right as it was. She didn't want to be the one to ruin it. As she looked around the beach, she saw figures, people and dogs, dotted along their own horizons. She didn't look at them for long. They continued to walk; she knew the sea wasn't far now. She saw a thin layer of water sitting on the surface of the sand, the sun and the sky reflected in it.

She turned around to look for her father, she could see him behind her, a little to her left, on sand she'd left untrodden, untouched. He was standing behind a figure, a blob on the landscape.

She skipped toward him, not minding the detour. She would get to the sea today eventually, though it was probably too cold for her to put her feet in. She could see now he was waving to her, his arm held high above his head, reaching farther than the trees.

As she got closer, she realized the blob on the landscape was a seal. She had been told by her big brother that there were seals around here, in Norfolk. And as she got closer still, she saw it wasn't a perfect seal. It had a hole in its side, flies were buzzing around it, and the sun hit its skin for just a moment, long enough for her to notice the flesh around the hole starting to draw back, weeping with some kind of liquid that wasn't blood, but wasn't water either.

She had never seen a seal before. Now she had never seen a seal alive before. She kept staring; she couldn't take her eyes away. Where had the hole come from? What did it mean? Her father's eyes were on her, and she could feel her head start to ache. A familiar ache. The one that came before tears, after sadness or anger.

She felt her father's hand on her shoulder, and she wanted to nestle into his stomach, to block out the seal, the endless sky, the endless beach, and see nothing but black, smell nothing but her dad's musty coat. Her tears were silent at first, cold and sticky as they crawled down her face. But then came the sobs, and she was embarrassed before they started, distraught when they did, and unable to stop. She couldn't imagine anything worse than being this seal right now. Decaying. Dying. Dead, already. With no one here to watch over it, no one but two strangers, one who didn't seem to feel a thing.

"Aleisha," Dean said to his five-year-old daughter. "You don't need to be upset. Things die all the time. It's not a big deal."

She wasn't upset. She wasn't anything. She looked at her hands. The policewoman was still sitting on the chair opposite her. Her mouth was opening, closing, as though she was speaking—mouthing words like "bad news," "found by a stranger," "so sorry"—but the room was entirely silent. And all Aleisha could think about was that seal—the memory was so distant, like words written by someone else in a novel, and yet she still felt her own heart ache at it. How could Aleisha have grieved for a seal, yet feel nothing when her brother, her Aidan, had been hit by a train.

She followed the policewoman into the hallway, let her out the door, her own face frozen in a surreal, cold, emotionless smile as she said goodbye.

She drifted into the kitchen like a ghost, walked toward the fridge. She looked at Aidan's Post-it notes, searching for a clue. As she read one, she took it off the fridge, listened to the soft peeling sound, and let it flutter to the floor. One by one. Until she started reading more quickly. Some of the Post-its just said one thing: *Beans* or *Bin bags* or *Washing-up liquid* or *Sandwiches for Mum*, and finally one said, *Back later, don't wait up. Love you Leish x*. She peeled faster and faster; he hadn't left a new note here. What would it say? *I'm heading out. Forever. Good luck.*

She lifted her foot up, and smashed it back down on the pieces of paper, like dead autumn leaves shriveling on the side of the road. She watched them, felt them crease and crinkle. She left them as they were.

There, poking out between the notes, half-hidden under the fridge, was a small shard of Aidan's special plate, with Peter Rabbit's ever-smiling face.

CHAPTER 30

MUKESH

"Hello, Mukesh!" It was the library assistant, Lucy. They had only spoken a few times when Aleisha was around, but Mukesh liked her nonetheless. She had a lovely smile. "I'm just heading out, but nice to see you! You're becoming a proper regular. What's that you've got there?"

Mukesh held *Little Women* out to her.

"*Little Women*! That's my daughter's favorite book, even now, and she's twenty-eight."

"It is really lovely. It reminds me of all my daughters. Their differences and similarities! My girls had squabbles and fights growing up, but they had always been the best of friends." Mukesh said all this in one torrent—his speech was almost rehearsed now after telling Nilakshi almost exactly the same thing the evening before. "I sometimes wish Naina had written a book of their lives, about the children, growing up."

"What do you mean?" Lucy asked, her bag on her shoulder, ready to go.

"Well, my late wife, Naina, she was around for most of the time with the girls, when we lived in Kenya, watching them grow up day to day. Sometimes, when I got home from work, everyone was already tucked up in bed and sleeping like babies."

"Did you feel you'd missed out?" Lucy's face was kind; she didn't make any effort to leave.

Mukesh realized he'd never really thought about it this way before. "Sometimes—but my Naina, she always told me we were a team. Every evening she would be waiting up for me, she'd tell me what had happened during the day. That was my favorite moment. I never *felt* like I'd missed it."

"That's so lovely, Mukesh!" Lucy said. She tapped him gently on the shoulder. "Thank you for telling me. Feels to me like *you've* got a book in you somewhere."

"Oh no! Maybe a Zee TV one-off series or something, but not a whole book."

Lucy chuckled at that.

"Where is Miss Aleisha?" He wanted to tell Aleisha how much of his wife he'd seen in the four little women in the book, and particularly in Marmee. And he wondered if Priya might grow up to be bold and brave and intelligent, just like Jo, the feisty sister. Jo loved books, and writing—she became a writer. Was that in Priya's future too?

"I'm afraid I'm not sure. I think Kyle might be on duty today, he's in the back, just ring the bell. Lovely to see you, Mr. Patel!"

Waving with one hand, he rang the bell with the other, and the young man Kyle turned up, carrying an armload of chunky books.

"Mr. Patel, isn't it?" he said, sweating slightly with his load.

"Yes, it is. Where is Miss Aleisha today?"

"She's not here, I'm afraid; I'm covering for her. How can I help?"

"Is she okay? Unwell?"

"I think she had a family emergency," Kyle said casually.

Alarm bells started ringing in Mukesh's head. "Her mother?"

"I'm afraid I don't know, sir."

Mukesh began to panic. "I want to make sure she is okay. I would like to visit her. Can you tell me where she is? Is she at home? With her mother? And her brother?"

"I can't give you that information, sir."

"But I am a friend. I am only being friendly. I am only worried about her. Can I help?"

"No, sir, unless she gave you her information herself, I cannot give you any details. It is against GDPR."

"Ah . . ." Mukesh tried a different tack. "She *will* have given them to me. She visited me just recently, you know? I will just have forgotten. You know, my memory . . . not as sharp as it once was. Definitely no need to worry about GD-whatsit." He tried to make himself look as frail, old, and helpless as possible. Sometimes it worked in his favor. He thought of what Marmee or Naina might do. "I just want to take her some food, something."

"I can't help, sir." Kyle started typing something on the computer. "I see you have a book here, reserved."

"I didn't put a reservation on."

"In which case, I imagine Aleisha did it for you. It is *Beloved*, by Toni Morrison."

Without a word, Mukesh handed *Little Women* over and let the boy do his job. As he passed the book over, he felt as if he was giving something up, saying goodbye. To whom? The March sisters? Naina?

As he watched Kyle take the book, his heart returned to Beth, the sister who became unwell, and her big sister Jo who loved her so much. He thought of the chapter where they went to the seaside, in the hope that the sea air would fix everything for Beth. Immediately, in his mind, the seaside Beth and Jo walked along was the same seaside he took his girls to in Kenya, when they were growing up. He remembered hot, sweaty days when he would come home early and take the girls to the lighthouse where they would get barbecued corn on the cob and sit by the sea. The girls would be so joyful, and Naina would be silent, just looking at the view, as Mukesh did everything he could just to entertain them and keep the smiles on all their faces. He wondered if his girls remembered those days.

Then, years later, in the summer, in London, on one of these hot, sticky days, Naina told him that she wanted to see the sea, to relive these memories. Looking back now, he wondered whether it was in the hope that the sea air might fix everything, just like Jo hoped in *Little Women*. That day, they had gotten the train to Brighton, with a packed lunch of hummus sandwiches, carrot sticks, some bhajis and tepla. Naina had prepared a flask of chai, a bottle of papaya juice, and added some cans of Vimto soda. They'd packed their tablets of chocolate in a tiny little Tupperware too.

The train journey was *exciting*—he remembered it well. He hadn't seen the sea for years, not since the girls were still young enough to come on holidays with them; even then, it had mostly been wet and windy because they'd stayed in England. On this trip, he felt that he and Naina were youngsters again, in the first few months of marriage, getting to know each other, when his parents had given them time and space, when they hadn't insisted on Naina helping around the house, or things being a certain way. He held Naina's hand on the train, and they both just smiled out of the window, watching the scenery rush by.

Naina loved the seaside. Seeing her by the sea that day, sitting on a bench reading her book, the sea breeze ruffling her hair, pulling out strands from her bun, he knew in that moment how lucky he had been, what a wonderful life he'd had with her. What wonderful children. His little women. How could he be this happy to just watch his wife, turning page after page, after years of marriage? How could he feel as though he was still as in love with her as he had been in those first few months of their life, learning new things about each other. And when they'd eaten lunch, overlooking the pier, avoiding seagulls, to the soundtrack of laughing, playing, squealing children, he'd told her he loved her with butterflies in his stomach, as though he was telling her for the very first time.

He hadn't known it then, but Naina only had a year and a half to live. It was the last time she'd see the sea. Looking back now, he was pleased they had gone to the beach, on a whim. But he wished he'd said he loved her every single day.

Now he knew, that just like for Beth, the sea hadn't breathed new life into her. But it had allowed them time, together, to reflect and remember. Reading about Jo and Beth on the beach, it broke his heart—for Beth's young life, and for Naina's too.

As he said goodbye to Beth, Jo, Meg, Amy, and Marmee, he accepted *Beloved*. He wondered what Aleisha would have said to accompany the recommendation. She was so good at helping him feel excited about every new offering when he was still saying goodbye to the old one.

"What is this about?" he asked the young man.

"I'm really sorry, I'm not sure—I've not read this one. But Toni Morrison—the author—she's just wonderful."

Mukesh nodded. "Thank you. Now I would like Ms. Thomas's address, please, thank you? I certainly need to tell her about *Little Women*—we normally talk about the books she recommends me. It helps me understand them, it's the full library service."

The boy shook his head. "As I said, I cannot give out that information."

"I am an *old* man," Mukesh said sternly—trying another new tack. "And I can cause a scene. If you don't give me her address, I will be *very* loud." Mukesh looked around the room. He spotted Crime Thriller Chris sitting in the corner again, and waved at him, momentarily distracted. Dotted around the library, there were three other regulars, a large enough number to cause Kyle *some* embarrassment.

Kyle looked around the room nervously.

"So. Will you help me?" Mukesh bellowed.

After a couple of beats, the tension in the library rising, Kyle ran his hands through his hair and sighed. "Okay, fine. But please do not say that I gave this to you, I'd lose my job."

So easy, Mukesh thought. Who could say he was just an invisible old man now?

Good job, Mukesh, Naina whispered cheekily in his ear.

He took the piece of paper from Kyle.

"Thank you, thank you, sir! You don't know how helpful you've been."

He turned to go, there was no time to waste, but something gave him pause. "In fact, before I leave, do you have a copy of *The Time Traveler's Wife*?" This book had comforted him when he needed it. He hoped Aleisha was okay, but the book might be a good distraction from whatever emergency she was dealing with.

"I'm sure we do." Kyle trotted off and came back a moment later, holding a copy of this special book in its plastic jacket.

Mukesh held on to it tightly, tucking the piece of paper with

Aleisha's address into the front cover, and wandered out into the hustle and bustle of Wembley.

Aleisha's road was new to Mukesh—he'd never even noticed it before, though it was just off the main high street. Though it was a terrace, it looked very different from his road, in a completely different style. It could be a world away.

He looked at Kyle's handwriting. It was hard to read, but he managed to make out the number. He kept walking. The house would be on his left. The sun was bright again, high in the sky, having broken through some thick black clouds earlier that morning.

He counted each and every house.

He could hear music blaring out of some of the windows, bass shaking the frames, and the panes as well.

He could see children playing in the street, kicking a football from one side of the road to the other. Mukesh felt his heart beat faster again, worried that the ball might come too close to him and he would either be hit or be expected to kick the ball back. Then, when he eventually passed the danger zone, he found he was standing outside the right house: number 79.

He was sure they would be home—Aleisha had said it herself: if she wasn't at the library, she was at home. But while the windows in the rest of the street's houses were wide open, these windows were closed. The front garden had nothing in it but bins and some weeds. Everything about the house was dull and gray, except for a flash of color in the window: the glittering reflection of a police car parked on the other side of the road.

The walkway up to the front door was lined with geometric tiles that Mukesh rather liked, but it was all rather unkempt. He could tell that this had been a loved space once upon a time, carefully created and looked after. He thought of his own garden, Battenburg paving slabs for ease, now sun-bleached and broken.

He went to knock on the door, but he was half-terrified of leaving a mark on this house. He waited, stepping a little way back from the door so he could look up at the upstairs windows, listening for any noises, checking for any movements. All closed. Curtains drawn. A silence that was heavy, pervasive.

Mukesh shivered despite the heat.

Perhaps nobody was in after all. He looked at the note again, wondering if he had gotten the right house. There was no mistaking the 7, and it was hard to misread a 9. This was 79.

His finger hovered above the doorbell, but for whatever reason, he couldn't bring himself to press it. No one was in.

Instead, Mukesh posted *The Time Traveler's Wife* through the letterbox—he would blame it all on Kyle if it was the wrong address—and walked to the high road to catch the bus.

As he walked away from the house, he felt lighter with every step, glad to be leaving those shut windows, the sense of something ominous breathing inside the house, worried for whatever lay within. An image of Manderley flashed in his mind from *Rebecca*; walking away from Aleisha's house felt like breaking free of that old place and the ghosts of the past it held, the secrets and fears. He shook his head, trying to banish the book's hauntings. Aleisha was fine, of course she was fine. Wasn't she?

CHAPTER 31

ALEISHA

The house was dark. The policewoman and her constable had taken every bit of light with them when they left. They'd had to step over a book facedown on the doormat to get out: *The Time Traveler's Wife*. They had all heard the thud as it was dropped through, and then they'd both taken a moment to stare at it, apathetic to its arrival.

Aleisha felt the silence of the house cascade around her. She took each step one by one, terrified to think about the next. When she reached the top of the stairs, her heart was beating out of her chest. As she placed her hand on the knob to Leilah's door, she felt its cold like a fire on her skin—for a moment, she was frozen to the spot. Aleisha couldn't hear anything coming from Leilah's room, but when she stepped in, she saw Leilah was standing upright, as if expecting her. Aleisha shut the door behind her. It was better to keep the whole world out.

"Mum, sit down." Aleisha rested a hand on her mother's shoulder. She could feel herself stepping into someone else's skin for this moment. Atticus—wise, imposing. Nothing would faze him. Jo March, the moment she learns Beth is gone—broken, angry. Pi, realizing he'd lost his whole family and had nothing but a tiger, which could turn on him at any moment, for company—all adrift. Nothing was quite right.

As she looked into Leilah's eyes, she saw her mum was searching for the answer already. Analyzing her face, Aleisha could see the policewoman sitting in front of her—she'd been calm. How had she been *so* calm? She had just broken someone's world.

Sharp pinpricks ran through her body, as though she was being lifted out of it. How she wished she could rewind time, rip out the last few pages of this story and rewrite them.

Aidan would walk through the door, trip over the book, tell her off for leaving things lying around. He'd head to the kitchen, take off the Post-it notes that weren't relevant anymore, and start digging around for some food. Everything would be fine, everything would be normal.

Nothing would be normal again.

Leilah's eyes stayed fixed on her daughter, boring into her.

Aleisha took a breath. For now, she could be Atticus. Relaying the facts. Stating the truth. Aidan had jumped in front of a train. Suicide. But Aleisha was sure that couldn't be true. She knew that feeling, standing on the platform, watching the train rush toward you. And that immediate, irrational impulse to propel yourself forward—wanting to know for a moment what it would feel like. To be hit by a train. But that was just a fiction, it wasn't real life.

Leilah watched her, and Aleisha couldn't know if the words were even making sense. None of this made sense. Aleisha just kept talking, until there was nothing more to say.

For a moment, the world stood completely still, as Atticus-Aleisha disappeared, leaving Aleisha alone in their place. Aleisha, whose heart was numb, who could *not* believe that anything like this could happen. She pushed herself forward, forcing herself to sit beside her mother. She ignored Leilah's flinches and held her mother's hand, as tightly as she could. Leilah's hand was limp, it had no life. Aidan had no life.

The room moved in slow motion—but the air had stood completely still. Breathless. Lifeless. Until Leilah began to scream. Leilah, she had been right, that night when Aleisha had come home to find her panicking, drowning. Leilah—her instinct. She had known. She had always known.

Leilah began to beat her hands on her thighs, until Aleisha moved them carefully onto the bed beside each leg. The sound of the beating was muffled, but Leilah's cries made up for their silence. Her voice tore through the house, tore through the rest of the world.

Her son was dead.

Her son was gone forever.

"Get out!" Leilah screamed at Aleisha, her eyes focusing for the first time. "Get out! I don't want to see you! Leave me alone!"

CHAPTER 32

MUKESH

The house creaked around him as he sat in his usual spot, lamps lighting up the space. As soon as he'd arrived home, he'd delved into *Beloved*, wondering if there was any sort of *clue* as to what Aleisha was going through within its pages. Had she left it as a sign for him? Or was it simply her next recommendation?

He'd been met, immediately, with another strange and eerie house, a house haunted with sadness.

He'd thought of number 79, Aleisha's house—at the time it had seemed like Manderley, the last ominous house he'd experienced through the pages of *Rebecca*. But now it was clear that Aleisha's house, with all its windows closed, its curtains drawn, shrouded in darkness, it was exactly how he pictured the house in *Beloved*—number 124. He *knew* it wasn't plausible, that a house in 1870s Cincinnati would look *anything* like a terraced house in Wembley built in the 1940s. But when the author described the haunting feel of number 124, he just pictured Aleisha's house—the windows shut, never to be opened, the silence echoing. But Toni Morrison allowed him to see inside the house in *Beloved*—he could *see* what happened there, he didn't need to let his imagination run wild. Inside 124, he met Sethe, and her last remaining daughter Denver, and immediately his heart hurt for them, living in a home that they felt they couldn't escape. Sethe's sons, Howard and Buglar, had fled the haunted house years before; even Baby Suggs, Sethe's mother-in-law, had been saved from its darkness by the next life, by death. Now it was just Sethe and Denver, alone. It was a house no one visited, a house no one entered. And Denver never went beyond the yard on her own. Her whole world was the house, her mother, and the ghost who lived with them. The ghost of her dead sister, Beloved.

Through every page, Mukesh wanted to throw himself into Sethe and Denver's world, to show them how alive and vibrant they were, how ready for life they could be, if they weren't being pulled back to trauma constantly by the ghost who could never leave them alone, who could never let them forget their past.

As he continued to read, the phone sat right beside him; he was hoping for a phone call from Aleisha. He just wanted to know she was okay. But with every page he turned, every noise, every car that drove past, Mukesh felt a shiver down his spine. He'd been sitting here for hours, just reading, unable to leave the characters alone, but the air around him was getting colder. Aleisha hadn't called. His worries weighed more heavily on him by the minute.

If this *was* a message from Aleisha, his heart ached at the thought of what she was trying to tell him. Was she, like Sethe and Denver, trapped in the house, unable to leave? What was keeping her there? Did she have a ghost of her own?

"Hello?" Mukesh picked up the phone, half-asleep, groggy. His alarm clock bleated 11:00 A.M. at him—later than he usually got up, but he'd been awake into the early hours, reading, searching for clues.

"Can you meet me?" the voice said down the phone.

"Sorry, who is this?"

"It's Aleisha."

Mukesh breathed in, he hadn't recognized her voice, she didn't sound okay. Number 124 floated to the forefront of his mind again.

"Aleisha, what can I do?"

"Can you meet me?" she repeated.

Mukesh nodded, though Aleisha couldn't see his assent. "I will come. Where?"

"I'm at the park, the one near the library." Her voice was hollow.

Mukesh shuffled to the telephone stand, where Rohini's Post-it notes sat waiting. "Yes, hold on, I am just writing it down." He didn't want to forget. He *couldn't* forget. His hand was shaking.

"Are you okay? Do you want me to call someone?" Mukesh asked.

"I have. I've called you."

Mukesh was silent. He hung up the phone and trundled as fast as he could to the bathroom. He got himself ready quicker than he ever had before.

At the park, Aleisha was sitting on a bench, *The Time Traveler's Wife* clasped tightly in her hands. Mukesh had taken forty-five minutes to get there, and he blamed the bus—stopping at every stop, letting on too many people so the bodies were squished together. He was ready to give his excuses and his apologies as soon as he saw her, but the look on her face told him she was somewhere else entirely.

He knew this must be about her mother. He saw Aleisha's face on the day she'd opened up to him, how sad, how *young* she looked. A seventeen-year-old girl shouldn't need to be strong all the time.

"Aleisha?" Mukesh sat down next to her tentatively. "How are you?"

She looked to her knees and shook her head. He could see her body doing all it could not to curl up into a ball and disappear.

"Miss Aleisha, what can I do? You can talk to me."

"No," she whispered, her voice breaking. She clutched her hand to her heart and Mukesh cautiously placed his palm on her shoulder.

"There, there," he said, hating the words as soon as they'd left his mouth. They sat side by side, Aleisha staring at the ground, Mukesh staring at his knees.

The silence stretched out for what felt like hours.

"My brother," she whispered. "He's dead. They said he jumped in front of a train." Each word exhausted her.

Mukesh took a moment to understand. "Your brother?" He said the words so softly, hoping she'd never have to hear them. Hoping he'd be able to change everything. But there was nothing he could do. He couldn't make it better.

Aleisha nodded. "I had to get out, of the house. I can't breathe in there. I can't—" She was struggling to catch her breath, until her breathing turned sharp, but shallow. "It doesn't make sense. He was fine. He was so strong. He looked after us all."

Mukesh squeezed her shoulder just slightly. He took a deep breath; he could feel his heart torn in two. He imagined Denver, fighting for her family, fighting to do her best to save her mother, to save her sister, Beloved—but he didn't have Denver's power, her intelligence; right now, there was nothing he could do. He couldn't hide behind someone else's words now, searching for an answer, he had to say something himself, say something *real*.

"I don't know what to do." Aleisha looked at him, pleading. Aleisha, who always told him what to do, what to read—she was asking him for help.

"Maybe, maybe you should go home. You should be with your mother, family."

Aleisha's shoulders drew into her body.

"I missed so much," she said. Her voice concealed a current of rage. "*Mum* missed so much. What were we doing? How could we have done this? I just had my head stuck in those *books*." Her voice turned into a shout—Mukesh skimmed the park to see if anyone was looking, but no one was paying them any attention at all. To everyone else, their lives were continuing—while Aleisha's life had come to a complete stop. She slammed her fist on the book, roughly pulling it open, scraping her nails down the pages. Mukesh strangled a gasp. "I was *crying* over people who didn't even exist, and all the time, my brother needed me, and needed my help, and I was blind. Completely blind!" She threw the book to the ground. Mukesh watched it land, facedown. He instinctually wanted to pick it up, to wipe it clean, to return it to safety. Instead, he turned to Aleisha—her face was screwed up, her eyes were shut.

"It isn't your fault." He could tell she wanted to disagree but had no energy to put up a fight. "I will call Nilakshiben. She will know what to do."

He hadn't meant to say the last bit out loud but Aleisha nodded.

She was looking at her shoes, brushing one toe over the other. Her fingers clutched the palm of her right hand, the thumb pushing in as hard as it could. She was checking if she still had the ability to feel, to understand the world around her. Hoping, praying, that this was just a dream.

Nilakshi arrived half an hour later with snacks in hand. She had picked up some salt 'n' shake crisps and some dhebra too. She offered the crisps to Aleisha, and when Aleisha asked instead about the dhebra, Nilakshi said, "Oh, just Indian food. You might not like it," but Aleisha tried it anyway. She ate the tiniest amount. No more than a fingertip-size piece. She claimed that was enough. Mukesh wasn't sure she had eaten for days.

Nilakshi didn't say anything to Aleisha, but she embraced her, without awkwardness, without asking for permission. "My beta," she said softly, and held on as tightly as she could. Eventually, Aleisha pulled herself away, gently. "I should go home." They all nodded, and Nilakshi led them to her car.

They drove to Aleisha's house in silence. As they parked, Aleisha stayed in the car, rooted to the spot. She was clearly terrified of stepping foot back inside—she didn't want to meet whatever was waiting for her there: sadness, emptiness, heartbreak. Mukesh didn't blame her. He remembered his own house when Naina died. He couldn't be in it. He couldn't do anything there. Rohini had taken it upon herself to sort everything out for him. She'd tidied Naina's things away for him, putting them in safe places, but making sure the house felt as if she was still there without reminding him that she was gone forever. He wondered who would do this for Aleisha. Where was her father? Would he come home to help?

A voice inside Mukesh—perhaps Naina—told him to distract Aleisha, to help her focus on something else, to get her through the present moment. "Aleisha?" he asked tentatively. "What did you think of *Little Women*? It's good, ne?"

Her eyes darted up at him, and he knew he shouldn't have said anything. "I don't *care* about *Little Women*, Mr. P!" she snapped, but clutched her hand to her mouth—willing the words to unsay themselves. Softer this time, she continued: "I've spent too much time in books. I need to start living again, or who knows if I'll fuck everything else up?"

She pushed herself out of the car. *The Time Traveler's Wife* was sitting on the backseat. They watched Aleisha walk away, taking a moment for herself before stepping into her house. Just as she turned around to close the door, she glanced at them both one last time.

Mukesh smiled at her—hoping she would understand that he was trying to send her all the strength he had in that smile, and to show her all she had in her young life to look forward to. He also wanted it to say something like, "I'm always here if you need to talk." Though he hoped she had someone closer.

After a few moments, Mukesh picked up *The Time Traveler's Wife* from the car seat, and took it over to Aleisha's front door, where he posted it through as gently as he could. She might not need it right now. But if in one moment, minutes, days, weeks, or months from now, it might prove a comfort, an escape—just like it had for him—it would be worth it.

CHAPTER 33

ALEISHA

"Aleisha, I've been trying to call you," Dean said down the phone, his voice laced with anxiety.

The glass of the screen felt like ice against her ear. "I don't know what to do, Dad," Aleisha whispered.

It was her habit to speak quietly on the phone, especially to her dad, but Aleisha knew it was futile—Leilah was upstairs, dead to the world in her room.

She'd tried to get Leilah out of bed today, because she knew she should. But she also couldn't bear being around her in the same way she couldn't bear being around herself. They were both to blame.

"I don't know what to do," she repeated, a tear tracking down her cheek. And it felt like the first time she'd been honest with her dad in years. "I don't know how to fix things."

"I know, sweetheart." His voice was cracking, but she couldn't bear his emotion. He didn't understand her. He didn't understand anything. "We can work this out together. What can I do to help? I can come over, help with anything. Just tell me. You don't need to take this all on alone, okay? I know what you must be going through. How is your mum?"

"Come over"—those words just reinforced to her that Dean didn't live here. For him, this tragedy was forever at a distance. He existed outside of Aleisha's world, outside of Aidan's world, and after the funeral, he would walk away to his own life. Aleisha could never walk away. She'd done too much of that already—she'd been too busy feeling sorry for herself, crying about her friends not being her friends anymore, living in other people's fictional worlds, to focus on her own, on Aidan's.

"No, it's fine, we don't need anything from you right now. Uncle Jeremy and Rachel are coming next week. They're bringing everything we need."

Uncle Jeremy and Rachel hadn't asked what they needed to do—they'd just done it, insisted. *Hun, we'll be with you in a few days, we will stay as long as you need. Xx R*

Dean didn't have a response to that. Instead he said, "Okay, I'd better go then . . . But, I love you, okay? We will make it through this. Tell me, if there's anything I can do. We will get through this, Aleisha."

Aleisha put her phone down. They hadn't been "we" for years.

As she hung up the phone, she saw three text messages from Zac. He'd been worried about her. She'd told him what had happened in brief, painful detail, but couldn't say anything else. He told her he was there if she wanted to talk, and had continued to send the odd stupid cat meme. She knew he was trying his best, but nothing felt like enough.

Aleisha picked at her nail varnish. Her eyes lingered on a photo on the mantelpiece. A photo of the four of them: Aleisha, Aidan, Leilah, Dean. Her anger began to dull, temporarily. When Aidan had thrown Dean's stuff out after he left, she'd been surprised he had kept that photo. He'd even dusted it. The final reminder of their family; the last piece of evidence they'd ever been a family of four. After she asked her mother, in a moment of madness, whether the photo bothered her, Leilah had said: "No. It was a happy time, and I can't regret happiness." That had stayed with Aleisha for many years.

She wanted to block out the world, like Leilah, but there was so much to do, so much to organize. Yet all she felt right now was numbness or bloodcurdling hatred for every happy smile, for everyone living life when her brother, her most important person, was dead.

The photo stared back at her, and she saw Aidan's face, his childhood grin, asking her one question: *What happened?*

"You jumped." *But I might as well have pushed you.*

Aleisha couldn't bear being in this house a second longer. It was too loud. Too quiet. Too empty. Too full. She left, not caring if Leilah called for her, not caring if her calls went unanswered. She was already living through the worst. How much further could she go? Today, she just wanted to walk. People laughed in the street. They didn't know Aidan was dead. Children played, shouted, screamed. They didn't know Aidan was dead. She passed a group of teenagers, jostling and joking, life stretching out ahead of them. And it hit Aleisha: those carefree school days that old people were always talking about, she wouldn't ever know them. So, she just walked, and walked.

Up the stairs she climbed, so many stairs, onto the platform of Stonebridge Park station. Finally, at the top, it felt like the top of the world. The platform was empty, almost deserted, in the middle of this blistering summer's day.

Bright colors, piled up at the edge of the platform, caught her eye. She saw flowers, envelopes, notes, letters fluttering in the wind.

She walked closer. The last place he had lived. *Aidan—Rest in Paradise.*

A Bakerloo train came into view, approaching her, and she imagined him throwing himself forward. She wanted to know if he stepped out, or if he jumped. She wanted to know what other people saw; did people scream, did people ask him to stop? Did people just continue with their day, grumbling about the train delay?

She looked at those flowers—all sorts of colors. At least three or four bunches. Reds, whites, pinks, blues. Some sunflowers too. He'd always loved sunflowers—ever since he was little. On her fifth birthday card, he'd drawn a picture of her and him standing next to the biggest sunflower ever. He'd titled it "Home."

She stood watching the petals blowing backward and forward, and she took a mental picture of them. Her own brother's memorial, of sorts. She was used to walking past flowers tied to lampposts, always thinking it was sad, a life taken too soon, but never lingering on it for more than a moment. But these flowers, they were different. Infinitely more beautiful, but also so small, too small, to even cope with the weight of Aidan's death. This didn't mark it. This wasn't enough to mark his death. She wanted more.

When she got home, she walked straight into her mother's bedroom—Leilah was still curled up on the bed, as she had left her. Aleisha's heart was stone. She hated Leilah, she hated herself, for everything they had and hadn't done, but she embraced her mother, wrapped her whole body around her, wanting to disappear, wanting to feel comfort, to feel close to someone, anyone, her mother, for a little while. She wanted to be away from this world, a world that felt completely alien and yet unforgivably unchanged too.

She picked up the copy of *The Time Traveler's Wife* she'd carried up the stairs, wanting to escape, wanting to soothe Leilah. But what good were books now? The characters she'd loved in them were fake, they'd never be able to fix anything. They'd never live beyond the page. But the person she'd loved who had existed in the real world, who'd fought for her, who'd encouraged her, who had given up so much for her—he was now gone.

Aleisha threw the book onto the floor beside the bed and drew herself closer to Leilah. She waited, she waited for her mother's body to fight against her touch. But Leilah didn't move. She just sobbed, silently—the only clue, the shivering of her body, her shallow, ragged breath.

CHAPTER 34

ALEISHA

Aleisha hadn't slept a wink. She hadn't slept for days, dreading this day, dreading how Leilah would react, what she would do.

As they stood by the car, Uncle Jeremy pulled Aleisha into a hug. "Aleisha," he said. "Just take your time, my love, okay? We're with you, every step of the way." She wanted to scream, shout, tell the world that all she wanted to do was leave Leilah, leave her brother's funeral behind, and run. And run. And never stop running.

Sensing her panic, Uncle Jeremy hugged her tighter, reminding her he wouldn't let her fall. Rachel stood by her side, holding her hand, making sure she didn't fall when she felt like crumbling completely.

"I've got you, Leish," Rachel said, squeezing Aleisha's knee once they got into the backseat.

She'd been relieved that Uncle Jeremy and Rachel had arrived a week before the funeral, so she didn't have to do this bit alone.

Eventually they were all in the car, on the way there, their eyes downcast, unable to look at the coffin traveling in front of them, but Uncle Jeremy stared straight ahead—keeping an eye on Aidan, without looking away once. He tried to make a joke, softly, under his breath, unsure: "Our boy always did like to travel in style. It's a Jaguar."

No one said anything in response; no one spoke at all.

When they arrived at the crematorium, they stepped outside, but Jeremy and Rachel walked ahead to give Aleisha and Leilah a moment together.

"I saw him today, crossing the road," Leilah whispered, speaking for the first time that day.

"Who?"

"Aidan."

"No, you didn't see him, Mum."

But Aleisha had seen Aidan too. Today, yesterday, the day before—she saw him everywhere. He was in the young man listening to music out loud at the bus stop, in the older man pushing his shopping cart, even in the eyes of the woman picking veg at the cash-and-carry. Aidan was everywhere.

Every time she saw him, he was there, alive, and well, but just out of reach. Then the fantasy would clear, and he left nothing but a memory behind.

The crematorium was full; people were queuing up outside unable to hear the service. But they were there for him, for Aidan. Everyone came to pay their respects to Leilah. Aleisha's mum smiled, she said thank you, but her eyes were a blank gaze. She was saying goodbye to her son.

Aleisha held her hand tight. Tighter still when Dean approached. Leilah squeezed her hand back, her fingers wrapped tightly around her daughter's—it was the first moment since Aidan had died that Aleisha had really felt there might be some glimmer of love left between them. They were in this together, whether they wanted to be or not. Dean kissed Leilah on the cheek.

"Our little boy . . ." Dean said, his voice cracked, his eyes downcast. She could see the grief written all over his face. He looked older. Full of regret.

Seeing him now, Aleisha realized just how much Aidan looked like Dean. Different color eyes, different color hair—Dean's hair had gotten even lighter, blonder, since she'd last seen him—but all the features, all Aidan's features, were Dean's.

Leilah let go of her for a moment, and rested her hand on Dean's shoulder. Her eyes were fixed on him. Aleisha watched as she comforted him.

After a few moments of silence, Dean walked away to stand beside his new family, with their bright blond and auburn hair. They all looked so different from her. No one would be able to tell that they were her half-siblings.

"Good of him to come," Leilah said. It made Aleisha want to scream.

Mukesh shuffled over just then. He'd never met Aidan, but he was here. He was wearing a slightly too-tight black suit, white shirt, and tie. When he greeted her, he had no words, because she could see if he tried to speak, he might cry. He simply handed Aleisha a piece of paper, a drawing, a child's drawing—but not stick figures, colorful, detailed. A woman behind a desk. A man and a young girl holding books. Shelves and shelves surrounding them.

Aleisha's breath caught. At the top, in handwriting that was trying to look grown-up, read the words: *We're thinking of you, Aleisha.* At the bottom, two different sets of handwriting, spelling out: *Love Priya and Mr. P.*

She looked up at Mukesh, her fingers gripping the drawing. There were no words left.

Aleisha kept her eyes trained on the photograph of Aidan at the front of the crematorium, standing in a blocky, gold frame, as Aidan's best friend, Guy, walked up to the microphone. She couldn't look at him—his voice was already breaking. In the photograph, taken about a year ago, her brother's smile was so wide. He was sitting on his car, freshly polished, his arms crossed, one eyebrow raised cheekily. He didn't know, then, that his photograph would be used to say goodbye to him, for his family and his friends to stare at, trying to hold on to the joy and hope he gave, while he was gone forever.

"I wanted to read out a poem, written by Aidan when he was eight," Guy said softly. "I remember he gave it to me as a gift, when I was having a rubbish day. He told me I needed it more than he did, and now I want to give it back to you all."

Sometimes the sky is gray
Sometimes the day's gray too
But behind every gray sky
There's always some blue

Guy let eight-year-old Aidan's words float in the air for a moment, before adding with a smile, "You know, he thought it was really profound"—there was a smattering of laughter—"but maybe he's right. I hope he's right."

Aleisha looked down at her lap, and squeezed Leilah's hand tight.

Nilakshi had offered to host a small gathering at her house for the wake, and Mr. P and his daughters had helped out too.

"Nilakshi," Aleisha said. "Thank you for . . . well, for all this." She glanced around the room, full of people. "And thank you to Mr. P too, for sorting everything."

"No need to thank us, Aleisha," Nilakshi said matter-of-factly. "Always let us know if there's anything we can do."

"Thank you. Is there, is there a place my mum can go, just to rest and get away from it all for a bit?"

"Of course." Nilakshi nodded. "Come, I'll show her." She directed Leilah from the corner of the room, staying as quiet and small as she could, to her spare bedroom, putting her arm gently around to guide her. Aleisha had never seen Leilah let anyone so unfamiliar get so close to her this quickly. For a moment, she felt a sliver of hope.

Noticing Leilah's absence, Dean wandered up to Aleisha. "Hey, sweetheart," he said. "How are you? How's your job? You've been working at the library, right?"

He didn't want to talk about Aidan—he didn't want to face up to whatever it was he felt guilty about; she didn't either.

"Fine," Aleisha said coldly. "Aidan would have hated all this attention." She waved to the blown-up photographs of Aidan's face (apparently Mr. P's idea). Aleisha loved seeing them, but knew her brother would have found a quiet corner to hide in.

"Yeah, I guess so," Dean said, slurping his coffee.

"Where's your family?" Aleisha asked, looking around.

"Oh, they left a little while ago. The kids were sleepy."

She didn't reply. After a few minutes of awkward silence, Aleisha spotted Nilakshi rejoining Mr. P, who was talking to Uncle Jeremy and Rachel. They were holding trays of canapés for sharing, but Mr. P was just helping himself.

"Are you okay?" Mr. P mouthed, glancing over at her.

Aleisha felt her eyes filling with tears, but gave a small nod.

"Who is that old guy? Was he invited?" Dean said, noticing Mukesh for the first time. "He's been giving me funny looks all evening."

"He's my friend—from the library," Aleisha said, her tone sharper than expected. "He's the best." Without waiting for a response, she just walked away.

Dean said goodbye an hour later. "Call me, whenever you need me," he said as he jingled his car keys. She watched him walk away, wondering if he wanted to stay. She helped Nilakshi carry used plates into the kitchen until she was shooed out. Mr. P had left already—she hadn't had a chance to say goodbye, or to thank him properly for the drawing, tucked carefully into her bag, next to Peter Rabbit's tiny little face. Feeling at a loss, she went upstairs to find Leilah sitting up on the bed, staring out of the window.

The room was tidy. It was a guest room with very few personal photos, and spare towels kept on an exposed cupboard shelf. The bedding was immaculate, and there were even throw pillows and a bolster. The pile of blankets Nilakshi had given her sat on the end of the bed, untouched.

"Are you okay?" Leilah asked.

Aleisha hadn't been asked that by her mother in a long time; she didn't have the words to respond.

They stayed together in that space in leaden silence. Leilah's fingernails cut into the palm of her left hand. They left bright, sharp indentations. The grooves turned blistering red. Aleisha watched as Leilah started to pick at her skin, slowly at first and then frantically. Leilah couldn't scream. People would hear. But she threw herself facedown on the bed and shouted wordlessly into a pillow.

Aleisha wanted so badly to do the same. But she needed to be the strong one now. Instead, she watched. In her mind, she saw Aidan, she saw Leilah, lying on the bed, joking, laughing, talking. In front of her, her mother screamed herself to sleep.

CHAPTER 35

MUKESH

Mukesh walked out of the house to a cacophony of children playing on the streets of Wembley, and convertibles driving fast up the road, whooshing past him. After a tempting pause outside Dosa Express, the smells of the limdi and jeera calling to him, he eventually reached the library. It was almost empty. It was one of the last few weeks of the summer holidays and all the kids and all the people were outside making the most of the sunshine that had just returned.

And there, sitting in her usual spot behind the desk, was Aleisha.

"Hello," he said formally.

There was a moment of silence; they both looked at each other nervously. It had been two weeks since he'd seen her. His eyes darted around, looking for something to say. He eventually landed on a pile of flyers at the front desk, with that same ominous slogan he'd come to know so well: SAVE OUR LIBRARIES. He looked quickly away, not wanting to think of anything else negative right now.

"My skin feels very dry, maybe burnt?"

Mukesh cursed his foolishness. He couldn't think of anything else to say.

"You and me . . . we don't get burnt," Aleisha said, confused, and Mukesh shook his head.

He thrust out an arm. "I may not be red, but the skin is sore. My Naina was right."

"Kyle's got some cocoa butter in the desk. Here, put this on. It'll soothe it. Are you okay?" Aleisha asked. The whites of her eyes were lined with red and her skin was gleaming with a thin layer of makeup.

Unable to respond, or to say thank you, he slathered on the cream. "My Naina must have had this, it smells familiar."

"Probably."

"Are you supposed to be here, Aleisha?" he said softly.

"I've got to work—routine is better. Normal."

"Okay, if you are sure . . . How is your mum?"

Aleisha shrugged. "My uncle and my cousin, you know, the ones you met, they're staying with us—just for a little while to help out. Mum's happy to have them." Mukesh thought she wanted to say more, but he didn't know what to ask. He was pleased that someone could be there to help take the load off Aleisha. She was seventeen, too young to be doing all of this on her own. Her brother was . . . *had* been twenty-five, and still too young to be caring for a whole family. "I want Mum to get some help," she continued. "To give *me* some help too. You know . . . speak to a professional. She's never seen a doctor. Aidan wanted that too. She's never ever spoken to anyone. It could help."

Mukesh wasn't used to people talking about such things, about the doctor, about *mental health* problems. He felt embarrassed, but Aleisha needed someone to be there for her. He could do that. He might not be super knowledgeable, but he could listen, or find another way to talk.

"I think . . . I think *Beloved* is helpful," he said cautiously. "The book. Did you read it?"

Aleisha's eyes shot toward him. "I don't want to think about books anymore."

"No, Miss Aleisha, I hadn't thought of it before, but books can help us too."

Aleisha sighed heavily. He saw her roll her eyes; she started to tap her nails on the desk impatiently and for a moment he was transported back to his very first day in the library.

"You see, *The Time Traveler's Wife*," he said. Aleisha's eyes were roaming around the library. "When my Naina passed away, that book had been a distraction, but it had brought me closer to her as well. But now, I think, more than that, it helped me process some things, you know?"

"No, Mr. P," Aleisha said sharply. "I don't know. I've spent the whole summer living other people's lives. I forgot to live mine, to look out for the *real* people around me."

"*Beloved*," Mukesh continued, trying to hide the tremor in his voice. "Did you read it? Denver. How does she help her mother?" Mukesh waited for a reply—but Aleisha was scrolling on her phone. "Okay, I'll tell you what I think. Denver realized that staying in that house, with her mother, with the ghost of Beloved, it wasn't helping anything. But Denver went out to get help from her community, from other women who wanted to help. She asked for help when her mother couldn't ask for herself."

Mukesh let the words hang in the air, and for a moment he felt a comforting hand on his shoulder. Naina's.

Aleisha kept staring at her desk. She refused to look up at him.

"Aleisha," Mukesh said softly. "Please try to remember that books aren't always an escape; sometimes books teach us things. They *show* us the world; they don't hide it."

That's a proper Atticus moment, Mukesh, Naina whispered in his ear, louder than ever before. He steadied himself against the desk for a moment.

Mukesh waited for Aleisha. She didn't respond and continued to scroll. Eventually, she let her phone sit beside her and just watched her screen.

Every so often, it would buzz and flash, sitting on the table in front of them and, while normally she'd turn it over, today she picked it up. Every single time. Her mind was somewhere else. It was understandable.

Mukesh didn't want to upset her, but he thought it would be better for her not to look at her phone. His daughters were always doing this too. Always looking at their phone in the middle of conversations, like they were never really present.

"What is it?" Mukesh asked, trying to keep his voice light.

Aleisha showed him the screen. A photograph of Aidan, a girl and a boy, both squinting in the sunshine. Aidan had sunglasses on.

"Lovely."

"It's not lovely—look what they've written underneath."

Mukesh could just about make out some typed words, but he couldn't for the life of him work out what they said. "I can't see," he admitted, and Aleisha read it out for him, hashtags and all.

"'Always there for me, always cared. Miss you, Aid. Won't ever forget you. #RIP #GoneButNeverForgotten #RestInParadise #Depression #TimeToTalk.'"

"That's a nice tribute to him," Mukesh said.

"No, it's not." She sounded furious. "It takes five minutes to do an Instagram post, if that. They're splashing my brother all over the internet, claiming a right to grief. They've even put the funeral on their story!"

Mukesh had no idea what that really meant—"story"—but whatever it was had clearly upset Aleisha.

"Who hashtags depression? They don't even *know* it's depression. And why the fuck would they tag him in it? Because he'll see it from wherever he is? Paradise?"

"I don't know what that means."

"Look." Aleisha passed the phone to Mukesh. "Scroll down." Mukesh did as told, his fingers fumbling about until the image started to move.

There were dozens and dozens of photographs of Aidan with various people—there were some photos of the flower arrangement spelling out his name, and he recognized Nilakshi's dining-room table with the food spread out all over it too. Everything. They had documented it all.

"For everyone to gawp at. Everyone. Even people who didn't know him. We wanted a *small*, intimate ceremony for friends and family, and now everyone has a piece of him."

One tear, just one, slid down Aleisha's cheek. She left it there so as not to draw attention to it. But Mukesh saw—he'd had three teenage daughters, all of whom had tried that same trick once in their lives, whether in response to the ending of *It's a Wonderful Life* (the saddest film ever), or because someone had decided to slap them on the way home from school because of the color of their skin and they needed to pretend that they were okay with it, that there was no one to blame.

"I'm sorry, Aleisha, it is just their way of paying respect, I think." Mukesh passed the phone back.

Aleisha began to obsessively scroll. She tapped a few things and started to type. He worried that she might be typing horrible emails to the people; he wondered if they would understand, if they would forgive her.

"My dad has put a photograph of Aidan as a baby up on his Facebook profile. He hasn't had any evidence of any of us on his Facebook since he got married again. Does a dead kid earn you respect, or something?"

Mukesh noticed that Aleisha's natural tone had vanished—she was enunciating in a way she never had before.

"Aleisha, I think you should go off these internet things. Please. For a little while, not just today."

Aleisha looked him in the eye for the first time since he'd started talking about *The Time Traveler's Wife*. Her face screwed up, she rubbed her eyes and she took three deep breaths.

"You're right," she said eventually, turning her phone facedown on the table.

Mukesh nodded—yes, he was.

They sat alone in silence for a while. Mukesh looked around him—it was quiet now, but he remembered seeing people, people he felt he knew, a little community he felt a part of.

He took himself away to a separate part of the library, wanting to give Aleisha some space, but not wanting to be too far away. He stepped back into *Beloved*—he'd already finished reading it, but he didn't want to ask for a new book. He didn't want to put the pressure on her right now.

He flicked through the pages of Denver's plan as she looked to escape the boundaries of their house, 124. Denver, who hadn't left the house in twelve years; Denver, who had a terrible fear of the outside world—she had gone for help. She'd overcome her fears, and thirty women from the community turned up to help Denver in any way they could.

He looked around the library—in a way, those first steps that had brought him here had been a chance for Mukesh to ask for help, a chance for him to reach out to a community. While he *had* left the house in twelve years, he'd not read a book in many. And he'd never set foot in the library, not until this summer. He thought of the leaflets, the slogan imprinted on his mind: SAVE OUR LIBRARIES. Naina had always been talking about it, saying how devastating it was for a library to vanish. He thought of all those things he'd taken to heart, whether it was wisdom from the characters in the books he was reading, or the familiar faces who smiled as he walked in, or Aleisha advising him, guiding him, or that feeling of being able to talk to Priya, see her grow into a reader . . . This library had come to mean something to him. It had begun to feel like home. And a place is only what it is because of the people who make it. That's what Naina always used to say about the mandir. And Aleisha had always said the library had meant something to Aidan too . . .

An idea hit him, a bolt from the blue, or perhaps from wise old Atticus Finch. He pushed himself up from his chair and stomped over to the front desk. "Aleisha?" he said. His voice was quiet, no more than a whisper. The library was still almost empty, but in his mind it was full of everyone he'd met, fictional and nonfictional, over this one summer.

"Yes?" Her reply came back sharply, and as soon as she heard it, he could tell she regretted her tone. "Yes," she said again, softly this time.

"You know this?" He held up one of the SAVE OUR LIBRARIES leaflets.

"Yes?"

"How are we actually meant to save our libraries, if we don't ask for help?"

"Er, Mr. P, I think that's what the leaflets are all about."

"Okay, fine, but . . . you know what I mentioned earlier, about Denver going to ask for help. What if we asked the community for help? Because, this library—it's been helpful for me. It has made me bolder, it has given me friends. And I am just one person."

"I'm sorry, I'm not following." Aleisha's face was expressionless.

"Sitting here in silence with others can feel much less lonesome than sitting at home surrounded by my family constantly talking over me. It is nice, *comforting*, to see the same people every week. And it feels like I've got so much out of it, because I've got people to keep me company. I am just one person, and I have gotten all of this from stepping out of my house, from leaving my comfort zone, just like what Denver did . . . And now, here I am, at the library . . . a place that feels like it *helps* me. Now, you always mentioned Aidan loved this place too. What did he like about it?"

"Peace. I think he found it peaceful. He could be alone here. But he hasn't come for years, unless it was for keeping an eye on me now and again. He was so busy."

"Okay, I understand. But this place, it was still very important to him, ne? And so many people come here for peace, or for friends. How would he feel about this 'Save Our Libraries' thing?"

Aleisha shrugged.

"Would he have been happy if the council closed this place down?"

Aleisha shrugged again.

"I don't think he would. I don't think *you* would."

Aleisha smiled. "No, you're probably right. But, I don't see what we can do? Everyone's seen the leaflets, and there's like a JustGiving page or something too."

"Okay, but I have a *better* idea." He waited for Aleisha to say something like "Go on, I want to hear it," but she didn't. He continued anyway.

"I know that you do lots of other things, like the book club stuff, I have seen the posters on the wall. But you must need to be busier, right?" Again, Aleisha remained silent.

"So, I would like to do a community drop-in morning, or afternoon, or whatever you think is best. You're the professional."

Aleisha rolled her eyes. "I'm not the professional. What do you mean?"

"No need for a library card, no need to take out books if you don't want to. We could use this reception bit for a coffee-and-cake-and-food thing; people always come for food, especially if it's free. Or even just a donation to charity. Every Wednesday perhaps. A chance to speak to people. And that can be the thing, talk to one new person every time you come. To help more people feel a little bit less lonely, and maybe help keep the library going. Because they don't *have* to sign up, but as soon as they're here, they'll want to, won't they? It can make it *popular* again!"

"You think enough people would come? They're not exactly a chatty bunch here, are they? Other than this one lady who comes on Tuesdays sometimes and she never stops talking."

"It's just a chance for us to ask for help, for the library, for each other too. Could we try? Could you ask? I think it would be nice—maybe people just need a little prod to talk to someone new."

"I don't know if my boss would agree. Wouldn't it just be the same people who come?"

"He will like it because it will bring even *more* people to this library. It will be 'Come for the cakes, stay for the books—and the new friends!' Isn't it? We could do flyers—but not like these sad ones." He held up the SAVE OUR LIBRARIES leaflet again.

She sighed. "I'll ask."

"And, I thought, this first one . . . maybe it would be nice to be held in memory of Aidan. Even if he didn't have the time to come here to sit and read in recent years, this place meant a lot to him. He wanted you to work here, didn't he? And it has helped you too. Hasn't it? I think it helped you. Maybe this is how to help his memory live on, beyond those Instagrab posts."

Aleisha nodded, a smile hiding in there somewhere.

At that moment, Crime Thriller Chris walked in, wearing a hoodie and jeans as usual.

"Chris!" Mukesh called over, his body zinging with excitement. "What do you think about a drop-in morning on Wednesdays at the library?"

Chris looked slightly taken aback—it was the most Mukesh had said to him in a long time; normally he just got a smile and a wave. "Errr, yeah, they're quite good, those kinds of things. My mum likes them. Coffee mornings."

"See!" Mukesh pointed at Chris, looking at Aleisha. "So, you will ask? Chris will bring his mother. This will be fantastic. I am excited." Mukesh was smiling from ear to ear, and Aleisha started to laugh. Chris shrugged, not sure what had just happened, and continued on his way to his usual spot.

"Naina would love this! She loved this kind of thing—and now *I'm* the one doing it. And not even at the temple."

Mukesh gave Aleisha a tap on the shoulder, bending down to her at her desk very slowly because his back was much stiffer than he remembered. Because for a moment, he'd forgotten that now he was an old man with aching joints. For a moment, he had felt completely and utterly brand-new.

CHAPTER 36

ALEISHA

Now she'd seen those flowers on the train platform through someone else's eyes, shared on social media, with forty-five likes. The petals were browning, they were dying. They weren't forever. Aidan was in these people's minds now, but like those flowers, he would one day be gone.

A drop-in morning in honor of Aidan . . . He would have laughed at the idea. He would have hated all the attention. But he had loved the library—he'd been so adamant she should take this job in the first place. The library had been *his* place for so many years. Maybe Mr. P was right. And it was some small thing she could do, something *she* could control, to keep his memory alive—and to prove to him that the library had come to be important to her too. She knew that's what he wanted. He wanted her to find peace here as well.

There was no time to waste—Mr. P wouldn't let this rest until it had been sorted. There had been that thing in his eyes: determination. He'd almost run out of the library, clutching *Beloved* to his chest, waving to her and to Call-Me-Chris Crime Thriller.

She gave Kyle a call, asked when he would next be in, if he was going to come for his shift later.

"Yeah, I'll be there."

"Great. Mr. P has had some thoughts about what we can do to spice this place up a bit."

"The library?"

"*Yes*, the library."

"Are you sure you're okay, Aleisha?" Kyle said.

"Yeah, I'm okay. Distraction is helpful. *This*"—she pointed to the screen, her makeshift flyer—"is strangely helpful."

Kyle nodded. "Sounds like Mr. P knows what he's doing. They do say with age comes wisdom . . . So how many shifts do you have left before you go back to school?"

Aleisha shrugged. "Just one more week, so five or six maybe."

"God, that's so soon. We'll miss you."

"Yeah, I think I've liked it here. Aidan said this would happen. That I'd *surprise* myself."

"What happened to 'This is just a shitty summer job'? You were so reluctant to actually do anything on your first day."

"I was. It *is* just a shitty summer job. But you know, it's *grown* on me," she said, the small hint of a smile on her lips.

It wasn't long before Thermos Flask Dev turned up. Aleisha felt a rush of adrenaline. She was grateful when Kyle set the stage for her, opening with: "Aleisha's got a great idea."

Aleisha felt all the attention in the room turn to her. Her mouth became dry, as if she was preparing to give a speech, and then Atticus came to her mind. Atticus, in the courtroom. He'd shown no signs of weakness.

She took a deep breath, and the words tumbled out. "We want to propose—" The word felt weird, but it was the right approach; Thermos was standing to attention. "We want to propose an open morning. We want to get more people in through the door. This place—it's got friendly family vibes; we should use that. Help people get in the spirit of things, help this library become the *center* of the community, y'know? A place to get people meeting, get them talking, opening up, discovering something new . . ."

"Look, Aleisha, should you be here? I told you, please take as much time as you need," Thermos Flask said.

"Distraction is good," she muttered under her breath, and then more loudly, she continued: "Anyway, so the open morning will be free for anyone to come along—they can meet new people, enjoy the peace and quiet, chat with friends. This place has always been a community hub—but it's been a little quiet lately. Let's change that."

Dev slowly nodded, unscrewing the cap of his thermos flask. "So, will people be encouraged to actually *join* the library too? That is a key thing for us."

"Yeah, definitely! Maybe Lucy or Benny could help out and give out flyers or something like that on the day. We want to show people what a great space this is, so they'll come for the cake, stay for the books—and the new friends."

"Great—that's exactly what we need to be doing. In all honesty, it's been a stretch keeping this place going for so long. The council are always worrying about budgets, especially when we compare our usage to the Civic Center." Dev took a long sip from his flask. "The knitting club was a great idea, but now we're just down to a couple of regulars—and only Lucy runs it, and she barely has the time. The book club, also not as popular as it used to be. But this . . . it might work. The library isn't *just* about books."

Kyle and Aleisha glanced at each other, a thread of hope between them.

"How about we try it out one Wednesday morning? Our quietest time!"

Kyle and Aleisha nodded.

"Perfect. I love it. This place, it's about connection. This idea . . . Aleisha, it really does get that. Love it," he said. "I think we should trial it—next week, see the turnout. We can always start it on a smaller scale—once a month, or every other month."

"A week doesn't give us a lot of time to spread the word."

"Well, you'd better get going then."

Aleisha looked at Kyle, who'd been sitting back and watching it all unfold. She smiled and he raised his eyebrows, giving her a double thumbs-up.

She couldn't wait to tell Mr. P.

CHAPTER 37

MUKESH

Beep. "Rohini, please can you come with some trays of food for next Wednesday, deliver them to my house Tuesday evening, maybe bring some of those samosas you make? That would be nice. It's for the library, an open morning. And *I* am helping organize."

Beep. "Vritti? I need your cooking assistance—do you have some nibbles you can bring for an open morning, for next Wednesday? Please deliver at my house on Tuesday evening. Something *hy-po-al-ler-gen-ic.*"

Beep. "Deepali, beta, please bring your special-recipe punch—you know, the one you make for special occasions—ready for an open morning on Wednesday at the library. Bring straight there, but come to help at my house on Tuesday evening too."

He hung up the phone, ticking off his three daughters on his list. He turned to Nilakshi, sitting in the living room, watching Zee TV.

"Nilakshiben?" he asked cautiously.

"Mhmm." She turned her head away from the TV for a moment, her ears still taking in the melodrama.

"Aleisha needs me to give out flyers, for the library." He waved the newly printed flyers at her. They were bright, cheerful. "Zac made them. They're very good, ne? So, what do you think about me spreading the word at the mandir? Will they laugh at me? Think I'm a lonely widower?"

"Mukeshbhai," Nilakshi said softly. "You are not a lonely old widower. And they know how much the library meant to Naina, they will know that you are doing this as much for that lovely young man Aidan as you are for her. You will have made her so proud."

Watching Nilakshi, he knew he had made his peace with everything. Nilakshi was his friend. And Naina, in some way, had sent her to him too—she had made sure their paths had crossed. She had brought them together, for company, in the same way as she had guided him to the mandir, and had left *The Time Traveler's Wife* as a sign. She had been right there, with him, from the very beginning.

He thought about distributing flyers at the mandir, what people would say; no one would expect this from Mukesh Patel. It didn't scare him, really, did it? This was for a good cause. The city was often a lonely place, and even in Wembley where lots of people knew each other, people still felt alone.

He thought then about posting them through people's letterboxes. Some people didn't like flyers, leaflets, that kind of thing. Could something as innocent as posting flyers through letterboxes get him in a chutney?

In a pickle, Naina's voice burst out at him then. *The phrase is "in a pickle."*

At the temple, Mukesh's courage finally plucked up, Harishbhai's youngest son was pushing him around for the day in one of the coveted wheelchairs.

"I need to have both hands free, for speed, you see," Mukesh had pleaded.

"All right, Mukesh, I'll do it for a tenner!" Harishbhai's son had bartered.

Mukesh was wheeled up and down the hallway, past the gift shop and the shoe zones and the toilets. He had given away only about three flyers so far. He had to change his approach.

Harishbhai's son was listening to something on podcasts and only acknowledged which direction Mukesh wanted to go in if Mukesh pointed or waved his arms dramatically. Mukesh was relieved he didn't have to make much conversation with the boy. Though he hated fitting the "old person stereotype," he loved the wheelchair and wondered why he hadn't tried it ages ago, especially when he could get someone like Harishbhai's son to push him around in it. He was going so fast!

Searching his brain for inspiration, Mukesh thought of TV programs like *EastEnders*, where people would shout in deafeningly loud voices, "*Read all about it!*" from their newspaper stands, or "*Two tomatoes for twenty pence!*" from their market stalls. He did a little cough, and started to shout, not too loudly because he'd be kicked out, but loudly enough to be heard, flyers waving in his hand above his head. "The Big Library Get-Together, don't miss it; all your friends will be there and will wonder where you are if you are not. Bring your children and your grandchildren!" It was miraculous, two women walked over immediately, curious. He had their attention! He handed flyers to them as he whizzed past, praying he hadn't given them a paper cut.

In the gift-shop aisles, there simply wasn't enough space for Mukesh and his chair and Harishbhai's son. Sensing that this might not be the right tactic, he asked Harishbhai's son to reverse as quickly as he could out of the gift shop, when they accidentally reversed into Rohini and Nilakshi. Together . . .

"Oh!" Rohini said.

"Oh!" Nilakshi said.

"Oh!" Mukesh said.

"Hey, I'm Harishbhai's son," Harishbhai's son said.

"What are you both doing here?" Mukesh asked.

"We're spending some time at the mandir," Rohini said. "We're going to go to a satsang. I got the day off work. Priya's with Robert," she added, preempting his question.

"Your daughter and I are getting to know each other even better!" Nilakshi said, her face bright.

Mukesh beckoned Rohini down to his level and he whispered in her ear: "Just like your mother, you are. Always welcoming to people."

Rohini beamed back, it was her way of saying, "If she's part of your family, she's part of mine too."

"Here, here," he said, and handed them flyers. "And we are asking for homemade food at the library too—so make sure you bring something! You got my messages? We need to keep the vegetarian food side up. I might even make my famous paneer."

Rohini and Nilakshi looked at each other. "Famous?" Rohini asked. "I thought you'd only managed not to burn it once . . ."

"Harishbhai's son," Mukesh said, wondering if the boy had a name, but appreciating Harishbhai's clear and strong sense of branding. "Let's go! Over there, there are a few lonely-looking souls who need a flyer. Food please, ready for Wednesday!"

And with that, they whooshed away over the smooth wooden floors, up the carpeted ramp, and onto the marble floor leading to the main mandir.

When Tuesday evening finally arrived, Mukesh was full of adrenaline. Rohini, Deepali, and Vritti were preparing all the snacks in his kitchen, and the twins were causing mayhem in the corridors. When Zac rang the doorbell, Mukesh was pulled back several years to one of Naina's fundraiser-planning evenings for which she'd always have a selection of snacks and other food prepared, "to keep energies up." He hadn't done anything of the sort. Thankfully, Zac was holding a sharing pack of Doritos with some salsa dip. Mukesh was incredibly grateful.

"My mum says never turn up to someone's house empty-handed!" Zac said.

Mukesh clapped his hands together. "You are a good boy!"

Zac seemed out of place in Mukesh's house without Aleisha. He kept asking Mukesh's permission to do things, like "Mr. Patel, can I use these plates for the Doritos?"

Mukesh nodded.

"Mr. Patel, can I get a glass of water?"

Mukesh nodded.

Then, "Mr. Patel, can I use your toilet?"

Mukesh said, "Of course, Zac. This, my home, is now your home. Do whatever you need."

Zac beamed at him in response, but still walked around the house tentatively, as though he didn't want to leave any trace of himself behind. Mukesh chuckled, podding some peas into a bowl, for the kachori, until Jayesh turned up, trying to use his grandfather and his bowl of peas as a climbing frame.

Nikhil arrived next, laden with vegetables from the shop. But as soon as he appeared in the doorway, he was summoned by Rohini: "Nikhil, we need you! Come here."

Nikhil stepped in reluctantly; Rohini had a notebook in hand.

"Yes," she said authoritatively. "Bring some extra ingredients tomorrow morning and I can fry it up just before we go. Nilakshi-masi said I could use her pressure cooker too." On uttering Nilakshi's name, she looked at her father and smiled. Mukesh smiled back, nodding through the pain as Jaya started to tap him with her tiny fists.

"Jaya, be nice to Dada," Rohini admonished. "Play gently." She obeyed for a second until her masi turned away.

Amid the mayhem of the living room, Mukesh spotted Priya curled in a corner, a book in her hand. He managed to free himself of Jaya, and Jayesh, and took his pea-podding over to her.

As he got closer, Mukesh could see Priya was reading *Little Women*. Again.

"Beta, you already read that?"

Priya nodded. "I know—but it reminds me of Ba. I just hear her voice. Plus, Dada, Ba always told me that sometimes when you really like a book, you need to read it again! To relive what you loved and find out what you missed before. Books always change as the person who reads them changes too. That's what Ba said."

Mukesh nodded. He understood.

Zac handed Mukesh a cup of tea and asked Priya if she'd like one too. In the background, Rohini said, "She doesn't drink tea," but Priya said, "I would love one please, Zac," so he passed her a cup.

Priya smiled, putting her book down, wrapping both hands

around her mug. She looked at her mother and playfully stuck out her tongue.

Mukesh wandered back to his chair and he sat down. He looked around the living room, completely full of movement, the twins back to running up and down the corridor outside too. He hadn't had this many people in his house since Naina died.

He thought of Aleisha, Leilah, in their silent home.

A Suitable Boy

by

VIKRAM SETH

CHAPTER 38

ALEISHA

"Aleisha, you look shattered."

"I guess I am."

"Look, why don't you go and have a nap before you go to work?" Rachel said, putting a hand on her shoulder.

"Yeah, maybe." Aleisha wanted nothing more than to sink into her bed and never get up. But her mind flew to her mum, who'd been doing exactly that for the last day or so. No, for *years*. "Let me just see how she is . . .

"Mum," Aleisha whispered, poking her head through the door. "Uncle Jeremy and Rachel are here, I'm going to sleep for a bit, okay? They're going to have some lunch in the garden. It's a really lovely day, would you like to join them?" She kept her voice as soft as possible.

Leilah was sitting up, staring at the wall ahead of her. "I'm fine," Leilah said. "Have a good sleep."

"She all right?" Uncle Jeremy was standing just outside the door.

"She doesn't want to come out. Honestly, there's no point in trying."

"No, my girl, there's every point." Uncle Jeremy stepped in. "Leilah, how are you? It's a lovely day outside."

Tomorrow was the open morning for Aidan at the library, and she didn't feel prepared at all. She was exhausted. Aleisha let her mind switch off and allowed her legs to lead her along the corridor, and into Aidan's bedroom. It was still, silent in here. Untouched. They hadn't gone through his things, Aleisha couldn't bear to touch anything. She wandered over to his bed, pristinely made. Despite the mess in the rest of the room, which wasn't very Aidan, her brother could never leave his bed undone. She lay on top of the covers, barely wanting to leave a mark. Her head hit the pillow and her eyes were drawn to a stack of books beside his bed, now with a thin layer of dust on the top, on each groove of the spines.

She turned over and stared straight up at the ceiling, willing sleep to overcome her. Suddenly her phone on Aidan's bedside table started to buzz: *Kyle.* Of course. She'd see him later for her shift at the library, anyway, so she turned it facedown. But her eye was drawn to Aidan's stack of books again.

There it was. How had she missed it? Nestled between the crime books, the Martina Coles, there it was.

The Time Traveler's Wife.

She thought of her copy, Mr. P's copy, resting beside her bed—forgotten and ignored.

Her heart caught in her throat. She pictured Mr. P, telling her about this book, about how it had helped him. *Books show us the world; they don't hide it.* She imagined Aidan, sitting in this same spot, reading it. Had she even seen him read it? How recently had he read it?

She took a deep breath, and unearthed the book, holding it so delicately between her hands. She'd been so sure she'd been hiding away from life. But maybe Mr. P was right—she'd *learned* from the books too. She'd seen what people had been through—couldn't she use that to cope too? And here it was in Aidan's room, on Aidan's bedside table. If he had ever read it, she wanted to read it too.

She turned to the first page of *The Time Traveler's Wife*; she forced her mind to go quiet, and she read the first line. One word at a time.

Later that day, in the deserted library, Aleisha sat alone at her desk—*The Time Traveler's Wife* by her side. She'd only read a few pages, but it had been like stepping into someone else's world, letting their emotions merge with your own, letting someone else guide you for a moment, so she could work out how best to guide herself. She'd been searching within the pages for clues of Aidan too—what had Aidan thought of Henry, and his ability to travel through his own life? What did he make of the love story too, and of Clare? Her particularly wealthy and snobbish parents. Aidan had always hated people like that.

"Hey," shouted Kyle from the kitchen. "Don't forget to give a final push for the library thing so we can draw in as many people as possible tomorrow—Dev just messaged me to tell me Lucy's daughter has given a few suggestions, putting it out on social media and whatnot." Aleisha groaned. She knew it was what Mr. P and Aidan would want too.

She looked at the big pile of leaflets for SAVE OUR LIBRARIES next to her, ready for the bin, usurped by the BIG LIBRARY GET-TOGETHER leaflets.

She scrolled through stories on Instagram so quickly she heard a millisecond of sound for each of them, trying to fill herself in on other people's lives. Bright lights, people in shorts jumping up, legs by the pool, legs by the beach propping up books, someone's cat's bum sauntering with J.Lo and Iggy Azalea's "Booty" played over the top. *Big big booty.* Hilarious. Her college friend pouting in front of the leaning tower of Pisa with his top off, too cool to do the standard pose of pretending to hold it up.

She was bored already, looking at other people enjoying life. Would she ever be able to post on social media without worrying what people would think of her, pigeonholing her as the "grieving little sister"? Before she had time to think, she took a quick video of the library—empty—and overlaid it with text: **COME GET THIS PLACE BUZZING TOMORROW 11 a.m.!**

She clicked "post" with a grimace.

Aidan would be shaking his head in shame at how uncool she was.

Her phone rang in her palms: *Rachel.*

"What's this about a library get-together? *Tomorrow?* First I've heard of it, why didn't you tell us?"

"What?"

"Just saw your story."

"You're quick!"

"Social media is my job, it's my job to be quick."

"Oh, it's like a community morning thing. Mr. P, you know, from the library, he suggested doing it for Aidan."

"I *love* that idea. Do you want to tell your mum? She's here."

Aleisha went silent. She didn't know what to say, didn't know what Leilah would think. Would she laugh at it? Worse, would she say nothing at all?

"Okay," Aleisha said, her heart starting to pound. She took a deep breath. "Mum?"

There was silence on the other end of the line. "Mum?"

"Leish, sorry, your mum had to go back up to bed. I'll tell her later, okay?" Rachel's voice was quivering; Aleisha could hear her nerves.

"Sure, thanks, Rachel."

Aleisha hadn't been expecting anything—she'd never expected anything at all.

"I have managed to get rid of ninety-nine flyers, Aleisha!" Mr. P gabbled down the phone.

"Wow, that's so great, Mr. P." Aleisha tried to inject enthusiasm into her voice. "I thought you might have gotten bored and just chucked them in the bin."

"Absolutely not! I even put a flyer up in my front window—I actually kept forgetting it was there, so when my old nosy neighbors come past and try to read it, I get very, very scared wondering what they are doing looking so closely through my window!" She'd never heard him so energized before.

"Mr. P, you're a joker."

"No, I'm being serious! I keep preparing myself to shout, '*Get off my property!*' Anyway, it must be a good advertising spot—I'm very proud! Do you have any flyers left?"

"Some, yeah, I guess I'd better take them out tonight." She bit her lip.

"Absolutely! It's *tomorrow* now. There's no time to waste."

As Aleisha hung up, she sat back on the sofa, next to her cousin, watching her uncle Jeremy with her mum. They hadn't mentioned the Big Library Get-Together again that afternoon. When Aleisha had come back from her shift, Rachel had muttered, "I'm sorry, I didn't want to bring it up with her. You know. Didn't want to step on any toes."

Uncle Jeremy had made his famous lamb stew even though it was really too hot to eat it today. Aleisha had devoured it anyway, and now they were all sitting in the same room trying to digest it.

It had been so long since they had been all together in one room as a family. Aidan would have loved to be here, but if he were around he would have played it cool, maybe gone out for a drink with his friends first.

No, she told herself sharply, she was misremembering him. For Aidan, family always came first. This would have come first.

"I've got to put out the last flyers," Aleisha said to her cousin, and tapped the pile that sat between them on the sofa. "Want to come?"

Rachel tapped her stomach in response. "Babe, I honestly don't think I can move."

Aleisha rolled her eyes jokingly. "Come on, walk it off." Her eyes actually said: *I really need to get out of here.*

"Yes, great idea, Aleisha. Go on, Rach," Uncle Jeremy said warmly. Leilah smiled weakly in agreement.

The two young women walked down the street, in silence at first. "Are you doing okay?" Rachel asked, and Aleisha could see her cousin's eyes were teary.

Aleisha took a moment to answer. She focused her eyes on the flyers. THE BIG LIBRARY GET-TOGETHER, it said in Zac's fancy bubble writing.

"I'm doing okay, yeah," she murmured. "I miss him, but that's normal."

Rachel took a moment to reply too. "He was the best. It just doesn't feel real, it's impossible."

"It doesn't make sense," Aleisha echoed on autopilot, replaying the conversations she'd had the day of Aidan's funeral. Shutting her brain off from the emotion for as long as she could.

They walked in silence again, until Aleisha felt her heart start to race. This kept happening recently. She knew in a moment she'd feel breathless. "You take these," she said, handing Rachel a wad of flyers, "and post them on this side. I'll go to the other side of the street and post them there. Any house, unless it really doesn't look lived in."

Rachel shrugged, and Aleisha crossed the road, relieved, taking deep breaths. She slowed down, feeling as though she might collapse at any moment.

In one house she could hear a dog barking, and she reversed as quickly as she could, nearly tripping over the fence. Her breathing quickened again, and she looked over the road. Rachel was posting some flyers and hadn't even noticed her cousin drowning in the searing summer air.

She took a deep breath. She didn't know what to do. She thought of Leilah, hiding away, keeping the truth from everyone. She was scared, she didn't want to reveal too much of herself. But she knew she needed help, Aidan had needed help, they all did. And Rachel, Rachel had been her best friend, once. And she missed her. She wanted her back. She crossed back over the road, her heartbeat slower now, the sweat on her brow evaporating almost immediately in the heat, and she linked arms with her cousin.

Rachel looked at her and tapped her hand gently. "I'm here," she said, as though she had heard every one of Aleisha's thoughts from across the other side of the road.

"Aleisha," Rachel said when they got in. The house was murmuring with quiet activity; Leilah was back in bed, Jeremy was washing up. "That Instagram post you did earlier, you should share it with Aidan's friends. Let them know about it."

"I don't think I can." Aleisha shrugged in response.

"Let me, yeah?" Rachel put her hand out and Aleisha handed over her phone, feeling a well of relief. "Last chance to get people excited."

"It's too late," Aleisha muttered, slumping down on the sofa.

Within moments, though, Rachel pointed to Aleisha's phone. Her feed was littered with people sharing the Library Get-Together post.

"See, Aleisha, I told you," Rachel said with a grin. Aleisha could just fixate on her phone, flashing in front of her, a new notification every few seconds. "People actually care, Leish. They care."

This was what her brother could do—bring people together, as he had always brought people together in his lifetime. To help them feel a little bit less alone.

CHAPTER 39

MUKESH

Beep. "Hi, Dad, it's Deepali. We're leaving soon—I'll see you at the library, okay! Jaya and Jayesh are coming with me. I'm bringing the punch."

Beep. "Hi, Papa, Priya is so excited about today! I'll drop her off with you first, as I will then go pick up the pressure cooker from Nilakshimasi's, for final preparations, okay? Priya has made some extra fairy cakes—so I'll bring them too, okay?"

Beep. "Hi, Papa, need me to bring any extra food or drinks and stuff? I can bring chairs too if that's useful for you guys. Let me know! Well done—I keep thinking Mum would be so proud of you, you know? She was always banging on about setting up an open morning at the library."

On the day of the Big Library Get-Together itself, Mukesh was amazed that there wasn't some kind of fanfare when he woke up. His daughters had packed up all the samosas, spring rolls, and vada of all types the previous evening, ready to go.

"Don't dip into any of this! Especially the vada, we only have a few, and I made them extra hot so *you will regret it*!" Deepali said to her father that night, as he approached the tray laid out on his kitchen table.

"You expect me to take them and not to eat them?"

"Yes, precisely that."

As soon as Deepali had gone, he just *had* to have one. Lo and behold, Deepali had been right, it had burnt even his lips and he knew that was never a good sign for the rest of the vada's journey. He chased it down with a glass of milk and several spoonfuls of yogurt.

He was looking forward to seeing who might come today—new faces, old faces, friendly faces. And he hoped Aleisha's mum would come today too, but it was unlikely. Leilah was struggling. He couldn't imagine how he would feel, God forbid, if one of his daughters or grandchildren died. He couldn't imagine waking up, leaving the bed, the house, ever again. The world would be so much darker without them.

He had ordered a new junior library card and preemptively taken out *Life of Pi*, *Beloved*, and *Pride and Prejudice* to give to Priya before the event. Now he just had to wait for her to arrive.

Mukesh tried in vain to read while he waited—but in the excitement, he found he couldn't pick up a new book. Instead, he read the first few pages of *The Time Traveler's Wife* once more—and the words instantly transported him to Naina. He remembered the time he'd first read it. How heartbroken he had been. But how different he felt now—how alive. And Naina, she was here, in these words, in this love story. She was here in his heart, with him every step of the way.

When the doorbell rang, pulling him from the story, Mukesh jumped up too quickly, his head feeling light. For the briefest moment, he had a feeling that Naina was at the door.

"Dada!" Priya called, stepping into the house. "Have you eaten a vada?"

Rohini, a few steps behind her, stormed through to the kitchen, zipping around the room, checking in every corner, every fridge compartment, for any snacks that had been forgotten. "Papa, did you?"

"No!"

"Yes you did." Priya giggled. "Deepalimasi said there were twenty-one, and now I count only twenty!" Priya stood over the tray of vadas, her finger raised accusingly.

Mukesh went pink.

"Right, let me take that." Rohini grabbed the tray. "I'm going to Nilakshimasi's now. Will you two be okay getting to the library on your own? How will you go?"

"I think we'll walk," Mukesh said firmly. Rohini nodded, formally, and trotted out of the door. A woman on a mission.

"So, Priya," Mukesh said. "I've got a surprise!"

"A surprise?" Priya said, a little cautiously.

"Yes." Mukesh pulled his canvas bag from the banister, and took out a little card and three books. He plonked them all in Priya's hands.

The library card said *Priya Langton*, in Aleisha's chubbiest handwriting.

"Mine?" Priya said, looking down at it. "For the library that Aleisha works at?" She looked up at her dada, hopeful.

"Yes, Aleisha wrote your name on it specially!"

"The books, are they all for me to read?" Priya laid them all out side by side on the stairs.

"If you'd like to. *Beloved* is maybe one for your mummy to read instead, but I wanted to give it to you so you know that it's a good one. Although it's a little bit scary."

"I've read *The Woman in Black*, that was scary," Priya said proudly.

"I don't know that one."

"Ba told me she read it once; she said she jumped out of her skin." Priya brought her hand to her mouth to suppress a giggle, but Mukesh saw her eyes glisten with a soft sheen of tears.

"Oh, beti," he said, embracing her. "Your ba would so love to see the wonderful young lady you are, Priya. You make her very proud." Mukesh's words trembled. "You make me very proud too."

They stayed in a hug for a moment, Mukesh resting his head on Priya's. The whole house, which had felt silent for so long, suddenly felt like home again.

"Dada," Priya eventually said. "Shall we get to the library?"

Mukesh looked at his watch, twenty past ten. "Oh, Bhagwan!" he said. "Yes we should! I'm meant to help set up!"

By the time they arrived at the library, twenty minutes before the start, Aleisha was already there with someone who looked very much like her.

"Hello, Aleisha! Do you remember me? I'm Priya," she said, skipping up to her. There was no sign of nerves today.

"Of course, Priya." Aleisha smiled, a sadness behind her eyes. "How are you?"

"Thank you for my library card," Priya prattled on, holding the card up to her. "I *really* like your handwriting."

"You're very welcome. You can keep your granddad company on some of his library trips, can't you?"

Priya nodded vigorously.

"Hi, Mr. P," Aleisha said, welcoming him over. He'd been standing a few feet away to allow Priya to have her moment. "This is my cousin Rachel," Aleisha said to Mukesh, who smiled and shook the young woman's hand.

"Yes, we met the other day," he said, noticing his accent getting heavier as he became increasingly nervous.

Two cars drew up outside, carrying Rohini, Deepali, Nilakshi, and Vritti. As soon as they'd parked, trays of food emerged from every door, and they carried them straight to the tables laid out specially.

"Why are the chairs like this?" Mukesh asked Aleisha. Kyle chipped in to answer instead. "You see, sir, it's actually more conducive to chatting, in clusters like this. Tables for people to eat outside, then people can browse the library inside—enjoy the peace for a bit! And we wanted this to be an open day for people to get to know each other."

"Actually, Mr. P wanted this to be an open day." Aleisha winked at Mukesh, and Priya giggled exaggeratedly, holding Mukesh's hand.

Gradually, people trickled over to them. Some of the regulars, carrying dishes of food, with friends and family, and some people who had clearly never been here before at all. There weren't *hundreds* of people, as Mukesh had been imagining, but there were at least thirty or forty. They had to bring out many more tables to accommodate the food. There were samosas of every kind, jerk chicken, chips with chilli sprinkled on top, mogo too, sausages wrapped in bacon, vegetarian sausages with rosemary that would later become Mukesh's new favorite, fairy cakes made by Priya, and quiche with something questionable inside it. Was it meat, or was it plastic? Cheese squares with cocktail sticks impaling them, and chutneys of all kinds. It was a feast.

At one point, the noise of chatter and laughter was unbearable, so Mukesh carried himself off inside for a while to settle into a chair. He looked around the library, seeing it as all the people outside might be seeing it. Stacks and stacks of books on shiny shelves that might once have been white, but were now yellowing, and chairs—some new and comfy, others not so much. He felt a calm wash over him. He was already looking forward to coming in again and relaxing in his favorite chair to read a new book when this day was over. He hoped that many of the people who came today for the first time would get to enjoy it too. And there, nestled among the bookshelves, comfy in her beanbag, sat Priya. She caught him looking, and beamed at him. He would never have imagined, just a few weeks ago, that this might have happened. He knew so much had changed, for better, and for worse . . . but this was one of the good moments, one of the loveliest moments.

Mukesh was nibbling on veggie sausages when he spotted Rohini with a paper plate in one hand and a mug full to the brim in the other.

"I brought you some more sausages!" she said loudly, over the din. "And some chai, homemade by Indiraba!"

"Indira is here?"

"Mhmm, *apparently* she's a regular—has been for a while now. I can't believe you never mentioned she came here. She's very chatty today," Rohini said.

"Indira, chatty? That's news to me! But in that case, I'll stay in here a little longer . . ." Mukesh laughed. "You know," he whispered, "the last time we spoke, it took me two hours to get away."

Rohini laughed. "Papa!" she admonished. "Just be kind to her, she is lonely. Isn't that what this whole day is about? Mummy really liked Indiraba, she always looked out for her."

Mukesh looked at his vegetarian sausage, twirling on its cocktail stick. "You're right." Rohini tapped him lightly but firmly on the leg, and Mukesh apologized.

"Anyway, Papa, I wanted to say sorry. I haven't treated you well. Always making decisions for you. But look around, you're doing brilliantly." She nodded her head over to Priya. "And Priya has said how much she's enjoyed spending time with you this summer."

Mukesh didn't know what to say. "And everything you've done for Aleisha, you've been a lovely friend."

Mukesh couldn't look at his daughter, he flushed with embarrassment. "I guess your mummy managed to instill something useful in me in the end."

"I worried that you needed someone to take care of you after Mummy died, but I didn't give you the credit that you could take care of yourself, and when I tried to look after you, I forgot how to keep you company. I'm sorry."

Mukesh smiled gently and squeezed his daughter's hand.

"I'm going to nip out and help Deepali escape Indira, but I hope we can see each other, spend actual time together, more often. Mummy would want that. I know that now."

Before Mukesh could say anything in response, Rohini had gone. There was nothing but a croak brewing in his throat—he tried to swallow the lump away before he had to speak to someone else.

He looked out of the window at the crowd of people, holding paper plates, stuffing food in their mouths, and chatting. He was so pleased to see the people from the temple weren't just talking to others from the temple, they were talking to anyone and everyone. The people he assumed Aleisha had invited—her friends, Aidan's friends—were even mingling with the oldies, and Mukesh's heart sang.

Then another car pulled up and out hopped Zac.

He smiled. Aleisha would be pleased.

And then Mukesh spotted a figure in the front seat, peering out of the window. Could it really be? He had to find Aleisha, to tell her. Leilah had come!

CHAPTER 40

MUKESH AND ALEISHA

Aleisha was filling the punch bowl. The ice cubes had melted quickly in the heat, and she worried that they hadn't enough in the library's freezer.

"Do you know that punch comes from the Hindi word 'panch'?" one old lady, dressed in a heavily embellished sari, said to her. She'd seen her around the library, she was always chatting away to someone in a corner, whispering in hushed tones. She'd had to tell her off once or twice.

"I didn't know that," Aleisha said, smiling at the lady. Her hair was pulled back into a severe bun with a net wrapped around it.

"Panch means five, and five is how many ingredients are in punch. How many did you put in?"

Aleisha shrugged, she didn't have a clue—Deepali had made it. At that moment, a young woman wearing a beret and a Breton top cut in. Aleisha knew she'd seen her around the library before.

"Indira!" the young woman said. "How are you? I've not seen you in ages."

"Oh, Izzy." The old lady beamed from ear to ear. "I know, my sciatica has been playing up so I've been on bed rest for a bit, but I'm back for the big day! Did you ever find out from that man at the library about your book list? Just like the one I found. I have been thinking about it for such a long time, beti."

Aleisha watched as the woman spoke at a hundred miles an hour. Book list? Aleisha listened in more closely.

"No, nothing yet. It's a complete mystery. I mean, we might never find out—but look how much we've gained from it. I might never have met you, Indira!" Izzy said with an over-the-top smile. "Would you like to try some of my kombucha? It's homemade. Sweetened with honey."

Aleisha smelled the kombucha, which stank in the heat, and took the opportunity to duck out. She filed away what she'd just heard about the list, reminding herself to investigate, when from behind the young woman's head, she caught sight of Zac's car.

"Aleisha!" Mukesh said breathlessly by her shoulder, pointing toward Zac. "Someone is here for you!"

She held her breath as Zac walked toward her, holding a casserole dish, and she tried to get a glimpse of the person accompanying him, her heart in her mouth.

"This all looks great!" he called. "Hey, come meet my mum."

Aleisha's stomach dropped—out of the car, carrying another dish, was a woman. A woman she wanted to be *her* mother. She hadn't expected Leilah to come. But she'd been hoping.

"Hi," Aleisha said as Zac's mum caught up with her. She was young and trendy with elegant blond hair. She was wearing high-heeled sandals and a sheer blouse that looked as if it was the wrong choice for a stand-up buffet. "Lovely to meet you."

"You too, my love. I'm just so sorry to hear about your brother. Zac told me. But this is such a beautiful idea. I hope my vegetarian tagine is all right for your grandfather." She nodded her head toward Mukesh, who was waving frantically at Zac.

"Oh, he's not my grandfather." She smiled. "Just my friend, and a regular at the library. But thank you, thanks for coming. It means a lot." Aleisha was happy to meet her, but she had to swallow down her disappointment. She wanted to go home, she wanted to drag Leilah out kicking and screaming.

Thermos Flask stepped out from the library doors, bellowing, "Gather round, gather round," and people gradually did as told, reluctantly ceasing their chat.

"Samuel! Don't pull that lady's dress. Come here!" one mother called to her son, just as the crowd had gone absolutely silent. "Shit! Sorry!" she shouted out. "Sorry!"

There was a brief chuckle, as Aleisha took a moment to survey the crowd. There were maybe around *fifty* here now, people of all different ages. She saw Breton Girl again, as well as the pink-haired regular, and Popular Science Guy . . . Wow, she hadn't seen him in ages. Benny and Lucy were tucked toward the back, with their families. She recognized some people from pictures on Aidan's phone, or from his social media, but most of them were brand-new to her. Others were clearly Mukesh's friends, but there were plenty of others Aleisha couldn't easily categorize. Then she spotted Chris Crime Thriller with his mum and dad, who both looked just like their son. All were hunched over slightly, hands in their pockets. When he caught her eye, he smiled and waved a copy of a book at her. *To Kill a Mockingbird*.

That felt like a lifetime ago. Crime Thriller Guy—the one who had given her the very first book, with that mysterious list between its pages. To this day, she still wondered, had he put that list together for her? Had he known?

"Thank you all for coming," Dev said, his eyes searching the crowd. He locked eyes with Aleisha and beckoned her over. She reluctantly shuffled her way to the front, catching saris and jackets and T-shirts as she went, feeling thoroughly embarrassed already.

When she arrived at the very front, her cheeks flushed and glowing with a thin sheen of sweat that she hoped everyone would just think was her natural radiance, Dev started looking for someone else too: Mukesh.

Mr. P took two steps forward and he was there right beside them.

"I would like to thank Aleisha, one of our brilliant librarians, and Mukesh Patel, a true Harrow Road regular, for thinking of this idea, and opening our little library up to everyone for the morning. We are so happy to have you all here, and we hope you continue to come for a drop-in on Wednesdays. Come for the cake—and stay for the books! I know we may not be the biggest library on the block, but we endeavor to make this space a peaceful and friendly place for our local community. We'd love to have your support, so we can keep this library going as an important part of Wembley's history, and its future."

Mukesh leaned into the microphone, his voice quivering. "Books are great!" he said, and a few people, including Deepali and Rohini and Priya, laughed. He stalled for a moment, wondering what to say, until, in the crowd, he spotted Naina—a complete vision of her, smiling, nodding encouragingly.

"I am grateful to Aleisha and Dev and the young man Kyle for helping me find a place that can feel like home. And, we want to do this as often as possible on *Wednesdays*. And you all know, Wednesdays are shopping days—so you'll be out and about, anyway. Why not pop along?"

Aleisha could tell he was nervous—he was stuttering very slightly—but he was certainly enjoying his limelight. He'd once said he hated being the center of attention—she was sure it had been a big fat lie.

"My Naina, my late wife," he continued, his eyes flying to his Naina, in the crowd. His eyes stung for a moment and he could feel a hollowing in his heart. "She loved books. I never understood books until I came here, but the library helped me feel closer to her. It is very important to feel a part of a place and a community, and I would like everyone to come and enjoy it here, just like me."

Aleisha nodded.

"And please don't forget to raise a toast, or take out a book, in memory of Aidan Thomas, a young man who loved this library very much!"

Mukesh handed the microphone back and stepped aside. He had said his piece, and there was silence all around. Rohini had a tissue held up to her nose, covering her mouth. He looked around once more and just for a moment, as the sun hit the cars in the car park and refracted through the library's windows, Mukesh could see all the characters he'd met along the way. There was Pi and his terrifying tiger, very out of place. Elizabeth Bennet, still playing hard to get, with Darcy a few steps behind. Marmee and her little women, linking arms together. Amir and Hassan, young again, carefree, running around with a kite in the car park. But, between them all, there was Naina—still smiling, her hands held together at her chest.

Aleisha and Mukesh were sitting in their usual spot by the window, the library now returned to its quiet state, the only evidence left of the day being the tin trays emptied of food and stacked up by the recycling.

"Aleisha?" Mukesh started, tentatively. "What did you think? Would Aidan have liked it?"

Aleisha had been asking herself the same question—she'd seen so many people here, laughing, talking to new people, even picking up flyers for the library itself. She wished more than anything that he could have been here to see it. "I think so," she said at first, before returning with, "No, you know what, he would have loved it."

Mukesh sighed shallowly, contented. "He would be very proud of you, beta," he said to Aleisha, looking directly at her. "You have done so much."

Aleisha felt emotion rise in her chest, threatening to burst out as tears and roll down her face. She hopped up from the chair, and wandered to a stray tablecloth, left forgotten on a library table. She shoved it into a canvas bag, not yet able to look Mukesh in the eye.

"Can I ask what the next book is? I want to read it," Mukesh said, sensing Aleisha's embarrassment, desperate to come to her rescue and offer a change of subject.

She nodded—for a moment, she thought she glimpsed Aidan, sitting on the chair next to Mukesh, reading *The Time Traveler's Wife*.

"Why don't you come in tomorrow and I'll suggest something for you?"

"Thank you, Aleisha." After a moment, he pushed himself up from his seat, slowly, carefully. "Well done on today, beti. Well done," he said, his smile infectious.

"Thank you, Mr. P," she replied softly, now wiping down some more tables, unnecessarily. Mr. P wandered out of the glass doors after tapping on the automatic-open button without a second thought, as if it was second nature. How far he had come. "Oh, wait!" she called out to him. He turned around, cautious. "Sorry, they asked me to remind you. Could you bring back *The Highway Code*?" Mr. P's face turned red, and he nodded hurriedly before wandering off.

Then her mind returned once more to the woman stepping out of Zac's car. She'd never imagined it would be Leilah, it was a distant dream, really. But today was meant to be about Aidan and she'd allowed herself to hope.

CHAPTER 41

ALEISHA

As Aleisha turned onto her road, she glanced at her house, expecting the usual shut windows, darkness inside, the curtains half-closed in every room. Rachel and Jeremy weren't back yet, their car wasn't outside—they'd gone to pick up some ingredients for dinner—and a panic started to bubble through her. Was Leilah okay? How long had they left her? She'd been so preoccupied by the planning for the event, she'd barely even stopped to think about Leilah being in the house on her own.

She started to walk more quickly, before breaking into a half-run. But when she approached number 79, there, sitting on the front step, was Leilah. The door was wide open behind her.

"Aleisha, I'm s . . ." she began, her voice fading away.

She was dressed head to toe in navy, in one of Aidan's hoodies and his tracksuit bottoms too. She began to push herself up as Aleisha moved toward her, but she didn't have the strength. Aleisha leaned forward and gathered her mum up in her arms.

Leilah and Aleisha stayed like that for just a few moments. But Aleisha took it all in. She wasn't angry anymore. She didn't have the energy to be angry. Aidan wouldn't want her to be. Now, she just wanted her mum back. She inhaled—smelling Leilah's coconut shampoo, and Aidan's stuffy, musty hoodie.

"Mum, it's okay."

"No, Aleisha." Leilah pulled herself away, gently. "I'm so sorry. I wanted to come. I tried. I just couldn't."

"Mum, don't worry." Aleisha wished Leilah had been there to see it, to see how many people had turned up, all the people who had been there for Aidan.

"Here," Leilah said. She pulled herself away again and dug out a piece of paper. It was a printout from Leilah's fancy printer—she could tell because of the thick paper, the detail in the lettering. It was an email.

"I signed up to the library," Leilah said. She smiled. "I know it seems stupid, but I've loved you reading to me. I hope we can do it some more. I know it might be a while until I get up and go there myself, but . . . I'm serious. I know how much your brother loved it too. Ever since he was little. And look." Leilah pointed to the bottom of the email.

1 book on reserve: To Kill a Mockingbird*, by Lee, Harper.*

Aleisha didn't know what to say. She hugged her mum even tighter. She knew this wasn't the end, it was only the very beginning, but she was conscious that Leilah was standing outside the house, on her own. She was here, and she wasn't shaking, she was breathing normally, she was making eye contact, she was trying.

"Maybe we could try to go together next week?"

"All right."

"After my doctor's appointment." Leilah kissed her daughter on the cheek. "I might need you there for that too."

Aleisha stopped, she took a deep breath and tried to keep her voice from cracking. "Mum, that's wonderful. I'm so proud of you." And she meant it, she meant every word. She wished Aidan were here to see this.

That evening, Aleisha and Leilah sat in the cool shade of the living room, the windows open, just a fraction, letting in a gentle warm breeze.

They'd spent the afternoon going through some baby photos, of Aidan, of Aleisha—they took it one at a time, but Aleisha watched as each photo prompted Leilah to light up, a memory to jump out at her. Beach holidays in the pouring rain, Aidan in the bath as a baby, foam on his head, Aidan learning to surf, Aidan and Aleisha's first school photo together.

When the photos had run out, when they started to hurt again, to remember he wasn't coming back, Aleisha opened the last book on the list: *A Suitable Boy*. She began to read out loud.

Immediately, Leilah and Aleisha were thrown into a wedding, where Mrs. Rupa Mehra was telling her unmarried daughter Lata that she would have to marry a boy that her mother was going to choose for her.

The book was vibrant, immersive, the wedding was alive in their living room—Aleisha watched as Leilah smiled along at Rupa Mehra's sternness.

"I'm not like that, am I?"

"Not always." Aleisha laughed.

For a while, mother and daughter were swept up in another story, centered on a mother and a daughter, and a quest to find this young woman a suitable boy.

"It's so *vivid*," Leilah said. "So many characters, with different backgrounds and beliefs—it's so clever, setting up all these strands. It's beautiful—I feel like I need to paint it."

Aleisha's eyes shot up. Leilah hadn't spoken about her art in months. Not wanting to ruin the moment that the author's words had created, she continued to read.

She wondered why this book was the last on the list, whether the list writer had ordered them for any particular reason. She thought about the journey the books had taken her on, the places they had transported her to—Maycomb, Alabama; Cornwall and Kabul; to the middle of the Pacific Ocean; to some shire in England; to Massachusetts; to Cincinnati; and finally Brahmpur, India. Through the reading list's characters, she'd experienced injustice and childlike innocence, terror and unease, guilt and regret and powerful, everlasting friendship, a dalliance with Mr. Darcy (*still* Zac came to her mind when she thought about *Pride and Prejudice*), resilience, independence, and determination through the little women, the repercussions of trauma and the power of hope, faith, and community. And now, with *A Suitable Boy*, a new journey was just beginning.

"What's that?" Leilah asked, peering at the pages.

Aleisha looked up. "What?"

"In the book?"

"They're just leaving the wedding now—Savita is the bride, Pran is the groom."

"No, I mean, at the back of the book, there's something there."

Aleisha stopped reading and flicked to the last page.

Leilah was right: tucked into the plastic dustcover was an envelope, creased yet flattened by the weight of *A Suitable Boy*.

She prized it out, carefully, as though it were a piece of buried treasure.

"What is it?" Leilah asked.

"An envelope. A letter, I guess." Aleisha turned it over to see if it was addressed to anyone.

Mukesh.

"Mum," Aleisha said. "I think it's for Mr. P."

"What?"

"The letter." She held it up.

Leilah squinted. "Do you think it's the same handwriting as the list?"

Aleisha pulled the reading list from her phone case, but she didn't really need to look at it. Its image was almost ingrained on her memory: every book, the curling *y*'s and *i*'s of the writer's careful script.

She handed them both over to Leilah, knowing her artistic mum had an eye for this kind of thing.

"Definitely. Is it . . . is it for *your* Mukesh? Mr. Patel?"

Aleisha shrugged and gently stroked the paper. "Well . . . let's find out."

"Okay, but don't lose our place."

Aleisha frowned, confused.

"In the book," Leilah said. "I want to know what happens next."

CHAPTER 42

MUKESH

Mukesh opened the door and a grin split his face in two when he saw her. "Aleisha! Did I invite you? I am so sorry, I forgot. I haven't cooked any food or anything, I am still so full from the buffet! Do you want to come tomorrow instead? Priya is going to be here—she would like to see you again, I am sure." He started to look around his house, analyzing whether it was guest friendly. "Or are you here for *The Highway Code*?"

"No, no, don't worry, Mr. P, we weren't meant to have dinner today. I'm just here, err . . . I've got something, I think it's for you."

She held up *A Suitable Boy*.

"Oh no! Aleisha. I know I am a much better reader than before, but honestly, that is *too*, *too* big for me right now. It will send me to sleep."

"First of all, Mr. P, what I've read is amazing so far. I think you'll like it, and by the time you finish it, Priya will probably be old enough to read it too." Aleisha laughed. "Here." She turned to the back of the book, pulled out the envelope, and passed it to him. "I found this. I think it's for you. But before you read it, you should probably know—" She gulped, suddenly nervous.

"You see, I found this list . . . A list of books. It's what we've been reading together."

"You wrote the books down? You are such a good librarian, Aleisha, the full service. How lovely," he said.

"No, Mr. P. They're someone else's book recommendations. I've been a bit of a cheat. You know how I said I didn't know anything about books?"

"Yes, you are a modest girl."

"No, Mr. P. I really know nothing, or . . . well, I *knew* nothing. But I found this list, the day you came in. And I thought . . . I don't know. I thought if I read them and they were all right, I could recommend them to you."

He looked down at the envelope again. "Mukesh." He said his own name as though he had never heard it before.

"I think it's from—"

"Naina," he cut in. "It's her handwriting."

"The list. I think it was Naina's."

She passed the list to him too. His hands were shaking. "And that letter, that letter is for you."

Mukesh looked up at Aleisha as though for the first time, as though taking in her face inch by inch, the envelope in one hand, the list in the other. Aleisha smiled, tapped her friend on the shoulder, and walked away.

As she crossed the road, she saw a young man standing ahead of her, leaning against a wall. For the briefest moment, she thought it was Aidan, his face turned into a smile—especially for her.

NAINA

2017

Naina had dropped off the second-to-last list; it was sitting under the copy of *To Kill a Mockingbird*. She hoped Chris might read it—it was completely different from the crime thrillers he usually read, but she thought something new might help him. He was hurting now. But books, they had the power to heal.

The library books were stacked on her bedside table. Her final library reading list. They were all her favorite books, the books she had grown up with, the books that had found her at the right time, that had given her comfort when she needed it, had given her an escape, an opportunity to live beyond her life, an opportunity to love more powerfully, a chance to open up and let people in. And now she had read them all once more, for the very last time.

Priya had been the one to suggest she leave a reading list behind. "Ba, one day I'd like a list of your favorite books. You are the best book person I know." She'd said it just in passing, as children often do, but the idea had stayed with Naina. She knew she was leaving—but she wanted to give something back. To Wembley. To the people who loved her. And the books had given her so much. Well, it was time to pass them on. She hoped that the lists would find their way into willing hands and hearts—in the supermarket, at the bus stop, in the library, at the yoga studio, in the community garden—and brighten them, even if just for a moment. With Indira's list, she knew she couldn't just give it to her directly—Indira was proud, she would laugh at the idea, discard it as soon as she was alone. It was maybe a silly idea leaving it in Indira's shoe rack, all crumpled up. But she was trusting fate to do the work for her. She hoped Indira would find her way to the books, maybe even to the library.

Now there was just one list left to give. And she knew who this one belonged to: Mukesh. He had never been a reader, but she hoped, after she left, he might start to wonder what all the fuss had been about for her. She didn't want him to be lonely, and he had a tendency to cut himself off from the outside world when he was sad. This way, she thought, if he did that, he might find some company elsewhere. Within the pages. He might find something to inspire him to meet new people, try new things, he might find some words of wisdom too.

She pulled out a piece of her letter-writing paper—this was her umpteenth attempt. Despite all the books she'd read in her lifetime, finding the words to say *I love you*, to the person she had spent the happiest years of her life with, seemed to be the hardest thing in the world.

She took a deep breath and began, her tears already blotting the paper.

Mukesh,

I've started this letter ten, twenty times and I never know quite what I want to say. Thank you. Thank you for loving me, for being my friend, my soul mate, for all our fifty years. I am so happy we found each other and raised our family. I am proud of the life we built. It has been small but it has been full of love. You have made it so.

I want you to know you will be okay without me. But push yourself, Mukesh, challenge yourself every day. Speak to someone new. Do something different. Teach our children about our lives before them, and look after them, and don't be afraid to let them look after you. Little Priya is shy—I found reading books with her helped her open up to me. I would love for you to try that too. She wants to be closer to you. And I want that for you both.

Find peace with yourself. I know you are angry, I know you are hurting. But my cancer is nobody's fault. Sometimes this is just the way life goes. If you are reading this letter, then I am gone, and the next part of your life is about to begin. Enjoy it, it should be just as special as the time we had together.

Be kind, be caring, be yourself, Mukesh. You are the most wonderful person I could ever have known. Don't be scared to love again if it finds you, and know I would be happy for you if you do, and remember, you can find family in the most unexpected places, and family will always find you.

All my love,
Naina x

P.S. These are the books that brought me closer to myself, that helped shape me and my world—I hope they'll bring you light and joy and, if you ever miss me, you'll find me within their pages. I love you.

P.P.S. I think Priya would love the books too—but maybe when she's a little bit older.

As she started to tuck the list into the envelope with the letter, she heard Mukesh's footsteps plodding down the stairs. She hurriedly sat on the envelope and tucked her pen away in the bedside table.

"Naina." Mukesh popped his head around. "Would you like some chai?"

"Ha, that would be lovely," Naina replied. Mukesh tiptoed

away as Naina pulled the envelope out from under her bottom. It was all crumpled and creased. She sighed, and tucked it into the back of *A Suitable Boy*. If any book could flatten out a letter, it was that one.

"Packet chai okay with you?" Mukesh called.

"Of course. My favorite," Naina said.

A READING LIST FROM THE AUTHOR

While the reading list in the book belongs to one character, there are so many more books I wanted to include, books that have changed the way I've thought about writing, people, the world. Books that inspired me, moved me, taught me more than any school lesson could. Books that made me want to be a reader and eventually a writer. This is my reading list.

Jhumpa Lahiri, *The Namesake*
Arundhati Roy, *The God of Small Things*
Zadie Smith, *White Teeth*
Chimamanda Ngozi Adichie, *Americanah*
Katherine Heiny, *Standard Deviation*
Rohinton Mistry, *A Fine Balance*
Hiromi Kawakami, *Strange Weather in Tokyo*
Angela Carter, *The Magic Toyshop*
Maya Angelou, *I Know Why the Caged Bird Sings*
Attia Hosain, *Sunlight on a Broken Column*
Ali Smith, *There But For The*

These books found me at just the right time in my life. I can remember each of them so vividly, I remember the characters as though they were friends, sometimes even family, I can remember exactly where I was and how I felt when I turned that final page. They've stayed with me ever since.

ACKNOWLEDGMENTS

This book has been so close to my heart for a long time, but it wouldn't exist at all were it not for so many amazing people. Thank you to my agent, Hayley Steed, who has been the biggest supporter I could have wished for. Thank you for believing in this book before it was even fully formed; for your editorial insights, expertise, and unwavering enthusiasm; and for guiding my anxious brain through the whole process. Huge thanks to the team at Madeleine Milburn Literary Agency, and a special shoutout to the rights superstars Liane-Louise, Georgina, and Sophie. You have been the perfect literary family—and this book is in the very best hands with you all.

To Charlotte Brabbin, my brilliant editor—this book would not be what it is without you. Thank you so much for your passion, for your creativity, for your attention to detail, your vision, and your belief in this book. Thank you to the whole team at HarperFiction, especially Becca Bryant, Hannah O'Brien and Katy Blott, Grace Dent, Isabel Coburn, Alice Gomer, Sarah Munro, and Laura Daley. I am in awe of all your talents! Thank you to Claire Ward and Andrew Davis for the amazing cover, and to Aleesha Nandhra for your beautiful artwork. To Rachel Kahan, my fantastic editor at William Morrow in the US, and to Virginia Stanley, Alivia Lopez, Jennifer Hart, Jeanie Lee, and the whole William Morrow team—thank you for taking such great care of this book stateside.

To my first readers—Hannah Wann, Amanda Preston, Niki Chang—your advice and your insight spurred me on. Rosie Price, thank you for your friendship and kindness and for helping me through all the bumps in the road.

To Ifey Frederick, for always being my rock and for keeping me grounded.

Noor Sufi, my partner in crime, you have been there every step of the way. Thank you for being my fabulous friend and this book's biggest champion—your excitement kept me going at so many points, and it has meant everything.

Thank you to Liz Foley and Kate Harvey, for all your words of wisdom.

To all my friends, for being the best cheerleaders and for picking me up whenever I've needed it, especially Abi, Mary, Rachael, Christina, Monica, Kitty, Radiya, Katie; and to Isobel Turner—for actually collecting lists and allowing me to put Izzy in the book!

To my colleagues and all the amazing authors I've worked with at Headline, Vintage, and Hodder—thank you for the guidance and support you've given me over the years.

To all the librarians and booksellers who make the book world what it is—you do so much for people and for communities. Thank you!

And finally, my family. Your joy about this book has meant the world, and it has made all my overthinking, the late nights, and the early mornings 100 percent worth it. Thank you to Dada, for always asking me what I was reading and for being the start of this story. Thank you, Ba, for your love and endless generosity; Jaymin and Jigar, for being great baby cousins and for telling me where all the cool kids hang out these days. Thank you, Auntie, for *so* much but especially for reading this book out loud to Granny and taking out the swear words. I'll forever be grateful!

Thank you to my parents for *everything*. Dad, thanks for always believing in me and for never letting me give up. You have read all the little stories and half-baked novels I've ever written, except for this one, because you want to buy it in a bookshop first. I hope you enjoy it and that it's been worth the wait. Mum, so much love to you for reading this story and for talking about my characters as though they're real. It has been the greatest feeling knowing you love it. The fact you're proud makes me proud too.

And to Granny—it brings me so much happiness and comfort knowing you read this book. Thank you for always asking me

"How's the writing going?" I never wanted to tell you "It's not," and because of that, this book is finally here. I miss you every day.

And to Will Handysides, I literally could not have written this book without you. Thank you for all you've done to make this possible—for putting up with my fretting, for reading and editing the book so many times, for being brutally honest and mega kind too, for letting me ask the same questions over and over again, for being a constant inspiration, and for putting up with my "creative" slobbishness . . . You're one of a kind. Thank you for being you.

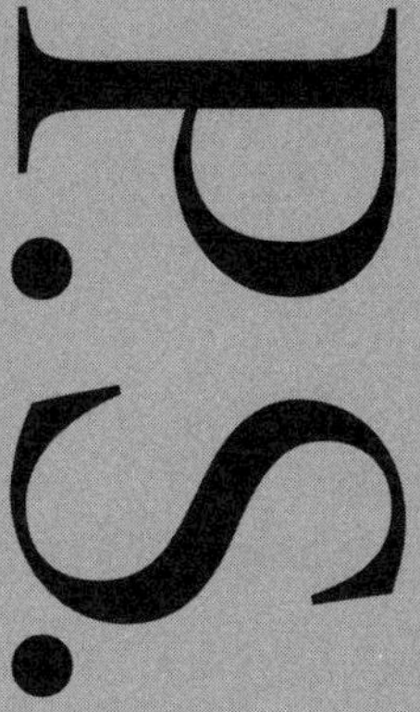

Insights, Interviews & More . . .

About the author

About the book

Meet Sara Nisha Adams

Photograph courtesy of the author

Sara Nisha Adams is a writer and editor. She was born in Hertfordshire, England, to Indian and English parents and now lives in London. *The Reading List* is partly inspired by her grandfather, who lived in Wembley and who immediately found a connection with his granddaughter through books.

A Conversation with Sara Nisha Adams

Q: ***You've said that* The Reading List, *especially the characters of Priya and Mukesh, was inspired by your grandparents and their London neighborhood. Can you tell us more about that?***

A: My maternal grandparents lived in Wembley, North West London, in the house my mum grew up in after her family moved to the UK from Kenya. I loved visiting them. The house held memories of my mum and her siblings growing up, family weddings, their grandchildren—my cousins—being born. The only thing that held me back was the language barrier. I never learned to speak Gujarati, the language my mum's family speaks, and so while I could broadly understand things, I couldn't respond in Gujarati. I was already quite shy, so I think this gap in my knowledge made me even shyer.

My relationship with my grandmother, my ba, was built upon our shared love of food—she knew my favorite meals and would cook them whenever I visited. I used to go to nursery school in Wembley too, and I remember my lunches always being delivered by my ba or mum. My dada, ▸

A Conversation with Sara Nisha Adams
(continued)

my grandfather, was also quite reserved, like me, and he noticed that I'd often tuck myself away with a book. He always made sure, before I left for the day, to ask me what I was reading. He'd take the book in his hands, read out the title to me, and ask me what it was about. It was the way into my world—I would talk about the book, but I'd also talk about myself. I came alive when talking about books.

These were small moments overall, but they hold such a special place in my heart—and the idea of *The Reading List* came to me when I asked myself, *What if my dada hadn't tried to reach me through books?* And that, in a way, is the start of Mukesh and Priya's journey.

Wembley itself feels like home to me too. I wanted to write about it because I've always loved being there—visiting my family; eating my ba's delicious food; spending time with my cousins; taking trips to the temple; walking down the high road to get my eyebrows threaded for the first time as a teenager (absolutely terrifying!); venturing out to Ealing Road to look at outfits for a wedding or to get the freshest vegetables for dinner; hanging around awkwardly as my mum and aunts chatted with an old friend or neighbor they spotted on the street, who would eventually turn to me and exclaim how much I'd grown.

For years I couldn't find a book that captured the London I knew, which was full of community: neighbors helping each other out, deliveries of Tupperwares of food, sharing of stories and recipes, long impromptu chats in the street that would then continue on sofas, with mugs or bowls and saucers of chai. I had read books about London's grand Victorian town houses, wealthy neighbors telling secrets at dinner parties, or young artists moving into the city to follow their dreams, but until I read *White Teeth* by Zadie Smith, I hadn't read a book that captured what I knew of London—North West London and Wembley, in particular. I wanted my first book to be about the place that held so many happy memories for me, and the place my family calls home.

Q: How did you choose the books on the reading list? Did you create the list first and then build the novel around it, or did you tailor the list to fit the novel as you were writing?

A: The list itself came to me almost instantly, when I had only a germ of an idea for the story! They are all books that I read as a teenager and that have stuck with me ever since. As a teen, I was always searching for books that would move or inspire me, beyond the novels ▸

A Conversation with Sara Nisha Adams *(continued)*

we were reading at school. Actually, I think a few of the titles on the list in the book were recommended to me by an English teacher from their own reading list. When I started including the books in the story, I realized each one needed to play some part in the characters' journeys—so in a way, I had to put myself in the characters' shoes and work out what would resonate with each of them at particular points in time, and why. It was a joy discovering books I've loved through new eyes, seeing what the characters loved about the stories and what they didn't like so much (This was the hardest part . . . It's impossible to be objective about stories that you hold so close to your heart!), because they couldn't just think exactly as I do!

A few of the books have moved around in the novel, to better fit the structure or the emotional arc—but, on the whole, the list appears as it first came to me. I think teenage Sara, reading *To Kill a Mockingbird* for the first time one hot summer, during the school holiday, would be quite amazed that the books that inspired her to keep writing and to keep reading all formed a crucial part of her debut novel.

Q: What kind of response did you get from readers when the book came out? Did people in your family recognize themselves in* The Reading List*?

A: I've had the loveliest response from readers—it's been by far the greatest part of my publishing journey. I've had so many messages from young women who recognize themselves in Priya or Aleisha, or from readers who have picked up *The Reading List* after a long time of not reading for pleasure at all who've been inspired to read more. Someone once said to me that as soon as a book is published, it belongs more to the reader than the writer—and I am so glad I kept this in mind from the beginning. I know not everyone will love my novel, but when I hear it has become someone's favorite book, or has helped them in a dark time, or has helped them feel seen in fiction, that means more than anything.

My family have been so wonderfully supportive of the book—none of Mukesh's family are exactly like my own family, but I think they will be able to see themselves in the joy of sharing food together, and in the overprotectiveness sometimes too! ▸

A Conversation with Sara Nisha Adams ***(continued)***

When I was little, my mum always used to say "Uh-ruh-ruh!" when she was disgusted at something, so I made her read out loud a passage where Rohini says that, and it was brilliant. My two little cousins (they're twenty now, so not so little after all!) both read the book—and they're two of my favorite people in the world. They grew up in the house in Wembley, so they recognized the way it was described, they recognized the places, the library—and after reading the book, they said it made them want to read more. That was the best thing to hear, ever.

Q: What's on your personal reading list right now? Is there anything you're reading and loving and want to tell others about?

A: I have read *so* much amazing fiction recently. As a fiction editor too, you'd think I'd want a break from reading on the weekends—but I can't get enough. I adored *Love After Love* by Ingrid Persaud, a story of found family—it is just beautifully written and full of warmth and wisdom. I also loved *Keeping the House* by Tice Cin—a novel full of strong, smart women, about the roles they play in their family and community in North London. It's lyrical, bold, and completely brilliant. And finally, *The Impossible Us* by Sarah Lotz, which I read holding my breath. A bighearted love story that is clever and funny and sharp.

Q: Tell us about what's next for you.

A: I'm currently working on my next novel, *The Shared Garden*, which is a story of community and an unlikely pair of friends who work together to restore their unusual shared garden to the community garden it used to be. I came up with the idea when I lived in a top-floor flat in Stoke Newington, North London, dreaming of a community garden to plant some vegetables or bulbs. Since I've started writing the book, I now live somewhere with a lovely garden and a great vegetable patch built by my partner, and there's even a community garden down the road, looked after by some of the loveliest neighbors I've ever met. It feels as though I did manifest my dream after all . . .

I hope when people get to read *The Shared Garden* they'll enjoy it, and the characters I've come to love, as much as *The Reading List.*

Reading Group Guide

1. Which books on the reading list have you read? Were any of them particular favorites of yours? Were any titles new to you?

2. When he picks up *The Time Traveler's Wife* after Naina's death, Mukesh reflects that "this book felt like one little glimpse into her soul, into their love, their life together." Is there a single book that would offer that same insight into your soul or your life? How does the experience of reading this book and the others from the list help Mukesh process his grief and loneliness?

3. Part of the reason Mukesh is compelled to begin reading is because his granddaughter Priya is an avid reader. The author, Sara Nisha Adams, says that this novel was partly inspired by the way she bonded with her own grandfather through their shared love of books. Are there people in your life whom you share the world of books with?

4. Aleisha's mother, Leilah, is often barely functional because of mental illness, and Aleisha always craves a

connection with her: "She believed the book . . . and the list . . . they might bring her mother back to her." Does Leilah draw closer to Aleisha as they read together? What does reading do for their fractured mother-daughter relationship?

5. Aleisha blames herself for Aidan's suicide: "I missed so much. . . . I just had my head stuck in those *books*." Was Aidan's death a surprise to you as well? Is Aleisha being unfair to herself?

6. In her despair after losing her brother, Aleisha thinks: "But what good were books now? The characters she'd loved in them were fake, they'd never be able to fix anything. They'd never live beyond the page. But the person she'd loved who had existed in the real world, who'd fought for her, who'd encouraged her, who had given up so much for her—he was now gone." Is this fair?

7. Mukesh later consoles Aleisha by saying, "Please try to remember that books aren't always an escape; sometimes books teach us things. They *show* us the world; they don't hide it." What did books teach or reveal to the different characters in ▸

this novel? Which books have had that effect in your own life?

8. Even though reading is a solitary activity, in this book it helps bring people together. How does the list affect the larger community where Aleisha and Mukesh live?

9. Aleisha tells Mukesh: "No one can ever really understand what other people have gone through. But people should try." Do books help foster that empathy? Do the different people in this book come out at the end having greater understanding of one another because they've really tried? What about Mukesh and his daughters? Aleisha and Leilah?

10. How does the experience of reading help push Mukesh toward Nilakshi? Is that what Naina would have wanted for him? Does her letter at the end shed light on her wishes?

11. What sort of future do you envision for these characters after this book ends?

12. If you were to compose your own reading list, which books would be on it, and why?